Praise for *Dark W*

"Dark Wine at Midnight is an innovative paranormal adventure that is dangerous, sexy, and gripping! Readers will be clamoring for more!"

~*InD'tale Magazine*

"Dark Wine at Midnight is overwhelmingly seductive with an aura of mystery and suspense. Enticing and surreptitious, [it] leaves readers completely speechless at the twists and turns Barwin takes us on this urban fantasy journey.... For those who really enjoy romantic novels with a mix of sultry, seductive scenes—you really should read this. For those who don't, I would still give it a chance! Mystery, thriller, action…these all await for your entertainment in Barwin's Dark Wine at Midnight!"

~*Bookmark Your Thoughts Book Review Blog*

"A smoldering Paranormal Romance.... Steadfastly smart and literate with a finely crafted narrative and captivatingly paced Barwin is a confident author who instinctively understands what fans of the genre demand and she gives it to them in spades."

~*BookViral Book Reviews*

"Dark Wine at Midnight fulfilled all my hopes for a story that would keep me engaged, and it did that with aplomb and sparkles. Barwin is a talented writer who tops out on all the markers that identify really good writing."

~*Sharon Bonin-Pratt's Ink Flare*

Praise for *Dark Wine at Sunrise*

"A paranormal romance worthy of the genre. Sensual, sophisticated and sinfully addictive!"

~*InD'tale Magazine*

"An intoxicating novel, packed full of thrills and spills. I loved it!"

~*A 'Wishing Shelf' Book Review*

"Barwin has delivered a novel with a well-constructed multi-layered plot and a nicely observed balance between action, intrigue and romantic tension. Dark Wine at Sunrise makes for a highly enjoyable read and is recommended without reservation."

~*BookViral*

ALSO BY JENNA BARWIN

The Hill Vampire Series

DARK WINE AT DUSK (Book 3)

DARK WINE AT SUNRISE (Book 2)

DARK WINE AT MIDNIGHT (Book 1)

DARK WINE AT SUNRISE

A Hill Vampire Novel
Book 2

Jenna Barwin

Hidden Depths Publishing

Printed in the United States of America
First printing & ebook edition, 2018

Hidden Depths Publishing
Orange County, California
www.hiddendepthspublishing.com

Cover design by Momir Borocki
Images used under license from Shutterstock.com and Depositphotos.com

Interior Design by Author E.M.S.

Editing team: Katrina Diaz-Arnold, Refine Editing, LLC; Trenda K. Lundin, It's Your Story Content Editing; Arran McNicol

Library of Congress Control Number: 2018932439

ISBN 978-0-9986549-4-2

1) Urban Fantasy 2) Paranormal Romance 3) Science Fiction & Fantasy 4) Romance

JOIN JENNA BARWIN'S VIP READERS

Want to know about new releases, and receive special announcements, exclusive excerpts, and other FREE fun stuff? Join Jenna's VIP Readers and receive Jenna Barwin's newsletter by subscribing online at: https://jennabarwin.com/jenna-barwins-newsletter

You can also find Jenna Barwin at:

Facebook: https://www.facebook.com/jennabarwin/

Twitter: @JennaBarwin https://twitter.com/JennaBarwin

Instagram: JennaBarwin https://www.instagram.com/jennabarwin/

Pinterest: https://www.pinterest.com/jennabarwin/

Email: https://jennabarwin.com/contact

DARK WINE
AT
SUNRISE

CHAPTER 1

Where is Henry?

Dr. Cerissa Patel fiddled with the strap of her purse, anxiety inching its way through her chest. Henry was supposed to be at the back of the council chambers next to his legal counsel, but the two reserved chairs sat empty.

She took a deep breath and let it out, trying to expel her worry. She wanted a glimpse of her boyfriend—her soon-to-be mate—to know he had fully recovered from the assassin's attack. She'd been separated from him for two weeks because of the town council's edict, which had placed him under house arrest and forbidden her from visiting him.

It had been two weeks of gut-churning, nail-biting, tied-to-a-train-track torture, and she couldn't handle another second of it.

She wanted to see Henry.

Now.

She twisted to look over her shoulder again. He still hadn't magically appeared.

A pale white hand belonging to Gaea Greenleaf patted her leg. "Relax," the Rubenesque vampire said. "Everything is going to be all right."

Would it? Cerissa wasn't so sure, but she silently faced forward, staring at the town council's empty dais. They hadn't made an appearance yet either. Where was everyone?

The all-vampire council was scheduled to decide two matters: Henry's punishment for violating the Covenant, and whether she could remain in the vampire-controlled town of Sierra Escondida.

As her grandmother from Surat would say, it made no difference whether you stood before a judge or behind a donkey, because the results were the same: you'd be buried in crap.

And the crap was already flying. Rumors had reached her ears—discontented rumblings in the community blamed her for Henry's transgressions. Just one of the many reasons she hadn't been allowed to testify at Henry's first hearing, which had been open to vampires only.

This hearing was open to the entire community, even the mortal mates who lived in Sierra Escondida, but she didn't belong with the "mortal mates" side either. She wasn't Henry's mate yet—or mortal, for that matter.

Henry was the only vampire who knew she was part of the Alatus Lux. The Lux were an ancient race who could shape-shift, but, in their native form, tended to be *confused* with biblical angels, which was why she hadn't shown him her Lux form yet. She didn't want Henry confused.

She brushed a piece of lint off her navy-blue skirt and unbuttoned the matching blazer. She'd dressed professionally in case she was summoned to testify in Henry's defense—although squeezing past the vampires and mortals on the tightly packed, pew-like bench wouldn't be easy.

The doors at the back of the room opened. She spun around to see who entered, and exhaled. It was only the town clerk. He marched up the center aisle and took his place to the left of the council's dais. Did that mean the proceedings would start soon?

Gaea patted her leg again, and on Cerissa's other side, Karen, her mortal friend, held her hand, but neither gesture was reassuring. The question still echoed in her mind.

Where is Henry?

Enrique "Henry" Bautista Vasquez hated being in the "Fishbowl." The small meeting room was a few doors down from the council chambers. It had floor-to-ceiling glass on two sides, which meant anyone in the lobby could peer in at him like he was some zoo animal on display.

He sat at the maple conference table with Yacov Eliahu on his right. His old friend Yacov was acting as his informal legal counsel. They both stared at the latest plea agreement, a deal designed to cut tonight's hearing short and allow Cerissa to remain within the walled boundaries of their private community. The town attorney, Marcus Collings, had drafted it.

Across the table, Marcus held out his fountain pen, offering it to Henry so he could sign the document.

"That's the best I can give you," Marcus said. "We both know you did exactly what you're accused of doing. Save yourself the embarrassment of having the whole mess paraded in front of the community and sign the damn thing."

Henry scanned the deal terms one more time and handed the paper to Yacov, pointing at the blank signature lines. Only two council members had signed it: Liza and Carolyn.

Yacov nodded. "I see that."

"Why is the mayor insisting I sign first?" Henry accepted the paper back from Yacov and laid it on the table. "There are three council member signatures missing."

Marcus shook his head. "The council is a bit divided right now. Some think I'm being too soft on you."

Marcus, Yacov, and Henry were three of the five vampires who had founded Sierra Escondida. According to Yacov, the mayor had accused Marcus of giving Henry preferential treatment because the trio had a long history working together.

"Soft?" Henry began, his anger rising. "You are extracting a fine from me larger than anyone has ever paid in the history of our community."

"Just be glad it's a fine, Henry." Marcus paused. "Look, if I have your signature first, they're more likely to approve the deal."

Henry gestured in the direction of the main meeting room. "Is the council on the dais?"

"Not yet. They're waiting in the other caucus room for me to deliver this."

Of the three council members who hadn't yet signed, Henry knew he could count on one vote in his favor—the vice mayor, Rolf Müller. They were business partners and co-owners of Vasquez Müller Winery. Rolf would never betray him. If Rolf signed the plea agreement, along with Carolyn and Liza, the deal would be binding on behalf of the council. It didn't matter what the other two members thought of it.

Henry took the pen Marcus offered and signed the damned thing.

Marcus swept up the plea deal. "You and Yacov take your place in the public chambers. I'll see you in there."

Marcus disappeared in the direction of the council's caucus room. Henry picked up his wolf's-head cane. He hated relying on it, but his gait was still unsteady. Blanche had fired six silver bullets into his gut two weeks ago, and the effects of silver poisoning lingered—so he used the cane. He refused to risk more humiliation by falling down in front of his community.

The chief of police, Tigisi "Tig" Anderson, met them in the hallway.

She was wearing her dress uniform and no expression on her face. Henry wasn't surprised. Tig's experience in both combat and police work had taught her to wear emotional armor.

"Founder," Tig said, giving him a nod.

"Hello, chief. Will you be escorting us?"

"I will. Evening, Yacov."

"Tig," Yacov said, giving a polite nod back and gesturing to the council chamber doors. "Shall we?"

Upon entering the crowded room, Henry ignored the residents who turned in his direction, instead scanning the room for Cerissa, finding her seated near the front between Gaea and Karen.

Cerissa turned around to face him. Their eyes locked for a moment and he felt himself drawn forward, desperate to touch her, to taste her, to finally claim her as his, but Yacov's hand clamped on his shoulder, pulling him back the few inches he'd moved.

Soon.

She'd be his mate the moment this circus was over. They looked at each other, eyes dancing, her longing gaze piercing his heart, and then the door behind the dais opened, breaking the moment. Cerissa whipped back around and he watched as the council made their way to their seats behind the u-shaped desk on the raised platform.

Ah, here come the jackals now. Marcus had better have gotten them under control.

Tig guided Henry and Yacov to two empty chairs and stood next to them. Henry focused on the mayor, who ruled from the center of the dais, surrounded by the other members of the town council like contestants on a game show. The mayor cleared his throat. Henry's gaze flicked to his Patek Philippe watch. Nine o'clock at night—time to get this charade over with.

The mayor banged the gavel on the wooden sound block.

"This special meeting of the town council of Sierra Escondida will come to order."

The room started to quiet down, and the mayor banged the gavel one more time, harder. The room settled into a tense stillness. The town clerk quickly called the roll; all five council members were present.

"Councilwoman Liza will lead us in the pledge," the mayor announced.

Liza rose, turning toward the American flag. Henry always thought she looked a little like Liza Minelli during her *Cabaret* era, with short

4

brunette hair cut in a perfect pageboy. Not a hair moved when she did. "Please stand and join me. 'I pledge allegiance…'"

He raised his hand to his chest, as did Yacov. Tig whipped off the chief's cap that covered her short afro and placed it over her heart in perfect form.

Henry said the words along with the rest of the community, his mind focused on the irony of it all. Most of the Hill's vampires hadn't been born in these United States.

Three of the council members came from Europe. Their assumed identities benefited from American citizenship, as did his, although he held greater claim than they did—born in Veracruz, Mexico, he had received a land grant in California when it was still under Mexican rule.

"…with liberty and justice for all."

Henry sat back down when everyone else resumed their seats, leaning forward on his cane, ready to rise again. The mayor waited for the shuffling noises to stop before announcing the first order of business on the agenda. Henry glanced once more at Cerissa, who was still seated with her back to him, before squaring his shoulders. He was ready to swallow his pride for her.

The mayor tapped his gavel once.

Henry was halfway out of his chair when the mayor said, "We'll begin with a report from our police chief on the recent attacks. Tig?"

Irritation rumbled in Henry's veins, and he wrapped his hand around the cane's brass handle, making a fist. The mayor was prolonging the proceedings for only one reason.

He's doing it at my expense to bask in the crowd's attention.

Henry wanted to interrupt the proceedings and take Winston to task for this affront. Instead, he restrained himself, resuming his seat as Tig approached the maple wood podium.

"Mr. Mayor, members of the town council," she said into the podium's microphone. "As you know, Blanche Larson has been unconscious since the night she attempted to kill Henry Bautista. After this hearing, Dr. Clarke and Dr. Patel are going to work together to revive Blanche. Until we can question Blanche, we won't know who she was working with or why she attacked Mr. Bautista."

Cerissa is going to try to revive Blanche? But why?

Henry didn't want Cerissa anywhere near that monster. Before he could consider it further, the name plate in front of the vice mayor lit up, indicating Rolf wanted to speak. The mayor called on him.

5

"What if we decide to ban Cerissa from the Hill?" Rolf asked. "Certainly you and Dr. Clarke can revive Blanche without Cerissa's help."

Henry gritted his teeth. So Rolf wanted to publicly wave his power around and make the threat one last time. *Fine.* The deal was done; let Rolf put on a final show for the crowd and convince them he wasn't Henry's lap dog just because they were business partners.

Tig turned in Rolf's direction. "The treatment plan to revive Blanche is Dr. Patel's. She came up with the idea. I would prefer to have Dr. Patel present for its implementation."

"I don't care what you *prefer*," Rolf shot back. "Can you proceed without Cerissa?"

Henry clenched his jaw tighter. Rolf was taking his exhibition a little too far.

"If the council decides we must, we will," Tig replied. "But Dr. Patel's insight may be helpful during the process."

Rolf sneered. "I don't see why you need a mortal's help when you have Dr. Clarke—"

"That's enough, Rolf." The mayor tapped his gavel once. "Let's keep this civil."

"But I was saying—"

The mayor shot Rolf a look. "We all know how you feel about Dr. Patel's presence on the Hill."

Uneasiness settled in Henry's gut. Rolf wouldn't betray him in this, would he?

"And if the vote goes your way," the mayor continued, "we can always let Dr. Patel stay for the procedure and then require her to leave."

What? Cerissa's spine stiffened. *Ban me from the Hill? If they think they can throw me out and still ask for my help....*

Cerissa glanced over at Henry and her breath caught in her throat. Of course she'd help. She had to find out why Blanche tried to kill him. She'd do anything to protect the man she loved.

The mayor waved dismissively in the vice mayor's direction. "The chief has answered your question, Rolf. Let's move on. Chief, is that all?"

"For now, yes it is."

"Thank you for your report."

Tig returned to the back of the room, standing next to Henry.

The mayor looked down at the desktop in front of him and gave the gavel one tap. "The hearing is hereby open. Enrique Bautista Vasquez, approach the podium."

Cerissa watched Henry move slowly to the speaker's podium in the center of the room using a cane to steady himself. He wore a dark suit with a royal-blue tie, his long obsidian-black hair tied back in a neat ponytail. Her fingers itched to unleash it.

Two weeks apart, and the moment their eyes locked, she forgot her fears. The intensity in his eyes reminded her of how he looked the last time they made love. His hair was loose, his abs flexed, his fangs out. As he sank deeper between her legs, she had wanted to feel his bite sink into her neck, but he'd held off due to a misunderstanding.

Her gaze refocused on him in the present when he faltered on his way to the podium, and her desire to help him kicked in. She scooted forward on the bench, ready to spring to her feet if he needed her. Gaea's arm snaked around her shoulders, holding her in place like an iron brace. Cerissa gave Gaea a sideways glance and narrowed her eyes. No one would stop her from protecting Henry, not even Gaea.

His beautiful copper-brown skin looked paler than it should. He held one hand across his stomach, protecting the area where silver bullets had been removed from his abdomen. Why hadn't he healed by now?

The crowd began murmuring again while Henry limped to the podium. The mayor banged his gavel to quiet the crowd.

Henry reached the podium facing the dais and rested against it, propping his cane to the side. Yacov stood at his elbow. Except for Yacov's long, frizzy brown beard, Cerissa would have mistaken the curly-haired vampire for a college professor, with his self-effacing manner and bow tie.

The town attorney stood and read the charges, keeping it short: two charges of violating the Hill's Covenant, and one charge of violating the North American Treaty. The last one came as a surprise. Apparently, taking her to a baseball game without a vampire escort not only broke the Covenant and its "Rule of Two," but also constituted "endangering the life of an envoy."

"Enrique Bautista Vasquez," the mayor said, "how do you plead?"

Yacov laid his hand on Henry's shoulder. Henry steadied himself and leaned forward to speak into the gooseneck microphone.

"Guilty," he said, his Castilian accent heavy in his one-word answer. He sounded resigned to his fate.

"Do you have anything to say in your defense?"

Henry shook his head.

"Speak up—for the record."

"No. Nothing."

The mayor looked to his left. Frédéric nodded. He looked to his right. Rolf did the same. Carolyn and Liza both frowned, clearly not part of whatever agreement the other council members had reached.

"We have given this matter great consideration. As you know, this council reinstituted the Rule of Two because members of our community have been attacked." The mayor paused, steepling his fingers together.

Karen leaned sideways, her auburn hair brushing against Cerissa's shoulder as she whispered, "He does that to look like a wise ruler—as if it changes the fact he isn't."

As Rolf's mate, Karen knew all the political gossip. Cerissa silently agreed with her—the mayor didn't look like a wise ruler. If anyone had asked her opinion, "pretentious buffoon" came to mind. But she didn't care what he looked like. His next words were more important than his looks.

"Now," the mayor continued, "we have a founder who has ignored our rules. At great risk to himself and Dr. Patel, he took Dr. Patel to Mordida alone without an escort, in violation of the Rule of Two, and that was after Dr. Patel had been asked to leave our jurisdiction. To this, he pleads guilty." The mayor paused and looked at something on the dais's desk. "He also pleads guilty to dating a mortal within our walls without first having taken her blood."

Heat flooded Cerissa's cheeks and sweat beaded on her hands. Did he have to say such personal information out loud? The mayor had given Henry permission to escort Cerissa to the dance, but apparently that didn't include taking her back to his house afterwards to make love. She wanted to crawl under her seat and not come out.

The mayor continued, "The council, after much debate, has decided to bring back a traditional punishment, one we abandoned in favor of more modern methods. It's apparent those modern methods aren't a sufficient deterrent."

The mayor tapped his steepled fingers together, taking time to sweep his gaze across the crowded council chambers.

"We are reinstituting the whipping post," he said.

No.

Cerissa froze in place, her pulse thudding, her mind racing, her heart crawling up her throat.

They can't. I have to stop this. They can't humiliate him because of me—

The mayor unfolded a piece of paper. "Enrique Bautista Vasquez. You are hereby fined two hundred thousand dollars and sentenced to a hundred lashes. The sentence will be carried out in the community amphitheater."

What the fuck? One hundred?

Could even a vampire survive that severe a whipping? Cerissa's fingernails curled into her palms, cutting the skin.

This can't be happening.

Fury sped through Henry, betrayal constricting his lungs. He looked from Yacov to the town attorney.

"That was not the deal," he said in a hoarse whisper.

The town attorney rose to his feet. "Mr. Mayor, the plea deal—"

"Can be ignored by the council. If he wants Dr. Patel to remain on the Hill, that's the new deal."

Yacov swiveled the gooseneck microphone, holding it in front of his own mouth. "We ask for a roll-call vote."

The town clerk clicked on his microphone. "You will answer with your vote when I call your name. Councilwoman Carolyn?"

"Nay. It's barbarism, plain and simple."

"Councilman Frédéric?"

"Aye."

"Councilwoman Liza?"

"Nay."

"Vice mayor?"

Rolf didn't respond immediately. He used his pinky to catch a strand of his light blonde hair and brushed it back, a gesture of contempt. Henry gripped the top of the podium tighter, already knowing the answer and hating himself for not foreseeing Rolf's betrayal.

"Vice Mayor Rolf?" the town clerk repeated.

Rolf looked directly at Henry. "Aye," he replied.

Henry glared back at Rolf, gripping the podium so tightly the wood cracked, the sound punctuating the silence. The moment crawled to a stop.

After all I've done for you, you would truly do this to me?

The town clerk continued, "Mayor?"

"Aye."

Without breaking eye contact with Henry, Rolf said, "Mr. Mayor, I have a motion to make. I move we conditionally suspend the whipping, but leave the fine in place. If there are any more breaches of the Covenant in the next two years by our revered Founder, the full sentence will be reinstated."

"I second the motion," Liza said before the mayor could react.

The mayor looked disgruntled. "We have a motion and a second."

"Oh, one other condition," Rolf said, almost too casually. Henry didn't believe it was an afterthought. "I want Cerissa removed from the Hill. She will not become his mate."

"No!" Henry's eyes stung as he felt his irises turn solid black with anger. "I'll be flogged before I let that happen. I only pled guilty to keep her on the Hill."

Yacov laid a hand on Henry's shoulder. "Henry, calm—"

"I will not. This is a farce, a mockery of justice."

"Order," the mayor yelled, banging his gavel.

"I will not be silent. I founded this town, and I won't let you twist its rules to force Cerissa out."

Henry kept his angry gaze fixed on Rolf. Now Rolf's betrayal made a warped kind of sense. Rolf distrusted Cerissa; his junior partner had made that clear enough. But until this moment, Henry hadn't believed Rolf would betray their sixty-five-year friendship over that distrust.

Liza raised a hand to catch the mayor's attention. "Do I have to second that part of the motion too?"

The town attorney leaned into his microphone. "No, you don't, but then the original motion to flog him will stand."

The mayor made a point of waiting, looking at each council member one by one. "Hearing no further motion," he finally said, "the punishment will be carried out in the amphitheater immediately after this hearing."

A muffled sound arose from the audience. Henry turned to see Cerissa struggling against Gaea's grip, but Gaea's hand was firmly clasped over Cerissa's mouth. He had to stop this before Cerissa did something they'd both regret.

He straightened his shoulders and faced the council. He'd take a hundred lashes before he'd let them ban her.

"Mr. Mayor, I accept the council's terms."

The mayor raised the gavel. "If there is no other business, I'll adjourn—"

Rolf's hand shot out to catch the gavel before it fell. "Fine, I'll amend my motion to suspend the whipping," Rolf said angrily. "Cerissa can stay.

But Henry has served fourteen days' house arrest. I move we make it twenty-one."

Henry scrubbed both hands over his hair, smoothing it back, fighting to regain control, his fury toward Rolf easing a notch. How could he trust Rolf after this? The younger vampire seemed to think being business partners and friends gave him the right to dictate Henry's actions. If anything, it should be the other way around. Henry's help was the only reason Rolf hadn't been kicked off the Hill long ago.

The mayor turned to Liza. "Do you second Rolf's revised motion?"

"Done," she replied.

"Before we vote, I got something I want to say to all y'all," Carolyn said in a slow Southern drawl. "Mr. Mayor, you didn't give us a chance to speak our piece, and I'll be heard on this before y'all vote."

"All right," the mayor said. "I'll call for discussion and recognize Councilwoman Carolyn."

Standing, Carolyn turned to glare at the three men on the council. "I said it in closed session, and I'll say it here now. Not one of y'all has ever been strung up to the whipping post. I'm the only one among ya who has, havin' been born to slavery and all. Until y'all feel the lash yourself, you have no business metin' it out as punishment. It's barbarism, and I reckon we shouldn't leave it hangin' over Mr. Bautista's head."

Cerissa couldn't agree more. Only Gaea's firm grip stopped her from applauding the councilwoman's speech.

The mayor looked like he had something to say, and then thought better of it. "Does anyone else wish to discuss this matter further?"

Carolyn resumed her seat, still giving Rolf and Frédéric the evil eye.

"I call the question," Liza said, not giving anyone else a chance to answer.

"Very well. You've heard the motion. Suspend the whipping but impose an additional seven days' house arrest." The mayor swept his hand in the town clerk's direction. "Call the roll."

The amendment passed. Frédéric joined Rolf and Liza in voting for it. Carolyn abstained, arguing once again that they shouldn't leave the whipping hanging over Henry's head.

Gaea removed her hand from Cerissa's mouth. "Now, child, may I trust you to be quiet?"

Cerissa let out a long exhale and nodded. Henry looked her way. She briefly met his crystalline brown eyes again, and longing seized her heart. He gave a slight bow acknowledging her. He then stooped over to retrieve his cane and followed Yacov out of the council chambers. Tig walked closely behind them. Cerissa's lips parted in a little sigh when she lost sight of him.

Karen tapped her on the shoulder. "Rolf's leaving on a business trip from here. Why don't you come back to my house after you're finished with Blanche? We can uncork a bottle and celebrate."

Gaea beamed at Karen. "That's an excellent idea."

"How about tomorrow night?" Cerissa suggested. "I don't know how long it'll take to revive Blanche. We may not finish until dawn."

"Tomorrow night it is, girlfriend. I'll be sure to stock something extra special from the winery."

"Sounds good."

And with Henry confined for another seven days, she might as well use the time to work on her biotech project. Cerissa turned to Gaea. "Now that the council has cleared me to stay, I'd like to schedule more investor meetings. I need investors in order to move forward with building the lab."

"You mustn't fret about that," Gaea said, patting Cerissa's shoulder. "Once you're Henry's mate, I'm sure community members will be lining up to invest."

Cerissa bit her tongue. That wasn't why she wanted Henry for her mate. She didn't need a man to succeed at business. "I'll contact the mayor myself. It's time to invite members from other communities to come here, so they can see the location we've picked for our project and hear my pitch."

Gaea gave an exasperated *harrumph.* "All right, Cerissa. I'll clear it with the mayor. Satisfied?"

It would have to do. Too much was out of her control, and she had to keep Gaea on her side. "Thank you, Gaea, that would be wonderful," Cerissa said, standing up. "Now, if you'll excuse me, I have a patient to see."

CHAPTER 2

Cerissa inserted a needle into Blanche's arm and started the flow of vampire blood. Her theory was simple: blood from the oldest vampire on the Hill might revive the comatose bitch.

Cerissa's back pressed against the silver grill as she worked in the cramped space on her side of Blanche's gurney. The chief had refused to move Blanche from the Hill's police station to Dr. Clarke's clinic. So they'd turned a jail cell into a makeshift treatment room.

Dr. Clarke hunched close to Blanche on the gurney's other side. The windowless concrete wall at his back was lined with silver mesh, and he held his elbows pinned to his sides to avoid touching it. Medical equipment sat on a small folding table at the foot of Blanche's gurney. Beyond the table, Tig stood watching.

Cerissa had changed out of her business suit and into surgical scrubs before beginning the procedure, just in case things got messy. From what happened the first and only time Blanche had awoken since her attack on Henry, "messy" didn't half cover it.

Blanche had screamed nonsense the entire time. Vicious swear words streamed out of her mouth in random order, her nails clawing at those trying to restrain her, her short blonde hair whipping back and forth as she snapped her teeth, trying to sink her fangs into anyone who came near her mouth. Then she passed out and had stayed that way for the last two weeks. Silver chains strapped her down in case she regained consciousness.

Cerissa watched the drip, drip, drip of blood in the clear plastic bubble. The infusion pump controlled the flow from the bag to the tube's collection chamber. Twenty minutes later, the first blood bag was exhausted, and no change in Blanche.

"Chief, could you hand me the next bag, please?" Cerissa asked Tig.

To reach it, she would have to squeeze past the chief. Tig opened the cooler and passed the bag over.

Cerissa connected the second bag to the infusion pump. As the clear tube filled with ruby-red liquid again, Blanche showed no sign of regaining consciousness.

Cerissa raised her gloved hand toward her own mouth and stopped. Gnawing on a fingernail was out of the question—no matter how comforting the nervous gesture might be. Instead, she rolled her lips under and bit them together, staring at Blanche's unresponsive face.

Why did you try to murder Henry? Personal grudge? Hired assassin? Part of the vampire dominance movement?

"Check her blood pressure," Dr. Clarke said, his acne-scarred face scowling at her.

"Will do." Cerissa scooched away from the metal rack that held the blood bag. In the tight quarters, she caught her foot on the gurney's wheel and grabbed the side bar before she hit the ground.

Note to self: never practice medicine in a jail cell.

Dr. Clarke narrowed his hazel eyes at her. "Get your act together, Dr. Patel. What's Blanche's blood pressure?"

Cerissa pumped up the cuff on Blanche's arm, watched the meter, and used a stethoscope to catch the first knocking sound of the systolic pressure, followed by the second. "Ninety over forty."

"That's low even for a vampire," he said. "I doubt this will work."

"The only way to know is to try," Cerissa replied, as she loosened the blood pressure cuff.

Dr. Clarke crossed his arms and shook his head. "This just doesn't make sense," he muttered. "I still don't see why Blanche is in such bad shape. What did Yacov do to her?"

Cerissa's stomach contracted like someone was practicing surgical knots on her duodenum. Neither Dr. Clarke nor the chief knew she was the one responsible for Blanche's injuries—although she had excellent reasons for splitting open Blanche's ribcage.

No one messes with my boyfriend.

A swell of anger loosened some of the knots in her stomach. She had stopped Blanche from killing Henry by morphing into a mountain lion and clawing out the crooked vampire's heart. Later, the vital organ had been shoved back in. Thanks to Henry's persuasive skills and Yacov's help, Blanche's mutilated chest was mended with vampire blood to keep Tig from learning the truth.

Cerissa licked her lips, her mouth dry, and checked the pulse rate monitor again, but Blanche's heartbeat remained unchanged from the last thirty times she'd checked it.

Dr. Clarke pulled back on Blanche's eyelids. Only the whites showed before he let go. Using a knuckle, he dug into Blanche's shoulder, trying a pain stimulus to wake her. Nothing.

"Let's give her the third bag," Cerissa said, keeping her mental fingers crossed. Blanche had to wake up and tell them why she did it. If not, how would Cerissa protect Henry from whatever or whoever was trying to kill him?

After the third bag emptied, Dr. Clarke dug his knuckle into Blanche's shoulder again.

Blanche's eyelids popped open. Her eyes moved from left to right, but the normally blue irises were grayed out, vacant of life—until they stopped on Cerissa.

Blanche let out a nails-on-chalkboard screech. Her pupils enlarged until her eyes turned solid black.

The chief pushed Dr. Clarke aside and gripped Blanche's arm. "What's wrong? We only want to talk with you."

Blanche's eyes continued to point in Cerissa's direction. The screeching continued.

"Are you in pain?" Dr. Clarke asked.

Another wordless screech.

Cerissa gestured to the ice chest. "Should we try human blood? With so much vampire blood pumped into her, her body may be trying to turn again."

Dr. Clarke gave a condescending sniff. "But unless we inject fang serum, she won't go through the change."

"I'm not suggesting we turn her," Cerissa said, speaking loudly to be heard over the next scream from Blanche. "We don't know what effect going through the turn again would have on her memories. But she may need human blood to counterbalance the effect of vampire blood."

"Do it," Tig said, and stepped out of the way, tossing Cerissa a bag of donor blood from the ice chest.

Using a needleless syringe, Cerissa tried squirting human blood into Blanche's mouth. Blanche gurgled, and then screeched again, the blood running down the side of her face.

Cerissa wrinkled her nose at the mess. "Can we give it to her intravenously?"

"No," Dr. Clarke replied. "It has to go through the stomach to be absorbed properly."

"We could try a nasal feeding tube."

Cerissa slid away to avoid Blanche's snapping mouth, swapping places with Tig, and found the tube and a large syringe in the medical supply box at Blanche's feet, handing them to Dr. Clarke. Tig managed to strap down Blanche's head without getting bit.

Dr. Clarke inserted the tube in Blanche's nose. "Chief, you may want to put on scrubs. There's an extra pair in that box," he said, jerking his head to indicate which box. "You don't want bloodstains on your uniform."

Tig still wore her dark blue dress suit, the jacket decorated with brass medals. "I have something better," she said, leaving the cell.

A minute later, Tig returned wearing a heavy black vinyl apron over her police uniform. It was long-sleeved, and the apron's skirt hung to her shins—the kind of apron a mortician might wear.

Okay, I don't want to know why she owns that.

Cerissa stayed back because she didn't want to get bitten. Being Lux, she had no idea what effect fang serum would have on her, and now was not the time to experiment.

Dr. Clarke filled the large syringe with blood and connected it to the tube. He slowly compressed the syringe, forcing blood through the tube and into Blanche's stomach.

After feeding Blanche two pints of human blood, Dr. Clarke's scrubs looked like they belonged to a splatter victim in a horror movie. Blanche regurgitated the blood as fast as he fed it through the tube. She continued to scream in between rounds of vomiting. Everything within range was coated red, with no improvement in Blanche to show for it. The air smelled sickeningly sweet, like someone had stirred sugar syrup with copper powder, and left the mixture outside to rot.

Cerissa took the next bag out of the ice chest, ready to hand it over.

Dr. Clarke waved her off. He stepped back, stripped off his gloves, and tossed them into the medical waste bin. The screaming intensified in volume. While putting on clean gloves, he said loudly, "I told you Blanche was too far gone. Her brain was without blood for too long."

Tig released her hold on Blanche. "If that's true, why is she so focused on Dr. Patel?"

"It's probably because she's the only mortal in the room," Dr. Clarke said, raising his voice a notch louder. "Blanche's brain is searching for food, even if she can't metabolize it."

"Can you do anything to stop her screaming?" Tig asked.

Dr. Clarke frowned. "Short of putting her down? No. She's probably in a great deal of pain. The trauma she suffered isn't healing right. There must have been a great deal of damage to her heart."

Cerissa dropped the unused bag back into the ice chest. She had to distract them—they were getting too close to the truth. "We could give Blanche a pain killer to alleviate the pain while she healed."

"Wouldn't work. It has to go through a mortal first."

"What if we asked a human volunteer to take a heavy opioid, and fed Blanche the volunteer's blood?"

Dr. Clarke shook his head. "She'd vomit it up again. It's not worth it."

Tig motioned for Cerissa to follow her out of the cell. They walked down the hallway, closing the heavy connecting door, which dampened the noise. Tig stopped and held up a finger, silently asking Cerissa to wait.

Cerissa clasped her gloved hands together, trying to control her nerves. Tig looked lost in thought, both beautiful and intimidating in her blood-covered apron, like an African version of Kali, the Hindu goddess of death and sex. Just like Kali, Tig made order out of chaos.

Cerissa's stomach rumbled. Why were they out here? Had Tig somehow guessed the truth about Blanche?

Tig's gaze refocused, fastening on Cerissa. "Should we try medicating Blanche as you suggested?"

Cerissa glanced back over her shoulder in the direction of the cell. "Ah, Dr. Clarke is right. It's unlikely to work if Blanche can't keep anything down. But we could still try giving her the drug intravenously."

"Dr. Clarke seems convinced it won't work."

"We have nothing to lose. I don't see how it would harm her, but then, I have no experience treating vampires."

"So the biotech lab you plan on building isn't researching vampire biology?"

Cerissa dipped her chin down in surprise, her eyes widening. "Ah, is that what you thought?"

"It was one of many possibilities we considered when you first arrived."

"My sponsor doesn't believe such research would be profitable. But given what's happened with Blanche, Leopold might agree to expand our business model. For now, we're focused on producing blood for the treaty communities."

"So there is nothing you can do to help Blanche?"

"I—" Cerissa began, and stopped. Maybe if she shoved enough of her aura into Blanche, it might calm whatever neurons were misfiring in Blanche's brain—and she could use her original idea as cover. "Before we give up, let's try giving her the painkiller directly."

Tig opened the door and motioned for Cerissa to go in first. Cerissa prepared the syringe while Tig explained the plan to Dr. Clarke.

"It's a waste of time," he said when Tig finished.

"Will it hurt her?"

"No."

"Then we'll try it."

At Tig's signal, Cerissa injected the morphine into Blanche's IV. Finished, Cerissa set the syringe aside and wrapped her fingers around Blanche's arm, focusing her aura like a laser beam into Blanche.

Blanche screamed once more in Cerissa's direction, and then her pupils shrank, her irises fading from solid black back to a dull blue-gray.

Cerissa leaned in a little closer, but not within snapping distance. "Blanche, it's Cerissa, remember me?"

Blanche kept staring blankly. Cerissa glanced at Tig, who nodded for her to continue.

"Blanche, can you hear me?" Cerissa asked, pouring out her aura. "Please, say something."

No response. Blanche's eyes were open, but the spark of life was missing.

"You and I were staying at Gaea's home." More aura flowed from Cerissa into Blanche. "Then something happened on Henry's front porch. Do you remember?"

Blanche let out a bloodcurdling shriek, and her eyes dilated, turning solid black again.

"Damn it," Cerissa said, stepping back and breaking the connection with Blanche.

"There was a moment there." Tig turned in the direction of Dr. Clarke. "Should we keep trying?"

He pursed his lips, and then said, "It's not worth it. We've done everything we know to do, plus Dr. Patel's idea."

"But Blanche is still awake," Tig said. "If there's any chance, I want to question her."

"Chief, she won't heal without blood, and her body is rejecting it. Her eyes may be open, but she isn't *there*. I'm calling it. Blanche is terminal and beyond repair."

Tig grimaced and exhaled loudly. "Okay, do it."

Dr. Clarke stuffed a wad of gauze into Blanche's mouth, muffling her screams. "Do you want me to notify her maker?"

"He's deceased. Go ahead and put her down."

"Wait." Cerissa held up a clean syringe. She may not have the answer to why Blanche shot Henry, but there was another question Blanche could help with. "We should take samples of her fang serum and blood to compare it to a healthy vampire. We might be able to determine what happened to her."

"Hmm," Dr. Clarke murmured. "Not a bad idea." He accepted the syringe Cerissa held out to him, shoved the needle into the large vein in Blanche's arm, and filled two stoppered tubes.

Cerissa took a specimen jar from the medical supply box and stretched the palm of a nitrile glove over it, tying the fingers around it to hold the glove on the jar. She handed it to Dr. Clarke.

"What do you want me to do with this?" he asked.

"Milk her fangs, the way a snake is milked." It was just a guess on her part. She hadn't examined vampire fangs closely enough to know how they functioned. "If Chief Anderson holds her head steady, you should be able to puncture the glove and pull gently forward. Hopefully, that will release the serum."

"An interesting approach—we'll see if it works."

He stepped away from the gurney to let Tig slide past him. Even with the strap across Blanche's forehead, there was room for the screaming vampire to twist. The chief held Blanche's head still and Dr. Clarke did the rest.

Cerissa took the sample jar from him and examined it against the overhead light. Not much, not even an ounce, but enough for a chemical analysis to determine what effect vampire serum would have on her.

To become Henry's mate, he had to bite her. She hadn't told him about the risks, and with this sample, she might not have to.

She removed the glove from the specimen container and screwed on the lid. Dr. Clarke then handed her the blood sample tubes.

"There's a lab in Mordida where I can test these," she said.

Tig looked at her sternly. "Those aren't leaving the Hill."

"Ah…"

"Dr. Clarke can test them. He has equipment at his clinic here."

19

"But I have access to advanced test equipment. I can run a full chemical analysis and gene sequencing. The more we know—"

Tig shook her head. "If we need special machines, then they can be rented and brought to the Hill. But those samples aren't leaving here."

"All right," Cerissa said, her stomach constricting again. There had to be a way. "Well, I'm happy to stop by the clinic tomorrow night and help you with the analysis, Dr. Clarke."

Dr. Clarke frowned at her. "That's not necessary. I can do it myself."

Damn. How was she going to get access to fang serum?

"Very well," she agreed. It's not like she could argue with them. Pushing too hard would make Tig suspicious. "If you don't need anything further, I'll go back to Gaea's house."

Tig slid past Dr. Clarke to stand by the cell door again, and she opened it for Cerissa to pass through. "Thank you for your help tonight. Under the circumstances, I appreciate your willingness to assist."

"I'm always happy to be of service."

Tig held out her hand for the samples. "I'm sure you understand why we can't let those leave the Hill."

Cerissa didn't hand them off. "The samples should go in a refrigerator right away. Do you want me to take them to Dr. Clarke's clinic? I'll drive by it on my way back to Gaea's house."

"No need to. We have a refrigerator here."

"Where is it?" Cerissa asked, slinging her medical bag over her shoulder and cupping the specimen container in one hand, the two blood sample tubes in the other.

Tig motioned for Cerissa to follow and then pointed down the hallway leading to the exit. "Through there, by my clerk's desk."

"Thanks."

Cerissa stopped at the small refrigerator. It was the size typically found under a hotel wet bar. Shielded by the wall, she peeked around the corner. Tig had gone into her office and closed the door.

Good.

Cerissa quickly unscrewed the lid to the specimen jar. Using a syringe she'd palmed up her sleeve, she drew back the plunger to sneak a sample of fang serum.

Tig's office door opened. "Cerissa, one other thing before you leave."

Cerissa fumbled the syringe, dropping it on the refrigerator rack, sliding it toward the back so the chief wouldn't see it.

"Yes?" Cerissa replied, her heart doing double time. She jumped up, twisting the lid onto the specimen container, hiding the motion with the palm of her hand.

Tig held what looked like a stake in one hand, a mallet in the other, still wearing the heavy black apron. "If you leave the Hill, please have Gaea notify me. Until you and Henry bond, you're only here as Leopold's envoy and diplomatic protocols are still in place."

"Understood. Thanks."

Tig cocked her head. "Are you okay? Your heart rate went through the roof."

"Ah," Cerissa began, looking for anything to explain why her heartbeat spiked. Spiked? *That's it.* She pointed toward the stake Tig held. "It's not every day you see one of those."

Tig raised the pointed hawthorn. "Sorry, I didn't think it would upset you."

"The idea of killing anyone…"

"You're a doctor. You save lives. I protect and serve, and sometimes that duty comes with this one. Goodnight."

Cerissa waited until the chief disappeared into Blanche's cell. She squatted back down, returning the specimen jar to the small refrigerator, capped the syringe, and placed it inside her medical kit.

She left the police station without looking back and got into her rental car. Nervous energy coursed through her. In fifteen minutes, she should have her answer. She just hoped it was the answer that let her become Henry's mate.

CHAPTER 3

GAEA'S HOUSE—TWENTY MINUTES LATER

Cerissa resisted the urge to tap her foot impatiently. She stood in the hallway outside her guest room at Gaea's Mediterranean-style mansion, trying desperately to detach herself from her hostess without seeming rude.

"When will they put Blanche down?" Gaea asked. Her fists were poised on her curvaceous hips, while her *eau de parfum* formed a no-man's zone around her.

Vampires usually eschewed heavy scents. Not Gaea. Cerissa's nose twitched at her version of chemical warfare. "I had the impression they were staking Blanche right away, after I left."

"That seems awfully quick. Are you sure they aren't going to hold a council hearing first?"

Cerissa gritted her teeth. How soon would fang serum deteriorate outside of a human body? She stepped into her room, blocking the doorway so Gaea couldn't follow. "When I left the police station, Tig was holding a stake. She seemed to imply the deed would be done right away."

Gaea *tsked*. "They shouldn't stake Blanche without the council's blessing. They don't have the authority."

"They seemed to think they did." Cerissa glanced at her watch. *Damn. I need to leave. Now.* "You may want to call Tig right away to discuss your concerns. You know, before they take any irrevocable action…"

"Yes, yes, dear, that's a good idea. Do you want to join me on the call? After all, you were there."

"I have a splitting headache, Gaea," Cerissa said, giving the first excuse that occurred to her. Her head did feel like a rubber band was slowly being tightened around it. "Blanche was…screaming a lot. Do you mind if I go lie down instead?"

"Of course, dear. I must imagine this has been difficult for you. Can I bring you something? A soothing tea, perhaps?"

"No thanks, I have aspirin, and I'm just going to rest."

She'd started to close the door when Gaea stopped her. "Are you sure you don't need anything? You've been through so much."

"I'm sure."

"Well then, don't forget the door hanger, dear. That way I'll know when you're up again."

Cerissa reached for the "do not disturb" sign and slid it onto the antique glass knob facing the hallway. The words were cross-stitched against a pattern of stars with a quartered moon. Like everything else in Gaea's house, the sign was a work of art.

"Thank you, Gaea," Cerissa said, closing the door. This time, she succeeded in latching and locking it without interruption. She checked the timer on her phone—twenty-five minutes had passed since the fang sample was taken.

Damn. Double damn.

She opened the crystal of her watch, tapped its face, and flashed to her private lab at the Enclave. She glanced around the rock-walled room to confirm she was alone. The lab—like the rest of the Enclave—had been carved from black and gray volcanic rock in a tall mountain, the volcano long extinct.

Stripping off her clothes, she morphed into her Lux form and donned a wraparound lab coat, which rode under her wings, leaving them free to hang down. The feather tips brushed the back of her knees.

She removed the syringe from her purse like she was holding the keys to the kingdom of heaven. Despite what she'd told Dr. Clarke, she sincerely doubted Blanche's injuries would change the composition of her fang serum.

Cerissa grabbed a glass tray from a nearby cabinet. It was about the size of a microscope slide, and she squirted a small sample of fang serum into the tray's dimple.

Barely two milliliters remained in the thin syringe. She placed it on the lab bench, carried the small tray to the analysis machine, and gingerly placed the sample into the machine's receptacle. She took a deep breath.

This had better work.

She tapped the front panel and slid through the menus, clicking checkboxes for the tests she wanted to run. The size of the sample, which would be destroyed in the process, limited the number of tests, so she had to choose carefully. Satisfied with her selection, she pressed the "start" key.

Returning to the lab bench, she opened a log on her computer using her neural link—the link only worked in her native form—and pictured in her mind the elapsed time: twenty-seven minutes. The data was entered automatically.

She fluttered the tips of her wings, her anxiety growing.

What if fang serum contained something poisonous to her? Her people could take human form and morph into any creature that had the same body mass, but substances harmless to a mortal might sicken her. She'd found out the hard way the first time she'd tried vampire blood.

That had been a rough night. Projectile vomiting was not something she wanted to experience again. But what if fang serum made her sick, too?

What then? Sex and biting went together for vampires. How could she become Henry's mate if she couldn't be bitten?

And even if the serum had no ill effects on her, what about the other obstacle standing in the way of their relationship? Her mission for the Lux had come with explicit orders from her superiors: she was forbidden from letting a vampire feed from her.

Frustrated, she sighed, the sound bouncing off the cavern walls. It was too late to turn the clock back now. The night she saved Henry's life, she had fed him her blood by cutting open a vein.

Still, she wouldn't officially be his blood mate until his fangs pierced her.

She fluttered her wingtips. Ruminating about it wouldn't solve the problem. Instead, she ejected her contact lenses, feeling more than hearing the slight *zzzt* vibration as the tentacles detached from her optic nerve. In her Lux form, the lenses never aligned with her pupil because they were too small for her large eyes and created annoying shadows in her field of vision.

She deposited the lenses into a compartment on the back of her phone. The lenses recorded what she saw and heard, but couldn't transmit directly or feed "live" images. She had to manually upload the footage using a transfer box, which was built into her phone.

The Lux Protectors—her superiors—noticed if she was slow in uploading her videos. In any case, watching Blanche scream should keep the Protectors occupied, debating the meaning for a day or two. She slid her finger across the phone's screen, initiating the upload.

The chemical analysis machine dinged. She set her phone aside and transferred the chemical analysis to her computer using her neural link.

Wow.

Vampire fangs should come with an FDA warning label. Floating in the serum were several chemical substances not normally found in the human body. Mortals were lucky the combination didn't prove toxic.

First up, a weak anticlotting agent to keep blood flowing freely, along with a mild anesthetic—both pretty predictable.

But along with the predictable were three unusual substances.

She told the computer to expand the first compound into a pictorial view. The complex CH and O chains of an organic molecule, each atom brightly color-coded in red, yellow, or white, with an occasional blue, floated above the console in 3-D mode. Slowly, she rotated the image with one finger.

Whoa, what's this?

Using the neural link, she retrieved the chemical structure of another compound, the Lux morphing hormone. When secreted, the morphing hormone modified her cellular structure, allowing her to change shape. She projected the morphing hormone next to the fang serum compound. Her memory was spot on—the structures were almost the same.

What is our hormone doing in a vampire's body?

She pulled up a backless chair, which allowed her wings to hang free, and eased onto it, her gaze fixed on the two floating molecules. Minor differences, very minor. But small differences could create big changes in how an organic substance functioned.

So what will it do to me?

The second molecule was a complete unknown. She flicked it with her mind until it, too, rotated above her console in 3-D mode and ran it through a simulation program, comparing it to how similar substances worked.

At most, it would cause a scent to be secreted from the victim's skin. The same way eating too much garlic could change a person's body odor. Then it struck her.

This is how they scent-mark their mates—how Zeke knew Henry hadn't yet had my blood.

Zeke had made an aggressive play for her affections, and failed worse than Count Paris did in *Romeo and Juliet*.

The third molecule almost matched a known psychoactive substance. *Hmm.* Could this be how the loyalty bond kept a mortal from disclosing to strangers the existence of vampires? A long-acting hypnotic compound, pumped directly into the bloodstream, resulting in temporary changes in behavior? And when a mortal mate left the community, the mortal's memory was altered, and their knowledge of vampires wiped away. This substance probably aided in that process as well.

She didn't have to worry about it. She was immune to vampire mesmerizing abilities, and morphing to another form, which she did almost daily, would filter the substance from her system.

But the first molecule, the one similar to the morphing hormone, created a bigger problem. She had no defense against it.

She examined the syringe—only a small amount of fang serum remained between the plunger and the needle. Should she try it? Experimenting on herself was a bad idea to do without someone here—anything could happen—but there was only one person she trusted with this information. She typed out a quick text message on her phone.

Five seconds later, her mission supervisor appeared next to her. "So what's the emergency?" Ari asked, glancing around the lab.

He must have been seated when he flashed. He straightened up, still in human form, and caught a cloth napkin to keep it from landing on the floor. He was dressed casually in board shorts and a t-shirt. At six foot four, he towered over her. He had the same dark, wavy hair and skin coloring as her human body, making it easier for mortals to believe they were cousins.

"I need help with an experiment," she replied.

"You pulled me away from dinner for *an experiment?*" He stared down at her, his deep green eyes angry.

"Dinner?" She glanced at her watch. "It's four in the morning in Florida."

"I was in Australia, about to enjoy a plate of grilled barramundi with a decent local Sauvignon Blanc." He waved the napkin at her and laid it on the lab bench. "Look, kid, you keep abusing the emergency code, and I'm not dropping everything next time."

"But this is an emergency. This stuff could lose its potency any minute." She lifted the syringe so he could see it. "And I couldn't call anyone else—no one else knows about me and Henry."

"Slow down—what stuff?"

"Fang serum. The active molecule in it is similar to our morphing hormone."

His eyebrows shot up. "No shit?"

"No shit." How could he doubt her work? She was a genius in the lab. "I ran the analysis myself moments ago. The similarities are striking."

He eyed the syringe. "And what do you plan on doing with that?"

"Don't worry, I'm not going to stick you with it."

He shook his head, and a dark brown curl flopped onto his forehead. "You're not going to try it on yourself, either."

"A small skin test—to see how I react. I didn't want to do it alone. *Ergo*, emergency."

"You are crazy, you know that?"

Crazy in love, maybe. She fisted her hands, propping them on her hips like Gaea did, except the Lux were stick straight, so there was no place to rest them.

"Will you help me out or not?" she demanded.

"Sure, why not? What could go wrong? You inject yourself with a strange molecule that's close but not the same to our own and you could morph into a Komodo dragon and never get back to native form, but who am I to question the great scientist?"

"Ari—"

"No, don't let me talk you out of the *stupidest* thing I've ever heard proposed. Go right ahead and screw up your entire life because you're *in love*."

Stupid? She narrowed her eyes and fluffed out her wings. *How else am I going to find out?*

She lowered the syringe and jabbed it under the shimmering blue skin of her forearm, moving the plunger a tiny bit. She didn't want to shoot the whole thing at once.

Her skin began to unbind, the small patch trying to change but having no direction. It swirled, forming and un-forming patterns of skin from the various species she'd mapped and morphed into before—scales, feathers, fur, human skin, and back to her own blue skin, a rapid kaleidoscope of colors and textures.

She focused on the area, telling it to stop. Morphing was like tightening a muscle. Lift a heavy object, and her muscle tightened.

So why didn't her desire to stay in one form stop the kaleidoscope?

Snatching a hypo from the lab bench, she dialed in a small dose of the stabilizing hormone. The stabilizer would keep her locked in one form. She pressed the hypo against her rebellious skin. The change stopped, the patch becoming human, an island of nutmeg-colored skin surrounded by shimmering blue.

That's inconvenient.

And it itched. Badly. Like a hundred mosquito bites. She scratched at it and the itching got worse. She morphed the rest of her body back to human form. The skin on her arm blended in perfectly and the itching stopped.

"So, kid, what does your mad scientist mind tell you now?"

"Something about fang serum makes it more potent than our morphing hormone."

"No kidding. You're lucky it wasn't permanent."

She rubbed at her arm. "Yeah, I'm going to have to study it further, once I get another sample."

"Why don't you ask that boyfriend of yours to help out?"

"He's still under house arrest for another seven nights. They have guards posted at his house around the clock for his protection. I can't flash back in to see him—not without risking discovery."

Besides, she wanted this solved *before* she saw him again. Explaining the whole thing to Henry meant confessing too many sins.

Ari yawned, stripped off his t-shirt, and morphed into his native Lux form. He caught his shorts before they fell off his hips and cinched the belt. Stretching his wings, he said, "Well, if that's it, I'm going to the caverns. Might as well get in some flight time as long as I'm here."

"What about your dinner?"

"It'll be waiting when I return." He motioned for her to follow him. "Come on, there's nothing more to do now. Change back and we can go flying together. The exercise will do you good—give you a break from your love-addled mind."

"You go ahead. I'll be along in a minute."

Once he was gone, she studied the syringe. A milliliter remained.

What doesn't kill you makes you stronger.

Still in human form, she shoved the needle into the vein in her arm, pushing the plunger, discharging the last of the sample.

A surge of lust overpowered her, followed by an uncontrollable urge to shift. She fumbled for her hypo, but didn't make it in time. She morphed, and her blue-skinned, six-fingered hand clutched air.

Oh, this is so not good. I can't morph while we're making love.

What would Henry think? One minute a mortal was in bed with him, the next, a blue-skinned being with long, straight hair the color of raw silk, and feathered wings to match.

And my blood—he can't drink my Lux blood.

He could feed on her blood when she was in her human form. They'd already crossed that line, and nothing bad happened. But her Lux blood? What would it do to him? Fear bubbled up from the pit of her stomach, washing through her like a bad chill.

What will he do when he finally does see me?

He had yet to see her real appearance. He had no idea she looked like a blue angel. Except...when he was lying on the floor after she rescued him from Blanche, while he waited for Yacov to arrive, she had impulsively morphed into her Lux form to fly away.

Had Henry seen her?

How stupid!

She should have waited in order to break the truth to him more gently. His religious beliefs were steeped in Catholic tradition. If he mistook her for an angel, would he believe their relationship was sinful?

It wouldn't be the first time she was rejected for her appearance. Of course, the first time it had been her *amma*—her mother—who was disgusted with her *human* form because she looked like her human father who was from India. Her human appearance was determined by his genes.

Amma would bemoan raising her daughter as a *human* while she pulled a hairbrush harshly through Cerissa's wavy, dark hair, which always needed oil to tame it, bending her head back cruelly with the effort. Cerissa's generation had been raised among their human families, locked in human form during their childhood. While *amma* had to assume human shape to carry out the masquerade, she seemed oblivious to that fact. Instead, she would run a finger over Cerissa's nutmeg-brown skin, skin that didn't shimmer when you touched it, and snap, *"Why couldn't you look like me?"*

The shame made Cerissa's head swim, and she fluttered the tips of her wings.

No, it can't be.

She had finally found something worth fighting for: a path for her life where she didn't bow to the dictates of the Protectors. She had embraced her own free will, chosen Henry as her mate, and his community as her home, and never considered what might happen when he finally saw her true form: he might not want her anymore.

Her throat constricted, her chest tightened, and her breathing became a thin whistling sound. She touched her watch, flashing to a plateau outside the Enclave, and found the North Star in the night sky—the same star that seemed to guide her to Sierra Escondida.

The tension eased and she took a deep, free breath. Her wings relaxed. Henry wasn't like her mother, or the Lux, or anyone else who had rejected her for not meeting their expectations. The way he fought to keep her on the Hill, no doubt lingered in her mind—he wanted her.

And she wanted him. They had other struggles ahead of them, but for the moment, she refused to let those obstacles cloud her mind. Instead, she envisioned his arms around her and couldn't wait for seven days to pass. By then, she'd find a solution to the fang serum problem.

She just had to.

CHAPTER 4

Henry woke when the sun set, relief and regret rising as he did. Last night had been a fiasco.

The council could have shown more compassion. They could have let him speak to Cerissa after the hearing. They could have given him a private moment alone with her. But Tig had taken the council literally, and she and Yacov had rushed him back home.

After two weeks apart and more than one misstep on his part, he hadn't had a proper opportunity to apologize in person to Cerissa. Sure, he'd sent her a clandestine note shortly after his incarceration began, but he owed her face-to-face amends.

The whole debacle had been his fault. He should have listened to her in the first place when she questioned his decision to go to the ball game without a vampire escort. His pride, his fear of being controlled by a woman, had stopped his ears from hearing her warnings.

Never again will I be so obtuse.

He took a deep breath. At least the council's judgment was behind him, the plea deal ultimately honored. He didn't like the threat of a flogging hanging over his head, but for two years, he could behave himself.

Yet the terms of his present confinement remained unclear. He'd been allowed no outside communications during the prior two weeks. But what about now? A quick exchange of emails with the mayor clarified the matter: he could have no contact with Cerissa, but he could make business calls. He read between the lines—the mayor was trying to keep Rolf happy.

As if Rolf deserved to be happy after the stunt he pulled.

They had co-owned the Vasquez Müller Winery for over half a

century. Was it time to end their partnership? Rolf's behavior over Cerissa was completely out of line.

Henry sent a quick email to his attorney, asking for a preliminary assessment of what it would take to end the partnership. It was all he could do for now.

He dined on a bag of donor blood, followed by a chaser of Yacov's blood—a daily dose to help him heal. With the passing of each day's sleep, the ache in his gut lessened. He climbed the stairs to his home office on the second floor, leaning on the rail, his other arm pressed against his stomach. By the time he saw Cerissa again, the pain should be gone.

As he settled into his office chair, the throbbing subsided, and he looked at the yellow legal pad in front of him. Written in the *Itálica* script the priests had drilled into him as a child during the early 1800s—those were some unpleasant memories—he considered the tasks in front of him. At the top of the list was Leopold.

Cerissa had been under contract to Leopold as his envoy when Henry met her. Through a fluke, he'd discovered her true nature, although he'd yet to see her full Lux body. In addition to her ability to change shape, she had enhanced senses and would live much longer than mortals did. Only he knew she was Lux. Even Leopold, who knew she was long-lived, didn't know about the Lux.

As Henry spent time with her, their dating had progressed through the usual phases, culminating in their first and only night of making love.

So beautiful, so sensual.

He didn't take her blood that night. Under the treaty, he could only take her blood if he had the approval of her sponsor. Leopold had extorted one point two million dollars for the right, except Leopold misled him.

Cerissa's contract allowed her to become mated in blood after giving Leopold notice. She had already given Leopold the required notice, something Henry didn't learn until *after* he paid Leopold for the right.

It was his own fault for failing to discuss it with Cerissa. Still, it was Leopold who was in the wrong. Leopold could not sell something he didn't own.

Henry continued to stare at the yellow pad of paper. One point two million—rebalancing his portfolio meant taking a loss due to a recent market dip. He had been willing to sacrifice the money to make Cerissa his mate, but the sacrifice had been unnecessary.

After brooding about it for two weeks, he was now free to do something. No one would make a fool of him—not even Leopold.

He picked up the phone, but twenty minutes later, it was not going well. Leopold would not return the money.

"We have always been on good terms," Henry reminded him. "You would destroy our friendship to make a profit on something you had no right to sell?"

"*Caveat emptor*, Henry. You should have checked with Cerissa first. You didn't research the matter—surprising, for you—but the money is mine."

"Misrepresentation is the exception to 'buyer beware.' What you told me was a material misrepresentation, Leopold. Very material. You had no right to keep me from her."

"By the treaty—"

"For purposes of becoming mated in blood, she was freed from your contract and thus by treaty. I expect you to refund the money by tomorrow evening."

"Expect all you like. Sue me, even. But if you do, consider how Cerissa will feel when I tell her the truth. You treated her as a prized cow to be bought and sold. Would you rather have her affections or your money?"

"She already knows about our deal. I told her weeks ago. Now whose good name is on the line?"

Silence. "Since she already knows, I have nothing to lose by keeping the money."

"Leopold, you are being entirely unfair—"

The *thunk* of an old-fashioned handset being slammed in its cradle cut him off. Henry checked his cell phone. Leopold had hung up on him.

I'm not calling him back.

He ripped the top sheet off the pad of paper, and on a blank page, listed the pros and cons of suing Leopold before a treaty tribunal. Was recovering the money worth the embarrassment?

Maybe.

But he wasn't the only one who'd be embarrassed if the matter became public. Cerissa may not want their dirty laundry aired, and he couldn't afford to screw up again. He'd bungled things enough already. His desires, his *pride* had to take second place to making her happy.

Besides, as Leopold's envoy, she owed Leopold a duty of loyalty. In a legal battle between her sponsor and her lover, which side would she take?

An email from Rolf popped up on Henry's phone. What could he possibly want? Henry read through Rolf's screed, his ire growing stronger.

Rolf wanted Henry to forsake Cerissa. Was this why Rolf voted to extend Henry's house arrest? So Rolf had seven more nights to harangue Henry into changing his mind?

That will never happen.

He clipped his phone to his belt and picked up his pen, returning to his dispute with Leopold, adding more pros and cons to his list.

The doorbell rang. He tossed his pen onto his desk's blotter and limped downstairs.

The entryway was dark. He flicked on the light switch, the wrought iron chandelier coming to life, and swiped the computer screen by his door, waking the security camera.

He had learned his lesson from Blanche's attack—never turn the brass deadbolt without first checking who stood outside.

He swung the heavy oak door open. "Good evening, Tig."

She removed her chief's cap, tucking it under her arm, the black bill facing him. "I got your message last night."

"Thank you for stopping by." After the hearing, he had discovered a piece of evidence, something that might help her investigation. "We can talk in the drawing room."

He stepped aside and allowed her to lead the way. The large room occupied half of the first floor of his Spanish Colonial home and had walnut-stained open beams across the ceiling, with a river-stone fireplace at one end.

He offered her the mahogany-framed leather chair opposite his, the armrests carved to resemble the claws of a large animal. Tig placed a leather folio on her lap, the edge of a computer tablet peeking out.

"Did you learn anything from Blanche?" he asked, taking his own seat.

She shook her head. "When Blanche woke, she was in full revenant mode."

He raised one eyebrow. Revenant? Really? Vampires unpredictably fell victim to the condition as they aged. Some compared it to Alzheimer's in mortals. But Blanche was too young to have the condition, unless being separated from one's heart could trigger it. Of course, Tig didn't know Blanche had been heartless—in more ways than one.

"Did she say anything you could use at all?" he asked.

"Mostly she screamed wordlessly, growled, and grunted. Dr. Clarke and Dr. Patel worked on her for over four hours, with no improvement. Dr. Patel's idea was a good one, even if it didn't work. She's going to be a big help on the Hill. I'm glad the council is letting her stay."

"As am I." He looked at his hands, his fingers interlaced over his lap. "With the hearing over, I don't understand why I'm not allowed to speak to her. The fear I might influence her testimony has passed."

Tig shrugged. "Council orders."

"But prisoners are allowed visitors at our jail."

"Henry, relax. It won't be long. Gaea tells me Cerissa is as anxious to see you as you are to see her."

He smiled. "That is kind of you to say."

Tig opened the folio, slipped a stylus out of the center loop, and awakened the sleeping tablet. "Anyway, whatever Yacov did to subdue Blanche apparently caused permanent damage. The doctors figured it was hopeless, so we had to put her down."

"A shame. I was looking forward to seeing her tortured to death."

"Dr. Clarke believes she was defective, her brain moving through early revenant, and that's why she staged the attacks."

Tig handed him the iPad. The screen was open to the doctor's report. He quickly scanned it.

"But you don't agree with the doctor?" he asked, returning the tablet to her.

"We searched her cell phone. It was a burner phone—minutes paid for in advance, no registration. She'd taken a photo, a selfie with you on the ground behind her."

"I have no memory of it." Most of the attack was like a distant nightmare, except for Cerissa—he would never forget seeing her beautiful face when he regained consciousness.

"Blanche texted the photo to another burner phone, with a message: 'Pay me.' We traced the receiving phone to San Diego, based on the cell towers it pinged, but it's been turned off and not used since the night after you were shot."

There was only one clear reason for that. "She was working with someone else, and when they learned I was alive, they stopped using their phone."

"Exactly. The history in Blanche's phone was sparse: a few text messages to the vampires who came after you at the baseball stadium, and a message to the San Diego burner phone, sending photos of you. That's it. The evidence points to San Diego as the locus of the conspiracy."

"I see."

"Now it's your turn, Henry. You emailed me about something you discovered."

He stood and went over to the fireplace, where he'd left a paper bag, originally intending to burn it. He reached into the bag, unfolded a piece of paper, and handed it to her. "I found this last night."

She took the page and held it to the light. Dried blood covered it, indecipherable text beneath the red crust. "Your blood, I assume?"

"It was in the pocket of my bathrobe—the one I was wearing when Blanche shot me. I was going to burn the bathrobe after the council hearing. That's when I found the email."

"I'll see if Jayden can remove the blood and enhance the writing."

"If it can be done, I'm sure Jayden can do it."

Henry had been on the hiring committee when Jayden Johnson was brought on as Tig's second-in-command three years ago. Since Jayden was Tig's mate, they couldn't let the chief make the decision. The committee was particularly impressed with Jayden's forensics skills.

"Seeing the email triggered a memory," Henry said, placing the paper bag down on the floor next to his chair. "The email is a fake."

"Fake?"

"Blanche stuffed it in my pocket to frame another community for my death and start a war between us."

"Who did she frame?"

"I don't know. Perhaps the email will tell you."

"Anything else?"

He paused for a moment, straining to remember. "Blanche spoke of changing things on a grander scale." He shook his head, frustrated with his spotty memory. "I'm sorry, Tig. That's all I recall until Yacov rescued me."

"That's okay. Tell me again how Yacov subdued Blanche. Her condition upon waking was so unusual, and we're trying to understand what happened."

"We were discussing my case when the doorbell rang," Henry said, repeating one of the white lies he'd told to protect Cerissa. "I assumed it was you and answered the door. Blanche fired immediately. Yacov heard the shots and circled through the kitchen, grabbing a large knife."

It had taken much imploring on Henry's part before Yacov agreed to the cover story. As Henry's representative at the hearing, Yacov was entitled to visit him at any time during his house arrest, making the story plausible. "Yacov snuck out the back door and surprised Blanche from behind. He slit her throat and sliced her open, or so he told me. By the time it happened, I was on the ground and not understanding very much at all."

"So Yacov didn't hear any part of this conversation?" she asked, her voice laced with skepticism.

"I am sure he told you he didn't."

Tig gave him a stern look. "I'm just double-checking all the facts—you understand."

Had he sounded defensive? He couldn't risk making the chief suspicious. "Of course," he said, lightening his tone. "I'm sorry I can't be of more assistance."

"It's okay. We'll work with what we have—and this helps." She slid a plastic bag out of her back pocket and dropped the crusty paper into it. "Did you see the message the mayor sent out?"

Henry unclipped his phone from his belt and scrolled through his email until he found the mayor's announcement.

"He's told the community that Blanche's death closed the case?" Henry asked, his voice rising in irritation. "This makes no sense. What about the text messages you found on Blanche's phone and her comments to me?"

"I'll fill him in on what you've remembered, but I doubt he'll change his mind."

What was Winston thinking? Lying to the community protected no one. Henry raised an eyebrow. "Then you'll just give up?"

"I'm going to keep investigating." She opened her hand and fanned her fingers, a gesture of *don't worry*. "I've been ordered to keep it low profile with the community. The council has been briefed, but the mayor doesn't want hysteria to spread."

"You mean he doesn't want you to contradict him."

"It's not only the mayor. The council's concerns are valid—they don't want this to turn neighbor against neighbor." Tig took a deep breath and let it out. "Speaking of neighbors, I've been going through the list of those who might carry a grudge against both you and Yacov."

"You're still pursuing that, then?"

"Until we have a better lead, Jayden and I are going to finish ruling out those on your list." She looked down at her iPad, using her finger to scroll through whatever she had opened. "What about Councilman Frédéric? What's his story?"

"Back when I was on the council, he requested permission to turn his mate, and the council denied the request. Yacov and I voted with the majority."

"When was this?"

Henry looked toward the ceiling, trying to recall the year. "Around 1929, maybe. I seem to associate it with the stock market crash." He returned his gaze to Tig. "Frédéric had only been vampire about twenty years. Too young to successfully turn anyone, so we denied it."

"Any sense he carries a grudge?"

"Aside from the fact he has his head buried so far—"

"Up Rolf's ass?" Tig finished for him.

Henry frowned at her. He disliked the crudeness of this current age. "I was going to say, 'buried so far in the sand he does not see what is around him.'"

"Which is?"

"After Maude died—"

"Maude was his mate?"

"Yes. After she died, his attitude changed."

The creases between Tig's eyebrows deepened. "Changed in what way?"

"After a time, he came to see we were right. He was too young and risked creating a defective offspring—a much worse outcome for Maude than death."

"Ah. Is that why he hasn't had a mate live with him in the sixty-seven years I've been here? He was too young?"

"In part. From what Rolf tells me, Frédéric was waiting until he was at least a hundred to seriously date anyone—he doesn't want to fall in love again and be disappointed. So he avoids it altogether."

"But he's over a hundred now. The ban on creating new vampires—"

"Has disrupted his plans, yes. But he supported the ban. He understood the risks we face if our population grows."

"Starvation or a devastating war for control of a limited food supply."

"Precisely. So, he put his own desires aside to deal with at another time. In the meantime, he has adopted many of the, shall we say, *conservative* viewpoints Rolf espouses. Like Rolf, he wants more restrictions on mortals who are brought to the Hill, and he believes we can't rely on the loyalty bond to keep them from telling other mortals about us—despite all evidence to the contrary. He also wants mortal mates confined to the Hill unless traveling with their vampire."

"I had the sense he always voted with Rolf, but I didn't realize this was the underlying reason."

Henry cocked his head to the side, considering carefully his next words. "Like I said, he doesn't carry a grudge against Yacov, me, or the others who were on the council at the time and voted against turning Maude. He has come to see the truth of the matter."

"Hmm," Tig said, tapping her stylus on the edge of her iPad. "Yacov is on the subcommittee on mortal rights. Neither Rolf nor Frédéric will be happy with the measures they've been discussing. Haley wants them to open a council seat for a mortal."

He cringed internally. *A mortal on a vampire council?*

"The council trusts Yacov," he said instead. "But the subcommittee wasn't what motivated Blanche. I've taken no public stand on mortal rights."

Although Cerissa had made him see the folly of treating mortals like second-class citizens—they should have the right to vote—but a council seat? Was that going too far?

Tig looked down at her iPad again, her finger scrolling down the screen. "You told me Rolf is your current heir—"

"And I also told you Rolf isn't behind the attacks."

"He's been displaying unusual behavior lately."

Henry clenched his teeth. *Yes, the trial.* It would be a long time before he forgave that particular betrayal. "Rolf may try to humiliate me, even have me whipped, but he would never try to kill me."

"Are you sure? Rolf has been off the Hill a lot. Most of his travel permits are for San Diego."

"I'm aware of Rolf's business travel. But I will reiterate: he would never murder Yacov or me."

"I wish I was as certain as you are, Founder." She swiped at the screen. "I noticed Marcus's offspring is also on your list."

"Ah yes, Oscar. He wants to rejoin our community. We've turned him down each time."

"I'm having the files pulled, but is there any reason Marcus should be on your list as well? Does he want Oscar back?"

"Marcus? None that I know of." Aside from the fact Marcus lost control of the council during plea negotiations, he and the town attorney had been friends since the mid-1800s, when Marcus was still mortal, decades before they founded Sierra Escondida. "He doesn't want Oscar on the Hill any more than the rest of us do."

She turned off her iPad and slid it back into her folio. "I did the background check on Oscar when he last applied for residency five years ago. I didn't see anything back then that raised concerns."

"And I know of nothing that has changed. Do you have any questions about the others on our list?"

"Not at this time." Tig's cell phone buzzed, and she glanced at it. "My apologies, but it's time for me to go. I have another appointment."

"If you need anything further from me, please let me know."

"I will."

She stood, and he accompanied her to the door.

"Your appointment," he said. "Something to do with the case?"

"No, I'm on my way to Ruthton. A new matter."

How could something in Ruthton affect the Hill? Ruthton was on the other side of Mordida, and didn't share any borders with Sierra Escondida. While it was within the hundred-mile "no hunting" zone, no vampire would violate that rule by hunting there, not with the council imposing punishments from the dark ages.

"Police business?" he asked.

"Unfortunately, yes." A grim look dropped like a curtain over her face. "It appears we have a serial killer in our backyard."

CHAPTER 5

RUTHTON POLICE DEPARTMENT—SAME NIGHT

Tig drove to Ruthton in the department's vehicle, a shimmery dark gray Cadillac. It was hers to use anytime it wasn't needed for surveillance work. As she passed the Hill's gates, she snorted to herself in disgust.

Henry was right. Blanche's death hadn't ended anything. Telling the community it was over was the stupidest decision she'd yet heard from the town council.

But she had to publicly support it.

Did she really want to work for such idiots? It seemed like her bosses became stupider the higher up the food chain she moved. It hadn't been that way when she started out as a mercenary for Phat. Now there was a brilliant strategist. She'd learned a lot from the vampire who turned her.

She huffed out a frustrated breath and ran a hand over her one-inch afro, patting it down as she glanced in the rearview mirror. The only reason she had any hair at all was because Phat had turned her vampire a few months after the death of her mortal husband. Maasai wives traditionally shaved their heads, except when in mourning.

She'd been born in Africa more than four hundred years ago and had the high, angular cheekbones and small, broad nose of her kin. Her chin tucked under slightly and her skin was the color of dark walnut wood, another trait of her people. The only ambition she had back then was to be the wife with the largest herd of cattle.

But after she'd been turned, she had lived as a warrior, a spy, and a mercenary. Now, she was a police chief who had to deal with power-hungry assholes and their politics.

If the Hill didn't provide such a stable home for Jayden, she would have considered moving. But there weren't many vampire communities where Jayden could get work as a police captain, with the commensurate salary and respect afforded his position here.

Thirty minutes later, still fuming over the council's idiocy, Tig strode into Chief Nguyen's office. She'd come alone—the Rule of Two didn't apply to her when she was on the job. She could travel to the neighboring cities without another vampire, and she preferred it that way. She didn't want anyone else knowing where she went or why—not until she had the hard evidence she was looking for.

"Chief Anderson," Nguyen said, moving from behind his desk, his hand extended to shake hers. "To what do we owe the honor of your visit?"

She shook his hand, not concerned he might notice her skin's slightly lower temperature. Most polite folk never mentioned it. "I'm here about the murder victim who was found at Hotel Ruthton."

His eyes grew wide. "Do you have a similar case in your jurisdiction?"

"I received an anonymous tip saying I should look into it. I'm following up." In truth, there was no tip. Her visit was prompted by something she had read on the police blotter tonight.

Chief Nguyen motioned toward the door. "You'll want to talk with the detective in charge of the case."

Tig followed him out of the administrative offices and to the detectives' bullpen, where Nguyen introduced her to Detective Moore. Moore didn't bother raising his lanky body when he greeted her. He had a worn look that matched the old, beaten desk he slouched over. Years of investigating the worst crimes could age mortals prematurely. She'd seen it many times.

"I'll leave you two to talk," Chief Nguyen said. "I have paperwork to complete. City council meeting tomorrow." He rolled his eyes toward the ceiling.

She understood his unspoken message and couldn't agree more. They both wasted too much valuable time on paperwork and politicians.

"Thanks, chief," she said, shaking his hand goodbye.

She turned back to the haggard detective, noticing his stained tie and mop of unkempt red hair. She tried not to let his sloppy appearance influence her opinion.

"Detective, can you brief me on what happened?"

"We're pretty sure we have a serial killer on our hands," he replied, leaning back in his chair to look at her. "Same MO as the two victims found in Carlyle, except this time our victim is female."

"That's unusual for a serial killer."

"True, makes it a wobbler. Usually they'll fixate on one gender." He shrugged his rounded shoulders. "We're calling him the Carlyle Cutter for now."

"He's male?"

"Yeah, we got lucky. Hotel surveillance camera."

"May I see the video?"

"Sure, have a seat," he said, gesturing to the guest chair.

He swiveled his computer monitor, opened the file, and hit play. A five-second shot of two people walking in and out of camera range played onscreen. The black-and-white video was low resolution and jumpy. Tig clenched her fists in frustration. The hotel should have upgraded their video system years ago.

The detective hit "play" again on the video and then paused it. On-screen, the light-haired woman wore a tight skirt and high heels.

"The woman was the victim?" she asked.

"Yup. It's hard to tell facial detail, but the hair and clothing match."

The other person in the video wore an oversized bomber jacket, the leather collar turned up hiding his neck and chin. A baseball cap covered his head, with not even an inch of hair showing. The bill tilted over his eyes and his hands were stuck in his pockets—hard to get a positive ID. For all she knew, it was someone from the Hill.

"You think the killer's male?" Tig asked. The Cutter was of average build, but not too tall. "Couldn't it be a large woman?"

"We showed the video to the hotel bartender, and based on the clothing, she confirmed he'd been in the bar. She said he was a white male. Scoot in closer, and I'll play it again," the detective offered.

Tig didn't need to move in closer to see it, but humored the detective. She stared at the video intently as he played it again. Could they identify something about the killer, even the rhythm of his walk?

Two more replays and no luck. She looked over at the detective. "Was the bartender able to describe him?"

"She worked with a sketch artist and gave up. He never came to the bar himself, his date did, so she didn't get a close look at him."

"Any DNA evidence in the hotel room?"

"Too soon to tell. The lab is going over everything."

"How close is it to the murders in Carlyle?"

"The cuts on the victim, the way he goes about mutilating the body, all identical." Moore closed the video window and opened another screen— photographs of the dead woman. "He's even using the same kind of knife."

"Surgical scalpel?"

"Nah, not from the size of the wounds." He hit the enlarge button and pointed to an area on the victim's torso. "The cuts aren't that clean."

"Victim was alive when it happened?"

"At the beginning," the detective said. "He's making what the medical examiner called 'twenty ritualistic cuts.' We haven't told the public yet, so keep that between us."

"Ritualistic?"

"Both bodies—same cuts, same locations." He pointed at the photo. "He starts with one cut above the right breast, straight line here, about an inch long."

She stared at the photo of the first wound. "How can you tell?"

"Blood clotted and dried on that one. He takes his time."

"And the rest?"

"He spells out 'NEVEr' on the stomach. Block letters, except the 'r' is drawn like a small 'r,' with the hook as a straight line. The word measures about six inches." He flipped through more photos until he came to a close-up of the r. "Underneath the word, he draws a shape like a diamond. If you count each cut in the letters, plus the one above the breast and the four sides of the diamond, you get twenty cuts."

"Fuck," she said. Even with everything she'd seen over a long lifetime, it seemed excessively cruel to her. "Sorry."

"I said worse when I first saw the body." He clicked to the next photo and zoomed in. "See the puncture wound there?" He pointed at the throat of the victim. "He punctures through the jugular at some point. ME isn't counting it in the ritualistic cuts, 'cause it seems to have a purpose. He bleeds them out. Tapping an artery like that, the heart pumps out the blood for him."

One puncture, not two. Were any Hill vampires missing a fang? She'd check V-Trak later.

"Why does he bleed them out? He's already cutting them when alive."

"Makes it less messy when he starts hacking off the fingers, we think."

"Fingers? Does he remove all of them?"

"All ten."

"Any clue why?"

"Just a guess: some asshole probably finger-raped him—it's like he's saying, 'No one will ever do that again.'"

"Does he take the fingers with him?"

"Nope. He lines them up on the nightstand all nice and neat." He changed photos to a wooden surface, marred by small blood pools in linear order. "When he's done, he stuffs them into various orifices."

The photo changed again to a close-up of the victim's mouth.

"Which is why you suspect sexual molestation."

"That's our thinking."

"But what about the diamond shape he carves?"

"We don't have a theory to explain it just yet."

Hmm. The only person she knew with a connection to diamonds was Yacov. He worked as a diamond cutter. But she couldn't see him doing anything like this. This kind of crazy would show up in other ways, and Yacov was way too sane.

Moore closed the computer window. The mutilated body disappeared from the screen. "Strange part is, he collects the blood and leaves with it."

This was the real reason she wanted to find out more. The victim's blood would fetch a high price on the vampire black market from all the stress hormones released in response to fear and pain. Drinking it would impart the same adrenaline-induced high created by the blood of a live victim who had been hunted and cornered.

She shivered at the thought. Had he stood over the body, sucking the blood out of each finger, the way mortals sucked juice from a crab's claw?

"The bodies in Carlyle were dumped in separate garbage bins, completely drained." Moore paused to take a sip of coffee. "Hey, would you like a cup? I started a fresh pot right before you arrived."

"No, thank you. Please continue."

"Do you mind if I get a refresher? Been a long day already." He stood, and she followed him to the coffee maker.

"Anyway," the detective said, as he poured himself more coffee. He hadn't bothered to dump out the dregs of the prior cup. "Something must have interrupted the perp this time. He didn't take the body with him. The bed was draped with plastic—it's like he could fold it around the victim and carry the evidence away with him."

"What about DNA?"

"I doubt it," he said, leading the way back to his desk. "The Cutter splashed a gallon of bleach on the body."

"How do you know he takes the blood with him?"

"The ME says there wasn't enough blood on the plastic tarp to account for all the blood missing from the body." He paused to sip his coffee. "Serial killers often take something from their victims. They'll fondle it and jack off, remembering the kill, but blood's an odd one, 'cause it spoils so quickly."

"Who rented the room?"

"It was under the victim's name."

"Anything else?"

"Not yet. We're waiting on the forensics lab." The detective gave a long, wide yawn. "The drug tests aren't back yet. I'll post the results when they're in. In the meantime, we're still searching for witnesses. Might get lucky—someone might have seen him when he left."

"When was that?"

"The doors are electronic; the hotel's system logs it every time one is opened. The last time the door was opened before the maids found the victim was five fifteen this morning."

Fuck. A good hour before sunrise. He could be a vampire. He could even be Zeke, one of her part-time officers.

Zeke fit the meager description and had a taste for adrenaline-spiked blood. He fed his habit by taking assignments as a government assassin in foreign countries. But would he torture and kill victims in his own backyard? If anything, Zeke was too smart for that, and from the reports she'd had, his kills were usually quick, nothing as bizarre as this. Still, even the smartest ones made mistakes when the compulsion overcame them.

"Do you have any video of him leaving?" she asked. She wanted another view of the Cutter, anything that would let her rule out someone from the Hill.

"Now that's the strange part," the detective said, his chair squeaking as he eased back in it. "The Cutter dodged all the security cameras on his way out. It's like he vanished from the room, which would be hard to do, lugging one and a half gallons of blood."

Not hard at all if he drank it first. "Would you mind making a copy of the video for me?"

"You think it could be someone in your jurisdiction?"

"There had to be a reason for the anonymous tip I received."

"Sure thing, chief. Won't take but a minute." He dug through a box of flash drives on his desk and inserted one into the computer. Less than a minute later, he unplugged the drive and handed it to her. "If you find the sick bastard, call me."

"Of course, detective," she agreed. But she'd pick up the phone only if the perp turned out to be mortal.

If the Cutter was a vampire, the council would never let it get that far. They'd order his death, and she'd take care of him herself. No mortal police agency would be the wiser. Not the best solution for the victims' families, but the Hill didn't have a choice—at least not if they wanted to keep the existence of vampires a secret.

She walked back to her car and tossed her cap onto the passenger seat. Scrubbing her hand over her head, she heaved out a loud sigh.

Like I don't have enough on my plate or anything.

She started the Cadillac and began the drive back to the Hill. She was looking at another all-nighter with no time for Jayden. This was beginning to seem less and less like the dream job she thought it was.

Sure, she had liked her job up to this point. At times it was a bit monotonous, but any job had that problem when you worked it long enough. And the Hill was a good place for Jayden, so long as her job didn't keep them apart too much.

So what loyalty did she owe the community? The thought niggled at her. She didn't want to uproot Jayden. But a change of careers might give them more time together.

She shook her head. One all-nighter wasn't a reason to leave. Still, if that was true, then why did she feel compelled to check the "help wanted" ads published online by the treaty communities?

Screw it. She'd check the ads when she reached her office. It wouldn't take long, and it might put the urge to rest. After all, she could afford five minutes for herself tonight. The Hill didn't deserve every second of her time awake, not when the council was acting as stupid as they were.

CHAPTER 6

The North Star was high in the night sky. A few clouds drifted by, but Sierra Escondida's undeveloped section had no street lights, letting the stars shine through. Seeing the North Star reminded Cerissa she was on the right path.

Only one more night and I'll be in Henry's arms again.

The crowd she led moved closer to the weed-strewn field, and she pushed aside fantasies of Henry. Right now, she had to focus on the forty potential investors following her.

Tonight's presentation would make or break her project. She wanted to hire an experienced marketing person to handle investor sign-ups, but Leopold had nixed the idea.

Instead, she had to convince this all-vampire group to fund her biotech research lab. They had traveled from various California and Nevada communities to hear her pitch.

The parcel they stood by was located on the public side of the Hill's wall, near the outskirts of Sierra Escondida's business district. The wall shielded the private vineyard estates from the general public. With her back to the crowd, she used a flashlight to point in the direction of the four corners.

"We plan on building our lab here," she explained. She gestured with the flashlight to the empty lot, spring weeds standing waist-high under the night sky. "We have a purchase option for this parcel and we've submitted a land use application to build the lab here. The town's planning department is currently reviewing it."

She turned to face the group again. "Almost sixty acres of vacant land—it will be easy to build the lab once we have sufficient investors and council approval."

The mayor sidled next to her and cleared his throat, bringing all eyes to him. "I'm sure if Dr. Patel obtains sufficient investors, the town council will have no problem approving the project."

His mouth shouldn't write checks he doesn't have the political capital to cover.

Three of the other town council members were present—only Rolf was missing. Carolyn and Liza seemed to like her, but she wasn't sure she'd have their vote. Rolf and Frédéric were outright hostile to her presence, and likewise, to the lab.

Such pointless animosity.

She wanted to *help* them, for goodness' sake. She tugged at the front of her suit jacket to straighten it, displacing her irritation on the fabric. She still hadn't forgiven the mayor for voting to whip Henry. At least he hadn't banked the political capital needed to carry it out.

When the mayor stopped speaking, she said, "Thank you, Mayor Mason. Now—"

"One minute there, Miss Priss." Councilwoman Carolyn waved her finger and stepped forward. "I don't want our grand visitors thinkin' we've already approved the project. I'm waiting until the town planners present it to us b'fore I make my decision, but I don't take to the idea of Henry expanding his business interests here—no, I certainly do not. This land should be saved for some of our younger residents. Let them use it to expand their businesses."

Oh damn. Carolyn had it all wrong.

"Ah, Henry isn't an investor," Cerissa said, and stopped, not wanting to say anything more that might hurt him in the eyes of his community. Leopold had refused to let Henry invest due to an old grudge between them.

Carolyn screwed up her face in disbelief. "Now, honey, there's no need to tell us a tall one. He's gonna be your mate. Of course he'll invest." The councilwoman paused for a moment while Frédéric whispered in her ear. "Unless he reckons it's a bad investment?"

"No, not at all. He wanted to invest. He asked early on."

"Then why ain't he?"

Well, so much for dodging the details. "Because Leopold won't let him."

Carolyn seemed to weigh this new information, and then let out a loud laugh. "Leave it to men. Leopold's afraid Henry'll have too much control over the whole darn thing, what with you becoming Henry's mate and all."

Others joined in Carolyn's laughter, and heat rose to Cerissa's cheeks.

The way some vampires viewed mortals ground at her stomach. No one controlled her—well, no one except her Lux superiors, but that would change soon.

As much as she wanted to set the record straight, perhaps it was better not to correct Carolyn's assumption. Henry had already been embarrassed enough by the hearing, and from what she'd seen so far, Henry's pride ran deep.

Before she could return to her prepared remarks, a man hidden by the crowd said, "Hey, I got a question."

Barney Morrison, the San Diego representative, pushed his way through the front row. "Why build your lab here?" he asked. "Why not pick one of the other communities?"

"We considered others, but Sierra Escondida offers the most advantages. Finding undeveloped land at a reasonable price is difficult to do. Distribution will be easy because we're near a major shipping center. And no other community controls an entire town like the Hill does."

Barney scratched at his chin. "Yeah, about that. I heard a rumor and I feel we have a right to know before we invest. So this question is for Mayor Mason. Is it true the Hill has plans to allow mortals to serve on your town council?"

What an asshat. She struggled to keep her face neutral, although she could feel her eyes narrowing. *Don't say anything—you can't be political.*

"Well, um, harrumph," the mayor sputtered, still standing at Cerissa's elbow. "Nothing so drastic as that. Just a small exploratory committee, I assure you. We're looking at ways to make mortals feel more like they are partners in our community."

Barney stuck his nose in the air, a look of distaste on his face. "In San Diego, mortals know their place. And it isn't as partners."

A few laughs, but most of those gathered had their lips pressed together in disapproval.

I'll review the video later, see if I can spot who laughed.

Members of the vampire dominance movement—the VDM—would hold attitudes similar to Barney's. The Lux had intercepted electronic messages that pointed to a nascent vampire movement to enslave mortals. So far, Ari's computer hacking hadn't discovered anything to connect the attacks against Henry and Yacov to the VDM. Still, she had to keep working her mission for the Lux—trying to discover if the VDM existed—until she figured out how to make a clean break from her people without losing her wings.

She took a deep breath and stepped forward, signaling her intent to resume speaking. "In a few weeks, I plan on traveling to each of your communities to talk with your members about investing in the lab. I can safely say the communities who invest early will receive preferential treatment when distribution begins."

A small murmur rippled through the crowd.

The lodge master from San Francisco, Victoria Rutherford, turned to her. "When will we be able to sample the goods? I mean, we could invest millions, and never see a drop of blood."

"Our prototype requires special equipment to survive. We can't bring it to California until the lab is built and support equipment installed. I could have samples shipped here, but there would be no way to prove their origin."

"You still haven't answered my question."

Damn. If the other representatives returned to their communities with negative views, the project was sunk. And after Carolyn's comments, Cerissa couldn't afford to fumble the question, but she didn't have a satisfying answer.

"How does this sound?" she said, tugging at her the hem of her suit jacket again and improvising on the spot. "Leopold will give you his personal guarantee. If we don't begin to produce a blood supply within five years, he'll reimburse each investor eighty cents on the dollar, tax-free, using money from outside the U.S. Between the tax write-off you'll have, and Leopold's guarantee, you'll make money even if the Biologics Research Lab never does."

Victoria appeared satisfied, and the crowd's energy relaxed.

Now it was Cerissa's mouth writing checks she wasn't sure she could cover. She just hoped she could convince Leopold to agree with her scheme before those checks bounced.

CHAPTER 7

FRÉDÉRIC BONHOMME'S HOUSE—LATER THAT SAME NIGHT

Tig took the chair Frédéric offered her. She'd never been in his study before. The man had an obsession with Greek gods, particularly Zeus.

Seven replica statues rested on a low hardwood credenza, including a bust and six full body miniatures, one naked. She wasn't an expert in Greek mythology, but she didn't need to be. The nameplates identified each figure as Zeus.

Even the painting over the credenza depicted Zeus on his throne, the other gods bowing before him.

She'd always suspected Frédéric had aspirations to become mayor. Was this the type of ruler he'd be? He wasn't someone she wanted to work for. If he got elected to the position, it would be one more strike against staying on the Hill, but she'd deal with it if and when it happened.

Frédéric smoothed back his long mustache, the ends so thin it reminded her of sprouting twigs on the acacia trees native to her Kenyan birthplace. His wiry brown hair was parted on the side and combed over, the waves creating a small mound like half an anthill. Tiny wrinkles appeared at the corners of his puffy eyes whenever he smiled. He had died at age twenty-nine in 1904, an era when people aged faster from working in the sun.

He took the chair across from her. "Your email was, shall we say, cryptic." His French accent was barely noticeable. "What is this about?"

"Do you mind if I record our conversation?" She started the recorder on her phone and placed it on the coffee table between them. She could have worn one of the lapel video cameras issued to her line officers, but recording only audio was less threatening to most people. After a few minutes, he would forget it was on.

He eyed the phone, looking unhappy. "I guess it's all right."

"Since you're on the council," she said, not giving him any time to change his mind, "you know they asked me to continue my investigation into Blanche's crimes quietly. I asked Henry and Yacov to make a list of people who might hold a grudge against them. Your name is on the list."

"My name?" He crossed his arms. "That's nonsense—why would my name be on their list?"

"Back in 1919—"

"Oh." He tweaked the end of his mustache. "Maude. It is because of Maude."

"Go ahead."

"Henry and Yacov voted against turning her." He snuffled, a sound like a pig rooting for grubs in the under bush. "They said I was too young."

Yeah, you were too young. The file listed his vampire age as fifteen years when he sought permission to turn Maude. Even in the early 1900s, most vampires knew the general rule: the younger the maker, the more demented the offspring.

She nodded, inviting him to continue.

"I met Maude when she was eight years old." His eyes took on a slightly glazed look as he recalled the past. "Such a precious child, so obedient to her parents. Her father tutored me in English when I came over from France. I believe it was in 1905."

She'd heard of robbing the cradle, but eight years old? Even her people had waited until a girl reached menarche. She glanced at her iPad. "You married Maude when she turned sixteen?"

"I waited until she was marriageable, yes."

"And she died—"

"In her fifties. A heart condition. I was devastated at the time."

"And how do you feel now?"

"I know where you're going." His voice was light, like a pleasant laugh hid behind his words. "I don't blame Henry or Yacov. They were right. I could have caused her real harm, turning her. Instead, I had her whole and well for forty years."

"But didn't you—"

He waved his hand, as if to silence her. "At the time, yes, I was upset with them. At the time, though, I was madly in love." He shrugged. "But my views have changed."

"In what way?"

He twisted the end of his sticklike mustache, a mannerism she'd seen many times—usually when he was being cautious about what he said. "We need to be *selective* in who we turn. Being in love shouldn't be the sole reason. Becoming vampire grants a large boon, and we should only bring over the best and the brightest."

"So you support the treaty restrictions?"

"How could I not?"

She looked down at the notes on her iPad and scrolled to another page. "The records from back then aren't clear. Who was your maker?"

"Eugénie. You wouldn't know her. She was staked the year after I was turned; another reason to leave France."

"What happened?"

"Wrong place, wrong time. A Catholic priest saw her returning to a cemetery, and killed her during the day. What can I say? It was unfortunate."

Hmm. Not worth pushing any further. She couldn't see a link between his maker's death and the attacks on Henry and Yacov.

He crossed his legs. "I'm surprised Henry didn't tell you about Anne-Louise."

"What about Anne-Louise?"

"Her sire is my grandsire."

Henry hadn't mentioned it. But then, why would he? Frédéric hadn't been attacked, so there was no reason to assume the connection held any relevance.

"Do you ever go to New York to see Anne-Louise?" Tig asked.

"My word, no. Distant relations, really. And I haven't been back to the big city since getting off the boat. Maybe someday I'll go back, see how it's changed after a hundred years."

"Then why did you mention her?"

"I've heard through the grapevine that she and Henry aren't on good terms. I wasn't sure you knew."

"The 'grapevine'?"

"My grandsire mentioned it."

Tig already had Anne-Louise on her list. Why did people in two cities—New York and San Diego—keep coming up again and again? Tig glanced at the phone to make sure it was still recording, and asked, "How often do you go to San Diego?"

"Occasional business trips. Not often. Why?"

"As I mentioned to the council, the shooters came from a prison in San

Diego. If you've visited other communities around there, you may have heard something—a reason why Yacov and Henry were targeted."

"Not a thing. I don't often visit the other communities. I'm too busy with my winery and being on the council—between the two, I don't have much free time." Frédéric stood up. "Now, if there is nothing else, I have work to attend to."

She got to her feet, gathering up her phone and iPad. He'd given the answers she'd expected. Even if he lied about carrying a grudge, she saw no reason for him to suddenly become a killer. It made no sense that he'd act on it now after all this time.

"If you hear anything that might help our investigation, please contact me."

"But of course." He twisted his mustache again. "You'll be the first to know. I want these attacks over with."

CHAPTER 8

CERISSA'S ROOM AT GAEA'S HOUSE—THE NEXT DAY

After wooing investors and keeping vampire hours for the last week, Cerissa allowed herself to sleep in. Her alarm chimed at four in the afternoon. She opened her eyes and excitement flashed through her.

Tonight, Henry was once again a free man.

She stretched, and then she saw it. A red orchid lay on the pillow next to her, with a note: *My dearest Cerissa, please meet me at my house forty minutes after sunset. Have dinner at Gaea's. You can have dessert with me. With deepest affection, Henry.*

She sniffed the orchid—a sweet scent, like jasmine, but more delicate. Warmth filled her heart, her head grew light, and she flopped back on her pillow, a big grin on her face. The invitation could mean only one thing: by dawn, they would be blood mates in the eyes of the community.

Four hours seemed too long to wait. She yearned to see his beautiful eyes and broad shoulders—so handsome, her hero. He'd been willing to be whipped rather than lose her, and her heart skipped a beat at the memory.

She raised the note to her lips, kissing his signature.

But what should I wear?

She bounded out of bed, throwing open the closet door. She riffled through her dresses. Nothing seemed right.

Why didn't I buy something special?

Karen wouldn't have this problem. She had tons of clothes. The night Cerissa slept at Karen's house, celebrating the resolution to Henry's hearing, they'd gone through Karen's closet looking for gently used formalwear to donate to the women who lived on Mordida's military base. The base threw an annual formal event, and a military salary only stretched so far.

Then it dawned on her. What she wore *under* the dress mattered the most. She opened her lingerie drawer and took out the same lacey set she'd worn the first and only time they made love. There would be opportunity for variety later. This cream-colored bra and matching thong had special meaning to them both.

In the same drawer was a negligee Karen had insisted Cerissa buy during one of their shopping sprees. *Hmm.* Henry hadn't seen it yet. She slipped it into her purse, along with a few other things, including her hypo. If her theory worked, she had a way to deal with fang serum.

She showered and went back to the closet, settling on a light spring dress. The dress had big flowers on a field of white, the short skirt flaring slightly from the waist, showing off her long bronze legs. Her stomach growled.

Time for dinner. Or is it still called breakfast if it's my first meal of the day?

She made a quick veggie omelet, and not just because Henry suggested she eat first. Her Lux metabolism required frequent meals to keep her comfortably in human form.

She read her email as she ate—Dr. Clarke had finished his analysis of Blanche's blood and fang serum. No change in composition that he could detect. However, the amount of fang serum was less than usual. Fortunately, he chalked it up to Blanche's dehydrated condition.

Thirty minutes after sunset, Cerissa went searching for her hostess. Peeking into the parlor, she found Gaea reading on her Kindle.

"Evening, Gaea. I'm going over to Henry's house."

"His house?" Gaea raised a finger to her chin, tapping it. "Hmm. Are you sure you're ready for this?"

"Absolutely."

"Really, dear?" Gaea furrowed her brow, a look of concern washing over her face. "Please come in and let's discuss this first."

"I'm not sure there's anything to discuss."

"Please?" Gaea said, patting the tapestry chair opposite her.

Cerissa glanced at her watch. She had time to humor Gaea and stepped into the cozy room, easing onto the chair.

Gaea set her Kindle aside and folded her hands in her lap. "You've been apart for three weeks. Perhaps you should take things slowly? Get to know Henry a little more. Talk over with him exactly what this means. I mean, I know how independent-minded you are, dear."

Ah, so that's her concern.

Not much different from Carolyn's attitude—hell, just about every vampire Cerissa had met exhibited the same attitude—that mating would put her under Henry's dominion. Well, she wasn't mortal and besides, that way of thinking was archaic. She'd have her own agency, even mated to a vampire.

Still, she could see how Gaea was just trying to look out for her, to be a good mentor. "Thank you for your concern, Gaea, but I've already waited too long."

Gaea shook her head. "Ah, young love. So impatient. I just hope he makes you happy."

"He does," Cerissa said, her smile warming at the thought of being in Henry's arms again. "Very much so."

Gaea chuckled. "In that case, I have something for you."

Gaea reached into her pocket and extracted a small glass vial with a black twist cap. Cerissa stood and accepted the vial, holding it up to the light—red liquid filled it.

"My blood," Gaea said. "You'll need it to heal the bite. I suspected you wouldn't wait."

"Oh, Gaea, thank you," Cerissa said, hugging the old vampire. While she would never use it because of her allergy, the generous gesture touched her heart.

"I'm so happy for you, dear. Really, I am. I just wanted to make sure it was what you wanted and not only what Henry wanted—men are, well, men." Gaea laughed lightly and placed her hands on both sides of Cerissa's face, patting her cheeks. "Now go on, get out of here. You don't want to keep him waiting."

Henry lit the long wooden match and, kneeling, touched it to the last candle's wick. He had prepared everything the night before. Small rectangular paper bags held tea candles leading up the steps to his front door. The candles cast a warm glow on the burnt-orange tiles.

He looked out at the mountains behind his house. The sunset colors were fading, the air crisp and clean, the early May weather perfect for their reunion.

He started to go back inside, and his vision wavered. He sat down abruptly on the hard porch—the same place he'd fallen after Blanche shot him three weeks ago. Sensory memories flashed through his mind: silver bullets pounding into his gut, his life's blood draining out of him, the Lord's Prayer on his dying lips.

He hated it when the memories overtook him with no warning. He hated the loss of control. But most of all, he hated having his home tainted by Blanche.

Earlier in the week, Father Matt had counseled him on how to deal with the nightmarish images. In the present, Henry pressed his hand against the cold tiles, letting the memories drain away, like electricity to ground, and said, "That is in the past. No one is hurting me right now. I am fine."

He felt silly saying it, but he refused to let Blanche sully his home, to drive him from it, to stop his plans. The first time he took Cerissa's blood would be in *his* bed and not some sterile hotel room. So he'd tolerate a little silliness to move beyond the past.

Dusting off his black slacks, he shook off the residual anxiety and returned to the kitchen. The fragrance of dessert baking greeted him. Chocolate may taste like cardboard to him—well, admittedly, except for wine, all food tasted like cardboard—but chocolate baking smelled delicious. He checked the timer. Six minutes left before it was done.

Over dessert, he planned to apologize and beg her forgiveness. Then he would confess something that still weighed heavily on him, to make sure she understood what it really meant. Only then would he be free to take her blood.

He peeked into the oven. Her dessert was almost done. He rinsed the mixing bowl and put it in the dishwasher. Leaning against the counter, he tapped his fingers, and then checked the timer again. Fifty-nine seconds left.

His phone buzzed. An email from his attorney had come in. Attached to it was a memo detailing how to dissolve his partnership with Rolf. The message wasn't optimistic. Henry had been in business with Rolf too long, and their assets were too intertwined. He would read the memo later. Right now, he refused to let business sap his excitement over seeing Cerissa.

He picked up his mug from the granite counter and took a swig. Earlier in the week Cerissa had sent him a box of clone blood disguised as a package from a local delivery service. It tasted far superior to the leftovers he usually dined on from the blood bank, but after a steady diet of clone blood, he'd noticed a certain blandness to it. He would ask her about it when the time was right.

Two seconds to go. He slid on the oven mitts and hovered, waiting for the bell to ding. When it did, he opened the oven door and stuck a toothpick in the center of the chocolate decadence cake. The toothpick's surface came out wet but not gooey.

Perfect.

He placed the baking pan on the rack to cool and turned off the oven. Double vanilla bean ice cream waited in the freezer to accompany his creation.

He checked the time again.

Maybe I should uncork the wine…

He removed the bottle of late-harvest zinfandel from the countertop rack. Guaranteed to pair well with dark chocolate, it would only need fifteen minutes to breathe. He expertly slipped out the cork and carried the wine bottle and two glasses to the drawing room. A small table sat in front of the fireplace. He placed the bottle in the center, arranging the glasses to flank the bottle and stepped back.

No, it didn't look right.

He moved the bottle to the left side, near the fireplace, and set the glasses in the center of each place setting. Better.

Should I light the firewood now or later?

The evening was cool enough for a fire. He sat on the raised river-rock hearth, struck a match, and used it to set the kindling ablaze. The same match lit a single white candle. He placed the short candle at the center of the table, a wreath of red orchids surrounding it.

He stepped back to take in the ambience he'd created.

Perfect.

The doorbell rang, and the five-tone chime ignited a rush of exhilaration in his chest. He tossed the match into the fireplace and raced to the door.

CHAPTER 9

HENRY'S HOUSE—MOMENTS BEFORE

Cerissa parked in Henry's circular driveway. Candles in small paper bags lit the way to his carved double doors. The Spanish-style house was a throwback to a bygone era, with its terracotta roof tiles, smooth white plaster finish, and dark brown eaves.

The last time she stood on that porch, she'd saved his life.

She pressed the doorbell, barely able to contain her glee, and rose on the balls of her feet, lifting her high heels off the ground before tapping them back in place.

The door opened. He stood there in a white dress shirt, unbuttoned at the collar, his muscular chest filling it out, the tight-fitting slacks he wore accenting his narrow hips, his hair held back with a black ribbon rather than his usual rawhide string.

His deep brown eyes locked with hers, and his pupils grew until his irises were solid black. Her breath hitched in her throat. He was a predator—a predator who had spotted his next meal and was already setting the table.

She loved that in him. The danger he represented thrilled her. Not that he'd ever hurt her, but still, the thought of belonging to this bad boy, feeling his fangs sink into her for the first time, sent an electric charge right through her.

Why hadn't he leapt into action? Was he waiting for her to make the first move?

Well, wait no longer.

She threw herself at him, wrapping her arms around his neck, her momentum backing him up into the foyer as she crushed her lips to his, the depth of her love spilling out through their kiss. Fear of losing him had torn at her heart, but the touch of his lips had finally set her fears to rest.

As his mouth hungrily devoured hers, she pulled on the ribbon, freeing his hair until it hung loose, and ran her fingers into his long strands, gripping them tightly, pressing against him. If she could have merged her skin with his to become one being, she would have.

His hands clutched her bottom. He lifted her and, with a little jump, she wrapped her legs around him, her dress's skirt flaring out, her purse dropping to the floor, and he took a step forward, supporting her back against the wall, never stopping their tongues' tango.

Yes, yes, yes.

He tasted better than the sweetest wine, and she was determined to drink all of him. She let go of his neck, holding on with her legs. Her fingers found the buttons on his shirt, which popped open easily, and she ran her hands over his bare chest, his nipples tight nubs underneath her palms.

He let out a low growl against her lips.

How she'd missed him. She'd missed his touch, his taste, his uncensored thirst for her.

She felt his fingers at the back of her neck and leaned forward to give him space between the wall and her back. He unzipped her dress and it fell forward. He lifted her higher, breaking their kiss, his lips planting frenzied caresses on the mounds of her breasts rising above her demi-bra.

"Oh, Henry," she said, brushing her cheek against the top of his head, the sparks inside her melting into a warm current, lifting her chest with lightness. She buried her nose in his hair and inhaled. His spicy cologne, a mix of clove, cedar, and other earthy scents, caused the sparks to shoot right to her core.

But there was something more; another luscious scent seemed to rise from him. She took another deep breath.

Mmm, chocolate.

"*Cariña,*" he said. "I've missed you."

She knew *cariña* meant "dear" in Spanish, and a little thrill went through her at the endearment.

"I've missed you, too. Enough that it looks like we might make love right here in your foyer," she said with a light laugh, holding back a giggle of joy that threatened to bubble up and overtake her.

He slowly lowered her. Her body slid against the bulge in his pants until she was on her high-heeled feet again. Her dress dropped to the floor.

He stepped back, gazing at her, scanning her from head to toe, and, with a sharp intake of breath, he whispered, "So beautiful."

"Do you remember?"

"How could I forget the first lingerie I ever saw you wear?" he asked, rolling his Rs deep in his throat, like a cat purring.

The sound pleased her. She had missed everything about him, including hearing him speak.

Holding out her hand for his, she met his palm. A quick squeeze, a press of fingers together, and his hand glided along her bare arm, leaving a trail of swirling electricity behind. He raised her hand to his lips, and her heart fluttered at his tenderness.

He reached beyond her to close the front door and started to lead her toward the drawing room. She stopped him to touch his stomach, circling her fingers around the area where he'd been shot. "How are you feeling?"

"I'm fine. Don't worry. All is well. Yacov has been very generous."

He did look better than the night of the hearing. "And there have been no new attempts on your life?"

"None. Even though my house arrest is over, Tig agreed to assign extra officers to patrol the area. I believe we are quite safe here."

She sighed, relieved to hear he had guards protecting him. "Then why are we going into the drawing room?" She glanced slyly toward the open balcony on the second floor. "Rather than upstairs?"

He slid his arms around her, resting his hands in the small of her back. "I thought we should talk first, *cariña*. Although with you looking like that, I don't know if I can concentrate."

She trailed a finger down his chest. "I could put my dress back on, but it seems a shame to start all over again."

"Then allow me." He slipped off his shirt and draped it over her shoulders. "Now we are evenly matched."

She slipped her arms into the sleeves. The cuffs hung past her hands, and she rolled them up.

He sighed and buttoned a couple of the buttons on his—now her—shirt, covering her breasts. "That only makes it worse," he said. "Seeing you in my shirt does something to me. I want to rip it off you and take you right here."

Seeing him shirtless, his well-developed pecs topped by tight, dark nipples, did the same to her.

"Come and get me," she said with a sultry smile, spreading out her arms.

"Don't tempt me." He took a deep breath and let it out. "We should talk first. And I made you dessert to enjoy. You should eat it while it's warm. So come with me and allow me the joy of feeding you." He paused, a glint in his eyes. "Before you feed me."

For the first time since entering his house, she noticed her surroundings. The foyer was softly lit by candlelight. Black wrought iron candelabra on floor stands held seven candles each. Fresh flowers in vases occupied every surface.

Her high heels clacked on the foyer tiles, changing to a deeper tone as she stepped onto the hardwood floor of his drawing room. At least ten more candelabra filled the large room with soft candlelight. His leather armchair, which normally sat in front of the fireplace, was gone, replaced with a small, round table covered by a white tablecloth, and two straight-back chairs from his dining room set.

He held out one of the chairs for her, and she lowered herself onto the soft cushion. He kneeled before her. "Before we go any further, I wanted to apologize, *cariña*. I don't know how I'll make amends for my missteps that resulted in our time apart, but believe me, I will try."

She cupped his face, brushing a stray strand of his straight black hair from his cheek. His eyes told her how much he needed to hear the words. "Yes, Henry, I forgive you."

A smile curved his lips. "Thank you."

He stood and leaned over, giving her a gentle, chaste kiss, and then poured a glass of wine for her from the open bottle.

"Please wait here while I get your dessert," he said with a nod.

Her heart skipped a beat at the thought of what was to come next, and her fingertips traced the vein in her neck. She wanted to feel his lips on her throat, and soon.

She picked up the twig of red orchids circling the center candle. The same delicate scent as the one she'd found on her pillow. A dozen long-stem roses sat in a vase on the nearby coffee table, in front of the couch. Smaller arrangements occupied the dark wood mantel above the fireplace. Black wrought iron sconces had been added to the white plaster walls, one on each side of the fireplace, aglow with candlelight.

The soft scent of vanilla rose from the table candle, mingling with the fragrant flowers.

He returned carrying a plate and a small pitcher. "I hung up your dress for you. It's in the hall closet when you need it again, and your purse is on the entryway table."

"Thank you, Henry."

With a graceful bow, he placed the plate in front of her. "Chocolate decadence cake. It should still be warm. I took it out of the oven"—he glanced at his watch—"twenty minutes ago."

"Oh my goodness," she said, looking at the deep, rich chocolate cake. A scoop of ice cream sat next to the single-layer wedge, and a circle of raspberries bordered the plate. The whole thing had been dusted lightly with powdered sugar.

So that's why he smelled of chocolate.

"I hope you enjoy it," he added.

He knew her weakness for chocolate. She took the first bite, rolling the flourless cake over her tongue, and closed her eyes, her whole attention on the burst of dark chocolate filling her mouth, the texture thick and creamy.

She opened her eyes. "That's almost as good as sex."

He smirked at her and raised one eyebrow. "We will see about that later." He poured the pitcher's contents into his own glass and topped it with an inch of wine. "A little wine mixed with blood. So I can keep you company as you eat and drink."

She took another bite, this time with a bit of ice cream and a raspberry. Pleasure darted across her tongue. She closed her eyes again, focusing on the way the rich chocolate was mellowed by the ice cream, the tart raspberry cutting the heavy sweetness.

"Try the wine," he suggested. "It's a dessert wine. You'll have to tell me if the reviewers are correct, that it pairs well with dark chocolate."

She swirled and sniffed the glass. Wow—it had a high sugar content. She took a sip. The sweet flavor was laced with hints of ripe blackberries.

"Yes, I'd say they are well matched."

"Excellent."

She glanced at the bottle. "But it's not from your winery."

"I haven't made a dessert zinfandel yet. Perhaps I should try." He took a sip, looking so sexy shirtless as he raised his glass. "You're right—it's not bad."

She slowly sank her fork into the dense cake for another bite. Despite her teasing words, the cake wasn't as good as being in bed with him. Still, she reveled in its richness, waiting for him to say whatever was on his mind.

It didn't take him long to start. "As I said, there is something I wanted to discuss. I know I mentioned Anne-Louise on our first date at the winery, but I wanted to make sure you're truly all right with the situation and all it means before we take the next step."

Oh, *now* she got why they weren't upstairs in bed and naked. And it looked like Gaea was going to get her wish, thanks to Henry and his incessant need to talk everything to death. Cerissa normally found it rather cute, except when it was delaying what she already knew she wanted. However, he'd given her cake—*chocolate* cake. She would happily sit through a chat as she finished it.

"What does your maker have to do with us?" she asked, and focused on the next bite of the fudgy delight.

"As you know, I'm still bound to her."

She gestured with the fork, a small circle in the air. "Because she continues to take your blood."

"I have no choice in the matter."

Well, wait a minute.

She wrinkled her forehead and laid her fork down, her cake half-eaten. The conversation had her whole attention now. "Explain one thing to me. Under the treaty, there isn't much she can force you to do anymore. There are a lot of protections for those made vampire."

"We wanted to be civilized—sexual slavery should be a thing of the past."

"It goes beyond that. I've had a lot of free time to read up on it." He slewed his eyes away, looking embarrassed to be reminded of their time apart. "Anne-Louise can't force you to work for her or surrender your possessions. She can only command you to return to her and accede to her demand for your blood."

"That is not only because of the treaty. It's one of the powers we possess as vampires. If I take a mortal's blood, I can call them to me and compel them to submit to my bite. It is the same bond between maker and their offspring. So long as Anne-Louise continues to take my blood, I must heed her call and submit to her bite. I cannot resist her."

"Have you tried?" she asked, the words spilling out of her mouth before she could take them back.

"Of course I've tried," Henry said, returning his glass to the table. How could she ask him that? "I don't want to be bound to her any more than you want me to be."

Cerissa's chin dropped and her mouth opened partway—she looked taken aback. He must have spoken too harshly. Reaching for her hand, he held it gently.

"I'm sorry, *cariña*. I didn't mean to let my frustration show. Please understand. I have no choice in the matter. I have tried to resist Anne-Louise time and time again, and I fail."

She furrowed her brow. "I don't understand."

"How can I make you see?" He clenched his jaw. He hated the compulsion, the way he lost control of his life at the whim of his maker. "When Anne-Louise calls me to her, at first I hear her voice in my head. It becomes a pressure that builds, until the pressure turns into pain, and the longer I resist, the pain turns to agony. And that agony does not stop until I comply, or until she rescinds the call, which she never does. I have tried to wait her out before, but she never stops. Never."

Cerissa squeezed his hand. "That's terrible."

"But, thank God, that is the extent of the compulsion. If makers could compel their offspring to do their bidding in all things, our culture would have evolved differently."

"How?"

"If a maker could compel *complete* obedience, armies of offspring would have been created. That didn't happen because obedience is not automatic. Anne-Louise cannot force me to do anything except return to her and submit to her demand for tribute. That is all she can force me to do against my will."

"*Tribute* indeed," Cerissa said, taking back her hand and using it to lift her wine glass. As she drank, the lovely ripple of the muscles in her neck held his attention. Finished drinking, she added, "I dislike your euphemism for taking an offspring's blood."

"Why?"

"'Tribute' suggests a voluntarily gift, a sign of respect, an honorarium. What Anne-Louise demands is anything but that."

Cerissa was right, but the term had been in use for centuries before he was turned. "It comes from the old meaning, when tribute meant a payment made from one ruler to another as a sign of dependence." He poured more wine for her. "I'm sorry you don't like the term, but that's what it's called."

She pursed her lips. "All right, I understand Anne-Louise has this power. But *why* does she keep you tied to her? Is she worried about becoming a revenant?"

He shook his head. "While some believe the blood of an offspring will delay the onset of dementia—that is not her fear." He looked at the table. Sometimes, the shame was too great to bear. "No, she uses it to blackmail me—for power over me. I've kept her demand for tribute a secret from my community, and she relishes holding the threat of disclosure over my head."

Cerissa's eyes got big. "Why give her that leverage? Why not just tell everyone she's demanding this archaic practice? Once it's no longer secret, her motivation to hang on will be gone, and then she'll free you."

He sat there in shocked silence. He could never do what Cerissa suggested. After taking a sip of his drink, he tried to put his thoughts into words. "I am a founder of Sierra Escondida. Can you imagine how the community would react—"

"I know you value the respect of your community, and you fear that if they learn of her hold over you, you'll lose that respect. But I don't understand why they would. It's not your doing, Henry. It's hers."

How could he explain his world—how power was power and weakness was weakness, regardless of the whys or hows of it.

"Henry, you do have a choice," she added.

He shook his head. "I do not. I would be perceived as weak, and that would jeopardize all the respect I've earned here. It would diminish my status—threaten my home and my business."

She looked unpersuaded. Would approaching the issue from a different angle convince her?

"Consider this: I could tell everyone and she could still refuse to let me go. Knowing her, she would likely do it out of spite. I would be demeaned, lose all the goodwill I've built, and still be bound to her."

She covered his hand with hers. "Oh, wow," she said, her eyes widening. "Anne-Louise doesn't play nice or fair."

"Or rationally. It has been a great source of, well…shame—to be tied to her for all these years."

"I'm so sorry you've had to live with that, Henry."

He raised her hand to his lips. "Thank you for understanding, *cariña*."

"Just because I understand doesn't mean I like it." She took in a deep breath and seemed to consider something. "How often will you see her?"

More often than I ever want to.

But how to answer the question truthfully, given Anne-Louise's mercurial nature?

He took a swig from his glass. "Based on the past decade, my guess is two or three times a year. We occasionally talk by phone, as well. She sometimes calls on me to take care of a problem for her. And in truth, I appreciate her counsel, when she is willing to be pleasant, which is rare. More often she is impossible and demanding and ill-tempered, and I am glad she is part of Leopold's community and not mine."

"Do you see anything changing? Any chance she might move here?"

"I doubt she'd ever try. She loves New York, loves the young men and women she finds there; the city is better hunting grounds for her purposes. Besides," he said, smiling a sheepish grin, "she cannot move here permanently without a majority vote of the homeowners association."

"And since you're still on the board, I imagine you'd block that vote?"

"You imagine correctly."

"How long? I mean, only a few nights at time, right? Just enough, for, you know…" She waved her hand at his wrist.

He shook his head. "One night, a few hours at most. We begin bickering as soon as we are in each other's presence. She tires of my 'insolence,' as she calls it, and dismisses me."

"It sounds like you've learned how to get rid of her quickly."

"Indeed I have." He paused. "Can you find this acceptable, *cariña*?"

Could she? Before they'd made love the first time, Henry had told her about Anne-Louise's demands. Although he'd provided more detail this time, nothing about it changed how she felt about him.

Yes, I can live with this arrangement.

She nodded in reply, and Henry immediately kissed her wrist, sending a flicker of heat over her skin.

But then she remembered something and a frisson of fear shot through her. Every time Anne-Louise bit, he'd feel a surge of lust. How to ask him the question without explaining she'd experimented with Blanche's fang serum?

"Henry, you'll, ah, you'll be faithful to me?"

The skin around his eyes tightened. "She cannot force me to lie with her."

"That isn't what I asked," she said gently.

"Of course I'll be faithful to you," he said impatiently.

If I don't trust him, this won't work.

Besides, she had believed him before when he told her the story of how he had been faithful to Erin, his prior girlfriend, notwithstanding

Anne-Louise's demand for tribute. He must have long experience resisting the potent aphrodisiac in fang serum.

She rolled her shoulders and tried to let go of the tension. She wanted to get the bite over with. The longer he pussyfooted around, the more anxiety crept up on her—she wanted to be past it, to know her solution to fang serum worked.

Or should she tell him about her problems with the Lux?

When his smile faded and uncertainty formed in his eyes, she decided to wait. There was something else bothering him. Henry, she was finding, was a brooder. And she could only imagine how much brooding he'd done in their time apart.

Perhaps for tonight, she could just soothe his worries rather than add to them. Her issues with the Lux would be there tomorrow.

"You'll recall," he said hesitantly, "I paid Leopold to buy the right to take your blood?"

Suspicion crawled through her. "Hasn't he returned the money?"

"No. I may have to sue him." He glanced toward the fireplace. "I'll call my attorney tomorrow about initiating the lawsuit. I wanted to find out how you felt about it before I did."

Dammit, Leopold.

"Hold off another night," she said. "I want to speak with Leopold first."

Henry frowned. "I don't need you to fight my battles for me."

"This isn't only your battle. Leopold violated my trust by misleading you."

He looked like he was struggling to reconcile two conflicting thoughts. "I see," he finally said, still sounding uncertain.

"Do you trust me?"

"Of course, but—"

"Let me do what I need to do. If he doesn't give back the money, you can do what you need to do."

He nodded once, sharply. She could see it was hard for him to relinquish control, but she was glad he was doing it—however begrudgingly—for her.

She took a deep breath. "Now, is that all? Because this is a strange way to run a seduction."

"Then allow me to remedy the situation." He rose, took her face between his hands, and gently kissed her, his lips cool and soft on hers, the kiss sending a pleasant quiver through her, a promise of more to come.

He looked at her intently. "If you're still willing to be my mate? I must confess, I'm not a modern man. I try to change with the times, but I don't always succeed. I promise to do better. I promise to try—"

In answer, she kissed him firmly, her tongue seeking out the taste of his mouth, the mingled flavors of sweet wine and sharp blood a prelude to what it would be like to kiss him after his bite, and she let the moment spin a little out of control.

With a deep breath, she pulled back to speak against his lips. "I am willing and I'm absolutely sure."

"Cerissa, I—"

She kissed him again before he could finish. She wanted this more than anything. For the first time in her life, she was putting her desires first, instead of her duty to the Lux. No way would he talk her out of it.

Breaking from the kiss, she took his arm and led him in the direction of the upstairs bedroom. As they passed through the foyer, she swiped her purse off the table. Its contents were crucial for what they were about to do.

"Cerissa." He stopped her when they reached the staircase, then turned to face her.

No more talking.

She leaned up to kiss him again, pulling his head down. He ravaged her mouth before suddenly pulling back again, resisting her tugs to keep him in place. She let out a little frustrated growl.

A small laugh escaped him. "Wait, wait."

"Henry, I want—"

He pressed a gentle finger to her lips.

"I'm trying to say, Cerissa, that I love you."

She froze at the words, her heart rate skyrocketing.

"I love you, Cerissa," he repeated. "I will always try to be worthy of you." He let his hand fall back to her waist. "That is the final thing I wanted to say."

Her breath hitched and she couldn't contain the bubble of joy that escaped in a kind of choked laugh. In that moment, she wanted him in a way she'd never experienced before, feeling like she'd be lost if he didn't become hers right *now*.

She hugged him tightly and whispered in his ear, "I love you too."

He kissed her fiercely, and when he released her, she saw his smile spread wide. In a kind of giddy, uncontrollable joy, they kissed and laughed and kissed all the way up the stairs.

CHAPTER 10

The sweeping staircase led to the master bedroom. When they reached the landing, he stopped and said, "Cover your eyes."

Now it was her turn to smirk. "I've seen you naked before."

He laughed, a deep sound of delight. "I have a different surprise for you."

Grinning broadly, she raised her hands over her eyes. The telltale squeak told her Henry had opened the bedroom door. She knew the squeak well—she'd stayed overnight in his master bedroom almost six weeks ago when she was recovering from a gunshot wound, one she'd received protecting him.

His hand wrapped around her arm, the other pressing at the small of her back. "Keep your eyes covered and let me guide you."

She had kicked off her high heels halfway up the stairs. Her bare feet registered the change in carpeting from the low weave of the hallway to a thick cut pile in the bedroom. She was about five steps into the room when he stopped her.

"All right, you can look."

The room was a soft sepia glow of candlelight. Every surface held a collection of ivory candles in different sizes, all protected by glass hurricane holders. Long-stem roses were scattered between the candles.

But that wasn't all. Her hand flew to her mouth in surprise. "Henry, this is all new furniture!"

"Erin used the old bed. I thought we should start out with something new."

She stood there staring at it all, frozen in the moment. Slowly, she glanced from the two posts and high, round back of the bed's headboard to

69

the two posts at the footboard. An elegantly woven comforter covered the
bed and large decorative sham pillows perched against the headboard.

The cherry wood furniture looked good against the paint color he'd
chosen for the walls—a pinkish pale brown, with the ceiling a snowy
white. Two nightstands flanked the bed, an eight-drawer chest with
mirrored vanity occupied another wall, and a couple of matching chairs
and a loveseat in complementary colors finished the set.

As a whole, the room warmly married traditional and modern style.

He'd even selected a king-sized mattress. Maybe he had listened to her
the night she saved his life—they'd need a big bed, even if it wasn't in his
basement sleeping room.

"Henry, you didn't have to do this."

"I want you to be comfortable here," he said. He slipped his arms
around her waist from behind. She sighed and leaned into his embrace,
feeling his erection pressing into her lower back. "If you don't like it and
want something different, I can arrange it."

"No, I love it. Thank you for doing this."

He spun her around and looked at her, his eyes growing black again. "I
am glad you're pleased."

He bent down to kiss her, but she put a hand to his lips.

Dammit. She hated stalling any further, but she didn't have a choice.
There was a reason her purse hung from her shoulder.

"Um, hold that thought and give me a moment," she said, hurrying
toward the adjoining bathroom.

As she started to close the bathroom door, he bowed to her. "Of
course, *cariña*," he said with a smile.

She shut the door, unslung her purse from her shoulder, and pulled two
items from it.

First, the short negligee—she slipped out of Henry's shirt, removed
her bra and thong, and donned the negligee. The sheer red fabric hid
nothing. Her breasts were at attention, the tips poking forward, the fabric's
brush against her delicate skin sending pleasant tingles through her.

She looked at the second item and her throat tightened.

The moment of truth.

Picking up her hypo, she dialed in the stabilizing hormone and
balanced the weight of the silver cylinder on one finger.

When she had experimented with Blanche's fang serum, she'd injected
a small dose of stabilizing hormone. The small dose had stopped the patch
on the back of her forearm from morphing continuously. The medication

had been absorbed by her skin locally rather than entering her bloodstream, and the dose wasn't strong enough to stop her from changing when she injected the remaining fang serum into a vein.

In theory, the maximum amount of stabilizing hormone allowed, injected directly into a main vein, would keep her locked in one form.

But it was just a theory—she had no way to test it in advance.

Shouldn't I just tell him first, before the bond?

He deserved to know the details of what she was—the longer she kept it secret, the bigger the fall when it did come out. But she didn't want to overwhelm him with the details. More importantly, she didn't want to delay their mating any longer.

They had plenty of time to get to know each other. Henry knew she was Lux, and that was the biggest hurdle of all. She'd share more details later, just as she would learn more about his very long past. She only knew a fraction of his story so far.

Small bites. We'll learn about each other a little at a time. That's how dating works.

She gave the hypo a toss, caught it in the air, and pressed it to the jugular vein in her neck. The medicine zinged through her system and her muscles relaxed slightly. She no longer had to keep a firm control on her appearance—the stabilizer took over that job.

This had better work.

While Cerissa was in the bathroom, Henry undressed and placed the crucifix pendant he wore on the nightstand. The bed needed preparing— he'd waffled earlier, and decided that having the bed ready for lovemaking presumed too much. He pulled back the comforter, neatly folding it onto the cushioned chest at the bed's foot, and piled the decorative pillows onto one of the chairs.

He crawled into bed and covered himself below the waist with the sheet. Propped on his elbow, he stretched out and waited for her.

The bathroom doorknob turned, the slight click of metal drawing his attention.

She emerged a vision in red. Her long mink-brown hair rippled across her shoulders, her green eyes sparkling.

His breath caught in his throat, and his old heart gave a brief *ka-thub*.

Her bare arm still bore the scar from the bullet she had intercepted protecting him. The scar was part of the illusion she maintained in her human form. Both sadness and gratitude flared in him at seeing the mark she carried on his account, but it was quickly followed by a shot of lust as she moved closer, the sheer fabric revealing her firm breasts and shapely hips.

"Come here, my beautiful one," he said, reaching out for her.

She stepped up to the bed's edge, one finger on her lips like she was considering something. Her look of confidence faded into uncertainty. The scent of her fear washed over his tongue like juice from an orange, both sweet and tangy.

Was she feeling afraid of his bite? The rapid thrum of her pulse called to him, and the animal in him wanted to pounce and devour her. Instead, he offered his hand, inviting her into the bed, and replaced her finger with his lips, a brief press against her soft flesh, holding back his passion.

The nightie she wore brushed against him as she leaned forward, electrifying his skin, its silkiness a prelude to the silky feel of her.

But he couldn't ignore her fear. The scent of it still lingered. "Is something wrong?" he whispered against her ear, as he rolled her over onto her back.

"I—" she began, tightening her grip on him. "How—I mean, *when* do you bite?"

He propped himself on his elbow to look at her, stroking her face with featherlight touches. "It's traditional for the bite to come toward the end, when you are fully aroused." He caressed her neck. "I'll be as gentle as I can."

She nodded and smiled, her eyes looking a little more confident.

He leaned over, and this time her warm lips parted, inviting him in. He swept his tongue along the roof of her mouth before thrusting in again to tangle with hers. Just talking about the bite had lowered his fangs. He took care to avoid puncturing her lip as he deeply explored her sweet mouth.

The citrus scent of her fear subsided, replaced with the erotic smell of her arousal—a scent like freshly ground cinnamon mixed with her feminine musk, the combination alluring. He deepened the kiss and ran the palm of his hand from her throat to the hem of the short nightie.

His erection pressed against her hip. Breaking from the kiss, he threw the sheet aside to remove that layer between them. A smile came to her lips as she surveyed his naked body.

"So handsome," she whispered, trailing her fingers across his chest and then tracing the outline of his muscles.

Through the sheer red fabric she wore, he tweaked her nipple and she let out a little gasp. Her hands gripped his shoulders while he cupped her other breast, massaging the nipple and rolling it between his thumb and fingers until she moaned deeply. He licked the free nipple through the silky fabric, the moisture melding it around the hard tip. Desire rolled through him. He licked the other one and her breath quickened even more.

Sweeping his fingers lightly across her taut belly, the sheer fabric a barrier between his fingertips and her soft skin, he reached for the hem and slid his fingers underneath, touching her tight curls.

He ran his thumb through her folds and lightly massaged the sensitive nerve bundle hidden between them, before sliding a finger gently inside her opening, followed by a second one.

Wet. Very wet.

He closed his eyes. His usually slow pulse pounded, his desire to plunge within her driven by her moist arousal. He wanted to claim her now, but he fought against the urge. Besides, the first time they made love, weeks ago, she had only orgasmed once to his twice. He owed her one.

Strike that—he owed her hundreds, but he'd start with one.

He curled his fingers to stroke her inner wall, his thumb continuing to draw circles. She moaned deeper, her body becoming liquid against his, her eyes fluttering open. The sight of her caused him to swell even more, the ache and desire nearly painful in its acuteness.

He rose to meet her gaze, not stopping the movement of his fingers, and her slick sheath squeezed his fingers. She wrapped her arms around his shoulders and brought him closer until her already parted lips met his. He took full advantage of it. His tongue repeatedly delved into her while his fingers continued to rub her slick skin.

She moaned against his lips. Suddenly, her back arched, and she cried out, the nub beneath his thumb swelling as her sheath tightened around his fingers.

Ecstasy played out on her face, a shining radiance emanating from her skin. She'd never looked more beautiful than in that moment.

He slowed his touch as her spasms subsided. "I told you I owed you a few more orgasms," he whispered.

"I'm not counting," she said with a light laugh between pants. "But I won't argue with you, either."

Hearing the satisfied, languid tone of her voice, the sexiness of it, caused his *pené* to throb. He nuzzled at her neck, placing light kisses there.

Her blood's scent was so close to the surface that he felt his control slipping, his fangs aching to bite.

Her hand wrapped around his shaft and she gently squeezed, splitting in two his attention and desire. But he wanted to be inside her when it happened, so he lifted himself from her neck and smiled at her crookedly instead.

She smiled back and reached for his hips.

"Patience, *cariña.* Your lovely nightie has to go first. I want to feel your skin against my body."

He slid her out of it and tossed aside the sheer fabric. His gaze traveled the length of her, pausing at her brightly painted toes.

So beautiful, mi amor.

She reached for his hips again, and this time there was no reason to resist. He kneeled between her legs, stretching his body over hers, and slid inside her, moving slowly, feeling every inch of that first thrust, the tightness of her sheath wrapped around him, and he homed in his attention on her movements, her rhythm. He was determined to give her a second orgasm, determined that she explode with pleasure when his bite finally came. In this, he and his hunger were aligned.

She loved the feel of his thick length filling her, plunging in again and again, rubbing against her cleft with each thrust of his hips. She bent her knees, lifting them high, allowing him to plunge deeper. Using one arm, he held himself up, leaving his other hand the freedom to massage her nipple. The sparks met in her core, building, growing, until she wobbled on the edge of the abyss.

When will he bite?

A sliver of anxiety brought her back from the edge. She ran her fingers along his back, feeling his muscles ripple with each thrust into her, and looked up into his intense eyes, the black pupils expanded to wipe out all color.

His unmasked desire melted her. She gave a little nod, and he lowered his lips to her throat. The touch of his tongue on her pulse, his breath against her neck, his fangs pressing her skin—all sent shivers of pleasure coursing through her.

The stabilizer has to work. It just has to.

"Cerissa?" he asked, his voice husky, his lips vibrating against her skin, his long, deep thrusts never stopping.

"Yes, Henry, yes," she said, and rose ever so slightly, turning her face away, the invitation unmistakable.

He growled and slid his fangs into her neck. So sharp, so careful, that she didn't feel the bite until after he was in. She let out a little sigh and sank back into the bed.

Finally, I'm yours.

Heat glided through her veins like lava trailing down a steep mountain, the color red filling her vision.

The fire hit her breasts, her belly, her thighs, and radiated inward to fill the area in between, lighting her ablaze with sensation, scorching her with pleasure, melting any last resistance, and she moaned. "Oh, Henry. Oh, my—"

The orgasm rocketed through her with far more bliss than her mind could handle, shattering her control.

He continued to thrust his hips as he drew in the first mouthful. Her blood tasted so fresh, so powerful, that he lost all sense of himself, all sense they were two separate creatures, and he moved in harmony with her, her rapid breaths close to his ear, until she called out this name and her tight sheath squeezed him in a series of rapid contractions, sending him over the edge with an explosion of his own pleasure.

When he returned to his senses, he focused on her. Her skin seemed to flicker, changing from shimmering blue to brown to blue and then back again. She clutched at his biceps, bracing like she was using him to force her muscles to contract, to prevent something from happening.

Suddenly, the flickering stopped. Her skin once again took on its gorgeous deep brown tones.

"Are you okay?" he asked softly.

"Wonderful," she said, closing her eyes.

He'd seen her flicker once before—when she'd been wounded protecting him, and at the time, he hadn't understood what his eyes had witnessed.

So why flicker now? Had his bite been painful to her? His past lovers reported the experience as pleasurable after the first sharp prick.

She didn't look in pain now. He leaned down to lick at the wound so the blood wouldn't drip onto the pillowcase. When the wound stopped bleeding, he laid his head on the pillow, facing her.

"You are mine now," he said.

"Yes," she agreed, sounding almost drugged. She grasped his hand and kissed each of his fingers. "And you are mine."

He hugged her tightly to him, cuddling her. Happiness enveloped him, a joy growing from the middle of his chest, spilling out to his fingertips—a feeling he hadn't felt in a long time.

After a few minutes, the rhythm of her breathing changed.

"Cerissa?" he asked softly.

When she didn't answer, he slid his arms out—she had dozed off. He brushed the tousled hair out of her face and gently kissed his sleeping beauty.

"*Mi amor*," he whispered, trying out the words aloud for the first time. His love.

Forever, mi amor...*forever.*

CHAPTER 11

THE ART GALLERY—SAME NIGHT

Tig looked around at the signs of a break-in: broken window glass, a tipped-over flower vase, and two empty picture hooks. The art gallery's owner, Chen Méi, stood in the middle of the showroom.

"I want you to investigate," Méi demanded.

"I'm sorry about the theft, but I don't have jurisdiction here," Tig said, trying to sound conciliatory. She may tower over Méi physically, but the artist had higher rank as one of the five founders of Sierra Escondida. "We should call Mordida's police. They can handle it. I'll talk with their chief, I'm sure they'll do a good job."

The petite vampire shook her head vehemently. Her long, straight black hair swished back and forth across her shoulders. "No outsiders."

"This isn't your home, Méi."

"I want no outsiders here. You do it, chief."

Tig looked around the room again. The front window had been broken and a few paintings stolen. Otherwise, the gallery looked like a pristine museum, with its walls painted white and its track lighting aimed at the artwork.

"Is there something here you don't want them to find?"

"*Pei*! I'm not afraid of any mortal."

"Then what is it?"

"That they are fools! Baboons! I don't want them gawking at what their eyes cannot truly see." She gestured toward the remaining paintings on the walls.

Tig tried not to roll her eyes. Although the gallery was open to the general public, Méi's current exhibit had a strong vampire clientele. The paintings focused on the most popular veins on the human body. Extreme close-up portraits were painted against very intense background colors— brilliant blues, bright reds, sharp yellows.

Some on the Hill called it vampire porn. One painting began below a woman's face and ended at her ribcage, with her hand gripping her own breast, her shirt collar pulled back revealing a low-cut bra. Three fingers dug into the breast and the index finger extended out, pointing right at the vein in her cleavage. Another showed a man's neck from his scraggly chin to his breastbone, his hand flipping the bird at the viewer, but in the process, pointing to a large, bulging neck vein.

Fangs were known to extend when looking at Méi's art.

All right, I get it. Méi didn't want her art exposed to those who couldn't appreciate its beauty.

Tig locked eyes with the temperamental artist. "If I help you, you have to promise to let me handle this—no retribution, understand?"

Méi gave a short bow in acknowledgement. It was the best Tig would get out of her.

"Okay, tell me what happened," Tig said.

"The alarm company called Razi this evening. I joined him after I woke."

"What time?"

"Razi said it was 5:42."

"Where is your mate now?"

"Talking to the insurance company."

"Méi, you'll need a police report for insurance purposes. I can't give you one; it's not my jurisdiction."

Méi stuck out her chin. "No outsiders."

"What if I call Mordida's chief, tell him what happened, and have Razi meet with Mordida PD. I'll do what I can to look into it, but officially, you'll have a report for your insurance company."

Méi frowned, her dark brown eyes showing both anger and impatience.

"Bunny ears, it makes sense," Razi said from behind Tig.

Tig kept her mouth shut. The first time she'd heard Razi call Méi a pet name, Tig had braced herself, expecting Méi to rip out his throat. Instead, Méi stoically accepted it. Anyone else would have been dead before they hit the floor.

"I spoke with our insurance agent," Razi continued. "We have to file a police report if we want our insurer to cover the loss. I've totaled it—at least ten grand between the two stolen paintings and the broken window."

Tig couldn't agree more. "Before we call Mordida PD, tell me what happened. Then you can return home to the Hill, and Razi can meet with the police."

Méi's face reminded Tig of a storm about to blow. Razi didn't wait for Méi to answer. "When I arrived, I found it like this. The glass was busted and two paintings gone."

"Anything else?"

Razi used a pencil to scratch between his long, beaded cornrows, which kept his afro-textured hair neatly styled. "I guess that's the strange part," he said. "They stole some stuff off my desk. A glass paperweight containing a peony petal, a photo of Méi and me, and one of the art reviews I had framed and hanging on my office wall—the one from last year, you remember, from the prior show."

Méi nodded. "They liked my art."

"Why would the thief take such personal items?" Tig asked. "Was there a picture of Méi in the article?"

"No," Méi all but shouted, stamping her foot, her accent thickening along with her anger. "No photos for interviews. Strict rule. Not allowed."

"Easy there," Razi said, stepping closer to Méi and slipping an arm around her shoulder. Razi looked back at Tig. "In all her incarnations, she's never allowed any member of the press to take a photo of her. The photo I had on my desk wasn't professional, just a snapshot of the two of us."

"Could the thief be an art reviewer who wanted to publish it?"

"I told you," Méi said, lifting her chin to look at Razi, "no more photos."

"Sure, bunny ears. No more photos here. Just at our home on the Hill."

Méi gave another curt nod.

"Do you have any copies of the paintings?" Tig asked.

"I'll email the jpegs to you," Razi said. "I took photos for our insurance records before we displayed the paintings. The insurance company said it's going to be messy, because the paintings have already been sold and paid for. Fact is, all this exhibition has sold. We were going to start packing it tomorrow for delivery, and make room for the new exhibition. The buyer's insurance will have to be contacted too."

With two insurance companies involved, everything had to be on the up-and-up. Technically, the buyers hadn't taken possession, so the gallery's insurance would likely cover it, still—better safe than sorry. "Did anyone else try to buy the stolen paintings? Any losers?"

"Rolf wanted them. He was outbid by Winston," Razi replied.

So the mayor and vice mayor were competing in other forums. Why didn't that surprise Tig?

"I'll talk with Rolf. Do you have any security cameras?"

"Why would I need a camera?" Méi asked. "I have an alarm."

Tig restrained herself from explaining why cameras were an essential component of any security plan; Méi wasn't known for her patience. "I'm going to call Liza and get her help dusting for prints, and we'll look for any trace evidence the burglar left behind."

"About time someone did something," Méi said.

Tig ignored the barb and phoned Liza. The councilwoman worked part-time as a reserve officer for the Hill's police department.

Méi left—she didn't need another vampire with her to go to and from her registered place of business. The Rule of Two had so many exceptions that the town council would never have nailed Henry with it if he hadn't signed the plea deal to keep Cerissa from being banned from the Hill.

Liza arrived fifteen minutes later. Working together, they got the job done quickly, finding fingerprints on the wall where the paintings had hung. Tig already had fingerprint cards for Méi and Razi—everyone on the Hill was printed before they could live there.

She fed what she found into the portable fingerprint scanner. The results were about what she expected. The machine identified Méi and Razi's fingerprints, no one else's.

There were a few smudges around the wall where the frames had been, like someone had worn latex gloves when removing the paintings. She took samples of the glove prints. If they caught a suspect with gloves stuffed in his pocket, the creases and other unique marks on the fingertips might match the prints. It had happened before. Perps were often stupid enough to use the same gloves over and over again, believing they couldn't be traced.

Thirty minutes later, the glass company arrived and replaced the window. Not long after, a two-man unit from Mordida's police department parked out front. Tig offered them the scant evidence she had collected so they wouldn't have to send an investigator tomorrow. The officers stayed long enough to take a written report, and she used Razi's photocopy machine to make duplicates.

She left when the officers did. She had more pressing matters on her mind—like finding Blanche's co-conspirators and determining whether the Cutter was a vampire, two cases that had seen no progress.

At the Hill's police station, she slapped the Mordida police report into a manila file, labeled it, and left it on her clerk's desk. Thank the ancestors Maggie had finally returned from sick leave.

Tig switched on her computer, returning to her investigation of Blanche, and an alert popped up. A week ago, after visiting the Ruthton police station, she'd preprogrammed the search terms. She opened the alert and read it.

Shit.

She trotted the short distance from her office to the indoor basketball court at the Hill's country club. An all-vampire game was in progress, with lots of spectators in the stands. She took the empty chair next to the mayor.

"Hi, chief," he said. "What brings you here?"

"I need to talk with Jayden."

Winston pointed at the scoreboard clock. "Another five minutes to halftime. You might as well relax and enjoy the game."

The clock was paused for a time-out. Having no better option, she observed who was in the stands. It was too large a crowd for a casual game. Then she remembered—this was the season championship.

Jayden stood by the blue team's bench, an African-American mortal surrounded by a team of vampires, both men and women, a real United Nations. He enjoyed coaching them when he needed to take his mind off police work. Vampires might be superior athletes, but they didn't always grasp the game's strategy. That was where Jayden came in.

A lot of money would be riding on these games in private bets. When the buzzer sounded, ending the time-out, Zeke got possession of the ball and made the basket from thirty feet out. The game was already at a score of 150 to 146. About average.

A few nights ago, Zeke had given her a list of names, alibi witnesses for the dates the Carlyle Cutter struck, which was the only reason he wasn't locked up. She planned on asking Jayden for help verifying them.

Her mind wandered back to the burglary at the gallery. Should she tell Winston about the loss of his painting? Usually she didn't discuss routine investigations with him, but his property had been stolen, even if he hadn't taken possession of it yet.

"Mayor," she said to get his attention.

His gaze continued to track the game. "Yes?"

"There was a theft at Méi's gallery today—the paintings you bought."

"Goddamn it!" he yelled. When the other spectators turned their way, he lowered his voice. "I bet it was that asshole Rolf. He wanted them."

"If Méi's gallery had security cameras in place, we would know who did it." Before Blanche's attack on Henry, Tig had asked the mayor for funding to install cameras on the Hill. Winston had nixed the idea of cameras at the guard gate, but had seemed amenable to other locations. "Have you given any more consideration to my request for security cameras along the wall?"

"Wouldn't be prudent," he said condescendingly. He faced forward and tracked the game again.

"Why not?"

He turned to her, narrowing his gray eyes. "We've told everyone the threat is over. There's no reason to buy cameras now." He turned back to the game. "Damn Rolf," he mumbled.

She stewed for the remainder of the first half. How could the mayor be so short-sighted? Another attack was still possible. Cameras would help catch the next perp.

When the halftime buzzer sounded, she said a brusque goodbye and climbed down from the spectator seats to where Jayden stood by the team bench.

"Captain, may I have a minute of your time?" she asked. Even though everyone knew he was her mate, they kept it formal when on official business.

"Will it take long?" Jayden asked. "I was going to discuss strategy with the team for the second half."

"I'll keep it short. Where can we talk in private?"

He led her to an office at the back of the weight room. The teams had ambled off to their respective lockers. After closing the door, he slid into the chair behind the desk and laced his fingers behind his shaved head.

She paced in front of him, explaining the burglary at Méi's, and concluded, "Why is Rolf on my suspect list for both the burglary and the attacks on Henry and Yacov?"

Jayden sat forward and rested his forearms on the desk. "After he helped rescue Henry at the baseball game, didn't you rule him out?"

"There was a delay between when the stadium scanned in Henry's tickets and when Rolf phoned me. If Rolf knew about the two vampires sent to kill Henry at the baseball stadium, he may have hoped we'd arrive too late. Henry would be dead, and Rolf would look as pure as Snow White."

Jayden shook his head. "That's a little too Machiavellian, even for Rolf."

She stopped pacing and grabbed a chair. "Something else happened tonight. I need you to look into Zeke's whereabouts."

"Didn't the mayor confirm Zeke's alibi for the night Norman was killed?"

"He did." The prison guard who'd been connected to the attacks had been murdered, his throat sliced open. It looked like Zeke's work, since Zeke's weapon of choice was a knife. But it couldn't be Zeke—at least not according to the mayor. "You met the San Diego detective who investigated Norman's murder, right?"

"Sure…"

"Call him tomorrow. The Carlyle Cutter struck last night in San Diego."

"How'd I miss that?"

"The reports aren't using his name yet. I have a search programmed for all murders with the Cutter's MO, all the ritualistic stuff he does." She took out her phone and tapped the community calendar. "Did you guys have a practice game last night?"

"No, we took the last two nights off."

She looked up from her phone. "Then you don't know whether Zeke was on the Hill?"

"I can ask him."

"Good. I already have a list of alibi witnesses from Zeke for the nights of the other Cutter kills. I want you to confirm their stories."

"No problem. I can do it after the game."

She tapped the phone and sent him the list. "You know, I should probably ask the gate guards for their logs and see who else was off the Hill on the nights the Cutter struck. I'll add it to my growing to-do list," she said with a sarcastic laugh.

"Leave that to me. I'll take care of it." Jayden walked around from behind the desk and stopped at the door, one hand on the knob. "Tonight's the last game of the season—I'm free after this."

"Good. When you're done checking out Zeke, call me and I'll meet you at home."

He raised one eyebrow suggestively. She liked his look. It held promise—a promise he could deliver on. She joined him at the door and lightly brushed his lips with hers.

"Until later," she said with a wink.

CHAPTER 12

SIERRA ESCONDIDA POLICE STATION—FIFTEEN MINUTES LATER

Tig stood in front of two cardboard boxes, which were sitting in the police station conference room. The room had chairs for eight and a long fake-wood laminated table. No computer, but she had her iPad and plenty of space to spread out documents. The squad room was already a bit cluttered with the evidence they'd gathered so far.

This room gave her a fresh start.

The warehouse supervisor had taken almost three weeks to locate the town attorney's files for two vampires who were on Henry and Yacov's "grudge" list. The warehouse claimed Marcus had mislabeled the boxes.

Yeah, right. No one took responsibility for their mistakes anymore. It was always someone else's fault.

She took the lid off the first box. At least the storage company had dusted the outside before delivering it. Inside, it had the musty smell of long-stored paper. With Jayden still on the basketball court, she had nothing better to do than to go through the old files.

The fake email Blanche had stuffed in Henry's pocket had been a dead end. On its face, the email was from Leopold to a member of the San Francisco community, giving the order to kill Henry.

But why attack Henry and Yacov? Of the five founders of Sierra Escondida, they were the only ones who'd been targeted. Were they attacked because of their status as founders?

For the first eighty years of the town's existence, the founders had controlled everything, including who could live there, who could be turned vampire, and who would be executed for Covenant violations warranting the death penalty. Now, the founders' powers were more curtailed, but they still served on the homeowners association board and controlled who could live on the Hill.

The suspect list included offspring of Abigale and Marcus—two other founders. Each of the offspring had been denied residency by the association board. But if the attacks involved a decision by the founders, it didn't make sense why only Yacov and Henry were singled out. It took a majority to deny residency, and so far, no other founder had been attacked.

Unless the art theft counted as an attack on Méi, the fifth founder?

Tig typed on the iPad's keyboard, adding the idea to her investigation plan, and then returned to the suspect list, flicking through the files until she found the one she wanted. She placed it on the conference room table.

Kyle Geerlingh. *Ah yes.* There were restraining orders out on him, forbidding him from visiting the Hill. He was stalking Abigale, his maker.

Abigale was a dominatrix. Each of her current mates—all seven of them—enjoyed her practices. Tig knew, because she'd had to vet them before they moved here. Each mortal had agreed in advance to everything Abigale did with them.

Kyle, however, predated Tig's arrival on the Hill. The file laid out the facts. After being turned vampire, Kyle didn't want to share Abigale with her other mates—he wanted Abigale all to himself. So Abigale had kicked him out. A majority of founders backed her, voting to ban Kyle from the Hill, and Kyle had resented it ever since.

Tig scanned the transcript of the public hearing, her eyebrows raised while she read the testimony. Abigale's special room had figured prominently at the hearing. It made for good drama when you mixed sex with some offbeat behavior, and added in a catfight or two. It reminded her of one of those reality television programs where they locked people into one house to see who would dominate.

Apparently, Kyle was a selfish man; turning him vampire only made him worse. At the time, Henry and Yacov voted with the majority to ban Kyle.

The photo in the file depicted a handsome blonde of Swedish ancestry.

Tig wouldn't have minded taking a bite out of him while he was human. She looked at the current address for Kyle. The New York Collective.

Hmm. It wasn't like she could hop a plane, barge in, and start investigating a possible New York connection. Should she call the Collective's security chief? She had met him before and didn't like him much.

Who to trust?

She tapped her iPad to wake it up and scrolled through the Collective's directory. One of the mortals listed as a daytime security contact was Anne-Louise's latest mate, Rick. He was also a detective with the New York Police Department.

Tig had heard talk that Henry's relationship with his maker was a troubled one, and not just from Frédéric. She hadn't seen her own maker in over ten years, but she was still on good terms with Phat. Then again, their relationship had not been born from sex and passion. It made the whole thing much easier.

Anne-Louise's name had been on the initial list of potential suspects. Based on the odds, a victim was more likely to be killed—in Henry's case, nearly killed—by someone they knew than by a stranger.

A call to Rick would be worthwhile, just to get a feel for their little triangle. Or with Cerissa in the picture, would it be a square? Either way, Tig could kill two birds with one stone: scope out Anne-Louise and ask about Kyle. She punched in Rick's contact number.

"Hello," a man answered.

"This is Tig Anderson, chief of police for Sierra Escondida. May I please speak with Richard Fiorello?"

"Speaking."

In the background, she heard someone talking—a woman's high voice with a trace of a French accent. "Who is it, Rick?"

"Just a moment," he said into the phone. "It's Chief Anderson from Sierra Escondida."

His voice sounded somewhat muffled.

"Has something happened to Enrique? Give me the phone," the panicked woman demanded. "Tig, this is Anne-Louise." Her voice was almost shrill. "Is Enrique all right?"

"He's fine. I'm sorry to disturb your evening, but I need to speak with Detective Fiorello. It's about a police matter."

"But nothing has happened to Enrique? You're sure?"

"According to the latest patrol report, all is well at Henry's house,"

Tig said without letting any smirkiness enter her tone. The report indicated Cerissa's car was still in Henry's driveway. Things must be going *very* well for Henry.

"*Dieu merci!* With the shootings and your call, I was concerned he was attacked again."

"I understand. May I speak with Detective Fiorello now?"

"Of course," followed by a muffled "It's for you."

"Hi, chief, I'm back. Sorry, but I've learned it's easier to indulge her than to fight it."

Rick's easygoing nature must be why his relationship with Anne-Louise worked. Henry was anything but easygoing. Tig exchanged a few more pleasantries with the New York detective before they got on a first-name basis. In the process, she told him what happened with Blanche, and about Henry and Yacov's short list of suspects.

"It's a long shot," she explained, "but I wanted to get your impression, since you also work security for the Collective. Has Kyle been acting strange lately?"

"With Kyle, it depends on what you consider strange. I don't keep track of him, but I have the impression he hasn't left New York City in a long time. I've run into him at various social functions."

"What about Blanche? Did she visit the Collective anytime in the past six months?"

"I've never met her. I'm going to have to pull her records from V-Trak to be sure."

"I'll send you her photo." She put the call on speaker and wrote out a quick email, attaching the image.

"Sounds good," he said. "I could snoop around, ask a few questions."

"That would help." She hit send on the email. "The photo is on its way to you."

"Super. I'll take care of it. Do you mind if I tell Anne-Louise?"

Tig paused to consider it. "I'd prefer it if you didn't give her any details. You can disclose you're looking into a New York lead, but don't mention Kyle's name."

"Not a problem. She and I reached an understanding when we first started dating. She knows I can't talk about my work. But would it be okay if I briefed our head of security?"

Tig pursed her lips, not liking the idea, but what choice did she have? "Officially, we've closed the case with Blanche's death."

"If you were convinced of that, you wouldn't have called."

Damned politics! The town council wanted it downplayed, but she couldn't let them tie her hands. "Go ahead and tell him—he's probably read the official version, since we had to announce it to the other communities once Blanche was dead."

"Will do."

"But let him know I called you first because of your connection to Anne-Louise. Otherwise he's going to wonder why I didn't call him."

Rick chuckled. "Yeah, good point."

"And tell him to keep it confidential. We don't want to start unnecessary rumors. It may turn out Blanche's death closed the case."

"You got it."

After saying goodbye, Tig made notes from the call into the investigation file. She kept a four-column table of suspects. Anne-Louise's impromptu performance had gone a long way to convince Tig to move Anne-Louise to the "not likely" column.

Tig returned Kyle's file to the box and moved on to the next name on the suspect list: Oscar Nolan, the town attorney's one and only offspring.

She opened the file. Marcus had turned Oscar after the town was incorporated, but before the first Covenant was signed in 1891. Marcus wasn't even forty in vampire years at the time, much too young to safely turn anyone. Not smart, but then, when one got the fever to turn their mate, even the smartest vampires succumbed. Oscar left the Hill shortly after he was turned.

Now Tig remembered hearing the stories. Oscar had used Marcus to become a vampire and then run off as soon as he was through the transition. *Ungrateful asshole.* Marcus let him go without a fight. If it had been her, she would have called Oscar back to her and kept him on a short leash, at least until she knew his feeding habits could be trusted.

Twenty years after leaving Marcus, Oscar applied for Hill residency, and the founders opposed it, including Marcus. Couldn't say she blamed him. Who wanted an ex-flame living in their neighborhood? She flipped through the file—about every ten or twenty years, Oscar applied again.

Wait, what's this?

In the past, the denial always turned on Marcus's testimony. But starting in the 1990s, Marcus had taken a neutral stance on Oscar's subsequent applications, the last of which was filed only five years ago. So why did Marcus change his stance? Did he want Oscar back? Tig couldn't imagine it. Their old relationship had to be dead embers by now.

She hadn't paid much attention to it at the time. Back then, Marcus didn't have a mate. Now, everyone on the Hill thought the assistant city attorney, Nicholas, would soon move in with Marcus and become his mate. The two had council permission to explore a relationship.

Nicholas had been hired six months ago with Marcus's recommendation, but it was Father Matt's bite that ensured the loyalty bond and kept Nicholas from telling outsiders about vampires. The priest had filled that surrogate role before on the *very* rare occasion when they needed to hire someone to work on the Hill who wasn't mated to a vampire. Once Marcus and Nicholas took the big step, Father Matt would bow out of the picture.

Tig rubbed her forehead. So would Oscar send assassins to kill Henry and Yacov for opposing his past applications? It seemed a bit extreme. The other founders had opposed the applications as well, except for Marcus, who abstained.

She used V-Trak to double-check Oscar's current location. He lived in Rancho Valley, a California town in Riverside County, and owned a winery there. Rancho Valley wasn't close to where the shooters had been incarcerated in San Diego, but it was closer to the prison than Sierra Escondida was.

According to V-Trak, Rancho Valley had a sizeable vampire population and Oscar had a leadership role. *Hmm.* The vampires of Rancho Valley didn't run the local government. Made sense, if he liked winemaking, that he would want to move back to the Hill—better security and more control.

Oscar's nest had been small when the treaty was signed in 1972, ending the war among the larger communities. His nest hadn't signed the treaty at the time, but then, small nests like his were left alone, so long as they hadn't aligned with either side.

But four years ago, shortly after his last application had been turned down, Oscar personally signed the treaty on behalf of the Rancho Valley vampires.

There was nothing in the file to suggest he had an active vendetta against Yacov and Henry. And without more, she couldn't go to Rancho Valley and start investigating Oscar any more than she could do the same with Kyle in New York. It just didn't work that way among vampires.

The buzzing of her phone told her a new email had arrived. The message read: "Do you want to place a bet for the South African soccer match this weekend? Your humble bookie, Petar."

She sat back in her chair. Henry's bookie had been on her short list of suspects, too. He'd been moved to the "not likely" column as well, simply because he had more motive for keeping Yacov and Henry as clients than for killing them. In the process of investigating Petar, she had extracted a promise from him to contact her if he heard anything.

The message could mean only one thing: Petar had news for her—news he couldn't trust to an email.

"Why, Tig, my dear, that was fast," Petar said when he answered.

"You have something for me?"

"Why else would I email you? But I'd like to meet in person. Phones are so impersonal. All those insects we hear about."

She grimaced. "Do you mean bugs?"

"Bug, insects—is there really a difference? Anyway, how does Wednesday night sound? I'll send you passes to my private club in Newport Beach."

She would have to borrow a plane. "Make it for two—I'll bring one of my officers with me, Liza Erhgott."

"As long as you trust her."

"I do." Liza had never done anything to raise any doubts. Next to Jayden, Tig relied on Liza the most.

Petar gave her an alias to use for the passes and said goodbye. The trip would cost her most of one night, but by the tone of Petar's voice, it would be worth the sacrifice. A bookie stood at the crossroads of an information highway she couldn't easily tap into.

She looked down at the file boxes. She'd done all she could with these historic records. The town clerk still owed her a few more files—nothing more to do until he delivered them. She moved the boxes back to the squad room. Jayden would be done with the game soon, and it wouldn't take him long to look into Zeke's alibi witnesses.

She pictured the way Jayden had winked at her and smiled to herself. Maybe it was time to try out the new bubble bath he'd given her. He was always buying her small, thoughtful gifts, and she had the perfect way to show her gratitude. The tub in the master bedroom was big enough for two—they could try it out together.

CHAPTER 13

Cerissa woke with a start. "Henry?" she called out. He wasn't in bed next to her. Where was he?

"It's all right. I'm here." He rose from the loveseat and snagged a white bathrobe from a nearby chair, draping it over his arm as he walked to her. The robe was like the one he wore—except his was forest green.

"I was dreaming," she said. "Someone was trying to take you from me."

He joined her in bed and wrapped his arms around her. "That will never happen, *cariña*."

If only his words could predict the future. But she wasn't going to spoil the evening by talking about the Protectors. She snuggled tightly against him, resting her head on his chest, his thick terrycloth robe soft against her face. She felt the beat of his heart through the robe—slower than a mortal's, but still strong.

The black wires of his earbuds dangled near her nose. "What are you listening to?" she asked.

He took his phone from the robe's pocket and punched an app, transferring the music to the speakers sitting on the dresser. "I listened to this a lot while we were apart."

It was an old blues song. The lyrics told the story of a young man alone late at night, lonely because his lover was out of town.

"It's such a sad song, isn't it?" she said. "You feel it in the song, the singer's angst at being alone."

"It mirrored my own feelings, being separated from you."

She placed her hand over his heart. "Deep down, you're an incurable romantic."

"Yes, but you mustn't tell anyone," he said, giving her a little squeeze.

"We can't ruin my brooding vampire image, now can we? Besides, no one on the Hill would believe you if you told them."

"It'll be our secret," she said with a smile.

Henry released her and slid out of bed, holding the white robe open for her. "It's new, but I washed it for you. I don't like wearing anything right out of the package."

She rolled off the bed and slipped into the robe, appreciating his thoughtfulness. The sweet scent of artificial sunlight promised by detergent manufacturers engulfed her. She ran her hand along the fluffy collar and wrapped the belt around her waist, the thick robe velvety against her bare skin.

She opened the balcony doors, the cool night air reviving her from her nap, the quiet night broken by the buzz of cicadas and the modulated chirping of tree toads. The view overlooked the pool and the guest house. A field of grapevines ran to the foothills, the scattered floodlights illuminating his vineyard. The music continued to play.

Henry stepped behind her and kissed the back of her neck. "Would you like something to eat? You should eat, to replenish your strength."

"In a bit. What I'd love is to see the rest of your house, if that's okay." She was looking forward to seeing his private space. During her previous visits, some parts had been off-limits.

The tour of the top floor didn't take long. She'd already seen the two guest bedrooms and the television room. He took her down the hall, which formed a balcony above the first-floor entryway, and turned the knob on a closed door.

His office was as big as the master bedroom, with a picture window overlooking the same view. He sat down against the large desk, perching his butt on the edge. The hardwood desk was so tidy—did he ever use it for business?

She walked over to his bookshelf. "Impressive," she said.

She picked up one of the gold medals displayed there and traced the words on the cold metal with her finger. *Double Gold.* The shelf was filled with trophies and awards his wines had won.

"I enjoy the winemaking business. It's been good to me over the years." He stood. "Would you like to see the rest of it?"

"Sure."

He took her to the room adjoining his office. Sparsely furnished, the narrow room could have been a walk-in closet for the office. No windows— she suspected it was lightproof.

"Do you ever sleep here?" she asked, eyeing the black reclining couch.

"On rare occasion. I feel safer in the basement crypts."

The crypts had steel doors, three deadbolts each, and reinforced concrete block walls. No wonder he felt safer there.

He led her through a doorway on the opposite wall to another room, which was also the size of the master bedroom.

It held enough clothes for an army.

Pants, suits, and shirts hung along all four walls, perfectly organized by style, color, and season. Another door opened into an immaculately clean bathroom, which shared a common wall with the master bath.

"You have excellent taste in clothes," she said, as they left the closet, returning to his office.

He looked pleased at the compliment and nodded in reply. "Now that we are intimate, no room is off-limits, but I would prefer you didn't use my office desk. I like things to remain where I place them."

She looked at the ceiling, biting her tongue. She already knew Henry was a neat freak. Maybe this was to be expected.

"All right, Mr. Meticulous," she said in a teasing tone.

"No, just discriminating." He caged her in his arms and backed her against the wall. "Which is why I choose you."

She tried to duck out of his arms, but he planted his feet on either side of hers, his hips pressed forward. She pushed at his arms—it was like pushing on steel.

Smirking at her, he added, "I can get you a laptop and connect it to the wireless router if you need internet access."

"I have my own computer," she said, still pushing at his arms. She wasn't ready to explain the computing power of her contact lenses to him. She gave up pushing and looked up at his handsomely cocky grin. "All right, where can I work if I need a desk?"

"You can use the library downstairs." He lowered his arms to her waist, pulling her closer, his breath whispering against her ear. "But whatever you need to be comfortable, just tell me. *Mi casa es su casa.*"

"Let's not move too quickly," she said rapidly, a small rush of panic speeding up her pulse. She could never fool the Protectors if she moved in here. Ari would have to edit out too much of what her lenses recorded. She took a breath to calm her voice. "That is, I mean, we have plenty of time to take things as they come. I still have the VDM to pursue, and I need more investors. So I'm not going to be able to spend every night with you. I'll have to work."

"I know, *cariña*. And I respect your obligations." He released one arm from around her and brushed his folded fingers across her cheek. "Is there anything I can do to help?"

She refused to use their relationship to get investors. But the VDM was an entirely different matter. "What can you tell me about the San Diego community? One of them said some nasty things about mortals."

"Who?"

"Barney Morrison."

He grinned at her, a look saying he wasn't worried. "Last I heard, Barney was happily married. I doubt he'd agree to turn mortals into slaves."

"But you could look into him, make sure nothing has changed?"

"It would be my pleasure, *cariña*."

"Thanks."

He gestured toward the wall between his office and the television room. "And I can always clean out the storage room and put in an office for you, if it would help—"

She held up her hands and stepped away. "Let's take things slowly."

"Of course," he agreed, his tone soft and warm. "I was only thinking of your comfort. Some evenings I may need to work for a few hours, too. And I want you to have access to whatever you need to succeed with your business plans."

"We'll figure it out as we go along." She took a deep breath, and then a thought took the wind out of her. She plopped onto his office couch. "Unless the community expects me to move in now? I mean, it's not that I don't want to be with you, Henry, I do. It's just that I'm still Leopold's envoy—"

He knelt in front of her. "It's all right. Being blood mates means we're exclusive. No other vampire can touch you without my permission, but—"

"Or my permission," she interrupted, raising both eyebrows.

"Of course, or yours," he conceded with a nod. "But as you know, it isn't a permanent bond. It remains our choice, exactly, what it means to us. So we can figure out what that is together."

"Oh, okay. I like that."

"As do I." He stood up and held out his hand. "Come downstairs with me. You should have something to eat."

They headed to the kitchen, where she took a seat at the mahogany table when he motioned her toward it. The *snick* of the refrigerator door sounded and he brought her a small tray of deli-style sandwiches and side

93

dishes labeled from a local caterer, and set them out for her, along with a bottle of champagne.

She smiled at the display. He had obviously thought ahead of her needs—he certainly didn't need food around.

He popped the cork on a champagne bottle and poured for her. "To celebrate our new status," he said.

She relaxed back and munched on half a turkey sandwich on wheat, watching the champagne's bubbles chase up the stem.

"Tasty," she said between mouthfuls. She washed it down with the champagne. While he refilled her glass, she sniffed the coleslaw carton.

Whew. She wrinkled her nose. Did the catering company own an onion farm?

She skipped the slaw and spooned some potato salad onto a paper plate instead—onion-free and better for a romantic evening.

"You've never told me how you became vampire," she said. Their earlier conversation had raised her curiosity. "Why did Anne-Louise turn you?"

He sat down across from her, a mug of warmed blood in his hands. "Well, there is the story of a young man's folly if there ever was one. It was October 21, 1825. I was in California to claim land granted to my family by Mexico. Once our house was built, I wrote to my father, asking him to send my bride—he had promised to make a good marriage for me. I received a letter back, telling me about Simona Rodriguez, which family she was from, and describing her. The letter included the name of the ship she would sail on, and the date she was expected to arrive."

Bride? Cerissa raised her chin, frowning.

He seemed oblivious to her reaction, his gaze focused on the mug of blood. "I rode my carriage into town and arranged for lodging. Two rooms, as we would not be together until the priest wed us. I went to the harbor every day, anxious to see who my father had chosen for me. The ship didn't arrive on time, and I grew bored. I convinced myself it would be wise to visit the local brothel, to expend some of my restless energy. I didn't want to be a beast on my wedding night."

Really? With his nuptials pending, he risked catching a disease?

Then she rethought it in the historical context. She'd seen firsthand the appalling lack of medical knowledge in the early 1800s. There wasn't much awareness of the risks back then, and culturally it was relatively common for young unmarried men to visit prostitutes. She grabbed another sandwich while he continued talking.

"There was a room at the brothel, a room where the men could mingle with the women, have a glass of fine whisky, and select the one they wanted. Anne-Louise caught my eye immediately. She was—is—radiantly beautiful. Curly salt-and-pepper hair. Much older than my twenty-four years, she had an air of sophistication and mystery about her. So unlike the woman I expected to marry."

He took a brief sip from his mug, and then continued. "She wore a loose dress falling against her curves to reveal a womanly figure. After I chose her, she led me to a room. We made love. It wasn't like anything I had experienced with a prostitute before. The sexual interest was as much on her part as mine. We made love a second time, and I did not leave the room alive."

Cerissa was fighting hard not to flinch at the description of their lovemaking when Henry's last words sank in. Her eyes widened. "Rather spontaneous of her. She had no idea who you were."

"She is like that. I was enraged when I arose from the death sleep to find out what she had done. All my plans, my bride, my family—gone. We fought, but I could not resist following her. I needed help to survive."

"What happened to Simona?"

"Anne-Louise insisted we leave right away—the area was not populated enough to serve two vampires, and I knew I could never return for Simona, not without risking her life, as I had little control around mortals at the time."

Wow. Okay. She swallowed hard on the last bite of her sandwich. "And you never learned later?"

"Thirty years passed before I returned to California. I checked the harbor manifests when I did. The logs showed Simona returned to Veracruz on the next ship." He took a deep drink from his mug and returned it to the table.

Okey-dokey. So he hadn't been married before. Or had he? "You didn't get married then—have you ever been married?"

He frowned, looking unhappy over the question. "No. Being what I am, I never felt it right to marry anyone."

He stared into his mug again, looking lost in self-doubt. The last time they opened their bodies to each other, they had revealed more of their souls. She wasn't surprised the same had happened again. Just like a wall protected the Hill community from outsiders, they'd each built up their own personal walls over the years. They'd break down those walls one brick at a time.

And despite those walls, she loved him, even though she still had so much to learn and discover, as if her heart knew the inevitability of their match even as her mind muddled through it. Creatures of longevity like them had all the time in the world, but so rarely experienced love.

Cerissa wouldn't take it for granted.

She stood and reached for his hand, inviting him into her arms. Sadness seemed to surround him. She held him for a moment, feeling him sigh against her shoulder.

"There's nothing wrong with you," she whispered. "I love you just the way you are."

CHAPTER 14

HENRY'S HOUSE—A MOMENT LATER

He buried his face in her long hair, holding her close and hiding his shame.

How can she say that? I'm an abomination.

As a newly turned vampire, he'd been repulsed by what he had to do to survive. Even now, he was haunted by the many things he'd done. They gnawed at his conscience like rats, never letting him heal, and some days the layers of raw guilt piled high enough to smother him.

"I mean it, Henry. I accept what you are."

How did he get so lucky to find her? Her words—her trust in him—was so rare and so easily given. She was able to accept him when he struggled with it.

He took a deep breath of her alluring scent. He could do nothing about the past. He could only move forward and try to be a better man.

He released her from the tight grip he'd held her in. "Cerissa, I have something for you upstairs. Bring your champagne if you like."

The box waited for him on the dresser where he'd left it. He motioned for her to sit on the small loveseat near the balcony windows. The drapes were still open, the moon visible in the distance.

He handed her the small, rectangular jewelry box. She opened it. Inside was a simple bracelet of amethyst and moonstone gems, set in yellow gold.

"It's lovely," she said, a large smile lighting up her green eyes.

He lifted the bracelet out of its box and, kneeling in front of her, fastened it around her wrist. "The moonstone tells other vampires you are now mated to someone from Sierra Escondida. They will be able to tell you are bonded to a vampire, but this confirms what their senses tell them."

"Karen wears a gold ring with a single moonstone," she said.

"Some prefer rings, others pendants. I guessed you might like this bracelet."

"I do."

She held out her wrist, clearly admiring it. The white stones were lovely against her dark skin, the deep purple of the amethyst alternating between them.

Seeing his bracelet around her wrist and his mark on her neck caused his chest to swell with pride. He was truly lucky to have her. He got up off his knees to sit by her.

She fingered the stones. "So this is what Zeke meant."

"Pardon?"

"The night of the baseball game, he confronted me, said I wasn't your mate. He said he knew because I hadn't been branded. I'm glad he hadn't meant it literally."

Henry kissed her hand, the bracelet sliding toward her elbow. "Different communities have different customs. Ours are more benign."

She snuggled against him on the loveseat and he basked in the warmth of her body against him, fully content in the moment.

Turning in his arms, she folded her legs underneath her and faced him. "Henry, I have what may seem like a strange request. I'd like to see your fangs."

A flare of unease ran up his neck. "Why?"

"Just curious. You've never let me see them up close before."

With good reason. He preferred to pass as mortal. But they were blood mates now, and her curiosity was normal.

"Give me your hand." He raised it to his lips and inhaled deeply. The roof of his mouth grew tight, there was a prickle of anticipation, and then the sensation faded, telling him his fangs were fully extended. Over the back of her hand, he leered at her. "A reflex action, triggered by the smell of your sweet blood."

"Interesting." She gently grasped his chin, turning his head. "Open wider."

"Cerissa, I—"

"Wait, don't talk. This is fascinating." She turned his head to the right, and then to the left, looking at his fangs from different angles. "How do they deploy?"

He pulled away, uncomfortable under her microscope. "They are hinged. There is a muscle, one that didn't exist when I was human—it causes them to extend and holds them in place."

"May I touch them?" she asked.

He hesitated. She tilted her head and looked at him as if to say "please." There was no judgment in her eyes. It was just her clinical curiosity. He'd have to accept the fact that he had mated a scientist.

"All right, yes, you may," he said, letting his voice express his reluctance. They were lovers, not doctor-patient. But tonight, he could refuse her nothing.

Using her index finger, she touched the roof of his mouth, pushing on the muscle, tracing its connection to his fangs. It tickled, and he had to fight the urge to close his mouth.

"I wonder which neurotransmitter triggers the extension?" she said. With her finger in his mouth, he couldn't answer, but guessed it wasn't a question aimed at him.

She ran her finger along the back of his fang, stopping at the tip. "Ow," she exclaimed. "I should have been more careful." She jerked her hand back and blood pooled on the tip. "Am I going to fall into a deep sleep?" she added with a laugh.

"Wrong fairy tale."

Blood welled from the shallow puncture faster than it should have. He caught the drop with his tongue. "Allow me." Taking her hand, he sucked on her fingertip, the enticing taste of her spreading out across his tongue. "To close the wound, I would use the blood of another vampire, except you're allergic to vampire blood."

"Yeah, Gaea gave me a vial of her blood before I came over here. It was very thoughtful of her." She morphed the wound closed. "Henry, you're aware vampire fangs inject a sexual stimulant, yes?"

"I have long suspected that."

She frowned. "How is fang serum any different from using a roofie?"

"If a vampire bit before obtaining consent to sexual activity, then you would be right. But the treaty forbids using our powers to rape mortals."

"Oh. So you can feed without consent, but no sex without it."

"Precisely. There are some locales where feeding on strangers is still permitted. However, the Hill has a hundred-mile 'no hunting' zone." He cocked his head and the corners of his mouth twitched up. "You aren't immune to its effect, are you?"

A blush rose on her cheeks. Turning away, she picked up her champagne glass and took a healthy swig.

"*Cariña*, look at me."

"No."

What was bothering her? She'd had bouts of shyness before. But why now?

"Please. Look at me."

She tilted her head and glanced over her shoulder at him. Had the moment of truth come?

I should tell him the real risk. I should tell him about the morphing hormone...

"There is no need to be embarrassed," he said. "If we are to be in bed together, we must be able to discuss things frankly. Enjoying sex is nothing to be ashamed of."

Oh damn. He wants to have that *talk.*

She scrubbed her hand across her face, her back still to him. Why was this part of having a human body so difficult?

His long fingers touched the back of her neck, working their way through her hair to gently massage her neck.

When she had first told him about the Lux, she'd explained there were three parts to their life-cycle: child, *karabu*, and *principatus*. The child stage had been the first sixteen years of her life. Then her body metamorphosed into a *karabu*, the intermediate stage. It wasn't equivalent to being a teenager—just the opposite. The *karabu* had mature minds detached from emotion. She'd lived two hundred and ten years as a *karabu* before metamorphosing into an adult and developing a normal range of human emotions and sexual interest. She'd only been in her adult phase for ten years. Enough time to experiment, but—

"Tell me what happened," he asked.

"Ah, happened?"

"Did a man hurt you?"

"Not in the way you mean. Any guy who tried to rape me would be minus his weapon before he got his zipper down."

"But something did happen," he said, continuing to knead her neck sensually.

Why was it so hard for her to talk about her pleasure? She kept her back to him. "The lovers I've had…well, one in particular…ah…he was kind of…critical of my…ah…sexual response. It's made it hard for me to talk about, well, about what I like…"

"Shall I find him and kill him for you?"

"Henry!" She turned around to face him, dislodging his hands from her shoulders.

"Cerissa, the man was a cad, an idiot who couldn't appreciate what he had." Henry's fingers brushed gently over her throat, running a path along the V made by her robe. "Every person is different, *cariña*. I plan on spending the next hundred years learning everything about your body, every inch, and how you like it touched, stroked, licked, or bit." He lightly caressed the top mound of her breast where it peeked through the robe. "Banish the cad from your mind, and I will replace him with memories far more pleasant."

Cad was a good word for him. The cad had reinforced her belief that all love was conditional—something she'd first learned from her mother. In his case, the love was conditional on how well she performed in bed. After that experience, she hadn't taken another lover. It was easier to put human sex on a shelf than deal with it.

She looked at where Henry's fingers rested on her breast and bit her lip.

"There's more to it, isn't there?" he asked.

She buried her face against his chest. How to explain to him a lifetime of experience?

"That guy was just the topping on the pudding. My *amma* was forced to rear me among humans, which meant I was kept locked in human form as a child. She hated having a human-looking child. She would push me away from her, disgust in her eyes. And the Lux weren't much better. Their love is conditioned on obedience, on fulfilling my duty to them. And then that guy—no one ever seemed to accept me just the way I am, for who I am."

Henry lifted her chin with one finger until she was looking into his deep brown eyes. His irises were so crystalline that light seemed to shine from them.

"I accept who and what you are."

"How can you say that? You've never seen my Lux form."

"I don't need to."

"But what if—"

"I love *you*." He caressed her cheek. "That's not to say I'm not curious, but I can wait until you're ready to show me."

Could he really love me unconditionally?

She had offered him the same unconditional acceptance—it didn't matter to her that he was vampire. Why couldn't she accept the same gift from him?

The light touch of his lips pressed against her forehead. "I am glad you enjoyed yourself tonight."

"Ah, something about the bite did help."

"Could it not be my animal magnetism and prowess in bed?"

"Henry, quit teasing me. This is hard enough without you teasing me."

"All right, *cariña*. As I said before, I have suspected fang serum contained a sexual stimulant, but I also thought it came from our ability to mesmerize, to relax our vic—to relax our lovers. Some experience it as an aphrodisiac, others as intensifying the sexual experience."

"*Intensifying* is a good word," she said, looking away. "Do you experience the same thing when you drink blood?"

"Only when I bite. Drinking bagged blood does not produce the same effect."

The idea crystallized in her mind and she raised her head to look at him.

"Backwash," she said. When she'd examined his fangs, she'd found a small groove behind the tips, like the opening in a sewing machine needle, but only on the backside. "Your fangs inject the serum, it mixes with my blood, and when you drink the mixture, you get some of the stimulant too."

"A reasonable explanation," he replied.

The only way to be sure was to experiment. "I want you to bite me before we make love, before we're lost in the passion of the moment."

He looked appalled. "It will hurt, and I don't want to hurt you. You are immune from being mesmerized, so I can't do anything to make you forget the pain. It's better for you if you are already aroused."

"Still, I'd like to try."

"But it's not good for you if I take too much blood in one night."

She grinned at him wryly. "It's not a problem for me. All I have to do is eat more food and increase my blood production. The advantage of being Lux—I'll be fine, as long as you don't drain me dry."

He exhaled with the deep-throated sound men made when they decided to do something against their better judgment, and stood, offering her his hand. She accepted it and faced him.

His gaze focused on the pinpoint wounds on the right side of her neck. "Why haven't you healed it?"

She touched her throat. "Because you gave it to me." A warm flush infused her at the memory. "Your mark. I want to let it heal naturally."

He moved her hair away from her other shoulder and, caressing her neck with his lips, slowly kissed along the side of her throat. The kisses sent shivers along her spine with each featherlight touch. With the next press of his lips, his fangs pierced a vein.

She let out a gasp from the sharp sting of the bite.

His mouth pressed sensuously, gently sucking, gooseflesh rising along her neck and down her back and arms. She tried to keep her mind detached, to track what happened, but volcanic heat swept through her.

She clawed at the knot in his bathrobe's tie, and then hers, until she pressed naked against him. Standing on her tiptoes, she slid herself along his length without letting him enter, pushing his foreskin further back. Slippery heat pulsed between her legs as she rubbed against him again and again, animalistic in her need for him.

He let out a noise, a cross between a growl and moan, and the sound shot lightning bolts through her, her heart pierced by him.

I love you so much.

With both hands, he grabbed her bottom, lifting her, and she wrapped her legs around his waist, her arms holding tightly around his neck. He carried her over to the bed and laid her down.

Still sucking on her neck, he entered her, her legs dangling over the edge of the bed. The heat from his bite caused sweat to bead on her skin, their bodies slick as his chest scraped against her hard nipples.

He released her neck and looked at her, his eyes solid black.

My predator.

The way he thrust into her, the angle he chose, rubbed against her core each time, building the tension. She flowed with it, seeking more contact, more pressure, until the explosion overtook her, and she crossed the peak, riding out the long wave, her muscles clenching him with each spasm until he cried out his own pleasure.

She lay there on her back, panting and looking at him, his long hair a wild, sexy mess. Hers must be just as bad.

"How was it?" he asked, between quick breaths.

"Intense." A warm trickle of blood ran along her shoulder and she felt his tongue lap up the liquid. "It's like I feel your passion, what the blood does for you. It hurts when we start off cold, but not much. And it gets very exciting, very fast."

He kissed her cheek and kept going, placing small, gentle kisses all around her face. She lay there, letting him express his feelings with his lips. When he slid off her, they worked their way up onto the bed to stretch out, and she rested her head on his shoulder, running her fingers over his pecs, finally screwing up her courage to ask, "How was it for you?"

He held her close to him as he spoke. "It's exciting—especially to do it the way we did when we still hunted mortals. It's too bad you aren't truly afraid of me."

She pulled back and looked at him. "That's a strange thing to say."

He ran his hand over her cheek, letting his fingers trail down her neck. "I wouldn't want *you* to truly fear me, of course. It simply would be more authentic if you were afraid—that is all I meant by it."

"Why?"

He drew her to him again and spoke softly into her ear. "There is just something different about the blood of a victim who is afraid. It's a minor thing." He sighed. "It's unimportant. Forget I mentioned it."

CHAPTER 15

HENRY'S HOUSE—MOMENTS LATER

He should have kept his mouth shut. He wasn't addicted to the taste of fear in his victim's blood, but he missed it, the same way he missed the occasional shot of whisky he'd enjoyed as a mortal.

She remained silent, resting on his shoulder. Was she mulling it over? Her scientific mind would no doubt file away his small comment for later—it was the natural curiosity in her.

He didn't look forward to that inquiry.

When she dozed off, he went downstairs and brought up another sandwich for her, setting the plate on the bedstand, along with a glass of cold water.

Asleep, she looked so peaceful that he loathed waking her. But she wouldn't spend the day here. She was quite clear she wasn't ready to move in—yet. If he left her be, it would give the impression he hadn't listened to her.

"Wake up, *mi amor*," Henry whispered. He didn't want to startle her.

She slowly woke, stretched, and asked, "What did you say?"

"I said, wake up."

"You said something else."

He caressed her face, loving the warm feel of her smooth skin on his fingertips. "I called you *mi amor*, for that is what you are now."

"My love," she echoed.

He kissed her, then handed her the robe and suggested she have something more to eat. Satisfied her needs were taken care of, he told her he was going to shower. "Dawn is less than an hour away, *cariña*."

In spite of what she'd told him earlier, she didn't want to leave. She wanted to stay with him in their own little world, one without the Protectors or the VDM to worry about.

The bracelet tickled her skin. She ran her fingertips across the stones, admiring them again. She didn't wear much jewelry, but she would always wear this.

Blood mates. She touched her neck. *Now the whole community will know.*

When Henry came out of the bathroom, he had a towel wrapped around his waist. He looked like a god to her, with his wet hair hanging loose across his broad shoulders, and his taut abs and strong chest on full display. He turned to pick up a tank top from the dresser, and the cutest butt she had ever seen was outlined by the towel tucked around his waist.

She went over to him. He took her in his arms and held her. She had not imagined how incredibly gentle he could be toward her.

"I want this night to go on and on," she said.

"As do I, *mi amor*. But now it's your turn to shower."

He turned her in the direction of the bathroom and gave her a light swat on the butt to get her moving. She looked over her shoulder and stuck out her tongue at him. He lunged at her, pretending to give chase. She ran laughing into the bathroom and closed the door.

When she came out of the bathroom, clean and dry, he was dressed in pajama bottoms and a tank top.

He stopped her to look at both sides of her neck. "Good. I didn't tear the skin. I haven't lost my touch."

"Don't sound so pleased with yourself, *Señor* Bautista."

"As long as you are pleased, that is all that matters."

"I am," she said, smiling.

"I hope in more ways than one."

"Henry!" She pushed away from him and covered her slight embarrassment by getting dressed. He had brought her dress and shoes upstairs for her.

Her discomfort over discussing her own pleasure would get easier over time. At the moment, it was nearly a reflex, one that seemed to melt away in the warmth of his understanding.

When she turned back to him, he was slipping the gold chain over his head until his crucifix hung against his chest.

She reached out and touched the hard metal body hanging on the cross. "I have never understood why Christians wear an implement of torture as a religious symbol."

"To remind us of what was sacrificed."

"It just seems so morbid to aggrandize suffering. It always reminds me of the powerlessness of God to stop the horrible things humans do to each other."

Henry frowned at her. "Their evil is not God's fault—it comes from Satan."

She stroked the gold cross again. "Christians project evil onto the anti-god. Not every religion does. Some embrace it all as coming from God—the wolf killing the rabbit is acting out God's thoughts. The Hindus—"

"Are you Hindu?"

"I'm Lux. We try to do what God does not," she said, the words flowing from her mouth uncensored.

But I'm choosing my own destiny.

If she succeeded in breaking free from the Lux, she'd no longer have a duty to protect humanity. Was she being selfish? Was there a way to do both?

Grow a spine.

She laid her head against his chest, close to the crucifix, sad to imagine anyone being sacrificed. Yet Henry found sacrifice to be so honorable. Why? Cerissa had been forced to sacrifice her own desires her entire life, and nothing about it felt honorable. Or was it only voluntary sacrifice that held honor? The sacrifices she'd made had all been thrust on her by the Lux.

He kissed the top of her head, interrupting her thoughts. "We can talk of this another time," he said. "Unless you want to stay—"

"You were right to wake me. I have work to do. It'll be easier if I return to Gaea's before you bed down for the day."

She stuffed the nightie into her purse.

He touched her neck lightly. "You should heal the bites. At least one of them. The Covenant only allows one bite per night. I wouldn't want Gaea to see two. Not unless you want to see me at the whipping post."

"Never." She morphed the skin on one set just so he could see it was done.

"Thank you, *mi amor.*"

As they walked to her car, a melancholy descended on her. "I don't want to go," she said.

He stroked her cheek. "I will see you tonight."

It could have been a question or a statement—she wasn't sure which. "Shall I meet you here?"

He slipped his hand into his pocket and took out a key. "If I am not awake yet, let yourself in."

Tears flooded her eyes. The brass key meant more to her than the moonstone bracelet; it meant he trusted her to be in his house when he was asleep and helpless.

"What is this? Tears? I hoped to make you happy."

"I am happy," she replied, hugging him and holding him tightly to her.

He tilted her head and kissed her. "Umm, salty," he said. She pulled back, smiling. "That's better," he added, caressing her lower lip with his thumb. "Now I have to go inside. Be careful driving back to Gaea's."

Sliding behind the wheel of her car, she squeezed his hand and let go. "See you tonight."

"Yes, *mi amor,*" he said with a slight bow. "Until tonight."

CHAPTER 16

After catching six hours of sleep, Cerissa took care of a few business matters and then flashed to New York. It was time she and Leopold had a major talk, one he'd like as much as a prostate exam with an ice-cold glove.

No one in Manhattan noticed when she stepped from a vacant alley onto a crowded sidewalk. Going from the quiet of the Hill to the sudden blare of horns, the screech of tires, and yelled curses felt like walking into a wall of sound, the cacophony crawling across her skin.

She hurried to the Collective's high-rise and signed in with the guard.

"You're not on the guest list for tonight," the guard said, looking from her driver's license to his computer monitor. He sat behind a small opening in the wall, like a receptionist at a doctor's office, but that was where the analogy ended. No doctor's office had a crystal chandelier and an antique Persian rug in its lobby.

"I'm on Leopold's permanent guest list. I'm still his en—I mean, his business agent."

"Yeah, but…" he said, pushing a few buttons on the keyboard, probably switching screens. "Let me phone him."

Less than a minute later, the guard hung up the phone.

"He's not answering. I should wait until Mr. Leidecker is available. I don't usually let anyone up when he isn't there."

She took back her license, letting her fingers trail across his hand as she did, sending a wisp of her aura into him. In the past she'd had trouble controlling it, blasting people with her charm when only a puff was needed. Did being sexually sated give her better control? Or did charting her own destiny give her a newfound confidence that improved her abilities?

"I'm sure Leopold won't mind if you let me in."

The skin around the guard's eyes relaxed and he pressed a button, buzzing her through the locked door.

"Thanks," she said, breezing past him and into the lobby elevator before he could change his mind.

She took the visitors' elevator to the tenth floor, got off and transferred to an elevator bank serving the higher-floor apartments where the Collective's vampires lived. Only vetted mortals were allowed above the visitors' floor. She punched in Leopold's code, pushed the button for the fifty-first floor, and watched the door shut.

He should change his code more often.

The elevator accelerated smoothly, arriving at his apartment, and the doors *whooshed* open. She stepped out onto the white marble floor of his private foyer.

Nothing had changed in six weeks. A Louis XIV cabinet with jasmine flowers inlaid against an ebony background still occupied the long wall leading to Leopold's living room. A tall white vase filled with bright yellow lilies sat in the center of the cabinet. Leopold liked decorating in black and white with an occasional splash of color thrown in.

He would have been shocked to see her there, but he was still asleep in a windowless closet. She pulled back the heavy satin drapes in his living room to look out over the New York skyline. The golds and reds of a gorgeous spring sunset didn't calm her growing ire.

Weeks ago, she'd concluded that Leopold's attempt to swindle Henry was nothing more than an old grudge. At the time, she'd briefly considered whether something larger was afoot, whether Leopold had ties to the VDM and swindling Henry was part of the larger plot plaguing Sierra Escondida's founders, but she had discarded the idea.

For six months while training as Leopold's envoy, she had resided in his guest room and never heard any rumors about enslaving mortals as food animals. The Collective's residents, including Leopold, seemed too content with their lifestyle to be a threat to humanity.

Her sponsor might want to tweak Henry's ego, play a few mind games at Henry's expense, but Leopold had backed her project so they could expand the blood supply without relying on mortals. Which led her back to her original conclusion: Leopold wasn't part of the VDM.

She turned away from the sunset and, using the crystal of her watch, transported two large cardboard boxes to his living room. She took a seat on the white silk-upholstered couch and opened her electronic tablet. She might as well get some work done while she waited for him to rise.

Ten minutes later, a door closed and she looked up. Wearing slacks and a t-shirt, Leopold stepped onto the black hand-woven carpet in his living room and froze. His eyebrows shot to his hairline, his brown hair slicked back with some sort of pomade. A thin, angular mustache outlined his upper lip.

The scrawny vampire crossed his arms and frowned, his look of surprise transforming to one of distrust. "Why Cerissa, my dear girl, I didn't expect to find you here," he said, his Dutch accent clipping his words. "How in the world did you get in?"

She *tsked* at him the way Gaea did to her and strode toward him. "You gave me your elevator's security code before I left for Sierra Escondida, remember?"

His pale white face looked confused for a moment. "Of course, you're right, as always, dear girl." He gave her a quick hug in greeting. "But I wish you had called first. It's a pleasure seeing you, but I do have plans for the evening."

"We have something important to discuss."

Taking her hand in his, he raised it, putting her bracelet on display. "And what is this?"

"You know what it is."

"Lovely. Simply lovely. The moonstone is nicely set off by the amethyst. Not as nice as the rubies our community uses, but lovely all the same. So who is the lucky vampire?"

"You know that, too."

"I believe I do." He motioned toward the kitchen. "Mind if I…."

"Go right ahead."

She followed him into the kitchen and climbed onto a tall stool at the kitchen island, laying her tablet on the cold black granite. The only exception to his black and white motif was the stainless steel range. The glossy cabinets were white, the refrigerator black.

The color scheme threatened to give her a headache.

His back to her, he tested the temperature of a slow cooker filled with water and dropped in a bag of blood. Nothing in his habits had changed. The pot was on a timer and automatically began heating the water each night before sunset.

"May I get you something to drink?" he asked, holding open the door to the wine refrigerator.

She shook her head. She'd rather cut to the chase. "Henry told me about your deal with him: one point two million dollars for my contract. I'm worth that much to you?"

He froze. After a fraction of a second, he closed the refrigerator door. "Cerissa, we both know you're worth far more than that."

"Except I'm not yours to sell."

He retrieved the bag from the water, cut off a corner, and poured the heated fluid into a wine glass. "Why didn't you tell me it was Henry Bautista you wanted?"

"Because it was none of your business."

"Henry and I go way back." He brought his glass over to the kitchen island. "If you had asked me, I would have advised against it."

"So instead, you tried to take advantage of him."

"You know me better than that. He asked to buy out your contract, which told me he hadn't spoken with you." Leopold gestured toward her with the wine glass, saluting her. "I was doing you a favor."

She shook her head. "I didn't know you indulged in self-delusion."

"Hear me out. Henry is a visionary, but he also has his flaws." Leopold paused to take a long drink from the wine glass. "He has a bad track record with women. By naming an outrageous price, I had hoped to force him into talking to you about it."

"He did talk with me."

"Only after he paid me. Beware, Cerissa. Henry was ahead of his time in the 1840s when he opened *Enrique's*. He showed us how we could fully assimilate into mortal society without revealing what we are, but he has made mistakes. Some of those mistakes still haunt him."

"He told me about Anne-Louise."

"There is more to it than that."

"Leopold, you're missing an important point." She tapped the hard granite with a fingernail. How could he be so dense? "If we're to be business partners, I need to trust you. This little game with Henry has undermined my trust."

For the first time since she met him over one hundred years ago, she saw fear in his eyes. He quickly downed the remainder of his glass.

"Why should it affect our relationship?" he asked. "I only sold him the right to take your blood. You're still my envoy."

"Not when you treat me like property. I gave you notice so I could become blood mated. I could just as easily terminate our partnership."

"You would use me that way? To find a mate and then cut me out of the lab?"

"Not at all. You breached our contract. What I don't understand is why, and don't say it was to protect me."

Leopold stared into his now-empty glass. "Why do you have this effect on me?" he asked.

She sighed, dialing back her aura. Using her charm was tricky. She could calm her subject, fill them with a sense of peace, and entice them to help her when they were on the fence about doing so. But she couldn't compel them to tell the truth, and repeatedly using her charm on a long-term acquaintance could backfire and cause her to become enamored of them.

The people we charm, charm us.

One of the reasons she stopped using her charm on Henry—she wanted to know what she had with him was the real deal.

This conversation with Leopold was too important to use her influence to make him *inclined* to speak the truth. He had to come to that decision willingly if she was ever going to trust him again.

"Why did you cheat Henry?" she asked again.

"Henry owed me a debt. A debt he never paid."

Not that again. She shook her head. "Henry owed you nothing. His restaurant—the shareholders voted to sell, majority rule. You made a profit, like all the other investors. Once a deal is done, it's time to move on."

"But I could have made twice the amount."

"Leopold, what is the difference if you're a billionaire or a trillionaire?"

"Nine hundred and ninety-nine billion."

"Which means nothing. I know your net worth."

"How do you—"

"Did you think I'd go into business with you without investigating you thoroughly?" She opened a window on her tablet and spun it around so he could see: his latest balance sheet. "You have enough money to live comfortably for the next three hundred years," she continued. "And my calculation assumes you don't earn one penny more. Look at the time you've wasted resenting the money you *might* have made. Time squandered. Not to mention it's destroying the friendship you once had with Henry."

"It was Henry who—"

"Sometimes enough is enough. Let it go, before you lose our deal, too."

Leopold placed his wine glass on the granite. The light *clink* of the crystal against stone broke the momentary silence. "And if I pay back the money?"

"We can put aside this minor misunderstanding and resume work on our project together."

He let out a long-suffering sigh. "Very well," he said. "Consider it done."

"Before the night is over."

"Of course, my dear. Anything else?"

She went over to his wine refrigerator and poured herself a glass of his best Cabernet. She needed some fortification before this next part. Ignoring the art of winetasting he'd taught her, she took a deep drink.

"There is one other thing," she said, her back to him. "I made a commitment on your behalf."

"What kind of commitment?"

She took another sip of her wine and topped off her glass. "Investors want proof—which we can't give them yet." She turned to face him. "Instead, you're giving your personal guarantee. You'll pay back eighty percent of any loss."

"I'll what?" he shouted.

"You heard me—you owe me after this stunt with Henry. Your guarantee." She saluted him with her wine glass. "Quite frankly, there's no risk on your end. The lab will be a major success once it's built—and you know it."

Before he could object again, she strode to the living room, where the two large boxes waited. He followed. With a sweep of her hand, she said, "For you. The latest samples."

She placed her glass on the coffee table, broke the seal on the top box, and tossed him a polyethylene pouch, the silvery-blue exterior hiding its true contents. "I'm still working out the process for mass-producing our clones, but I believe you'll be happy with these samples. Particularly the ones packaged in red." She tossed a red one to him as well. He picked it out of the air. "I suggest you reserve those for when your lover is around and in the mood."

"My lover? Whatever do you mean by that?" Leopold asked, sniffing the red one. His fangs extended, visible over his lower lip.

"A surprise," she replied with a smirk. "And I have a hunch you'll find it a pleasant one."

Using apheresis, she had collected twice the number of red blood cells than normal blood, and packaged the results in the red bags. She had given some to Henry weeks ago when they first started dating. The effect had been powerful and immediate when he had sampled it, and she'd jokingly called the concentrated blood Viagra for vampires.

Leopold tore the serrated corner off the bag. He sniffed the opening and then took a hesitant sip. His eyes lit up and his tongue traced the residue from his smiling lips. "Agreed. I'll give the investors the guarantee you want—if you send me a box of these reds ones once a week."

"Once a month, and we have a deal."

"Done."

"And be cautious in your use. I don't know what the long-term effects are."

"I'll happily play guinea pig for you."

A short while later, she boarded the elevator, waving goodbye to Leopold and wondering whether he'd drink the rest of the bag alone or wait for his date.

From the same alley, she flashed back to the Enclave to pick up a few things, and then on to Henry's home. Thanks to the time zone difference, she made it to his porch at sunset.

The dark brown entry doors were constructed of ornate inlaid panels, carved as sunbursts. She ran her fingers over one sunburst, tracing the center swirl, the shadows of dusk deepening. Her joy at seeing the sun set over the southwest mountains wiped out the stress of dealing with Leopold. She slid the key into the door handle's shiny brass lock.

My key.

A light, airy feeling of happiness grew in the center of her chest as she pushed the door open. She carried a small bag holding her bathing suit. After she'd left Henry's house in the early morning hours, he had texted her: "Bring a swimsuit tonight."

She also carried a box of clone blood. Leopold had gotten the lion's share as a consolation prize, but she'd saved some, and took the blue pouches to the kitchen, leaving them on the counter, since they didn't need refrigeration.

She hadn't brought any red ones.

From what she'd seen so far, Henry didn't need any encouragement.

CHAPTER 17

Henry heard Cerissa moving about in the kitchen as he shaved. He caught himself humming a tune, stopped, and smiled to himself. He'd risen happy, unusual for him, and rushed through his evening rituals, showering in his basement dressing room. He changed into the clean clothes he'd selected last night, shorts over his swimsuit and a tank top. Before going upstairs, he checked his phone for business email.

Good. Nothing needs my immediate attention.

He opened his personal email and saw an alert from his bank. Leopold had initiated a wire transfer—one point two million dollars was on its way to Henry's Swiss bank account. Cerissa must have persuaded Leopold. Henry felt a momentary rush of pride, and then, just as quickly, a dark thought passed through him.

Why did Leopold listen to her and not me?

He wrinkled his forehead while his conflicting feelings battled for supremacy.

I got what I wanted. Why am I dissatisfied? Because she's done something I couldn't?

He clipped his phone on his belt and climbed the basement stairs, straightening his shoulders, trying to snap himself out of it.

I'm too confident in my manhood to be threatened by Cerissa's success.

It was true, but perhaps having a girlfriend who was a force to be reckoned with would take some getting used to. Then again, he'd told Cerissa last night he wasn't a modern man. For her, he'd try, but he knew how easy it was to backslide into his old-world attitudes.

He strode through the kitchen and traced Cerissa's sweet scent to the drawing room. "Good evening, cariña." He took her hand and pulled her into his arms to kiss her. "Have you eaten yet? If not, I'll make you dinner."

She smiled at him. "An offer from Chef Bautista I can't refuse."

"I had the delivery service stock the kitchen during the day. Let's see what they brought us."

A quick look in the refrigerator, and he decided to make his spicy baked chicken. It wouldn't take long. He started the oven heating, took the ingredients out of the refrigerator, and washed a bell pepper, then gave it to her to slice while he prepared the rice.

"Leopold returned the money," he said, placing a pot of water on the stove.

The *thunk* of her knife hitting the cutting board stopped. "Good. We can put it behind us." She resumed slicing the pepper. "He said he was doing me a favor."

"Leopold was going to give you the money?" If she needed money that badly, he'd have happily given it to her directly.

"No, he wasn't going to give it to me, although he would have funneled the money into our project. We still need capital."

"Then what was the favor?"

"Leopold believed his demand would spur you to talk with me," she said. "To tell me of your plan to take my blood." She kissed his cheek, her hand holding half a pepper. "Anyway, it's over. Forget about it. I have."

Forget about it? Not likely. Leopold hadn't made his demand to spur Henry to talk with Cerissa first. At the time, Leopold had accepted payment, knowing Henry hadn't yet discussed the matter with Cerissa.

"Quit stewing about it."

She was right. He was brooding. "As you wish," he replied.

He laid the boneless chicken in a glass baking dish, seasoned it, and covered it with a can of stewed tomatoes. He scooped up the sliced pepper, layered it over the seasoned chicken and tomatoes, and handed her an onion to dice. When she finished, he spread the pungent squares over the chicken and peppers, added more stewed tomatoes, and placed the baking dish into the oven.

Thirty minutes later, the timer dinged and he removed the baking dish from the oven and spooned the chicken and vegetables over white rice, then served her at the kitchen table. He warmed one of the blood pouches she'd brought and poured it into his favorite metal coffee mug.

"How was your day?" he asked, then took a sip of his blood and sat down across from her.

"I bought a car," she said, her face brightening. She took her first bite of the chicken. "Henry, this is wonderful. You really are an excellent chef."

"Thank you," he said. "And thank you for this." He indicated the coffee cup and took another sip of the warmed blood. "So, tell me. What type of car did you buy?"

She took out her phone and showed him a picture of a four-door economy model. "The trunk is a little small, but it's comfortable and unobtrusive. The dealership helped with the return of the rental car."

"I see." A standard, ordinary car, like so many on the road today. He could have bought her a much more elegant sedan.

She cocked her head, looking puzzled. "You don't sound happy."

He took another deep drink and then smiled at her. "On the contrary, I'm happy you purchased a car—it means you plan on staying." Her green eyes lit up again at that. They looked almost catlike when they did. "What did you do with the rest of your day?"

"When I finished at the dealership, I went back to my lab at the Enclave to check on the clones." She took another bite of the chicken. "And I boxed the most recent harvest before going to see Leopold. Do you like this batch?"

He sipped at the blood and rolled it around in his mouth. "Good. Very good." He closed his eyes to concentrate on the flavor—how to explain it to her? "It's missing something, though."

"Really? It should be genetically identical to human blood," she replied. "Wait—is it a blood factor? The clones are O negative. We started with that blood type because O negative is the universal donor. We plan on marketing to hospitals as well as the treaty communities."

"That isn't it. Blood type doesn't alter the taste. There is no difference between A positive and B negative. I suspect the blandness is caused by what you feed them. The flavor of blood depends upon the diet and health of the donor. Meat eaters taste different from vegetarians."

"Oh. So someone who ate a lot of spicy food—"

"Would taste different, yes."

She looked puzzled for a moment, and then laughed. "No wonder you like to cook for your mate! You're seasoning your food."

He looked away, heat creeping across his face—the blood he'd drunk made it possible for him to blush. "Indeed," he said. "You have figured out my deep, dark secret, but I would not put it so crudely."

"Karen believes you like to cook to nurture your mate."

"There is some truth in that." He took her hand in his. He should be honest with her—the small stuff counted. "But there is some self-interest in it as well."

"So if I had to guess, you like onions and bell peppers."

He smiled. "The snap imparted by peppers and onions reminds me of foods I used to eat as a child."

"Then it's good I like peppers and onions, too," she said, and took another bite of the chicken, which was covered in them.

"Even if it did not flavor your blood, I would enjoy bringing you pleasure by cooking for you."

"As I do for you, when I provide you with blood from my clones." Her eyes lost their focus, like she was considering something. "Next time I'm in my lab, I'll have to see if I can find a way to 'season' your drink for you. The clones are given liquid nutrition, but it's not flavored. I wonder if I can introduce the flavors you like…" She trailed off, as if pondering the problem.

Finished with her meal, Cerissa took her plate to the sink, rinsed it, and put it in the dishwasher. Would it make a difference if she added natural flavor to the liquid nutrition the clones received?

From behind her, he asked, "Do you feel like an evening swim?"

"That sounds lovely." She could think about flavoring clone blood later. "My bag is in the drawing room."

"Let's collect it. You can change in the pool house. I asked Tig to limit the patrols this evening, so we'll have privacy while we swim."

She had noticed his casual attire earlier—unusual for him—but held off commenting on the shorts and tank top, guessing he'd already dressed for swimming. His jet-black hair hung loose, brushed back, flowing past his shoulders.

He accompanied her to the pool house and left her to change on her own, closing the door behind him. A good thing, too. If he had stayed, she had a feeling they would have forgotten about the pool the moment she stripped. She changed into her white bikini with matching cover-up. Karen had, of course, picked it out for her. Then she weaved her hair into one long braid and joined him outside.

He had already turned on the pool lights. Classical Spanish guitar music played over the outdoor sound system. His tank top and shorts were draped on one of the chairs. She took off her cover-up and put it next to his. The early May night air caused light goose bumps to bud on her arms, and she morphed her skin to increase her resistance to the cool breeze.

He stepped up onto the diving board wearing tight black swim briefs trimmed with a vivid blue piping. She hadn't realized it before, but he had what she thought of as a swimmer's body, with his broad, muscular chest and narrow hips. The stretchy swimsuit material left nothing to the imagination.

She couldn't help herself: she kept staring at the bulge outlined by the tight suit.

He executed a perfect reverse one and a half tuck dive, entering the water so smoothly that the surface hardly rippled. She smiled to herself. He was showing off for her.

Rather than turn the evening into a diving competition, she skipped the diving board and jumped in from the edge of the pool.

As she surfaced, the night air stung her face, but the contrast between the warm water and the cooler air felt good. She hadn't noticed a pool heater. Did solar panels on the roof of the pool house do the job?

Wisps of vapor rose from the pool's surface to create a fog-like effect. Through the fog, she looked around and, not seeing him, dove under the water again. She found him sitting on the bottom of the pool, his long black hair floating around his head, the underwater lights making it look like a halo.

Vampires could hold their breath for long periods of time, so he could spend as much time underwater as he wanted to. She swam down to him. He cupped her face, kissing her briefly before they both surfaced.

"Nice dive," she said, treading water. He was already swimming toward the ladder to get out for another one. She backstroked to the shallow end, listening to the music. The gentle pluck of the individual guitar strings created a melody that evoked feelings of tender longing in her. Henry definitely had a knack for setting the scene.

This time, he did a perfect swan dive, but he didn't surface in the deep end. She stood in the shallow water, and in spite of the lights, she had trouble tracking him underwater until he came up behind her and bit her backside.

She jumped. "Henry! That's not fair!"

It wasn't a vampire bite, just a quick nip to show his ability to sneak up on her. He disappeared underwater again. She tried watching for him, so he couldn't do another covert attack. Then it dawned on her. She had a better way to deal with his playful aggression.

She dove under, discarding her bikini and slowly morphing. She swam the circumference of the pool, staying in the dark shadows at the deepest end. By the time she had completed the change, he was standing up in the shallow water searching for her. She swam underwater past him and perched on the broad half-moon entry steps.

The rough cement felt cool against her scales.

"Over here, big boy," she called out, doing her best to sound like Mae West.

Henry turned to see a mermaid in his pool. Not the sort of mermaid found in children's cartoons. No, this one was naked from the waist up, with big, full breasts, dark hair trailing down her shoulders and across her back, and a svelte, scaly fish tail colored bright green with swirls of pink and turquoise.

It wasn't her native Lux body. He'd seen her six-fingered Lux hand and knew her skin was a shimmering blue in her true form. The mermaid's hand had five fingers and was a pale green. The face was reminiscent of Cerissa's face, with one exception. Bright pink and yellow lines circled her eyes like a brilliant sunburst. It put him in mind of a Caribbean princess parrotfish, one he'd seen at a local aquarium.

Did this mean she was more comfortable with the idea of revealing herself to him—even if it wasn't her Lux body? Perhaps their talk last night had reassured her.

She slapped the water with her tail and his eyebrows shot up. It wasn't one tail—it split in the middle to form two tails.

She pushed off, swimming fast. As she passed near him, she flicked one of her tails in the direction of his butt, catching him off guard with the sting of a gentle swat.

An invitation like that he couldn't ignore. He dove under and pursued her around the pool, exhilarated by her game of chase. While those tails definitely gave her an advantage—she swam faster than him—he could stay under without coming up for air.

He started gaining on her.

She circled one more time and then landed on the steps in the shallow end, splashing the water with her tails to keep him at bay.

A little water wouldn't deter him. He braved the spray and grabbed her by one tail, pulling her toward him until he had her floating in his arms.

She was slippery and cool to the touch. When he had a good grip on her, he lifted her out of the water and walked up the pool steps.

"Henry, where are we going?" she asked, a slight edge of panic in her voice.

The unexpected taste of her fear shot a bolt of excitement straight through him. It wasn't his intent to scare her. She was in no danger, as he had a firm grip on her, but the sweet-tart scent of her fear washed over his tongue and he felt the sting of his irises turning solid black.

He carried her around the walkway bordering the pool and stepped up onto the diving board walking its length.

"Two can play at your game," he said, holding her out over the water.

"Henry," she squealed, laughing and kicking her tails.

He gave her a gentle toss into the deep end, and she twisted in midair, diving under in one smooth motion. He followed her in. She could stay underwater for quite some time, but he was determined to show her that *he* was the master of the chase.

The trick for him was to avoid both tails, either of which she could use with expert precision.

He had fun with her whenever he caught up with her—a pinch here, a squeeze there, a little tickling. Then he'd pull back and let her take off again so he could give chase once more.

Truth be told, he missed the hunt, and any game of chase seemed to fill a need that wasn't met by the more domesticated mating rituals they'd shared last night—however pleasurable they were.

After a few more circles through the deep end, she swam up onto the stairs.

"I give up," she called out, laughing and trying to catch her breath.

He swam up beside her and rested on the stairs next to her. Elated, he announced quite seriously, "I do believe I won that round."

"Next time it's water guns at fifty paces and we'll see who wins," she said between breaths.

"So what prize do I win?" He leered at her in a mock-villain way before slipping his arms around her and pulling her to him.

She pushed back at his chest. "You'll have to claim your prize later. I don't think fish blood is on the menu."

He considered that for a moment. As much fun as it might be to land such an exotic fish, the mermaid's blood didn't smell right to him. "Very well. Do you want me to retrieve your swimsuit for you?"

"No, I can get it." She pushed off and dove under.

She found her swimsuit at the bottom of the pool. Surfacing, she wondered if she should put it on there or just walk out naked. He must have caught the sense of her dilemma, because he climbed out of the pool and held up a towel for her. She swam to the shallow end, only realizing then that she was still in mermaid form. Now she'd have to morph in front of him.

He accepts me. I have to trust in that.

She gave in and let her body change to match the map of Cerissa she held in her mind, pushing through the squishy feeling. It felt like sinking into a mud bath face first. Fairly quickly, legs replaced the tails, scales gave way to human skin, and her hair was once again in a long braid. She walked out naked and a shiver ran through her, goose bumps covering her skin. He enveloped her in the towel and kissed her.

"You are lovely as a mermaid," he said, his arms still around her. "Does this mean mermaids exist?"

"They did. They're extinct now. Humans hunted them until they all died out."

He looked less than happy at that news. "I'm sorry," he said. "Having seen you as one, I wish I had met a real mermaid."

She didn't want him unhappy over the demise of mermaids, but something about his reaction reassured her. He seemed to accept her ability to morph. She wrapped her arms around him and hugged him tightly.

He nuzzled her ear, taking a nip at her lobe. "Perhaps I should claim my prize now."

"You're serious?"

"Yes, I won."

She stepped back and saw his eyes were solid black. A pleasant tingle shot through her. "You're so cute when your eyes get like that."

"Cute? Cute?" He gripped her arms, pulling her closer. "No one who has seen this look would dare call me cute."

His fangs were out.

Uh-oh. She hadn't used the stabilizer yet.

"Hold that thought," she said. "I'll be right back."

She made a mad dash into the guest house and found her purse. Moments later, she returned. The outdoor heaters had been lit, the air around the deck warming. He was laying dry towels on one of the pool chairs.

Did he plan on making love outdoors? The idea thrilled her.

He turned to look at her, his eyes turning black again. "Are you ready to tender your unconditional surrender now?"

"Well…" she began, backing up, one heel raised, like she might run.

He closed the distance in a flash and grasped the towel wrapped around her. His solid black irises bored into her.

"I asked you a question," he said, a lusty smile curving his lips, a playful threat in his voice. "And your answer?"

She smiled coyly. "Why, yes, I believe I am."

The moment the words left her mouth, he tugged the towel off her and sank his fangs into her neck. He was so quick that she hardly felt the bite, but the heat flowing through her heart—now, that she felt all the way to her toes.

CHAPTER 18

Beethoven's Fifth played from the phone in Tig's pocket—Jayden's ringtone. She left Liza sitting in the police department's conference room and stepped into the hall.

"Where are you?" she answered. He hadn't been at the house or the office when she rose for the night.

"San Diego. When I called the detective this morning, he invited me down for the day."

"Good job. I'm glad you jumped on that."

"So am I, because you were right. The detective here is now convinced. The most recent killing was the work of the Carlyle Cutter."

"I'm surprised it took them this long," she said, leaning against the hallway wall.

"They didn't want to alarm the public, but they released it to the media today—they couldn't avoid it any longer."

"Were you able to confirm Zeke's story with his alibi witnesses before you left the Hill?"

"Gaea called me right before sunrise. She had played poker with Zeke at Jose's Cantina for the timeframe of at least one killing. He can't be the Cutter."

That's a relief. Zeke had a taste for adrenaline-spiked blood, but so far, he'd relied on his own kills—the kills he made for the government—to feed his habit.

Tig had given Zeke a stern warning last week when she asked him for a list of people who could alibi him for the nights the Cutter struck. "You better not be buying the stuff locally," she had told the cowboy. "The council will stake you if you're buying adrenaline-spiked blood from the Cutter."

Zeke had turned whiter than he normally was. "No, ma'am. I don't buy it. Never have; never will. Can't trust those chiselers who sell it."

"Tig," Jayden said, his voice slicing through her reflections. "You still there?"

"Yeah, I'm here. I have to meet with Méi tonight. She wants a status report on the burglary investigation and I have nothing for her. Liza and I were just discussing it. When will you return home?"

"Tomorrow night. I got a call from the prison records clerk. I'm going to stop by the prison to see him before I drive back."

"Sounds good," she said. "And Jayden? Thanks for all your hard work. I couldn't do it without you."

They said goodbye, and Tig walked back to the conference room. She filled in Liza on what Jayden had told her. The conference room phone lit up, a New York area code on the display. Tig raised an eyebrow at Liza and punched the button to accept the call.

"Hi, Tig, it's Rick Fiorello, from New York."

"I'm going to put you on speaker." Tig tapped the button and slid the phone between her and Liza. "I'm here with Liza Ehrgott, one of my reserve officers. She's also on the town council. Do you have news?"

"You can scratch Kyle off your list," he said.

"How can you be so sure?"

"He hasn't left New York for over six months. I went over the Collective's security records after you called. Kyle has returned each morning to sleep in the building. The Collective's logs are very thorough."

"No chance they could be faked?"

"None. We have entry-door surveillance video for the past month. I spot-checked it."

If only the Hill kept such accurate records. Tig's request for security cameras wasn't going to happen anytime soon. "Kyle could still be behind the attempts on Yacov and Henry," she suggested.

"I doubt it," Rick replied. "I asked around. Kyle has found a new lover. She works the Alley and, as he puts it, 'she's everything he's ever dreamed of.' I've seen them together. He's her puppy dog, and I don't mean that figuratively."

"The Alley?"

"An area in the city known for its dungeons. She has a regular clientele of submissives, but she's now dedicating herself to Kyle at night. He's absolutely enamored—all he does is talk about her."

"Thanks, Rick. It was worth a shot."

"Anytime. Anne-Louise is anxious, which is unusual for her. I'll be happier when this is resolved."

"Agreed. What about Blanche?"

"No record of her arriving or leaving the Collective's building in the past year."

"Thanks. Please call if you learn anything new."

Rick said goodnight and Tig disconnected the call. She pressed her lips together in disappointment. They were running out of viable leads.

Liza leaned back in her chair. "Well, I guess we can rule out Kyle."

"I don't know whether to be relieved or not. The other names on the list are turning into dead ends too. Of the list of residents who requested permission to turn a mate, one resident is dead. I spoke with two of the others, and neither of them sounded like they carry a grudge. I've even interviewed Frédéric."

"Frédéric? Now there's an asshole," Liza said, a look of disgust on her face. "Fucking Eurotrash, just like the mayor and Rolf."

Tig tended to agree. The council was a little too European for her liking. The mayor, Rolf, and Frédéric had all been turned within the past two hundred years, and immigrated to America from Europe. Carolyn was now the only person of color on the council. She'd been a slave and dying had been the only way to escape. Liza was a poor white girl from Minnesota, and in the 1940s—twenty years after she was turned—she invested heavily in plastics and made a fortune.

Everyone knew the boys tended to hang together.

"What about the vampires ordered staked by Henry and Yacov?" Liza asked.

"Two died without progeny. I'm still trying to find their makers. The other three—well, I phoned both their children and their makers. None of them sounded like they gave a shit, and none of them had a connection to San Diego."

"What about applications turned down for residency?"

"I have the names, but I've been trying to figure out an excuse to call them. It's one thing to look into old closed crimes, see if there is a connection to the assassinations. But past applicants? They aren't under my jurisdiction. We don't have any evidence pointing at them, nothing that ties them to Blanche, no basis to demand they cooperate with an interview."

"I see your point."

"And Oscar is the leader of his community. I have to tread very carefully with him."

"Has Marcus helped?"

"I plan on talking with him soon."

Tig had even asked the council to put out a fake bulletin to announce a new opening on the Hill. It would have given her an excuse to call all the old applicants, see if they were interested in applying again. If the applicant said yes, she'd have an excuse to ask them the kind of pointed questions she wanted to ask, and it wouldn't raise suspicions. It would just look like she was updating their background check.

She couldn't make them suspicious or they might clam up and refuse to talk.

But the council turned down her idea.

"I do appreciate your vote supporting the ruse," Tig said. "And Carolyn's."

Liza flicked a lock of her short brunette hair behind her ear. "Yeah, but without *the boys*, it got us nowhere. We're back at square one."

"Not quite. I received a cryptic email from Petar and called him back. He wants to meet in person, tomorrow night. He wouldn't talk over the phone." Tig handed Liza the iPad, showing her the email. "I want you to go with me."

"Where to?"

"Newport Beach. We'll take the mayor's jet. Petar wants to meet at a private club."

Liza looked skeptical. "But he's still a suspect, isn't he?"

"He's not a prime candidate, but it doesn't hurt to meet him in person, to get a feel for him. We'll see what he's turned up."

CHAPTER 19

Jayden stopped by the motel's front desk to check out. The place was so cheap that it didn't have an in-room remote system like the fancier hotels did, but it was conveniently located twenty minutes from the prison.

In spite of the motel's worn-out look, the room hadn't been half bad, and it was walking distance from a local pancake house. After a tasty breakfast, he arrived at the prison in a good mood. Blueberry waffles were better than all the antidepressants in the world. Not that he was depressed—he loved his life with Tig.

The administration office for the prison was located outside its gray walls, so there was no security to hassle him, another bonus. He strolled into the office, a smile of confidence on his face. He had this unshakeable feeling—whatever the clerk had discovered would be the break they needed.

His good mood did not last long.

"Ah-choo." The clerk at the counter sneezed and blew his nose loudly. "Damn virus."

"Sounds like you've got a bad one. I won't take much of your time."

The clerk propelled the wadded tissue toward the trash can, which hit the rounded white pile and toppled out. He grabbed another tissue from the box.

"I took this daytime cold medicine, but it isn't doing shit." The clerk indicated a bottle of yellow liquid on his desk. "I may give up and go home."

He sneezed, blowing a hole through the new tissue.

"Look," Jayden said, "I don't want to keep you here any longer than necessary, so let's get to it. Did you find the three missing exit forms?"

126

"Oh, those." Sneezy tapped at the keyboard on the counter near the computer monitor. A violent sneeze overtook him, but he managed to turn his head away from Jayden. "Sorry." He swiveled the computer monitor so Jayden could see it—an internal email. "Our computer geek said someone tampered with the computer system. They got through our firewall, found the exit reports, and deleted them."

"How could he tell?"

"She. Suzy says the computer's indexing table shows the records were scanned in, even though the image files were erased."

"Was Suzy able to tell who did it?"

"Not yet. It was hacked from the outside. She found the hacks—three unauthorized entries into the system."

"Was she able to recover what was erased?"

"Nah. The hacker was good. Killed the report images and emptied the trash. Shouldn't have been able to. Takes administrator-level privilege to permanently delete files held in the trash folder. System was designed to prevent that sort of thing."

"So we're at a dead end?"

"Nope." Sneezy reached for something on his overly cluttered desk and picked a file folder right out of an unorganized stack. "The paper doesn't get shredded until we confirm the images are scanned in correctly. It took me a while, but I found the originals in the bins of paper scheduled for pick-up by the shredding company."

"That's great news." Jayden accepted the file and looked at the reports, not believing what he read. Norman, the murdered guard, had been the one to escort each perp out.

Shit. Could Norman have identified the other members of Blanche's cabal? With him dead, they'd never know.

At the end of each report was a section denoting who picked up the parolee on his release date. Jayden laid the reports side by side to compare them—all identical. A check mark was ticked next to "religious organization" and the blank line filled in with "New Path Church."

Jayden glanced up at the sound of a loud sneeze. "Sorry," Sneezy said, wiping his nose with a tissue. "You want copies of those forms?"

"Yes, please."

Sneezy used some hand sanitizer before running the reports through a scanner. He removed the paper from the printer and laid it on the countertop.

"Thanks," Jayden said. "Here's my card. Call me if you learn anything else."

"Can't say I hold out much hope, but I'll try."

"Call me, even if it's to say you're at a dead end. And thanks for your help."

"Hey, no problem, man." Sneezy inhaled sharply and let out another violent "achoo." Wiping his nose again, he said, "I sure hope you don't get what I've got."

Jayden picked up the printouts. "Don't worry about me. I never get sick. I take a regular immune booster."

"You'll have to send me some."

"Sure." Jayden laughed. He'd never send the poor clerk his secret elixir. An occasional taste of Tig's blood kept him virus-free. "For now, try chicken soup."

"I drank so much chicken soup yesterday, I cluck when I piss."

Driving back to downtown San Diego, Jayden pondered the reports. Why had Blanche become involved with a religious organization? Could New Path be involved in killing Yacov and Henry, or was the organization simply a charity group involved in transitioning parolees to the outside and had nothing to do with the attacks? It seemed like every lead just created more questions.

NEWPORT BEACH—THAT NIGHT

Tig gave the name she'd been told to give: "Susan Anderson, party of two."

The hostess at the Newport Beach club ran her finger down the names on the reservation list and stopped when she came to it. "Welcome to the Magic Mansion," the hostess said. "Here are your maps. Please stand over there and tell the wizard your fondest wish."

Tig stepped over to the animated character on a video monitor.

"I wish to enter," she said. Not her *fondest* wish. Her fondest wish was to find Blanche's co-conspirators, but she'd settle for getting in to see Petar right now.

The animated wizard waved his wand. A trail of twinkling stars pointed to a wall, which slid back to reveal an elevator. When they arrived at the next floor, Tig and Liza followed the map.

They soon found the room where Petar displayed his talent. He worked at a half-round table with a plain green felt top—the type used for dealing blackjack. He wore a sharp black tuxedo with the House of Dracul crest pinned to his pocket.

Pretentious sot.

Tig guided Liza to a nearby bar, suggesting they wait there for Petar to finish, and waved off the bartender. Years ago, one of her private clients had hired her to figure out how a dealer was stealing from the client's casino. In the process, she'd studied sleight-of-hand card tricks so she could spot them. Petar's spiel was pretty standard.

"Now put the card back in the stack," Petar told one of the spectators, who sat at the round side of the felt-covered table. Tig could see the card—the eight of hearts. "And don't forget your card."

The young woman whispered to her friend, giggled, and looked back at Petar.

After his song and dance—throughout which Petar flirted with the young woman—he fanned the deck to demonstrate her card had disappeared and pointed to a sealed envelope lying on the table, untouched throughout the trick. At his coaxing, the pretty spectator opened the envelope, which held the eight of hearts.

A typical card force.

When Petar finished the trick, Tig slid off the barstool and stood behind the spectators. Petar raised his eyebrows before returning his gaze to the audience seated around him.

"I play private parties," he said, handing the pretty spectator his business card. "Call me. For any reason. Or none."

He stood with a bow and motioned to Tig. She and Liza followed him past a door marked "For magicians only" and into a cramped dressing room.

"We can talk in here," Petar said, closing the door behind him.

Tig looked around. A mirror outlined by bright lights filled one wall, a makeup table jutting out from it. Lockers and a couple of chairs took up the remaining space. Tig sat on one of the chairs while Liza leaned against the makeup table.

"I was surprised you wanted to meet at this club," Tig said.

"Few know of my hobby." He eased onto the other chair and adjusted his tux coat so it hung gracefully. "Better we meet here than at my office. I don't want anyone aware I'm talking with you."

Okay, that made sense. "Well, it's a long way to come. I hope you have something good."

Liza planted her hands on her hips. "Yeah, John Wayne Airport has turned into a real bitch. We had to keep circling while the tower brought in commercial flight after commercial flight."

Petar nodded with a leer. "The area's crowded, but it makes for good hunting."

Liza's face lit up. "This area isn't covered by the treaty?"

"Only part—the beach area from Huntington Beach to Long Beach is claimed. But central OC is wide open for live feeding." He gave her a fangy smile.

Liza looked at Tig. "Maybe we could…."

"Maybe we couldn't," Tig shot back, growing impatient. What had gotten into Liza? It was time to focus on their real reason for being in Orange County. "What do you have to tell us?"

His eyes had a condescending look of secret knowledge. "Well, now, Miss Police Chief, it's like this. Something's going on in Southern California. One of my clients told me there's tension between the unaffiliated nests and the treaty communities."

"Anything to do with San Diego? Blanche was heading there next."

"Nothing specific. I also heard there's a power struggle on your little Hill."

"Did you get any names?"

"Your vice mayor and his cohort were mentioned."

"Rolf Müller and Frédéric Bonhomme?"

Petar nodded. "Rolf and Frédéric—those were the names I got. Word on the street is Rolf wants to replace Winston as mayor, and Frédéric is kissing Rolf's butt so much an image of his lips should be tattooed there."

Anyone on the Hill could tell you that.

"Did they say how Rolf planned to accomplish his goal?" Tig asked.

"Nothing about the shootings, if that's what you mean, but I've also heard something even I find disturbing, and nothing much disturbs me these days."

"Go on."

"Some underground group wants us in charge."

"Us?"

"Our kind."

"In charge of what?"

"The world."

Tig's eyebrows shot up. Was Blanche's comment about war connected to Petar's rumor?

"And just how do they plan on taking over? We can't go out in daylight. Kind of makes it difficult to rule over mortals."

He fanned his fingers—a gesture implying the reason was self-evident. "My source found the whole thing quite comical. Decimate the mortal population, keep the rest for food."

Shit. That didn't sound good.

"Is Rolf involved?" Tig asked.

"Didn't come up."

"Did you press *your source* for more information?"

"Look, chief. We need to get something straight right now. People will tell their bookie things they won't tell their priest, but I have to be careful. I can't be too interested or they stop talking. So if you want whatever information I can get, we have to take this slow and easy."

"You had us fly here for that? You couldn't tell us by phone that an underground group of vampires plans on taking over the world?"

"You never know when the phones are infested."

"Bugged," she spat, not hiding her irritation.

"Yes, that. And I thought we should get the terms of our arrangement straight first. I provide you with information and you provide me with...."

"Money."

"Precisely. Now, how much money do you want to place on the South African soccer team? Worst players I've seen in years. I do need to make a living, you know."

CHAPTER 20

SIERRA ESCONDIDA—SAME NIGHT

Cerissa punched the disconnect button on her car's steering wheel, ending the call with Henry, and signaled her left turn into the Hill Chapel's driveway. Tonight, Henry's winery had a special tasting event scheduled for local restaurant owners. The winery was making a concerted effort to convince more local restaurants to feature their wines.

Karen, as public relations and marketing director, would be there to host. Normally, Rolf would have been the owner present to co-host, but with him out of town, the duty fell to Henry.

Last night, after Henry had claimed his victory prize, he told Cerissa she was welcome to attend the event, but he wouldn't have much free time for her. His guests expected him to spend most of the evening glad-handing through the crowd.

Since Gaea had invited Cerissa to an event at the Hill Chapel, she had suggested to Henry they get together after midnight.

He sounded quite pleased by her suggestion.

How would they top the past two nights? Making love on the chaise lounge under the stars had certainly been exciting. Something about him exuded an edge of danger. She'd loved the way he had taken what he wanted, but at the same time, made sure she was satisfied—very satisfied. He seemed to learn more about her body each time they made love.

Her fingertips touched the smooth skin of her neck where he'd bitten. She'd relented from her decision to let his bite heal naturally. Instead, she healed it the next day so he'd have a clean canvas on which to place the next one.

She parked in front of the chapel and shook off her fantasies. She'd never attract investors reeking of arousal—or perhaps she would, but they'd be the wrong kind of investors.

The chapel's beauty helped center her. Constructed from gray river-rock, the one-story building looked peaceful and inviting, right at home in its rural setting. A covered walkway, grape vines entwined around the wooden lattice, adjoined one side of the chapel, and she followed the walkway to the meeting rooms in the back.

Gaea had suggested Cerissa arrive early so she could meet Father Matthew Blaine, who ran the meeting. Before leaving Gaea's house, she had checked his dossier so she'd recognize him. He was both an Episcopal priest and a trained psychologist. If only she had dossiers on all treaty vampires in North America. It would make her job much easier. So far, she just had background reports for Hill residents.

The door stood open. About thirty chairs were arranged in a horseshoe pattern. A single chair was at the horseshoe's opening near a big dry-erase board. Father Matt stood at the board writing: "What is the nature of God?"

She had a sinking feeling. Gaea had coaxed her to attend, stressing what a good opportunity it was to meet potential investors. Cerissa hadn't realized it was a religious meeting. But then, what did she expect if it was held at the Hill Chapel?

Hmm. Maybe this wasn't such a good idea after all.

She would have to be careful—becoming involved in a religious debate could alienate potential investors.

The priest turned around. "You must be Dr. Patel."

He offered his hand to shake, and she took it. "I am, but call me Cerissa. And you must be Father Blaine?"

"Matt is fine."

"All right, Matt. I guess I'm a little early."

"I told Gaea I wanted to talk with you. Do you mind stepping next door?"

He escorted her to a cozy kitchen where coffee was brewing, and suggested they sit at the small, utilitarian table to talk. Brushing her dress underneath her, she took the chair across from him. His brown hair hung straight, stopping at his strong jaw line, and he wore a closely trimmed beard. Gold wireframe glasses outlined his eyes.

Wait—glasses on a vampire? Then it struck her—Matt looked like a young John Lennon, but thinner.

Matt crossed his legs and laced his fingers over his knee. "You've been provided with a copy of the Covenant?"

"When I first arrived."

"The Covenant governs our way of life here. You'll want to read it again to ensure you're aware of the rules. There are certain protections built in, safeguards to protect the mortals who live here."

"I understand." To prove her point, she met his gaze. He wasn't permitted to mesmerize her—not that it would have worked on her anyway.

The corner of his lip twitched, his eyes shining with humor. The meaning of her actions wasn't lost on him.

"We don't tolerate any abuse or mistreatment," he continued, resuming his professional persona. "Using vampire powers to compel, ah…to compel a mate to submit to being bitten is akin to domestic violence, and prohibited."

Cerissa cocked her head, considering this information. So what Anne-Louise did, calling Henry to her, demanding his blood, would be illegal if Henry was mortal?

"Should a problem develop," Matt continued, "you may come to me or

133

Gaea rather than filing charges with the chief of police. Your choice, of course. The council has appointed us as, well, intercessors. You can speak to either of us in confidence and we won't report it to Tig unless you want us to."

She crossed her arms. "I'm glad the community has safeguards built in, but you needn't worry about me. Henry would never mistreat me."

"Of course, but we need to have safeguards in place, regardless. We all fight demons, being what we are."

"Demons?" she asked, furrowing her brow. Vampires weren't demons.

"To put it in more modern terms, vampires are much like addicts. They crave the blood of a victim—it becomes all they think about until obsession overcomes reason. We want to protect our mortal community from any kind of *addict* behavior."

"But vampires have to drink blood to survive."

"I'm talking about hunting behavior. Feeding is different from hunting."

"I don't see the difference."

"Feeding can be done without harming the donor. Hunting is about engendering fear in the donor. Those who hunt are addicted to the taste of a victim who is afraid of them."

"You believe it's an addiction?" she asked. During her envoy training, no one had ever put it this way.

Matt gave a knowing smile, framed by his neatly trimmed beard. "Vampires can survive on banked blood and the occasional intake of animal blood, but most of my clients struggle with the temptation to hunt—they want to feel the exhilaration and power coming with it, to reaffirm they aren't truly dead."

"But live feeding is allowed by some communities. I heard others in New York talk about hunting for a one-night stand, so long as the victim isn't injured."

"That isn't the kind of hunting I'm talking about. Some communities still allow live feeding, within reason and safety, of course. We don't allow it locally unless the mortal and vampire live here and are mated. We prefer to vet consent, safety, and risk before allowing it."

"But I don't see how hunting can be considered an addiction," she said, her voice carrying her skepticism. "It's so integral to the vampire personality."

"Drinking blood is integral—needing the 'high' of adrenaline-spiked blood and the fear-inducing hunt from which it comes is an addiction," he replied.

Is this what Henry meant? How my blood would taste different if I was truly afraid of him. Still, she'd seen no sign Henry was addicted to such blood. It was a passing comment, nothing more.

Matt uncrossed his legs and leaned forward, his fingers still interlaced. "And sometimes mortals come here for the wrong reason."

"Which is?" She looked away, concerned. Matt was Henry's confessor. Certainly he hadn't told Matt about her mission for the Lux.

"Just like addicts, vampires can seem very seductive, particularly to those mortals who see the vampire's inner pain and believe they are the ones to stop it. It doesn't work. A mortal can't rescue them from what they are."

"I'm here to build a research lab, not rescue anyone. I mean, there's nothing wrong with being a vampire."

"That's a healthy attitude to have." Matt paused. "But just remember, if anything comes up, I'm always here to help."

Why was this making her edgy? He seemed convinced she would need his council at some point. She trusted Henry not to hurt her, and she had no desire to rescue him, except from the likes of Blanche. Maybe she was reading too much into the conversation. Matt must give this orientation to all new mortals, to emphasize his role as an intercessor on the Hill.

"Do you realize you speak in the third person when you talk about vampires?" she asked, trying to turn the conversation in a new direction.

"When I'm conversing with a mortal, I tend to." He touched his beard and quickly returned his hand to his lap. He seemed self-conscious about the habit.

"I must admit, I was surprised when I learned about you and the chapel."

"Contrary to popular myth, vampires are not minions of the devil. Or if we are, I've not received any direction from the dark lord." He chuckled lightly.

"I never thought so," she said, smiling back. "But I'm glad you have a sense of humor about it."

"In this job, I need to. Some people have a rough time with the transition to vampire. Particularly those who were turned without their consent—they may feel ashamed of what they've become. Having a spiritual foundation can help them find an ethical way to live. Given what we are, it can be challenging at times."

She suspected as much from hearing Henry's story about Anne-Louise. "Did you get your training before or after you were turned?"

"Before. I was convinced liberation theology was going to change the world—it's about seeing theology through the eyes of the poor, about changing power structures so everyone has food, shelter, and medical care."

"And yet here you are, ministering to the rich."

He laughed—a warm sound. "Death can be ironic." He glanced up at the wall clock and she did too. Nine o'clock. He stood up. "Thanks for meeting with me. We should probably get back in there. It's time to start."

She stayed behind to pour a cup of coffee, adding a healthy dose of sweetened vanilla creamer.

That went fairly well.

Matt's openness meant the community accepted her as Henry's mate and trusted her with their secrets. She walked back to the meeting room. Hill residents and their mates, most of whom she'd never met, filled the room.

Matt turned toward the group. "Let's begin." He waited a beat while those still standing found chairs. "Based on where we left off last time, the question for tonight is this: If we presume God exists, what is the nature of God?"

"Well, my dears," Gaea said, "we cannot discuss the nature of God without first conceding the name used implies certain characteristics. The term 'God' presumes a masculine being. But in my CO, the goddess was primary."

Cerissa leaned over to the young woman next to her, who wore a name tag with "Haley" written on it. "CO?" Cerissa whispered.

"Culture of origin," Haley whispered back, and raised her hand to speak. Matt called on her. "Even Genesis 1:27 concedes humans—male and female—were created in the image of God, so God must be both male and female."

"Wait a minute," Mitch said. "Jesus was male. That has to mean something."

Mitch had all the characteristics of a permanent resident, right down to the pale skin and the deep ridges in his fingernails.

Father Matt stood and wrote "gender" on the board. "Does the divine have gender, and if so, which one, or both?"

Gaea waved a finger. "Wait one moment, Matt. Don't you mean 'sex,' not 'gender'? After all, gender roles are a social construct. For example, in the sixteen hundreds, only men wore high heels."

"Really?" Haley interrupted.

"For horseback riding, dear. They even dyed them red, a color signifying wealth—long before what's-his-name designed those red-soled shoes you like to wear." Gaea gestured toward Haley's high heels. Haley blushed and uncrossed her legs, tucking her feet under her chair. Gaea continued, "But by the last century, society determined that only women should wear high heels based on their gender. That's why sex is the word used when referring to, um, different parts."

Matt nodded with a smile and added "sex" to the board. "Of course, Gaea, good point. In a way, you're asking whether God or Goddess has reproductive anatomy similar to humans."

Really? Interesting.

The Lux had only one sex, closer to human females than males. Was it because her people were unisexed? Or were those who arrived here four thousand years ago all the same sex?

Most likely the latter, since they were unable to breed among themselves, even in human form. A unisexed species would have to carry both sperm and egg, or they would quickly die out. But the Lux didn't carry both in their native form, which was why they had to mate with mortals.

When Yacov spoke, Cerissa's focus returned to the discussion. She hadn't met Henry's friend yet, although she recognized him from the hearing.

"A principle of my belief is that the creator does not have physicality." Yacov tugged at his long beard. "Even the Torah, in using 'he' or 'him' is speaking in human language, which itself is limiting. It uses human terms for the creator because that is all we can comprehend. From my perspective, the creator has no sex or gender."

"And my point is," Gaea replied, one finger poised in the air, "the very term we use to name our experience of a deity includes with it certain preconceptions. If we always hear a male pronoun, we will presume men are closer to being the image of the divine than women."

"To view the creator as either male or female would be to create an image of the creator, which is forbidden for my people," Yacov said.

"I agree with Yacov, even though I'm Christian," Haley said. "Just because Jesus was male doesn't mean God is male."

Mitch crossed his arms. "Yeah? Why wasn't the messiah female?"

"God's a pragmatist. Back then, women were second-class citizens."

"They still are, honey," Aeesha quipped, and everyone but Mitch broke out in laughter. Based on the size of the diamond on Aeesha's well-manicured hand, which rested on Mitch's knee, she was his wife as well as his mate. A lovely moonstone pendant hung at her neck.

When the laughter died off, Mitch asked, "But what about the 'Our Father' prayer?"

Matt took over. "Haley is correct—it must be viewed in its cultural context. Hebrew kings were called God's son. In that context, it wasn't radical to refer to God as Father. They believed Jesus was the next Davidic king. Besides, the Aramaic word was *abba*—which meant papa or daddy, as well as the more formal father. He was teaching them about the relationship—he wasn't saying God was male."

Cerissa resisted the sudden urge to raise her hand to share her viewpoint. Her father had been Hindu. As a child, she had learned about both gods and goddesses. But her feelings about human religions had always been mixed.

The amount of violence and oppression committed in the name of religion—particularly violence against women—had turned her off at a young age. During the European witch hunts, Lux members in female form had been burned at the stake, unwilling to reveal their true natures by morphing to escape. And the way women of her childhood village were thrown on the funeral pyres of their husbands…

She shuddered at the memory. Not that she'd ever mention it in a group like this.

Frédéric politely raised a finger to signal his desire to speak. The council member looked stuck in the past, with his long, Salvador Dali-esque mustache pointed at the ends.

"Another attribute to consider is power," Frédéric said when called upon. "Just look at the ancient Greek religion. They didn't view their gods and goddesses as all-powerful. Even Zeus had to bend his will to fate."

"So you'd add to the list 'power'?" Matt asked, writing it on the board. "And that 'God' is *not* omnipotent."

"More than that. Their deities had many human foibles. The only difference between Greek gods and mortals was Zeus and his contemporaries had greater power. Like us."

Cerissa frowned. The chair next to her rattled—Haley had crossed her arms and legs again. Guess she wasn't a fan of Frédéric's, either.

Gaea's mouth gaped open. "Now, Frédéric, you're not suggesting we're gods…."

Frédéric laughed warmly. "Not at all, Gaea, not at all. Although we're more powerful than mortals, it doesn't make us gods. I'm simply making the point that not all cultures associated omnipotence with their gods."

"So back on topic," Matt said, looking uncomfortable. "Power is a factor we must consider when discussing the nature of God."

Cerissa looked closely at Frédéric. Although he'd been polite while correcting Gaea's assumption, his example gave a glimpse into how he viewed mortals. But he wasn't exactly alone in thinking himself superior to mortals—other vampires shared his old-fashioned ideas. Would he go so far as to support the VDM? Cerissa would send a message to Ari later— look into Frédéric, just in case.

After an hour had passed, Father Matt adjourned the group. Haley stood and offered to introduce Cerissa to the others.

"But before I do," Haley said, reaching into her purse and pulling out a glossy folder, "I have a feeling you might be interested in this."

Cerissa turned it over to read the front. *Committee for Guest Resident Rights* was boldly printed at the top, a colorful photo of a vineyard as the background. *Guest resident* was the accepted euphemism for mortals who lived on the Hill.

She quickly stuffed it in her purse and glanced around.

Did anyone see me accept it?

She agreed with the committee in principle. When she started dating Henry, she'd told him things had to change on the Hill if she was going to live here long-term. But she wasn't ready to get in the middle of a political controversy. Just like arguing about religion, politics could alienate potential investors.

"Ah, thanks," Cerissa said. "I'll read it later."

"If you have any questions, call me."

"I do have one. Even if things change and you get to vote for who's on the town council, I mean, what's to keep your vampire—"

"Vishon."

"What's to keep Vishon from controlling how you vote?"

Haley gave her a *what planet did you come from* look. "Has Henry been feeding you that nonsense?"

"He didn't, I mean—"

"Vampires can't mesmerize us into doing their bidding with a few limited exceptions, and how we vote isn't one of them."

"You're positive?" Even with fang serum, Cerissa couldn't be mesmerized. She had no way to verify it. And although the Covenant forbade using vampire powers to control mortal mates, she suspected not everyone on the Hill obeyed that law behind closed doors. Otherwise, why would Matt have been so insistent on meeting her in person?

Haley scrunched her eyebrows together. "Let's say they try to use one of their *limited* powers. They can't control the consequences. Sure, after they've had our blood, they can call us, you know, make us return to them. Well, Vishon tried that once. I told him he ever tried that again, he wasn't tapping any of this," she said, pointing at her neck. "Don't worry about what will happen when we get the vote."

"If you say so."

Haley gestured for Cerissa to follow. "Let's grab some coffee. I'll introduce you to Aeesha—you'll like her. She's a hoot, you'll see. Mitch can't control anything thing she does," Haley added with a wink.

Someone had moved the coffee pot into the meeting room. Aeesha and a few other mortals were chatting in front of the refreshment table. Vampires were huddled on the other side of the room.

It's like the circle broke in half.

Haley introduced Cerissa around the group, and they picked up their conversation as if her arrival hadn't interrupted them.

Cerissa stood there listening, trying to figure out how to politely ask if they were interested in investing, when Gaea swept up like a whirlwind. "Cerissa, my dear—if you'll pardon us, Haley, I want to introduce Cerissa to someone."

"No problem, Gaea," Haley replied. "I was about to scoot out of here. Give me a call, Cerissa. We can get together for lunch sometime."

"Sure."

Gaea grabbed Cerissa's arm and propelled her across the small meeting room.

Okay, I wanted to meet everyone, but this wasn't the way—

"Yacov, oh Yacov," Gaea said. "I don't think you've actually met Henry's new mate, have you?"

Cerissa came to an abrupt stop in front of him.

"Dr. Patel," he said, offering his hand to shake. "I'm Yacov Eliahu."

Cerissa accepted his hand. "It's a pleasure to meet you, but call me Cerissa, please. I was impressed by what you had to say."

"Thank you, Cerissa, but I must tell you," he said, placing his hand over his heart, "I'm nobody important, so you may not want to waste your time here on an old man like me."

"Now, Yacov," Gaea said, "don't mislead Henry's mate." She gave Cerissa's arm a friendly squeeze. "Cerissa, Yacov is someone you should know. He may be interested in your research lab. I'll leave you here to talk with him. Or do you need a ride home?"

"I have my car here—I'm going over to Henry's after I leave," Cerissa replied.

"Don't stay out too late," Gaea said, clucking at her as she sauntered off.

Ugh. Gaea's mother-hen tendencies were starting to wear thin. Or was it a subtle way to tell Yacov that Cerissa and Henry weren't living together yet?

"Our Henry is a lucky boy," Yacov said. "I've heard much about you since you arrived. Having an envoy on the Hill has the community all atwitter."

She smiled weakly. "After the hearing was over, I hoped I was yesterday's news."

He laughed. "Indeed, you have provided much-needed gossip for our small community. I, for one, think you being here is a good thing. Our community has proven vampires can live peacefully with mortals. Just ask my wife of fifteen years."

"I would love to meet her. Is she here tonight?"

"No," he replied, shaking his curly-haired head. "The group discussions are my passion, not hers—a good thing, too. All couples need their own interests."

"And theology is one of yours?"

"Indeed. She is a religious woman, but doesn't enjoy the level of debate I do."

"How did you meet your wife?"

"When I go to Los Angeles on business, I visit the local temples. I met her at one of the singles mixers. Beautiful and smart. I have no idea what she sees in me, but then, who am I to question the wisdom of the creator in bringing her to me?"

"She sounds like a woman of good taste."

He smiled, and his honey-brown eyes shone brightly. "I like to believe so."

With Gaea now gone and no one in earshot, Cerissa leaned toward him, lightly placing her hand on his arm. "Thank you for everything you did for Henry," she said. "And for me."

"It was nothing. Really."

"Henry has healed so quickly. He wouldn't have without your help."

"Now, my dear girl, Henry and I go way back. He has helped me over the years, and I have helped him. It's what friends do for each other."

"I'm glad he has a friend like you."

"And I'm glad he's found a special young lady like you to bring joy back to his life." He took her hand and patted it, much like an older man would. "It's been a pleasure meeting you. I hope you and Henry are very happy together. And do send me the prospectus on your business venture. I'm always looking for a good investment." He handed her a business card.

"Thank you, that's most kind of you."

"And now I see the learned father trying to get my attention. I will say goodnight, and see you here another time."

Most of the others had left while Cerissa spoke with Yacov. She took out her phone, emailed a prospectus to him, pocketed his business card, and headed to her car. Then it occurred to her. Leopold wouldn't let Henry invest.

Would Henry resent it if his friend got to do something he couldn't? Next time she was in New York, she'd push harder. Eventually, Leopold had to give in.

CHAPTER 21

GAEA'S HOUSE—THE NEXT MORNING

Closing her eyes, Cerissa let the shower's spray wash over her face as she ran her hands through her hair, smoothing it back with the flow of water. After the chapel meeting, she'd met up with Henry and then returned to Gaea's house around two in the morning. Eight hours of sleep and now she had to get ready for a long day ahead of her.

Henry had provided her with information about Barney Morrison. Still married, but "hen-pecked," according to Henry's source—Henry suspected Barney's attitude was based in resentment, not a desire to subjugate all mortals. But Barney's comments merited digging a little deeper into his background.

The warm shower relaxed her. Standing under it longer was tempting, but she had a long list of tasks to accomplish, and food was first on the agenda. Once dry, she fastened on her bracelet and stepped into a pair of boyshort panties Karen had encouraged her to buy. Cerissa had to admit that the pale seafoam-green lace looked good on her.

A sudden flash of light told her she was no longer alone.

"Ari, what are you doing here!" Cerissa exclaimed, rushing to get her silk robe so he wouldn't see her half-naked. "You were supposed to meet me in Mordida."

Her cousin smirked at her. "Body modesty? Really, Ciss, it's one thing to morph into human form, but you don't have to adopt all of their attitudes."

Cerissa pulled the robe tightly around her. "Next time, call before you pop in."

"I did, but you didn't answer."

"I must have been in the shower. But that's no excuse." She shook a finger at him. "Wait until you reach me."

"Sure thing, Ciss. Didn't know you'd be so touchy about it. You weren't when we were *karabu*."

"We're adults now. So why are you here?"

"Mind if I kick back while we talk?" All one hundred and eight-five pounds of him bounced onto her unmade bed.

"At least take off your shoes."

He kicked off his worn loafers and made a show of surveying the room. "This wallpaper is hideous. How can you stand living in this floral nightmare? And what idiot took a vintage carved headboard, whitewashed it, and hung an anemic crystal chandelier over it?"

"Don't look at me. I didn't pick it out."

"It's so—so feminine," he added. "In a creepy sort of way."

She crossed her arms and walked to the foot of the bed, glaring at him. "Ari, you aren't here to critique Gaea's taste in interior design."

"That's true, sweet cheeks," he said, lazing back on her pillows. "You haven't worn your lenses much since Henry's release three nights ago. Ya got to get back with the program, Ciss."

Cerissa cringed. Ari was right. "But I sent you the video of me and Matt, and the chapel meeting. Doesn't that count?"

"Yeah, about ninety minutes' worth, and I had to use a chain saw to edit the footage when you talked about Henry. The Protectors are going to start asking tough questions, and soon."

She didn't need them nosing around her operation. But what could she do? "I can't wear my lenses when I'm with Henry. I'm not going to violate his privacy."

Ari rolled his eyes at her. "You don't have to record the dirty deed."

"It's not like Henry tells me the itinerary before we get together. It's all kind of spontaneous. What if I blink wrong and accidentally turn on the camera while we're in bed…"

…or on the chaise lounge, or on the floor, or wherever else we make love next?

The idea horrified her.

"So what?" Ari said, looking faintly amused. "Do what you did the first time at the dance—duck into a restroom and remove your lenses. I can tell you, it's not uncommon for women to do that. Empty the bladder, that sort of thing. Henry won't suspect a thing. And no chance of accidental recordings that way."

She was already taking a break to inject the stabilizer. She could remove her lenses at the same time. But recording the rest of her conversations with Henry? Ari didn't need to hear every little thing they discussed, even out of bed. Still, saying no outright might piss off Ari.

"I'll consider it," she said.

"Hey, you gotta to do more than consider it. This isn't only your project—my butt's on the line too. We have to keep pushing out product. Your videos have helped the Enclave understand the vampire communities better. You can't stop now, or they'll suspect something's wrong. If you want my help with your cover-up, we need to keep sending videos to the Protectors."

Damn. How was she ever going to have the type of relationship she wanted with Henry until she broke free from the Lux?

"Fine," she said. "I'll start wearing them again. I'm meeting Karen for target practice. I'll record whatever she has to say about the community."

"Good. Now tell me. What's so special about sex with a vampire?"

A hot blush overtook her. "That's none of your business."

"Come on, you can confide in me."

"I'm not discussing my sex life with you."

"All right, but the day will come—when it does, you'll turn to *moi* for advice."

As if she'd ever take advice from Ari again. His bad advice had gotten them into this mess in the first place.

"Can we talk about business instead?" she asked.

"Sure. You can tell me over lunch."

She scowled at him. "I don't have a lot of time."

"Then we should get going. Where do you want to meet?"

"How about the Navajo?" She gave him the address. "No garlic. I can't eat garlic and be around Henry."

"Aaah, the things we do for love."

She grabbed the closest bric-a-brac from the nearby table and threw it at him. He blinked out of sight; the ceramic girl holding a basket of flowers landed safely on her pillow. She scooped it up, returning it to the table.

She'd started to untie the belt on her robe to continue dressing, when caution got the better of her. She took her clothes into the bathroom and dressed there. Even Ari wouldn't pop into a bathroom unannounced.

She checked her makeup in the mirror. Then she saw it. No wonder her cousin was all up in her face about vampire sex. Henry's bite from last night had been visible the whole time she spoke with Ari. She hadn't yet healed it for the day.

How mortifying.

She quickly morphed it. No more evidence of last night's tryst. She ran her fingers over the skin, missing the reminder.

The Tex-Mex food at the Navajo was good. Cerissa enjoyed her meal while she listened to Ari talk about the latest gossip from the Enclave. Keeping track of the political machinations of the Protectors was almost as fun—or depressing—as watching human politicians, depending upon your point of view.

When Ari finally stopped talking to shovel food in his mouth, Cerissa turned the conversation back to the VDM.

"I need you to get background checks on six vampires for me," she said.

"Okay, I'll bite. Why?"

She grimaced at his bad pun. "When I gave a presentation on the lab to some out-of-towners, a vampire named Barney Morrison talked about mortals knowing their place, and five others laughed. I checked the presentation video and identified them."

Ari's eyebrows rose and he pantomimed twirling a Simon Legree mustache. "What, were they like, *bwahahahaha?*"

"You're not taking this seriously."

"Hey, there's no crime in finding something funny."

"No, but turning mortals into blood slaves would be a crime. Can you do the research or not?"

"Hmm. I've got a tracer program running—I'll focus it on them. Send me the names of the lucky winners."

While Ari stuffed another forkful of enchilada into his mouth, Cerissa took out her phone and swiped the main screen to reveal the Lux communications system hidden beneath it. In a few clicks, she forwarded the information to Ari.

He glanced at his own phone. "Got it. But look, Ciss, you've got your fingers in a lot of pies right now. You gotta figure out your priorities."

"You're my supervisor. A little guidance here, please?"

"Next time, don't waste your time reviewing the videos. That's my job."

Cerissa chewed that over for a moment. She hated when Ari was right. "Yeah, but I thought it was important—"

"Then send me an email." He slurped down his margarita and licked the salt rim. "You do your job and I'll do mine."

"And you see mine as…?"

"Okay, let's break it down." He held up one finger. "You've got to find a way to deal with the Henry situation before the Protectors find out." A second finger joined the first. "You need funding for the lab to fix the vamp's long-term blood supply problem." A third finger rose. "And now, you're not just *watching* to see if the VDM might be real, you're trying to hunt them down. So which will you focus on first?" He made a mock show of gazing at the three fingers he held up and then pointed one at her. "If it was me, I'd go back to *watching and recording* like I told you to in the first place, and focus on getting the Henry situation fixed."

"I've been trying to figure out how to broach it with the Protectors, get them to see that my bond with Henry helps their cause." She sighed. "Suggestions would be welcome."

"Noted. And in the meantime, continue working on getting the lab funded. You do that, and you should be fine."

"But I can't just drop the VDM. That's what's keeping the Protectors at bay, isn't it?"

"*Information*, Ciss. That's what keeps them from banging down the door. What about this chief, Tigisi what's-her-name? Does she know about the VDM?"

"I don't know. We got nothing out of Blanche, and the Council said the investigation on her was closed."

"Hmm, I'll look into that, I think."

"Thanks, Ari," Cerissa replied.

When they parted, Ari hugged her. "Wear your lenses again and you'll be fine. From what I've seen, all your investor presentations have been topnotch. It'll work out okay. And it's a good thing vampires are susceptible to your Lux charm."

"All except Rolf."

"Never say never, kid. Keep on trying—you might get through to Mr. Asshat."

CHAPTER 22

SIERRA ESCONDIDA—THAT AFTERNOON

After lunch, Cerissa drove back to the Hill, waving at the guards as she passed the gate. They knew her car by now, which was just one more sign that the Hill accepted her.

She drove along the main two-lane highway, passing field after field of leafy vines. Tiny green grapes hung in clusters on the vines. Even the Cabernet grapes were green at this early stage.

Rolf's property was as expansive as Henry's and fronted the main highway. She parked at the curb by Rolf's corral and got out. Right on time, Karen's black Escalade stopped at the end of the driveway, and Cerissa climbed into the passenger seat of the luxury SUV, excited to see Karen again.

A slight whine emanated from the back seat. She glanced behind her at

Mort and Sang, strapped into their harnesses. Both German shepherds were amazingly gentle for guard dogs trained by Rolf.

"Zeke won't mind we're at his place during the day?" Cerissa asked, fastening her seatbelt.

"Nah. He gave me permission to use his firing range anytime." Karen turned the Escalade onto Robles. The main road ran through the valley, and its name meant "oak" in Spanish—fitting, as oak trees dotted the low, rolling foothills.

"I'm glad you suggested target practice," Cerissa said. "I need to keep up my skills."

She had been trained in most modern weapons, but even with the advantage her lenses gave her, regular practice was the key to accurate shooting.

A couple of sharp barks erupted from the back seat. "Mort, quiet," Karen commanded. Mort dialed it back to an excited whine, his nose pressed to the side window. "Good dog," she said. "If he sees a jackrabbit, he goes crazy. He loves to chase them. Hasn't caught one yet, but it seems to be his reason for living."

Cerissa reached back over the seat to pet each dog. Mort calmed as she stroked his thick, coarse fur. He was almost solid black, with hints of light brown fur near his belly. He rewarded her by licking her hand.

She gave Sang equal time, scratching behind her ears when the dog leaned her head forward. Sang was more traditionally marked, with blonde fur topped by a black saddle.

"Why did you learn how to shoot?" Cerissa asked as she petted the dogs.

"When I was a kid, my family's vineyard was pretty much out in the middle of nowhere. The sheriff's office was a good half-hour away, so Dad made sure all us kids could use a gun."

Karen turned off the main highway, onto a driveway leading to a dirt road. She pulled over and parked under the shade of a tall oak tree, fallen leaves covering the dirt.

Zeke's ranch was in an area where the valley flattened. His one-story home had been built near Robles Road. A barn and fenced corral for horses sat behind the house, and further out, a herd of cattle grazed on wild grass, the new growth bright green with small yellow flowers interspersed.

Cerissa stepped down from the SUV and took a deep, relaxing breath. The crisp scent of sage mixing with musty oak filled the air.

Karen opened the back door on the driver's side and unstrapped the dogs. Mort immediately took off, romping toward an open field. Sang patiently waited while Karen unhooked the seatbelt holding the dog's harness in place, and then jumped from the back seat, sniffing around, but she didn't follow Mort.

"Let's get the stuff out of the trunk while the dogs stretch their legs. I'll call them back before we start shooting." Karen opened the gun safe and took out the practice guns, handing Cerissa a basket with a tablecloth. "Spread the tablecloth out, so I can put this stuff down."

Karen indicated a picnic table near the firing range, and once the cloth covered the table, she laid out two handguns, ear protection, and ammunition. A man Cerissa didn't recognize waved at Karen from the corral.

"Who's that?" Cerissa asked, using her contact lenses to search dossiers to identify him, but he was too far away for the facial-recognition software to work. Not only did her lenses record, they allowed her to look up information downloaded to a nano-processor embedded on them.

Karen waved back at the guy, and he went back to feeding the horses. "He's married to one of our residents and takes care of the horses for Zeke and Rolf during the day."

They sat down at the picnic table and started loading ammo into the gun cartridges.

"I brought the Glock 19 for you because you've used Henry's," Karen said, "but we can trade off."

"That sounds like a good plan." Cerissa pulled back the slide on the Glock, checking that the chamber was empty. "You carried a gun when we went horseback riding. Why?"

At the time, Karen had mentioned her concern over wild animals. Cerissa had wondered if there was another reason, given how quickly Karen drew and fired in the direction of the assassin.

"Just a precaution," Karen replied, shoving a full clip into her Beretta and flipping on the safety.

"Against wild animals?"

Karen smirked. "Sort of." Then her look grew serious. "Look, most of the vampires on the Hill have been here a long time and are committed to their form of civilized behavior, but occasionally one will get rowdy. They all fight bloodlust, and sometimes, one of them just kinda snaps. I like being prepared. Even a lead bullet will slow them down until they clear their head or until another vamp handles it, you know?"

Cerissa reeled a little from this new information. "How frequently do they just snap?"

"Well, I've never seen it here," Karen said. "But Rolf warned me. And you stay in the communities long enough, and you'll hear rumors. Of course, no one ever officially confirms it, but I'm sure it happens. What really keeps them from killing is their Covenant. They want to keep living here, they like the benefits, and they won't risk being ostracized or staked. But never forget, being with a vampire *is* somewhat like being with a wild animal. They're never tame—they're only acting in their own self-interest."

"Father Matt called them addicts."

"Pfft," Karen scoffed. "As if that excuses it when one of them crosses the line and someone gets hurt. I know when gossip is more truth than not. But still, you're probably safer here than out there." She pointed in the direction of Mordida. "I mean, you heard about that serial killer, right? You need to be extra careful going into town."

"Do you think it's a vampire?"

"Nah. Nothing in the rumor mill so far."

Cerissa returned the Glock she held to the table, an idea forming. "Karen, can I ask you a question and not have it go anywhere further?"

"Sure. I'm a gossip, but I know when to keep my mouth shut. And I can keep a secret, especially for a friend." Karen pulled her auburn hair back in a ponytail and fastened it with a poufy band. "Tell me what's bugging you, and maybe we can work it out together."

"Thanks." *I should have asked her about the VDM before this. Ari may think I should only observe, but when an opportunity presents itself...* "Have you... I mean, is there anything you've heard recently that's disturbing?"

"Like what?"

"Any, ah, political unrest?"

Karen gave her a squirrely look. "You mean the mortal rights movement?"

"No, I meant among vampires."

"Oh. Rolf is going to run for mayor, but that's par for the course. He's run in the last four elections. Why?"

"Well, if Leopold and I put all this work into building the lab, we don't want a new war to interfere..."

"Got it. That's why you don't want anyone to know you're asking. You could start rumors just by asking the question, and no one will invest if they think war is coming." Karen paused. "But if it helps, I haven't heard a thing. Everyone says Blanche was trying to kill Yacov and Henry to make an opening on the Hill for herself, not start a war."

"Really?"

"Yeah. I haven't heard anything to the contrary so far. And these guys, they've gotten kind of complacent under the treaty. Like I said, sometimes one will get out of line, but as a group? They're like a contented, lazy cat lying in the sun."

Not good. In coyote country, it was never safe for a cat to let its guard down. Being complacent meant they weren't watching out for the next threat. The VDM could walk in and take over before they knew what had happened.

Karen stood up. "And you can ask me anything, anytime. If you want it kept quiet, I will. We're friends. You mean a lot to me."

Karen put an arm around Cerissa and gave her a hug.

"You mean a lot to me, too," Cerissa said, hugging her back tightly. She'd gone so long without any true friend other than Ari, and it filled her with joy to realize she now had another close friend in her life. "And thanks for the info—I really appreciate it."

"Anytime." Karen handed Cerissa a set of ear protectors and shooting goggles as she added, "Okay, let's do this."

Karen called the dogs. Mort ignored her and kept sniffing at the ground, rapidly swerving in a random pattern, trailing after whatever scent he'd found.

"We jokingly call it doggie deafness," Karen said with a laugh. "That damn dog can hear the rustle of the dog food bag from behind closed doors, but my voice across an open field, no, that he can't hear." She slipped a dog whistle out of her jeans pocket and gave four sharp blows. Mort came running at full speed, his long pink tongue flying in the wind.

Once Karen had Mort corralled, she tied both dogs to a tree on the other side of the Escalade. "I bring them because I want them accustomed to the sound of guns," Karen told her, "so they won't get spooked in an emergency, but it's hard on their ears, so the car and distance provide a buffer."

Cerissa followed Karen to the outdoor firing range. A makeshift wooden counter marked the firing line. Seven yards away, the targets were fastened to bales of hay.

They took turns practicing. Cerissa gripped the Glock, one hand under the butt to support it. The gun was large, but her fingers were long, and she liked its weight; it balanced well in her hand.

She managed to hit the bullseye ten times without using her lenses to help her. Four shots landed within the outer circles, and two went wild, missing the target. Not bad, overall. But Karen had put her bullet in the center fifteen out of seventeen shots.

Damn. I need to add regular gun practice to my already jam-packed schedule.

Four more clips later and she hit the center circle each time. She even tried Karen's Beretta, and was fairly accurate with it, though the Glock remained her favorite.

Karen finished her last clip and glanced at her phone. "Time to head back."

They gathered the guns, put them into the Escalade's gun safe, untied the dogs from the tree, and fastened them into their harnesses in the back seat again.

"I wanted to ask you about Frédéric," Cerissa said, getting comfortable in the passenger seat. Weeks ago, she'd asked Karen about Rolf's travels to San Diego—all on winery business, according to Karen. But Rolf and Frédéric seemed tied at the hip, and Frédéric's comments at the chapel meeting had bugged her.

"Aren't you full of questions today," Karen said, putting the car into gear. She drove off, the tires kicking up dust on the dirt road. "Why do you want to know about Frédéric?"

"Ah, he seems opposed to my project. I'm trying to figure out what might sway him."

"Don't worry about him." Karen waved her hand like she was swatting a fly and turned the car onto Robles Road. "He's harmless—does everything Rolf tells him to do."

"Are you sure? I went to one of Father Matt's groups, and Frédéric was quite condescending. He talked about Greek gods and how they were more powerful than mortals—just like vampires are."

"I bet that went over well." Karen snickered. "But there's nothing to worry about. He's got this fixation on Zeus, and he's boring as hell on the subject. It's all he talks about when he visits. Sublimation, you know?"

"No, I don't."

"His wife died in the late 1940s. He's Catholic—you know, old-school late 1800s French Catholic. The nuns got a hold of him when he was a child, and wow, did they screw up his head. And when the Second French Republic was formed— No, I think it was the Third French Republic. God, you have to know your history, living with vampires. Anyway, his dad wanted to see the monarchy restored because the church feared losing control if us *commoners*"—she said the word in the snootiest way possible—"took over."

Karen stopped the Escalade on the pavement behind Cerissa's car. "Anyway, where was I? Oh, right. So after his wife died, Frédéric swore he'd never take another mate, never marry again."

"Never?"

"Yeah, he takes the whole *till death do we part* to a new extreme." Karen wagged a finger in Cerissa's direction. "You know the crazy way Frédéric's mustache looks? All waxed like two curving wires sticking out to his ears? I heard Frédéric styled it that way after his wife died. It's so silly looking that women avoid him. If you ask me, he's afraid of falling in love again. So he spends all his spare time in a fantasy world, living in ancient Greece. That's where the obsession comes from. He's harmless; he just doesn't know how to deal with grief—or the fear of being hurt again."

"Thanks. I appreciate your insight."

"No problemo. But there's more, and this is only for your ears. Rolf thinks Frédéric's dating again. So don't be surprised if his ideas soon mellow a bit."

Cerissa waved goodbye and got into her car. As she did, she replayed Karen's remarks. The death of a beloved spouse, especially for an immortal, could be a traumatic event.

Poor guy.

Maybe Karen was right—finding the right woman to love might mellow his attitude. Still, his viewpoint about mortals bothered her. She sent an email to Ari, asking him to look into Frédéric. Not that it made much difference—Ari had already researched the town council members and found nothing disturbing.

Finished with work for the day, she drove over to Henry's and showered there using the master bathroom. The sun had set by the time she finished dressing, and she checked her email. The town's planning department had written to say her land use application was complete; they didn't need any more information from her.

She clutched the phone to her chest, excitement streaming through her. That meant the lab project was moving forward. Environmental review was the next step, and could take as long as six months to a year, which would give her plenty of time to get the funding wrapped up before they started building. When the environmental impact report was finished, the town council would decide whether to grant approval.

In addition to the town planner's message, two other welcomed emails had arrived, one from Yacov and one from Gaea.

Both wanted to invest in the lab project.

She did a Kathak dance around the bedroom, a happy dance she'd learned as a child in India, the rhythmic foot movements causing her bracelet to jingle on her wrist.

She couldn't wait to tell Henry the good news, and ran downstairs to the kitchen. He was still in the basement, talking loudly, almost on the verge of yelling, his voice audible through the floor—probably on the phone. Something must have happened.

A short while later, the basement door slammed open.

"I am going out," he abruptly told her when he strode through the kitchen.

"What's wrong?"

He didn't stop. She followed him to the front door. The keys to the Viper were already in his hand.

"A matter has come up," he said, then rushed out the door and closed it loudly behind him.

CHAPTER 23

HENRY'S HOUSE—MOMENTS LATER

Cerissa stood there, staring at the closed door, her eyebrows raised, her mouth open.

What the hell was that about?

If Henry needed space, he would have gone riding in the hills on his motorcycle. He'd done that once during their short time dating, but if he took the Viper, he was either going into town, or meeting with someone on business. Perhaps there was some problem at the winery he didn't want to share with her.

What to do with herself? She hadn't planned on being alone tonight.
Oh well.

She checked the community's website on her phone—no social events were scheduled, so she couldn't use the time to meet potential investors.

Should I go back to the Enclave's lab?

Not a good choice—she tended to lose track of time there and didn't want to end up missing Henry when he returned.

Sighing, she made a quick dinner, and after eating, went upstairs to the television room. Nothing was recorded on the DVR she wanted to see without him. She scanned through the program listings. A newer Dracula movie was available. Henry must have viewed it during his three weeks of confinement, because it had a checkmark by it.

The television room seemed empty without him. She decided to watch the movie on the smaller TV in his office. When he came home, he was likely to go there first. Besides, she wasn't going to be working, so she wouldn't disturb his pristine desk. She stretched out on the leather couch, waiting for him.

Except the movie ended before he returned.

What to do now? She hadn't read the stuff Haley had given her. She should—Haley might ask her about it the next time they ran into each other. Cerissa found it in her purse and returned to Henry's office. With her head propped on a throw pillow at one end of the couch, she began reading about the mortal rights movement.

Impressive. Haley's group had done an excellent job laying out their arguments. The Protectors would be interested in it. She was almost finished reading the mortal rights proposal for restructuring the Hill when the front door slammed. She sat up.

Hmm. That didn't sound good. Should I stay here or go downstairs?

Before she could make up her mind, Henry opened his office door and marched past her to his small bedroom, stopping in the doorway. His gaze moved from her to the carpet. She'd left the glossy "Guest Resident Rights" brochure on the floor while she plowed through the denser material.

"Must you read that insipid polemic?" he demanded.

"I want to know what's going on in the community. They make some good points."

"They have no idea the chaos their *good points* would cause."

"Henry, we talked about this before the ball game. I won't be treated as a second-class citizen. You said you understood." She looked at him, letting her puzzlement show on her face. "Why the bad mood?"

155

"I do not need to be in a bad mood to question why you would read such trash."

Trash? Were they about to have their first fight? This soon? If they were, it wouldn't be because of her—she refused to take the bait.

"You were upset before you saw what I was reading. What's really wrong?"

"I didn't expect to find you in my office."

"Are you saying I can't be in here unless you are?"

He let out a long exhale. "No, *cariña*, I didn't mean it that way." His tone had softened and he scrubbed a hand over his face. "I'm sorry, you're right. I'm not in a good mood. Perhaps you should return to Gaea's."

She furrowed her brow, cocking her head. She'd been around humans enough to know it was rarely the first issue, or the second. Something deeper, something big, must have upset him.

"What really happened?" She rolled off the couch and walked toward him. He backed up and began closing the door to his windowless bedroom.

Okay, that is just strange.

Then she caught a whiff of something—lavender with an overlay of female pheromones—and a wisp of fear ran through her. Her hand shot out to stop him from closing the door. "Henry, I can smell a woman on you. Who is it?"

"You are imagining things."

"No I'm not." The wisp of fear grew into a steady stream. He was hiding something. She wrinkled her nose, sniffing the air near him. "Definitely female."

"I'm going to shower."

"No you aren't, not until you tell me what's going on."

He started to turn away, but she grabbed his shirt collar to keep him in place, popping the top button in the process. Two red fang marks stared back at her.

The heat of anger crawled up her neck and bloomed on her face. Neck bites were never used on the Hill to donate blood when a vampire was injured—the embrace felt too close to sex.

Now she understood how Erin felt. Erin had left him after he came home with a similar bite. That meant...

"Anne-Louise?" she demanded.

"Yes."

"You son of a bitch." Her anger skyrocketed, shooting fire through her chest, and she clutched his shirt collar tighter. "Why didn't you tell me she's here? I deserve to know."

Henry jerked his collar out of her hand. "Do not swear at me."

"I'll swear if I damn well please. You won't make this about me."

He straightened his collar, making an effort to look indignant, and turned away.

"Not so fast," she said, following him through the small bedroom and into the huge closet. "We aren't finished talking."

He pulled the shirt over his head, taking the chain of his crucifix with it, snarling it around one of the buttons of his shirt. He angrily untangled it, grasping the crucifix in one hand, and glared at her. "I do not have to stand here while you screech at me."

"I'll lower my voice, but you'll answer my questions."

He turned his back on her, continuing to undress.

Why did he try to hide the visit from her? They'd discussed the situation *ad nauseam* three nights ago. Threads of jealously and doubt began to weave together with her anger, and she couldn't stop the question from forming on her lips.

"Did you have sex with her?"

"No!" he barked from between clenched teeth. Without warning, he swung his fist, driving it into the closet wall inches from her. Chalky debris fell to the floor.

She brushed some of the dust off her sleeve, ignoring his attempt to intimidate her. "You sure?" she asked.

He stripped off his pants and faced her naked. "Do you doubt my word?" he growled.

"Then why is her bite *there*"—she pointed at his neck—"and not on your wrist?"

"It wasn't my choice." He turned away from her, fuming.

"*Henry.*"

He strode into the bathroom, stepped into the shower, closed the glass door behind him with a *clank*, and turned on the water.

While he showered, she dialed her anger back a notch. Okay, she believed him. He hadn't had sex with Anne-Louise. He'd been faithful.

But his maker had no business biting his neck, and he had no business hiding it from her.

Cerissa exhaled, releasing a little more anger. They both came with individual duty-bound baggage, hers to the Lux, and his to his maker. Hell, even if she broke away from the Lux, in a hundred years, she'd still have to find someone with whom to have a child. He knew this already; they'd discussed it before they made love the first time. And when the time came, she damn well expected him to be understanding.

For *them* to work in the long-term, they had to find a way to deal with his tie to Anne-Louise. She simply didn't think it'd be this hard—or that they'd be tested so soon.

She waited, leaning against the cold bathroom wall. For now, she'd stop her accusations. But he needed to learn he could not lie to her, not even by omission. At least, not without consequences.

Henry turned the hot water all the way on, leaving off the cold. The water turned his chest sunburn-red, his body healing it almost as quickly, the pain lingering, an echo reminding him he deserved to be scalded for hiding the truth from her—the truth he still hid.

Anne-Louise's scent rose with the steam, evoking centuries-old memories, memories that flooded through him unbidden: the whorehouse's rough linen sheets on his back, his maker's fangs piercing his neck, his life draining away with each swallow she took, her blood on his lips as he drank from her, the impotent rage he felt the next night he woke.

The *puta* had stolen everything from him, and she continued to take from him. No matter how many treaties he negotiated, no matter how he tried to use rules to limit the hold she had over him, at bottom, he was powerless to stop her.

He placed the small blood vial he'd palmed onto the soap tray and scrubbed off her scent, bowing his head into the shower's burning spray, closing his eyes.

None of it excused how he treated Cerissa.

The faucet squeaked as he turned it off. He grabbed the towel he'd hung over the shower door and dried off, his nakedness still concealed by the opaque glass. Shame pricked his skin, and he wrapped the towel around his waist.

"Anne-Louise texted me this morning, before I retired for the day," he said from behind the shower door. "She had arrived on the Hill last night without warning me she was coming. She had heard you were now my mate, and threatened to come over here if I didn't immediately come to her."

And none of it excuses my behavior tonight.

Cerissa remained silent, so he continued. "I had spoken to Anne-Louise right before I saw you in the kitchen. I didn't know what she would do if she came here. She has never cared before who I took as a lover. Suddenly, she cares."

He opened the shower door, which made a wet popping sound, like a stopper had been pulled from a bottle of wine. He stepped out of the shower and shut the glass door, the towel still wrapped around his waist.

"So I went to see her. She demanded tribute. We argued." He shrugged. "The subject doesn't matter—she can pick an argument over how I say *hello* to her. She is just that way." He grabbed another towel and used it to wring the water from his hair. "Then I came back here."

He faced Cerissa. Anger still flashed in her green eyes. "I'm sorry," he said. "I should have told you the truth from the beginning."

Her silence continued.

"You were reading that insipid literature." He turned back to the mirror, unscrewed the lid on the blood vial, and poured vampire blood over the bite. The skin healed instantly. "I'm sorry I vented my anger at her on you."

"Whose blood?" she asked, stepping closer to him.

"Rolf's." He took a tissue from a box on the counter and wiped off the excess. "I may not have handled things well tonight, but she has this way of *disturbing* my peace of mind."

"Why do I feel like you haven't told me the whole story?"

"Cerissa..." he began, his eyes avoiding hers. He didn't want to discuss it right now. It might be nothing; it might never come to pass.

"What did Anne-Louise really want?" she demanded.

No choice now. He owed her the truth. "Anne-Louise wants me to return to New York with her."

"For how long?"

"She didn't say. A night, a year." He shrugged. "It's up to her."

"A y-year? She could do that?"

He ran a comb through his hair, which was a stringy, damp mess. "She can compel me to stay with her, yes. She has before, a long time ago, but I believed we were past this."

"When were you going to tell me? When you were getting on a plane for New York?"

"Anne-Louise is mercurial. She could change her mind..."

"Henry, I can't move back to New York. The lab project will fail if I do. What are we going to do?"

"Pray she relents. There isn't much I can do. If she insists, I must follow her."

"Why does she suddenly want you with her?"

He stared at the sink. "She would not say."

"When does she leave for New York?"

"This morning. The mortuary service will transport her to New York during the day—we settled that much."

"Then you'll take me to see her tonight."

The mirror reflected the appalled expression on his face. "No," he said. "That's not a good idea."

"You weren't honest with me, so now we do this my way. Call her and tell her we're coming to see her." She paused. "Where is she staying?"

"Rolf's. His guest house."

"Wonderful," she said, throwing up her hands. "Rolf knows. How humiliating."

With that, she left the bathroom, leaving him alone with his guilt and fear. He bowed his head, praying for wisdom. He couldn't let Anne-Louise separate him from Cerissa. No matter how hopeless it had been in the past, how Anne-Louise always seemed to get the better of him, he had to find a way to resist her so he could stay here with Cerissa.

But how?

CHAPTER 24

SIERRA ESCONDIDA POLICE STATION—SAME NIGHT

Tig stared at the interactive whiteboard in the police station's squad room. Projected onto it was her most recent flow chart, which summarized the facts and key dates for the attempted assassinations. Behind her, spread out on a long worktable, lay most of the documents and photos she'd compiled, along with her laptop. The laptop was attached to the whiteboard and controlled the projection.

Using the whiteboard's software, she could write text on the board with a stylus, or move images and words around with a touch of her finger. The edits were automatically added to the flow chart's electronic file.

Yes, the town council usually didn't mind paying for gadgets. And this was one great gadget. Too bad displaying the information this way didn't reveal anything new.

When she heard the station's outer door buzz, she sniffed the air, detecting the familiar scent of masculine musk and her favorite aftershave.

Jayden.

"I'm in the squad room," she called out. She hadn't seen him since he'd returned from San Diego during the day.

His shoulders slumped as he plodded in, and she closed the squad room door behind him. With no one else around, she took him into her arms and kissed him. He returned the kiss, but tension wafted off him like dust in a hot savannah wind.

"How was your day?" she asked.

He shrugged, looking at the paperwork on the table. "You got the reports I left you?"

"Yeah, I did." Had something about the case made him tense? The longer it took to solve a crime, the less likely they'd find whoever was behind it. But like most cops, he usually had no problem expressing his frustration. Rarely did she see him bottle it up like this.

Or was he just tired? Two nights out of town shadowing the San Diego PD would leave anyone exhausted.

Maybe if she got him talking about the case it would improve his mood. She touched the whiteboard to open a different computer window. "I'm trying to make sense of all this."

At the top of the board, she had written V-1 in bold. V-1 was the mastermind—they were both sure there was one. A lateral line to the left connected V-1 to Blanche. Another line led from Blanche to a photo of Norman, the dead prison guard, linking the two—Blanche had been in Norman's apartment, and was probably his girlfriend.

Another lateral line, this one to the right, led to the three shooters, with links from the shooters to New Path Church. She had added the link after Jayden emailed her the results of his prison visit. The church had picked up each shooter on their release dates. The guard and the three shooters were linked back to the San Diego Prison. One dotted line ran from Blanche's name to New Path, with a question mark by the line.

Even the Carlyle Cutter had his own space at the lower corner of the board.

Pointing at the Cutter's entry, Jayden said, "Why include him? We're not positive the Cutter's a vampire, or that he's connected to the attacks. It could be a human serial killer with a blood fetish."

"He's creating adrenaline-spiked blood. Why would a mortal do that?"

"Why do any of us stupid mortals do what we do?"

She turned and stared at him. *Where did that come from?*

"Jayden—"

He held up his hands. "Look, I'm sorry. Ignore what I said."

She sat on the edge of the table and tilted her head to the side. *No, there's more to this.* His scent was off; he smelled like wilting flowers on a grave. He smelled like...sadness.

"What's going on?" she asked gently.

"I guess you didn't see this."

He pulled a folded paper out of his back pocket and handed it to her. She opened it. A two-sentence message: *Fuck and suck—that's all a mortal's good for. No council seat.*

"What the hell? Where did you get this?"

"Someone stuck it under my car's wiper blade. But I wasn't singled out. Every vehicle in the town hall parking lot had one."

"Sit down." She pulled out a folding chair for him. He stood there for a moment, and then lowered himself onto the metal seat. She grabbed a chair for herself, turning it around to face him. "I'm sorry this whole mortal rights subcommittee thing is affecting you. It's brought out the worst in some vampires."

He scrubbed his hand over his face. "I shouldn't let it get to me. It's just..."

"Tell me," she said, trying to sound calm when what she wanted was to curl her hands into fists and pound the shit out of whoever had left the flyer. "We haven't talked much about the subcommittee."

"Thanks, but you know I don't give a shit about politics. I like my job. I like what I do. They couldn't pay me enough to be on the council. But..."

"But what?"

"I don't know. Something about the note got me here." He tapped at his chest, just above his heart.

She nodded. "It's like all the other racist shit you've had to endure."

"Yeah," he said with a sigh, his shoulders slumping even more.

"I told the mayor I thought mortals should have voting rights on the Hill."

"Thanks," he said, still staring at the floor. He sat there silently while seconds ticked by.

Why didn't her support make him happy? She was on his side in this battle. Unless it wasn't just about sides?

"What're you thinking?" she finally asked.

He shook his head. "It's not worth talking about."

May the ancestors help us—she wasn't good at this touchy-feely stuff, but she couldn't let it fester. She took his hand and squeezed it. "We should talk if it's upsetting you."

He shook his head again, like he was trying to persuade himself out of something.

"Come on," she said. "Tell me."

He didn't want to talk about this shit. Hell, she probably carried more baggage than he did. Her life hadn't been easy either. First her husband died, and then she was pulled out of her Kenyan village and turned by Phat, who forced her to work as a paid mercenary. And now she had to keep a whole community of vampires happy, while tracking down whoever was behind the recent attacks.

Why should he weigh her down with his petty complaints?

"Jayden—"

"It's not important, Tig."

"Let me be the judge of that."

He ran his hand across his shaved head. *No way out of it now.* When she set her mind to something, nothing stopped her.

"Okay," he said, and paused. *Shit,* he hated talking about it. She eyeballed him as if to say, "Go on."

"Okay, I told you how I was a pint-sized kid?"

"Until you hit puberty and started working out with weights."

"Yeah, a late growth spurt, but even now, I'm shorter than my dad." He could still see his father towering over him, a barrel-chested man with a perpetual frown. "He served as a Los Angeles deputy sheriff."

She raised one eyebrow. "So..."

"He was ashamed of me." Jayden stared at the worn industrial carpet. Between foot traffic and coffee spills, the thing looked damn ratty. Maybe they should ask the council for new carpet. If he couldn't vote, the least they could do was to keep his workplace in decent shape.

"Fathers are grateful for sons." Her words intruded on his reflections. "Maasai fathers always prayed for a boy child."

"Not if we're runts. They don't want us if we're runts." He kept staring at the carpet. "I was the smallest kid in my class. When I was in the seventh grade, they took our class picture on the school front steps. Dad looked at the photo and handed it right back, unhappy. I was in the first row, the shortest of the short."

"That doesn't mean he was ashamed of you."

"Oh, yes it did," he said, meeting her gaze. "He told me I'd grow up to be a bookworm like Mom, which was the worst insult he could think of. And the other kids felt the same way when it came time to pick teams. There wasn't anything I could do to change my height."

Tig looked off into space for a moment. "Just like there's nothing you can do about being black...or mortal."

"Yeah. I don't want to be on the council, but to tell me I can't because I'm mortal, because of something I can't change—it's the same shit all over again. I'm not good enough the way I am."

"As far as I'm concerned, you're more than good enough. You'd do better than most of the current council members. You're smart, you're organized, and you get things done. Most of the council is so stupid, when they step in dung they can't figure out where the smell is coming from."

Having her support meant everything to him. It was one thing to say she thought mortals should get a vote; it was another to tell him he was as good as any vampire—that he *was* good enough just as he was. Sometimes, in this town, he needed to hear—needed a reminder—that the woman he loved saw him as an equal.

Everyone else could go to hell.

"Thank you," he said, cupping her face and leaning over to kiss her. Tig's lips parted and he took full advantage of it, deeply seeking the taste of her after two nights apart. "God, I've missed you," he said, hugging her to him.

"The feeling's mutual." When Tig released him, she scanned his face closely. "Look, if you're not happy here, we don't have to stay."

"And not solve the puzzle? I want to figure out who's behind this." He motioned toward the whiteboard. "If we leave, we won't find out who the Cutter is."

"True. But Jayden—I mean it. We don't have to stay if this shit gets worst. You say the word, and we're gone."

He gave her a heartfelt smile. It was good to know she had his back. "I hear you, Tig. But let's solve the puzzle first."

Good. For once, she'd said the right words. He needed to understand—his happiness was more important to her than this damn job. He glanced over at the flow chart and seemed ready to move on. Standing, they both walked over to the whiteboard.

She still wanted to strangle the asshole who had passed out the flyer. She shoved it into her back pocket—she would check it for fingerprints later. Paper wasn't the greatest surface for lifting prints, but the latest development in rubber-gelatin lifters made it easier. Maybe she'd get to pummel someone after all.

"Well then, back to my original question," she said. "Why would a mortal drain their victim?"

"A guess?" he asked. "Mortal serial killers get off on the pain and fear of their victims. Bleeding out someone, watching their victim's eyes as their life's blood flowed out of them—I've read profiles of other serial killers, and this is consistent behavior. But if the DNA comes back corrupted, we'll have proof a vampire is involved."

She went over to the table, shuffled through the paperwork, and picked up the lab report. "The Carlyle police found no DNA, corrupt or otherwise. Have you received the lab results from San Diego?"

"Not yet. The San Diego ME has her hands full right now. Nasty shooting. Six dead, two injured. They're overwhelmed."

"Six dead?" she repeated. "That's a high body count."

"A man went into a restaurant today and gunned down almost everyone inside. The police suspect the husband of one of the waitresses, but it happened so fast, the killer left before the police arrived. The lab's working overtime trying to identify him. The Cutter's been pushed to the bottom of the food chain."

"Fuck," she said. "When are we going to catch a break?" She tossed the Carlyle lab report back on the table.

"Are you going to brief our buddies on the council?"

She gave a derisive sniff. "Not yet. The gate logs arrived while you were gone. I looked through them. Rolf and Frédéric were off the Hill each night the Cutter struck. I don't yet know why."

"Together?"

"They drove separate cars, but they left around the same time."

"I see your problem. But there was only one puncture wound. Rolf and Frédéric have both their fangs, and no one in V-Trak is tagged as missing a fang."

"Yeah, but the perp may have used a needle to puncture the artery and drain the victim, to drink it later."

"Possibly," Jayden conceded.

Tig considered asking Jayden to look into Rolf and Frédéric, see if they had alibis for those nights, but investigating council members was too sensitive to delegate. She'd get to it eventually.

She went back to the whiteboard and tapped the silhouette of Blanche. "New Path picked up the shooters from the prison. How is Blanche connected to New Path? Aside from the fact the church is local to San Diego."

Jayden picked up a stylus and used the pull-down menu to select a color she hadn't used. "What if there isn't a vampire behind this? Sure, Petar heard a rumor about a vampire-led conspiracy, but what proof do we have? It could as easily be a religious group using ex-cons as vampire hunters." He wrote "Vampire Hunter Conspiracy" in blue next to V-1 at the top, and drew a vertical line between them, separating them.

"Then why was Blanche involved?" She couldn't imagine a vampire hooking up with mortals to kill her own people. "And why was she trying to start a war between the Hill, New York, and San Francisco?"

Jayden scratched at his neck. "Yeah, my idea seems far-fetched. The way mortals are being used—sacrificed—we figured it had to be a vampire behind it in the first place. Maybe the church bribed her, or she had a death wish."

Tig added a big question mark under "Vampire Hunter Conspiracy," showing her doubt. "If Petar's rumor is true, then New Path's involvement makes more sense, and it follows that a vampire must be behind New Path."

"What about the others on the Henry/Yacov list?" Jayden asked.

She touched the whiteboard and the suspect list appeared. "I spoke with Frédéric four nights ago. He doesn't sound like he carries a grudge. If anything, he sounds like he's swung the other way—he's firmly in the 'no new vampires' camp." She'd drawn a dotted line through his name. "Did you know Frédéric and Henry have the same grandsire?"

"Let me check V-Trak." He went over to the computer. A few seconds later, he said, "Yup, the same grandsire. But what does it tell us?"

"I don't know. Family isn't the same for vampires—being cousins wouldn't matter to them. But if someone was coming after their grandsire's progeny, a revenge thing, then Frédéric and Anne-Louise could be in danger as well."

Jayden turned to the computer, and as he typed, the link between the three appeared on the whiteboard. He then swiveled back to face her. "But how do you explain the attack on Yacov? We'd have to do a family tree to see if Yacov has any blood connection to Henry's grandsire."

"Add it to the investigation plan. You can pull the info from V-Trak later. If there is a connection, we should warn them." She double-tapped the whiteboard by Frédéric's name. A document linked to his name opened. "Do you remember the recent amendment to the Covenant, the one Rolf proposed?"

"Vaguely."

She gestured to the document, a copy of the motion Rolf made. "Rolf wanted a firm hundred-year rule—can't turn a mate until a vampire hits their hundredth year. No exceptions. Frédéric backed him on it."

"But no one can turn a mate, not while the treaty ban is in place. Why pass a useless law?" Jayden asked. "Wait, that means if Rolf wants to turn Karen, he's out of luck—he's been a vampire for, what, seventy-five years?"

"Close enough. Yeah, I don't get it, unless he doesn't want to turn Karen."

Jayden touched the whiteboard, dragging Rolf's motion to hover over Karen's name, connecting the document to her. "Maybe he proposed it so she wouldn't bug him about it, in case the treaty rule was lifted."

Now there's an interesting idea.

This was why Tig loved working with Jayden. Their minds chased each other around until they tumbled onto new theories. Bouncing thoughts off him was so much better than staring at the board alone.

"Henry's heir" was already written by Rolf's name, and Tig added Jayden's idea underneath it. "Anyway, I put Rolf on the list even though Henry and Yacov didn't. We don't know Rolf's whereabouts for the night Norman was killed."

"You should add Karen's name to the list of motives, too."

"Karen?" Tig didn't hide her surprise. "Why?"

"Karen told me she went out on a date with Henry before she hooked up with Rolf."

"Henry didn't mention Karen."

Jayden picked up a file and pulled out a one-page report to hand her. "It was shortly before Henry asked Erin to move in with him. He was seeing both of them, picked Erin, and then introduced Karen to Rolf."

Tig looked over the report. "You think Rolf's holding a grudge over getting sloppy seconds?"

"Not that sloppy. Karen says she never made it past, ah, first base with Henry."

Tig understood the American idiom. After considering the information, she wrote Karen's name with a question mark as motive, although greed and power seemed to be bigger motivators for Rolf than jealousy.

"Shit," she said. "Rolf tried to ban Cerissa from the Hill—was he afraid Henry would change his will again, make Cerissa his heir?"

"But then how do you explain the attack on Yacov?" Jayden slid his fingers across the board to bring forward a map. "San Diego is the focal point. We need to look into the San Diego and Rancho Valley communities—the ones with ties to the three vampires on the Henry/Yacov list."

Tig leaned back against the squad room table. Oscar and a few others still hadn't been ruled out. "I've been trying to figure out a way to do just that—I can't just show up in a treaty community and accuse them of hostile acts. Wars have been started over less." She swiped at the whiteboard to bring back the list of suspects again. "What if I'm wrong and Petar is involved? Could Rolf be in business with Petar?"

"Seriously?" Jayden asked.

"Yeah. Why not?" She circled her hand, gesturing at the whiteboard. "When you look at this mess, anything is possible. But our better lead right now is to track down the church. Petar's comment is still bothering me. If Petar is telling the truth."

"Let me get my research." Jayden dashed out of the squad room.

Tig sat down at the keyboard, the screen now blank. He returned a moment later.

"Okay," he said, spreading out sheets of paper on the table so she could see them—pages printed from a website. "Their only address is a PO box in San Diego. They have a web presence. 'Finding a New Path in Life' is their slogan. No incorporation records. I can't say why, but reading their website—I have the sense they want to attract people who were lonely. 'Be our friend' was another slogan. Something about it felt strange."

Tig stopped typing, her fingers hovering above the keyboard. "They aren't on the state's website as a tax-exempt organization?"

"They aren't registered as a church or as a 501(c)(3)," Jayden said. "They may not offer a tax deduction to donors. Have you checked with Father Matt? See if he's ever heard of them."

"That's a great idea, thanks. I'll call him later." Why hadn't she thought of it? Then again, it was another reason why she and Jayden made a good team.

"As far as I can tell," he said, "they only have a website and a PO box."

She typed in the address with two fingers, and the computer froze. The whiteboard program wasn't cooperating. She pounded on the escape key. New technology was great—but only when it worked.

"Here, let me," he offered.

She stood, and he took her place at the keyboard. For someone who never learned touch-typing, she typed pretty fast with two fingers, but she had no patience when machines turned obstinate.

He restarted the program and typed in the URL. The website appeared on the whiteboard.

She walked to the board. "They can't create a website using a fictitious name without filing some paperwork. They at least need to register a DBA."

"I checked with San Diego's Recorders Office—they didn't have a '*doing business as*' certificate on file."

"Who's the URL owner?"

He keyed in a quick search for "WHOIS." "We're in luck. They were too cheap to pay for privacy protection."

If they'd paid for privacy, she'd need a search warrant. "So, who is it?"

He scrolled through the report. "Someone with a sense of humor. It's registered to the Reverend Jim Jones. He's the same guy on the website's contact page."

"As in *the* Reverend Jim Jones?" she asked. "You mean the cult leader who killed his followers with a cyanide-poisoned kids' drink?"

"The same name."

"The military recovered his body, right?"

Jayden ran an internet search. "According to his Wiki, Jones' gunshot body was among the dead. The Air Force conducted the autopsy—no chance he's a vampire."

"That's good," she said. "I can't believe anyone would turn Jim Jones."

Jayden typed in the information, adding it to what they had learned about New Path. "I'll note it for now, but it's probably either a coincidence, or a case of someone having a warped sense of humor." Finished, he tapped on the open window with the Wiki article, bringing it to the front. "Huh, you learn something new every day. You know the idiom, drinking the Kool-Aid, came out of the Jonestown deaths, right? But according to Jones' Wiki, a different soft-drink brand may have been used."

Tig frowned. Something about the whole thing bothered her. Jayden opened the search box for V-Trak, projecting the results on the whiteboard. There were plenty of registered vampires with the last name Jones, but no Joneses with the first name Jim or James. Then again, no one would be stupid enough to use their real name, would they?

Tig looked at the paper file. "The website was registered about ten years ago. They've been functioning for a long time. Can you tell where it's uploaded from?"

"No. We should hire a computer expert to find out."

"Wait." She dropped the file onto the table. "I've got an idea. They have an email address, right?"

"Yeah—"

"Use a dummy account and send an email offering to make a donation if they'll meet with you. See how they respond."

"New Path may be run by mortals," he said. "A religious sect that's figured out vampires exist."

"And led by Jim Jones? No." She shook her head adamantly. "Mortals would know how damaged his name is. They would never use it if they were serious. More likely, it's a vampire with a warped sense of humor."

Then she remembered Petar's words.

Rumors of a movement to put us in charge...

She abruptly sank onto the chair behind her, like a lead weight had pulled her down. She couldn't believe it, even as she spoke the words.

"The reference isn't a joke, Jayden. It's a message." She shook her head. "Jim Jones killed all his followers. And this time, his followers aren't drinking a kids' soft drink when they die."

CHAPTER 25

ROLF'S GUEST HOUSE—AFTER MIDNIGHT

Cerissa curtsied when Anne-Louise opened the door of Rolf's guest house. Her anger had become tempered with fear: fear of losing Henry, fear of losing her new community, fear of bungling everything.

And here I thought the Protectors were my biggest problem.

"Countess, please pardon my intrusion," she said in French. "It would be rude if I didn't introduce myself before you left this morning."

By speaking French, she excluded Henry from the conversation. He only spoke English with the Countess Anne-Louise d'Hardancourt Brillon de Jouy. The countess's Spanish was terrible, and his French wasn't much better, but during the drive over, he'd agreed with Cerissa's strategy. This type of negotiation had to be conducted in the native language of the dominant player—and Anne-Louise held most of the cards.

But not all of them.

Cerissa stayed in the curtsey. She pushed her aura in the direction of Anne-Louise, keeping her eyes focused on the beautiful vampire.

Much more beautiful than I am.

The countess wore a chic dress with a red lace bodice and floor-length white linen skirt. The skirt gathered in at the waist before flowing gracefully over her hips. Her hair was salt-and-pepper gray, with big soft, curls held off her face by carved wooden clips, and her hazel eyes shone with a certain sparkle—whether from a natural passion for life, or as a result of becoming vampire, Cerissa wasn't sure. Pale white skin bore the same agelessness as most vampires, so Anne-Louise didn't look old, but she did look more mature than Henry.

Why had she dressed so elegantly to feed from him? Or did she desire another kind of tribute?

The countess stared back, looking wary. "Enrique, why have you brought this creature to my doorstep?"

Henry crossed his arms. "It wasn't my idea."

"Obviously. Doesn't she realize what danger she is in?" Anne-Louise asked, baring her fangs in Cerissa's direction.

Karen's comment about vampires "snapping" shot through Cerissa's mind, but she didn't move.

Henry stepped between them, almost butting chests with Anne-Louise. "You will not touch her," he said. "She is mine."

Anne-Louise flipped her fingers dismissively. "And what's yours is mine."

Heat radiated across Cerissa's face, her jaw muscles locked.

I'm no one's property.

"Do not try to scare her with your lies," Henry said, his voice lowering in register, his tongue rolling the Rs. "You know better."

Still holding the curtsey, Cerissa slightly lowered her eyes. "Countess," she said in French, "Leopold would not be pleased if you tried to harm me."

Anne-Louise stepped back and crossed her arms. "Why you impertinent little she-devil." Her gaze moved pointedly from Cerissa to Henry. "Well, Enrique, I must say she does have courage, this one. Not like the whiney thing you had before her."

Henry extended his arms to grab the doorframe on each side, giving Anne-Louise no room to maneuver around him. He took a step toward his maker, challenging her.

Older and stronger, Anne-Louise would win any physical battle. Cerissa's anger toward Henry melted a little—his willingness to protect her, to defy his maker, to take a beating for his defiance, thawed her heart.

But this wouldn't be solved through violence. Cerissa kept her aura directed at Anne-Louise.

Anne-Louise gave a little chuff, a puff of air like the sound a tiger makes. "You might as well come in." She gestured at Rolf's house. "I don't plan on providing Rolf with his night's entertainment. He has his spy telescope trained on us."

Cerissa nodded politely and rose. Henry stepped aside to allow her to enter, but he followed closely on her heels, shutting the door behind them.

They walked through the entryway into a small parlor. A blue velvet settee, framed in carved wood, stood opposite two chairs, with an oval coffee table between them, periwinkle flowers hand-painted on its surface and coated in a shiny varnish.

Cerissa raised an eyebrow. Would the delicate furniture survive the meeting?

Henry stood next to her, glaring at Anne-Louise, his chest thrust forward, his fists clenched at his sides. The look of challenge he gave was unmistakable. He was prepared to fight to the death to protect his mate.

Then he dropped his gaze and stepped back.

Cerissa's heart fluttered—he was honoring her request, trusting her, giving her a chance to work things out with the countess.

Anne-Louise gave a dismissive shrug and stepped gracefully through the room to one end of the settee. Lounging back onto an embroidered pillow, she made a show of spreading her full white skirt so it draped around her.

Cerissa waited for Anne-Louise to finish posing, and then perched on the opposite end of the settee, leaving Henry to take one of the chairs. Her father's mother used to say in Hindi: *If you live on the river, befriend the crocodile.* But how to befriend this particular crocodile? The only thing they had in common was Henry.

"Tell me about—" Cerissa began in French.

Anne-Louise motioned for Cerissa to stop. "Speak English," she said. "I want him to understand what we are saying."

Cerissa nodded. "Tell me about yourself, countess."

"Aren't you here to talk about Enrique?" Anne-Louise asked, her English betraying a French lilt. "To talk me out of taking him back to New York?"

"We can talk about him later." Cerissa sat with her back straight, her hands folded in her lap, giving her best imitation of being harmless, keeping her aura pouring out to enfold Anne-Louise. "I'm interested in learning about you and your life. Leopold told me you were married to Count de Jouy and became vampire after he died."

Anne-Louise narrowed her eyes. "Why would you want to know more about me?"

"We should get to know each other, since I'll be joining Henry in New York." Cerissa kept her voice calm, a friendly smile plastered on her face.

"And what leads you to believe you're welcome to join him?"

"I'm his mate."

"I don't care." Anne-Louise waved her hand like a beauty queen on a parade float. "There is no room for you in my apartments."

"I'm sure Leopold will make a guest room available for me. What I can't figure out is why you're trying to separate us."

"You think I'm jealous of you?" Anne-Louise asked with a disdainful laugh. "If I wanted him, you wouldn't be able to keep him from my bed. He's only with you because I refuse him."

Yeah, in a pig's eye. If antipsychotics worked on vampires, I'd write you a prescription for a year's supply.

"Why don't you tell us what this is really about?" Cerissa asked, meeting her gaze.

Anne-Louise turned briefly to glance at Henry. "I don't have to explain myself to you. I'm his maker—that is reason enough."

Cerissa looked down at the bracelet on her wrist, and an idea rose in her mind. Anne-Louise had started their conversation wanting to talk about Henry. So let her. "What was he like when you first met him?"

Anne-Louise sat back, seemingly startled by the question. "Enrique? Such a serious young man. Did he tell you how he came to be at the brothel? He was waiting for his bride's ship to come in."

"He told me about it."

"He did? He was honest with you? How refreshing." Anne-Louise laughed, a high sound, like the tinkling of glass chimes. "It was such a spontaneous decision to turn him. He was so beautiful, and we were so good in bed together, I wanted to keep him to myself. He has never forgiven me for it, even though he still loves me."

Really? Did he love Anne-Louise? Or was it hostage syndrome? As a fledgling vampire, he needed protection—he had no one else to turn to.

Cerissa looked over at Henry. He sat still as ice, his face a mask, his eyes focused on his fingernails.

The countess turned in Henry's direction as well. "He must love you very much to agree to sit through this."

"And I love him." She tugged at the moonstone bracelet, turning it on her wrist. "I would hope to have your blessing."

"You are *arrogonte*, aren't you? Why should I give it?"

"Because I'm no threat to you."

Anne-Louise's eyes bloomed with fire. "Of course you're no threat to me."

Cerissa inclined her head in a slight bow, conceding the point. "It would make him happy to know there is peace between us. Especially since I'll be with him in New York."

"You think I care about his happiness?"

"Yes, I do." She rotated the bracelet one more time, before releasing it, letting it hang naturally. "I have no intention of interfering in your claim on his blood so long as you respect my position—he has promised to be faithful to me."

Anne-Louise laughed sarcastically. "He has?"

"He has. I have spoken at length to Leopold about this."

With Henry's permission, Cerissa had phoned Leopold and, after he swore to keep it confidential, told him about Henry's situation with Anne-Louise.

"According to Leopold, there are rules making it possible to live peacefully with the situation, and one of those rules is I go where Henry goes."

"You are very much like Enrique. Always speaking of rules. Always making rules. One of the reasons I had to get away from him." The countess thrust her nose in the air. "Perhaps you will be good for him. It will let him see what it's like to be on the other side of someone's rules."

Cerissa tried not to smile. "One thing puzzles me. Why do you want Henry in New York? Rick will not be happy."

"How do you know of Rick?"

"Through Leopold."

"Does no one respect my privacy?" Anne-Louise said angrily. "If I want Henry at my side, Rick will have to live with it."

"And why do you want Henry at your side?"

Anne-Louise glanced back to Henry. *"Pour le protéger,"* she whispered so softly that the words were like wind in the trees.

Cerissa's jaw dropped. "To protect him from what?"

"From whoever is trying to kill him."

"But Blanche is dead. No one is trying to kill him."

Cerissa wasn't sure she believed her own words, but it didn't matter. She was in the best position to protect Henry. She had to use whatever persuasion might work to keep him here.

Anne-Louise looked unconvinced. "Tig called Rick, asking questions."

"I'm sure Tig is just being thorough. The council announced the matter was closed. Besides, taking Henry to New York is not the way to protect him. If there is still a threat, the killer may be based in New York. He's safer here."

"He will stay in my apartment and not leave. Much safer still."

"But the Collective would have to approve Henry's residency. Given Henry and Leopold's history, I can guarantee this: Leopold will vote no on any request to allow Henry to live in your apartment. Unless you plan on moving out of the Collective, Henry cannot stay as a guest for more than a few weeks."

"Maybe I'll put him in a hotel near the Collective. That way, I can keep him there longer."

"Surrounded by strangers? With maids who have the key to his room? You're not making him safer."

Anne-Louise gave Cerissa an appraising look. "You are not at all like Erin."

"And you are more beautiful than I could have imagined."

Anne-Louise glanced in Henry's direction again, her face softening. "You believe he's safer here?"

"I do."

Anne-Louise angled her head, her face dropping all expression. "And what would Leopold be willing to give me to let Henry stay here?"

Cerissa dialed her charm back to zero. She couldn't use her aura to seal the deal. The risk of buyer's remorse was too great.

But she wasn't above using bribery. "Leopold mentioned something about an application to the Collective's board—you want to remodel your apartment and expand into an adjacent empty apartment?"

"Leopold has opposed my application."

"Leopold is willing to drop his opposition, and abstain from the vote, if you agree to limit your visits with Henry to twice a year, a maximum of one night each visit, unless Henry wishes to stay longer. Leopold needs me here in Sierra Escondida, not in New York."

"Leopold thinks he can buy me off so cheaply? I have the right to keep Henry at my side."

"Not without me there, too," Cerissa said, shaking her head. "And one other thing. The Hill has certain protocols in place. When a vampire donates blood, they use a wrist."

"Why should I care?"

"This is Henry's home, and their laws apply."

"He would never complain to his council because he doesn't want them knowing."

"All these years you've never told anyone either. You must have your own reasons for keeping this private." Cerissa rubbed one of the moonstones on her bracelet. Calling Anne-Louise's bluff was risky, but it had to be done. "Perhaps you don't want your current lover to hear how you indulge in neck bites—such an intimate space to invade on a former lover."

"*Merde*," Anne-Louise whispered. "Well, if you want a deal with me, Leopold must vote in favor of expanding my apartment, not just abstain."

"Done. You'll have his vote of approval." Leopold still owed Cerissa for extorting money from Henry—this would make them even. Then another idea occurred to her. "If you want, I could ship Henry's blood to you. You wouldn't have to come here."

The corner of Anne-Louise's lip turned up a in a snarl. "Don't push your luck, little girl."

"I thought it would save you time—"

"Then think again," she snapped. "I want fresh blood."

Cerissa held up her hands. "All right, all right, but the other terms…"

Anne-Louise brushed her hand across her skirt, smoothing out some imaginary wrinkle, and then looked at Cerissa, her eyes narrowing. "If I give my agreement, Tig had better keep him safe."

"She has so far. And I won't let anyone harm him either."

"As if a vampire needs a mortal to protect him."

Cerissa clenched her jaw. She'd already saved Henry from death—three times. She took a breath. "There is one other thing I'm curious about. Why do you stay here? I have to be blunt—Rolf and I are not on the best of terms."

"That Rolf can be a nasty one, can't he? Always acting so superior. You'd think he was the first vampire ever made." Anne-Louise punctuated her point with a chuff in the direction of Rolf's house. "But where would you suggest I stay? The last time I was here, before Erin left him, I stayed at a dreadful hotel in Mordida. Rolf offered me the use of his guest house this time." She brought her hand to her mouth and squinted, like something still bothered her. "Then again, maybe Enrique should come to New York for a week or two. To be sure no one is after him."

Cerissa's pulse sped up, panic seeping through the cracks in her composure. "Don't you want to expand your apartment? Leopold will only agree if you let Henry stay here."

"I will talk to Leopold myself," Anne-Louise said, the corners of her mouth forming a sly smile, a look of superiority on her face. "Now that I know what's on the table, I don't need his envoy to make the bargain."

CHAPTER 26

Damn. Without her aura, the deal was falling apart. Cerissa had nothing else to offer, and turned to Henry, plastering an expression of *what do I do now* on her face.

The slightly glazed look drained from his eyes, and he studied his fingernails again. "Anne-Louise, there is something else you want."

"My own room at your house?"

His eyes flashed black. "You will not be getting that. But I'm prepared to make another offer, to sweeten Cerissa's proposal."

"And what might that be?"

"We could build a house on my property for you to stay at when you visit here. A *small* house." His gaze stayed glued to his fingernails.

Cerissa's eyes widened. He'd be willing to do that to remain here with her?

Anne-Louise scowled. "Your mate would agree to this?"

Cerissa slowly nodded. "It's better than being under Rolf's nose."

"So, my dear, you follow the old Machiavelli adage—'Keep your friends close, and your enemies closer.'"

"You are not my enemy."

"That has yet to be seen. I may give you my blessing, but I'm not surrendering him to you. He will still come to me three times a year."

"Two times," Cerissa corrected her. "And wrist bites only."

Anne-Louise smiled smugly. "As you say, he can always *choose* to visit more often. And if he built a house for me, it would be more convenient for me when I'm here."

Cerissa inclined her head. Not to mention it would keep their arrangement private, which would make Henry happy too.

"Fine," Anne-Louise said. "Enjoy him. You may have better luck taming him than I did."

"Oh, I don't believe he needs taming," Cerissa said, a slight grin forming as she recalled their game of chase in the pool and what happened afterward. "I rather like his wildness."

Henry cleared his throat and Cerissa looked over at him. He appeared less than pleased. Whatever had possessed her to be so bold?

"One other thing," Henry said, his gaze locking on Anne-Louise's eyes. "In addition to the terms Cerissa laid out, since the guest house will be on my property, it will be under my rules."

"Your rules?" Anne-Louise said. "Whatever do you mean?"

"You will show both Cerissa and me the respect we deserve," he said sternly. "You'll give us privacy. You won't do anything to interfere with our relationship." Henry's gaze returned to his fingernails. "And I have the right to add to those rules."

Anne-Louise frowned and gave a miffed sound. "*Mon Dieu*, I'm not sure who's getting the worse end of this deal, but all right, I'll agree to Henry's rules when, and only when, I'm residing at his guest house."

Cerissa would rather have that promise in force at all times, but for now, it was the best she could hope for. "Why don't we go over there tonight to select the location, since you're leaving this morning?"

The Viper was a two-seater, so Cerissa asked Karen to drive her back to Henry's, arriving after Henry and Anne-Louise. Bidding Karen goodbye, she caught up with Henry and slipped her arm around him as they walked toward the wooded area. Henry put an arm around her, and Anne-Louise walked by his side, not touching him.

Good. We aren't going to be locked in battle over this.

It was a five-minute walk along a dirt path to the remote uncultivated area to the east of Henry's house, nearer to the Hill's wall. Anne-Louise quickly picked a location and decided she wanted her house to face southwest, so she could see the moon rise from the backyard patio.

Henry's existing pool house—in the opposite direction—was connected to his house by an underground passageway. Cerissa suspected the last thing he wanted was Anne-Louise appearing unexpectedly from the basement, which was why he hadn't suggested his maker stay there.

When they were through, Cerissa said goodnight and kissed Anne-

Louise goodbye on both cheeks, wishing her a safe journey back to New York, and gave Henry a closed-lipped but unhurried kiss.

"Take your time," she told him, squeezing his arm affectionately. "Visit with Anne-Louise."

"Are you sure?"

"Absolutely." After the way she'd accused him of cheating on her, she wanted him to know she trusted him. "If you get back late, I'll see you tomorrow evening."

Henry stood at the edge of the woods, watching Cerissa return to the house, his respect for her deepening. She'd gone into the lion's den and come out unscathed—Anne-Louise hadn't even raised a paw to hurt her.

And working together, they'd accomplished something he hadn't been able to do alone.

"You may finally have chosen well," Anne-Louise said, breaking the silence.

He looked at her in the moonlight. She hadn't changed at all from the night she killed him.

After all these years, how did he really feel about his maker? He had held his silence when Anne-Louise declared he still loved her. He didn't want to break Cerissa's rhythm—the negotiations were going too well at that point.

During his early years as a vampire, he had been under his maker's spell. And then she'd do something so infuriating that he swore he'd never let her get close to him again. She had a way of tweaking his pride for the sheer pleasure it gave her, as if she was compelled to demonstrate she was the boss of him.

In an abstract way, he could step back and see the allure that had first enticed him to choose her in the brothel. But now, it was just an echo of a memory. If the bond hadn't tied him to her, would he have ceased all contact with her? Or would they have found a new respect as equals, and become friends?

With their history, he wasn't sure it was possible.

Anne-Louise motioned toward the Viper. "Shall we?" she asked.

He took her back to Rolf's, taking his time in returning. He even managed to hold a civil conversation with her about the latest New York gossip until she dismissed him.

Dawn was two hours away when he returned home. The light was still on in the master bedroom. Had Cerissa waited for him rather than returning to Gaea's? The door was open, but he knocked anyway.

"Come in," she said. She was lying on top of the bedspread, reading. She had changed into yoga pants and a t-shirt.

He kicked off his shoes and stretched out on the bed next to her. "No more lies," he said, taking her hand in his. "I will never hide the truth from you again."

She squeezed his hand. "Thank you, Henry."

He pulled her closer and pressed his lips gently to hers. How could she forgive him so easily? He couldn't bear to look in her eyes, so he rolled onto his back.

"I don't know what to think," he said, talking to the ceiling. He folded his arms across his stomach and crossed his legs at the ankles—the position he slept in during the day. "I don't see how you can accept the situation with Anne-Louise so easily."

Her hand brushed along his sleeve. "Then don't."

"Don't what?"

"Don't think about it. Just let it be. We've reached a friendly solution. Don't overthink it."

"But aren't you jealous?"

"I trust you."

"After tonight, I don't understand how you can."

"Maybe with time you will."

He continued to stare at the ceiling. He had something he needed to say, but finding the right words was difficult.

He turned to look at her. "Anne-Louise was wrong, you know. I don't still love her. If I ever did."

She patted his arm. "She said it to rattle me."

"I still don't see how you can accept all this."

"Henry, you've been a part of Anne-Louise's life for close to two hundred years, yet you promised to be faithful to me. Should I assume you lied?"

"No."

"Then you love me."

"Yes."

"So, where's the problem?"

"I wouldn't be as understanding if you remained close to an ex-lover."

That's an understatement.

She looked at Henry lying next to her. His gaze was once again focused on the ceiling. "In a hundred years," she began, "I'll have to find someone with whom I can have a child. I expect you to be as understanding then."

Henry closed his eyes. "I don't want to think about a hundred years from now. My own years seem to be weighing heavily on me tonight."

"Why don't you roll over? You look like you could use a back rub."

He pulled off his shirt and rolled onto his stomach. She took the massage oil bottle out of the nightstand drawer and, straddling him, worked the unguent into his shoulders, its jasmine scent rising as she rubbed. His tight muscles relaxed under her fingertips.

Her anger over his earlier behavior had ebbed. He wasn't used to thinking of his mate as an equal and a partner. It would take time for him to adjust, to change his ways.

But he had already changed a little bit. He had trusted her to negotiate on their behalf, first with Leopold, and then with Anne-Louise. That was a lot of control for him to give up, and that was all she needed for now.

His back glistened with oil. She ran a finger down his slick skin, enjoying the sight of his naked back, his large deltoids rippling under her touch, the fascia loosening as she worked along his spine. She stopped at his waistline. She didn't want to ruin his beige slacks with oil.

She slid off him and he rose without warning, grabbing her and rolling her onto her back. Laughing, she managed to keep the bottle upright despite his sudden attack.

"Careful, Henry, or you'll spill oil on the bedspread."

"Then I will buy you a new bedspread." He took the bottle from her hand and stretched across her to place it on the bedside table, displaying his well-muscled chest. "There, now the bed is safe but you are not."

He kissed her, pinning her wrists above her head, tightly holding them together in one hand.

Giggling, she wiggled to free herself. He rolled on top of her and his body held her down, her movement rubbing his hard length against the sweet spot through her thin yoga pants.

His soft lips caressed her jaw line, her neck, her collarbone. He stopped there and rose to look at her, his deep brown eyes serious.

"For now, you are mine. All mine."

"Yes, Henry. I'm all yours."

His free hand snaked under her t-shirt. She let out a gasp when he rolled her nipple between his fingers.

Raising her head, she caught his lower lip, sucking it into her mouth, feasting on the tender flesh, scraping her teeth across it.

He growled. Lust shot through her at the sound. A heated flurry of motion followed. They flung their clothes off the bed, their naked bodies coming together.

Lying limp in his arms afterward, she relived the thrill she felt when he fed on her blood. And then a small thought rose unbidden, disrupting her happiness.

Did he wish she could feed on him like Anne-Louise did? Biting him was one thing Cerissa could never do; her allergy to vampire blood made it impossible.

She touched his neck. Her finger traced the spot where Anne-Louise's mark had been.

The image of Anne-Louise's lips on any part of his body, even his wrist, caused Cerissa's jaw to tighten, and the hair on the back of her neck to rise.

She didn't want to admit it. She thought she'd let go of the feeling when she forgave him. But maybe—just maybe—she felt a little jealous after all.

CHAPTER 27

TIG'S HOUSE—THE NEXT NIGHT AT SUNSET

Tig sat up in her sleeping room and stretched. The sun had only just set, her eyes barely open. She looked at the bare wall across from the small bed. Jayden had urged her to paint the walls, decorate the room, but it seemed ridiculous. She only slept here.

What was that noise? A knock?

She stood and unlocked the three deadbolts on her room's steel door, letting herself into the hallway of their house, surprised to find Jayden waiting for her on the other side. He offered her a tall glass of warmed blood. She drank it and followed him into his bedroom.

Perhaps she shouldn't have been surprised. His time away in San Diego had left them both hungry for each other, and they had yet to satisfy their hunger in full.

He dozed off after they finished making love. She slid out of bed, trying not to disturb him, and pulled the sheet over his naked butt, sad to see it covered.

Jayden's mood had improved since he found the flyer last night. She had checked it for fingerprints—nothing. She'd even asked around, but no one could identify the asshole who distributed it.

She wished she could do more to make Jayden feel better, but she had no time. There was less than an hour before her appointment with the town attorney, a meeting to discuss renewing her contract. Salary negotiations were one of the more modern rituals the town observed. She hated the whole thing. The council should pay her what she was worth.

She turned on the shower and stepped under the spray. The timing of tonight's meeting couldn't be worse. In spite of their public stance, they knew she had yet to catch Blanche's co-conspirators.

As a trained mercenary, she'd never had time to accumulate possessions, the result of being on the move constantly. A change of clothes, a daytime resting place, and a willing source of blood—or an unwilling source, if push came to shove—were all she needed.

She had been paid in gold or jewels for that work and had a decent nest egg spread out among various European safe deposit boxes. Converting it to currency and bringing it into the states meant sacrificing a percentage to taxes. She hadn't needed to yet. The Hill had waived her buy-in fee as long as she remained under contract to the town.

The lease on their house alone ate up a third of her salary. And on the Hill, money mattered. She needed baskets full to maintain the lifestyle or to change communities. The average buy-in price was over five million dollars, and that was just to get through the door. If she ever wanted to change communities, and not be a hired hand for the rest of her existence, she needed a serious bankroll, much more than she currently had squirreled away.

She stepped out of the shower and wiped the steam off the mirror. Staring back at her was the face of her kinswomen, the people who spoke

Maa. The base makeup she applied matched the bluish undertone of her black skin. She used a peach lipstick on her thin lips, selecting the pale color because it looked more professional than fuchsia. After applying some oil to her short, kinky hair, and fluffing it with a pick, she changed into her dark blue dress uniform with matching tie and was ready to go.

She parked outside Jose's Cantina. The tasteful neon light announced the owner's name. She had never met Jose—he'd died many years before she joined the community. When the homeowners association built the new country club, old-timers raised a ruckus, protesting the demolition of Jose's. Ultimately, they compromised and built the new country club around the bar. The town attorney had insisted they locate his office at the country club, down the hall from Jose's. He was there more often than he was at town hall.

She entered the bar and strode past one group of residents. A cutthroat game of poker was in progress. Rolf, along with several regulars, tossed chips into the pot, and he smirked in her direction. As vice mayor, he knew why she was there to meet Marcus.

The door to the private conference room where Marcus waited was opened. Some of the younger mortals on the Hill thought Marcus bore a striking resemblance to a young Bradley Cooper, his dishwater-blonde hair slightly long and combed back. He had a flair for style, his clothes always fashionable for the times.

He sat at the table, smoothing out his perfectly trimmed mustache with two fingers. Tig had seen the handlebar mustache he died with only once, at an emergency council meeting, one called on such short notice that he had no time to trim it into a more modern look.

After they exchanged a few pleasantries, she placed her phone in record mode and asked, "Before we get started, do you mind answering a few questions about Oscar?"

"Oscar who?"

Why was he being coy? He had to know who she meant. "Oscar Nolan. I've read the file," Tig said. "I know you turned him in in the late 1800s, right before the town was incorporated, and against the advice of the other founders."

"Then you know there's no love lost between us."

"If that's true, then why did you stop opposing his applications?"

Marcus tugged at the corner of his mustache. "Conflict of interest. In this era everyone is concerned about the *appearance* of conflicts, so I thought it better to abstain."

"Then you don't want him to return to the community?"

"Absolutely not." He tugged on his mustache again. "Now can we focus on the real reason we're here?"

Hmm. Something bothered him about discussing Oscar. She'd seen him tug at his mustache like that when stressed—it was his tell. But his reaction could just be the bad blood of ex-lovers.

"One more question: any reason Oscar might have it in for Yacov or Henry?"

"Aside from voting against his application, which is why I assume you're asking. The answer is no. Now is that all?"

"For now," she said, touching the "stop recording" button on her phone and returning it to her belt clip.

He withdrew a black binder from his briefcase and set it on the table. "I've looked over your proposal for a new contract. I must say, you're asking for too much."

"Let's not kid ourselves, Marcus. The town can afford it. Between sales and property taxes, we are one of the wealthiest cities per capita. You have very low overhead. No schools to support, no social services. The town has the money."

"It's not the money alone." He handed her a list of police chiefs in the state and their annual salaries. "We don't want to draw attention to ourselves. Paying our police chief a high salary would put media attention on our town."

"People squawk about what public servants make," she said, flapping the list in his direction, "yet when they want something from us, they want it now—they don't care if we're understaffed."

"Look, our residents don't begrudge what you're paid. But paying more—"

"When the council first asked me to come here, I named an outlandish fee. You know it and I know it. They paid it without blinking, because you need someone who understands the vampire mind and hasn't succumbed to it. Besides, my extra duties policing our neighboring cities for unlawful vampire activities are outside the scope of a normal police chief's job. I should be compensated well for my work."

"With the press monitoring public employee salaries, we can't get away with it."

She leaned toward him, her eyes narrowing. "There are ways to do this. The homeowners association can pay me for my extra services. Consider it my day job," she said, with a tight grin. "And the council can double Jayden's salary and relieve me of my support obligations—the town can fund his trust account."

"Won't work," Marcus said, shaking his head. "Each of us is responsible for our mate's trust account."

"What does it matter if the money comes directly from my bank account or is paid to Jayden's trust account by the council in lieu of paying it directly to me? Jayden would still have the funds should our relationship end before he dies."

Marcus tugged at the corner of his mustache. "The council isn't convinced the job is worth what you're asking."

"Not worth it? I have four full-time police officers under my command on the Hill, including Jayden. I have all the administrative headaches of supervising these mortals, and I have to listen to complaints from their vampires if I need them to work overtime. Plus I supervise the mortal police officers who work for our police substation in the business district—all while keeping them from guessing what we are. As you can imagine, it isn't always easy."

"Tig, I—"

She rapped her knuckles on the table. *No, he doesn't get to interrupt.* "Not to mention I have excellent relations with the chief of police in Mordida. The mutual aid agreement I negotiated gives us access to their larger crime lab. With what I'm saving the town, I'm well worth what I'm asking."

Marcus didn't reply when she stopped. It didn't matter; she wasn't backing down. "So who would you get to replace me? Zeke Cannon is fairly reliable as a reserve officer, but given his extracurricular activities, are you sure you want him running your police department? The only reason he's still on the police force is because he agreed never to take black op assignments within our jurisdiction. Who else is there? Rolf has made it clear he doesn't want my job. Liza doesn't want it either—she likes her free time too much. I even suggested we share the job. She's refused."

Marcus sat back in this chair. "I must be frank with you. The council is considering bringing in someone who's more experienced with police investigations."

"They're what?" Her fist banged down, almost cracking the maple table.

He raised his hands. "Take it easy."

Yeah, she'd take it easy, right after she told them all to fuck off.

"We understand you were hired for your military skills," he continued. "The council made you chief of police to use up your contract after the treaty was signed. They've kept you on because the police work hasn't been demanding, and we couldn't be sure there wouldn't be future threats of war, but forty-five years have passed since the treaty was signed. Some are afraid you haven't made the transition to civilian life well. With the attacks on Yacov and Henry—well, they want to bring in someone more experienced with this sort of thing."

She sat there seething. She'd tolerated their politics all these years, but this was too much. "First they tell me to keep the investigation quiet, now they want to replace me because they aren't satisfied with my progress. Who? Tell me who on the council is pushing this."

"I can't discuss with you what happens in closed session."

She leaned forward, locking eyes with him. "A name. Who's leading the charge to get rid of me? You aren't stupid. The assassin could be part of our community."

He broke eye contact first. "I can tell you it isn't the mayor. You work closely with him, and I wouldn't want you—"

"Rolf. It's Rolf Müller, isn't it? With Frédéric backing him?"

"Now, Tig."

"That's Chief Anderson, Mr. Town Attorney." Tig restrained her desire to lunge across the table and snap his neck. It wouldn't kill him, but it would shut him up. "You know I'm qualified to lead this investigation. If it isn't Rolf pushing this, who is it?"

"I'll get back to you after the next council meeting. That's all I can say." He stood, indicating the meeting was over.

She grabbed the proposal binder. Waving it in his face, she said, "If you don't want me leaving for another community, you'll pay it."

She threw the binder on the table and stormed out, closing the door behind her, and then stopped. She had to get her rage under control before she returned through Jose's Cantina. She wanted to see how Rolf reacted when she came through—she wouldn't slink out through the country club exit. She wouldn't give him the satisfaction.

Deep breath. Exhale. Calm down. There. Keep it easy.

She walked into Jose's. The poker game was still going. They were all intensely studying their cards, as if vampire powers included the ability to change a bad hand to a good one. Too bad it didn't work that way.

When Tig strode past Rolf, he didn't even glance her way.

She drove back to the police station. The extra money she wanted would hardly compensate for all the politics she put up with. She was tired of kissing the mayor's ass. Winston could be a pompous fool at times, even for a vampire. If she had to tolerate their idiocy, the council should pay her handsomely for her trouble.

Tig parked the police van and pounded her fist on the steering wheel. *Careful*, or she'd break the damn thing. *Think.* Had it all been a bargaining tactic? Were they trying to make her believe she was replaceable so she'd take less? *Damn it!* She slapped her palm on the dashboard. This was a stupid game for them to play, not with an assassin still on the loose.

She charged into the police station, grabbing the mail on her clerk's desk. She slammed her office door behind her, thumped into her desk chair, and rifled through the mail. Nothing worth her attention. She threw it aside. It hit the basket and slid out, scattering across the floor. Someone else could pick it up tomorrow. They didn't pay her enough to do it herself.

She opened the file on the shootings. Bring in an expert investigator, would they? She would show them. She'd solve this, and Rolf and Frédéric had just moved to the top of her list. She took a deep breath, letting the anger flow out of her with each exhale. Anger clouded her brain—it was good for fire in the belly, but she needed a cool mind to piece together this puzzle.

Start with Rolf. Besides her suspicions, what evidence did she have he might be the mastermind? So far, she hadn't found any connection between Rolf and Blanche.

She dug out the autopsy report on the shooter from the first attack on Henry. They'd been horseback riding on some of the trails by Rolf's vineyard when the sniper shot at Henry from the bushes and hit Cerissa instead. Tig had fired back, getting the sniper in his gun arm, but Rolf's bullet was the kill shot.

Had he done it to make sure the shooter wouldn't be alive to identify him? Not enough to hang him with. But his trips to San Diego—why did he go there so frequently? He could have a perfectly good reason having nothing to do with the attacks, but Tig had yet to hear it.

Marcus's comment about hiring someone new kept circling through her mind, like a hyena chasing its tail. She eased back in her chair, the germ of an idea forming. Instead of the council hiring someone to "help" her, she could hire someone—someone to follow Rolf. She couldn't charge it to her department's budget. It had to come from her pocket. Otherwise, Rolf would find out and scream retaliation.

Wait. She had some asset forfeiture money in the slush fund. The money came through joint police operations, when assets were seized and sold in drug cases. Her department had helped out and been cut in on their share, and she could allocate the money any way she saw fit—it wasn't reported as part of her budget. She didn't have to use her own money after all.

A short time later, Tig hung up the phone and smiled to herself. Help was on its way—her idea of help, not Rolf's. Her comrade Ufa would arrive in five nights.

Now, what about Frédéric? Maude wasn't his motive—it would be too inconsistent with his current politics—but she might as well check his travel permits against the gate logs and see if they matched up, make sure he was returning each night and not making any unpermitted trips or sleeping elsewhere during the day.

She had already checked the gate logs for the nights of the Cutter's kills to see who was off the Hill on those nights. Now, she would expand her research of Frédéric's travel, see where he was when other key events occurred.

Come to think about it, she needed to do the same for Rolf. Compare Rolf's travel permits for the last three months against the gate logs. And maybe she should include Marcus on the list.

No, being an ass in negotiations wasn't a reason to investigate someone. That was her anger talking.

She left a note for Maggie, asking her records clerk to do the research on Rolf and Frédéric, and strode out the door. She wanted all the facts neatly correlated before she asked them why they were gone each night of the Cutter's killings, so they couldn't wiggle out.

She still had to deal with the council's stupidity over her contract. Her dress uniform immaculate, her cap in hand, she marched the short distance to the mayor's office and entered without knocking. She resisted the urge to slam the door after her.

Winston looked up from his desk, a single eyebrow questioning her presence. When she didn't move, he gestured toward the guest chair.

Ramrod straight, she took the seat and waited for him to begin the conversation.

"What can I do for you, chief?" the mayor asked. "A little early for our weekly meeting. Have you had a break in the case?"

"Not yet. Captain Johnson recently found out the prison's records had been hacked, which is why we hadn't learned about the guard's involvement before he was killed."

"Sounds like a good lead. Anything else?"

"I met with the town attorney this evening."

"Oh, that." He leaned back in his chair, crossing his hands over his substantial stomach. "Chief, you have to understand. The council is on edge. They're afraid our strategy will backfire if we don't catch the real culprit, and soon."

Our strategy? It wasn't *her* strategy. She handed him an envelope. "My letter of resignation. I'm giving six months' notice. When my contract expires, I won't renew it. You should have enough time to find my replacement."

"Now, chief, there's no reason to do anything this drastic. The council just thought we should hire someone to help you with the investigation, behind the scenes, of course—you'd still be in charge." Winston picked up the envelope. "We haven't lost faith in you, my dear. You're an important part of our community. Please, take this back." He held it out to her.

"I've had inquiries from other communities. If you'd prefer, I can resign tonight."

He sat there, holding the envelope out to her. When she didn't take it back, he dropped it on his desk. "Let's take a deep breath, shall we? We weren't going to hire anyone without your approval. We just thought you could use the help."

"Your idea, maybe, but it's not Rolf's. My guess is he has Frédéric's support. If he gets one more vote, he'll have his majority, and he'll bring in his own man. There can't be two generals—I learned that a long time ago."

"Rolf isn't going to bring in his own man. The council won't let him."

"Then I want a vote of confidence from the council."

"There's no reason to—"

"If I'm going to run this investigation, it's time you told the community the truth—Blanche's death didn't close the case. Either you vote, in public, to support me—"

"And if the vote is against you, your contract terminates immediately, leaving us with no one."

"Marcus would never have mentioned it unless the council was serious. I suspect you have candidates already lined up."

"I told them this was a bad idea. I told them. Tig, please. There is no one else in line for your job. Take back your resignation." He slid the envelope closer to her.

"Vote of confidence, now. And if I solve this before the six months are up, I'll stay, but you'll double my salary and benefits. You'll include those terms as part of the vote."

Winston made a noise like a cat choking on a hairball. Sure, it was hard to swallow, but the council had played the game. She dealt it right back at them. Double or nothing.

"Now, Tig, my dear, we can't do that."

"Mr. Mayor, you'll address me by my title. Chief—not 'Tig,' not 'my dear.'" She stood. "And that's my final offer. You have one week to accept." She turned and marched out. She only slightly slammed the door when she left.

CHAPTER 28

HENRY'S HOUSE—TWO NIGHTS LATER

Cerissa glanced out the library window. Henry stood near the gazebo, leaning over a high-quality telescope. Anne-Louise had left a few nights ago, and since then, he'd been sweet and attentive.

Now he was outside behind his house, engrossed with something in the sky. Upon rising, he had fed, immediately unpacked his telescope, and asked Cerissa if she minded waiting while he observed a planet.

No community meetings were scheduled for tonight. No potential investors were in town. She'd been killing time, using the ornate desk in his library to work. Her tablet was open to the most recent lab report on the modified human clones. Her colleagues at the Enclave sent reports on a daily basis—tedious but necessary work.

One clone had a high fever. She wrote back recommending a change in antibiotics, suggesting they isolate it from the others. She didn't want drug-resistant bacteria sweeping through the entire population. It should have been impossible. There should have been no way for one of those bacteria to infiltrate the Enclave. Still, she had to be cautious. They might lose the whole population if she wasn't careful.

She checked the rest of her email, surprised to see one from Anne-

Louise. Henry's maker had obtained a prospectus from Leopold and wanted to make a sizeable investment.

Stunned, Cerissa sat back in her chair. With Anne-Louise's money, they were almost half-way there. Leopold still adamantly refused to allow Henry to invest, and she hadn't pushed the issue further.

How will Henry react? She twined a lock of hair around her finger. *Anne-Louise in, him out. Is that why she did it? To yank Henry's chain?*

The buzz of her phone signaled the arrival of a message from Ari. She read his text and swallowed hard. She had anticipated this, but on top of Anne-Louise's news, his message stared back at her like a storm warning during monsoon season.

She got up and peered through the library window. Henry was still preoccupied with his telescope. She pulled the drapes so he wouldn't notice her absence. After texting Ari back, she took the hall past the kitchen, avoiding the drawing room so Henry wouldn't see her through the glass-paneled French doors, and found Ari waiting on the front porch.

"We can talk in here," she said, leading Ari through the foyer and into the large open kitchen. She took a Coke out of the refrigerator and placed the can on the kitchen table for him, a glass filled with ice next to it.

He popped the tab on the Coke can. "I got called into the Protectors' Assembly and grilled," he said after she took the seat across from him. "Questions like, why is she spending so much time around Henry? Why isn't she wearing her lenses all the time? The gaps I've had to cut out are making them suspicious."

She glanced over her shoulder to make sure they were alone. "What did you tell them?"

"Nothing yet," he said, and took a swig from the can, ignoring the glass. "Kid, you have to get serious about this. Instead, you're sitting here playing house and not thinking about the consequences."

"Hey, that's not true. I've been working hard on my cover—we now have about half the investment dollars we need for the lab."

Using her phone, she pulled up the latest email from Anne-Louise and showed it to him.

"That's not what I meant." He handed the phone back to her. "Your blood bond with Henry is the problem."

"They call it a loyalty bond, not a blood bond."

"I don't care if they call it nirvana, *it's* the problem."

"I know, but I haven't found a solution yet."

"I thought you were making that a priority? Even over the VDM?"

"I…"

"Come on, fess up. You were avoiding it."

"I wouldn't put it that way."

"I would." He took another gulp of his Coke and let out a loud burp. "Well, it's a good thing for you I've put my brilliant mind to figuring it out, then, isn't it? I have a solution, at least partially."

"So? What is it?"

"Drum roll, please."

"Ari!"

"Fine. We need to bring Henry under your protection."

"Wait a minute," she said, her mind racing to figure out the consequences. This sounded so not good. "I can't bring someone under my wings. I'm not a Guardian."

"Yeah, you're a Watcher—"

"But it's more than that—no Lux has ever protected a vampire before."

"Which weighs in your favor, Ciss. When we tell the Protectors about your relationship with him, we have no idea how they'll react. If the deal is done, they can't do anything about it."

"Where did you get the crystal?"

"Better you don't know." He laid the crystal injector on the table in front of her. "Ya gotta do this. I'm thinking of you, kid."

After Ari left, she hurried outside to join Henry by his telescope. He was bent over the eyepiece, the telescope's tripod positioned at the edge of the swan-white gazebo near the pool. Moon-flower vines threaded through the gazebo's latticework of wood.

All the outdoor lights were off, leaving the night sky awash with bright stars. She looked for the North Star, but couldn't find it, and gave up.

Henry was leaning over the telescope. In spite of being upset, she couldn't resist taking a moment to enjoy the view of his butt in tight jeans. A small leather-bound notebook lay on a nearby glass table—in his beautiful old-fashioned handwriting, he kept a log of his observations.

She trailed her fingers along his bent shoulders, waiting for him to take his eye off the eyepiece and acknowledge her presence. "Hello, *cariña*," he finally said, giving her a quick peck before returning to his observations.

She stretched out on one of the cushioned lounge chairs under the gazebo. "Henry, I hate to disturb you, but I need to talk with you about something."

"Hmm," he replied, continuing to adjust the telescope, his arm muscles tightening as he twisted the knob. The tank top he wore gaped at the arm, giving her a peek at his well-chiseled pecs. She'd rather take him upstairs to bed than tell him about Ari's concerns.

Maybe we should wait. Ari's idea is crazy. When the Protectors find out, I'll be in deeper crap than I already am.

She slid off the lounger. "I'll come back later."

She'd almost made it to the French doors when Henry said, "Give me a moment." He paused to adjust the scope again. "There. Come see."

She sighed and returned, taking his place, her eye to the viewfinder. "What am I looking at?"

"There are times when I have fleeting doubts you are what you say you are."

She turned around and stuck her tongue out at him.

"A mature response," he said.

"One you deserved. Are you going to answer my question?"

"Jupiter. Another red spot is forming, a companion to Jupiter's great red spot. The white spots are caused by cyclonic storms. There is still much debate about what causes the red ones."

She stepped away from the telescope. "I can tell you're excited about this viewing. We can talk later."

"We have thirty minutes before the spot is at Jupiter's centerline." He took her hand. "What do you need to discuss?"

"Well," she said, suddenly feeling apprehensive. Best to start small. "My cousin Ari wants to meet you."

"I wondered if I would be allowed to meet your relatives."

"Let's start with Ari." Henry already knew her *pita* had died when she was a small child. And she'd told him all she planned to about her *amma's* lack of interest in her life.

"I assume Ari knows what I am?" he asked.

"Oh yes, but this isn't a social call, I'm afraid. He wants to put you under our protection."

"From whom do I need protection?"

She looked away, focusing on the vine-covered rolling hills in the distance. Why was it so hard to say out loud?

You can do this. Little pieces, bite sized. It's only two words.

"Cerissa, whom do I need protection—"

"Ah, well…"

"Cerissa." He placed his hands firmly on her shoulders, turning her to face him. "Tell me who," he insisted, his eyes almost solid black.

"Ah, the Lux," she squeaked.

"Your people? Why?"

She dipped her chin, avoiding his eyes. "I've explained we have sort of a military structure, haven't I?"

"You haven't explained much," he said impatiently.

"Well, it's not as rigid as a human military, but we have rank, and Ari and I are young, so we're like junior officers. Ari's older than me, so he has higher rank within our classification."

"What classification?"

"We're called Watchers."

"And above you?"

"Messengers, Guardians, and finally the Protectors. Guardians are generals, and the Assembly of Protectors is like Congress. The Assembly listens to the Guardians and decides policy."

His pupils were slowly receding, letting the brown show again. He didn't say anything, so she kept going. "As we grow older, we'll move higher in rank. If we're lucky, we'll become Protectors too, and—"

"Cerissa, why are the Lux a threat to me?"

"Umm...you see...because we don't know the identities of the VDM, my assignment included certain orders. I was forbidden from entering into a relationship with any of the subjects I was observing—intimate or otherwise."

"Otherwise?"

She cringed. "No biting. They didn't know what fang serum would do to me."

Henry rocked on his feet, grabbing the back of a nearby chair to steady himself.

"Don't you think you should have told me this before?" he asked, trying to keep from raising his voice. "Are you in danger from your own people now, for breaking their laws?"

She looked toward the patio flagstone. "Ah, well..."

"You are, aren't you?" *Madre de Dios.* Henry shut his eyes. How could he protect her if she didn't confide in him?

"No, I'm not in trouble—at least, not yet," she said in a rush. "You see, my cousin and I had a small miscommunication. Ari's my supervisor on this project, and he suggested I seduce you, which was a mistake on his part, so he's been protecting me. But he thinks this will fix it—all of it.

That's why he wants to put you under our protection."

"Do you believe I need protection from your people?"

"I don't think so, but you never know what they will do." She rubbed her forehead, like she had a headache. "I'm not explaining this well."

He took her hand and guided her to the lounge chair, sitting down next to her. If he got angry, it would only make it harder for her to tell him the truth. "It's all right, Cerissa. Take your time."

"By putting you under my protection, it also protects me. But it's not without consequences—it's only fair that Ari explain it to you."

Henry's gaze moved heavenward. Could the threat from her people be real? He'd had his doubts about them before.

"What does it entail if I accept this protection?" he asked.

"A small device is implanted, usually in the wrist. It's a tuned crystal."

"Magic? I will have nothing to do with witchcraft."

"Not witchcraft," she said, with a small smile. "You know what an integrated circuit chip is?"

"A component in computers—"

"Integrated circuit chips are made of silicon. Silicon's a crystal. When we developed a, well, a similar technology, we called it a crystal rather than a chip, because it was made of a crystalline material. It's placed under your skin to protect you."

He pursed his lips, pondering the idea for a moment. "I assume Ari will be coming here to meet me?"

"Yes."

"And when does he want to schedule this meeting?"

"You're taking this all rather calmly."

"No one ever tells the whole truth right away," he said, trying to sound patient. "Once I learned you weren't human, I expected to find out more about you as we spent time together."

He hadn't been open with her about Anne-Louise's visit—he was in no position to chastise her for withholding information. Well, maybe a *little* chastisement.

"I must admit, I'm not happy it's taken you this long to tell me," he added.

She looked at her feet again. "I'm sorry."

He sighed and glanced toward the telescope. "So when does Ari want to meet?"

"This evening. He's in Mordida. He didn't give me any notice."

Why did she look so worried? Was there something more she wasn't telling him? He wrapped his arms around her, bringing her in close. "It will be all right, *cariña*."

"I hope so. If I could just make progress finding the VDM and stop whatever war they have planned, the Protectors would back off—"

"Wait. The VDM." He sat back so he could see Cerissa. "After Blanche shot me, she said something. I didn't make the connection, it didn't occur to me until you mentioned 'war' just now. Her scheme, the people she was working for, they had some grander plan to conquer the communities, to pit them against one another and start a war—"

"Does Tig know?"

"I told her about Blanche's comment, but not the VDM. Tig has quietly continued her investigation, trying to find Blanche's cohorts."

"Now it makes sense—why Tig contacted Rick, why she kept investigating despite the council's announcement." Cerissa took her cell phone out of her jeans pocket. "I need to text Ari about this. Should I tell him you've agreed to meet with him about the crystal?"

"Of course." He glanced at his watch. "But can Ari wait until after ten o'clock? Jupiter won't be this close again—this is the best view I'll have all year."

"I'll tell him to arrive at eleven."

"That would be fine. Thank you, *cariña*."

She stood to leave, but he grabbed her about the waist and pulled her onto his lap. "You don't think you get to go without kissing me first, do you?"

He gave her no opportunity to respond. Had Jupiter not been at its apex, he would have made love to her right there on the patio recliner. Instead, he reluctantly brought the kiss to an end.

Her smile made her beautiful eyes seductive. "After Ari leaves, will you return to stargazing?"

"No, the best view will be over."

"Then perhaps we might..." She didn't finish her sentence, and instead brushed a finger against his tank top, circling his areola, tantalizing him with her touch.

"Perhaps we might," he agreed. His lips met hers again. "Until then."

CHAPTER 29

Tig drove past the gates headed toward Mordida, fuming and royally pissed over the Hill's politics. Two nights ago, Marcus had insulted her skills during salary negotiations, and now Méi was being a pain in the ass, demanding Tig do something immediately about the stolen paintings.

Maybe she should lock the doors to the police station and disappear for a week. Get some rest, ignore council politics, and gain a new perspective. Let someone else handle her job for a week. They'd beg her to come back.

Yeah, right. If she did that, she might never return.

She sighed. She wasn't ready to throw in the towel just yet—at least not until the council responded to her demands. And with any luck, one problem would be crossed off her list tonight. The art thief hadn't left behind fingerprints, but the culprit's intelligence ended there. He had posted the paintings for sale on Craigslist.

Real stupid.

Since the burglary, Jayden had monitored pawnshops and online ads, and tonight, they'd hit pay dirt. Using a dummy account, she'd responded to the ad, asking to see the painting in person. The seller agreed to meet her at a Mordida coffee bar tonight.

Only problem was that Méi saw the same ad, which prompted the nasty phone call. Tig had resisted the urge to tell the Founder to go fuck herself. But only barely.

What Méi didn't know was Tig was already on top of it. Wearing plain clothes—black slacks, and an off-the-shoulder tan knit pullover—Tig looked like a hipster, good enough for undercover work. She drove an electric-blue Mercedes Roadster she'd borrowed from Liza, with Jayden and Liza following in an unmarked police car.

Had she not been so irritated, Tig might have enjoyed driving the powerful convertible. Maybe she'd borrow it from Liza on date night and take Jayden for a scenic drive.

The coffee bar was a half block from Méi's gallery. Was the perp that stupid? Tig parked out front and then sized him up in the five steps it took her to get from the door to his table. He sat with the painting wrapped in butcher paper, propped on a chair. He didn't look the type—he looked like a skinny chipmunk, and based on his yellow buckteeth, she suspected he'd stolen the painting to pay for drugs.

"Did you place an ad?" she asked the chipmunk.

"Yeah. You wanna buy a painting?"

Tig pointed to the wrapped object. "May I see it?"

"You got cash? Only gonna unwrap it if you got cash."

She removed her wallet from her pants pocket and took out four hundred dollars, laying the bills out on the table. He reached over to the painting, his hand shaking, and lifted the tape at one end, folding back the paper revealing Méi's signature—three Chinese characters. That was all Tig needed for probable cause. She flipped her wallet around, revealing her badge.

"You're under arrest," she told him.

The chipmunk rocketed to his feet, his wooden chair making a loud *thunk* as it hit the tile floor. He took two steps before she had him. In one smooth move, she tripped him, pinned him to the ground, and slipped on the handcuffs.

Liza and Jayden were through the door before the coffee bar patrons got in her way.

"We're police, everything's okay," Liza said, holding her badge high, both her and Jayden dressed in their dark blue patrol uniforms. "This man is under arrest on suspicion of burglary and selling stolen property." Liza stopped next to Tig, still speaking to the crowd. "We'll have him out of here quickly, and you can go back to enjoying your coffee."

Pulling the chipmunk off the floor, Tig marched him to the unmarked police car, while Jayden and Liza followed with the painting and the money. Tig bent him over the hood of the car and searched him. No weapons, but she found his wallet.

"Take Liza's Roadster," she told Jayden, tossing him the keys. "Write a search warrant and get it signed by a judge." Shaking the guy, she shoved his driver's license in front of his nose. "You still live there, chipmunk?" He bobbed his head, looking too frightened to speak. Tig passed the driver's license over to Jayden. "Search his home. See if you can find the other painting and the stuff missing from Razi's office."

"Roger that, chief," Jayden said. He placed the painting in the trunk of the police car, shrugged on his leather jacket, grabbed his crime scene kit, and took off in the Roadster.

Liza scowled. "If he scratches it—"

"The town will pay to have it repainted. Now get in and drive us a few blocks away." Tig shoved the chipmunk into the car's back seat and got in next to him. "We're going to have a talk," she told him.

The chipmunk didn't say anything. The back seat shook with his shivering and his anxiety smelled like a sour dishcloth. Liza parked them on a nice, quiet block with a dead streetlight.

"Okay," Tig said, staring at him, "did you steal the paintings?"

"D-don't I get a lawyer?" the chipmunk asked, his voice wavering.

"Maybe later. Right now, you'll answer my questions."

"I don't gotta."

It was times like these that Tig wished vampire powers included the power to compel a perp to talk. Still, she had other ways. Taking his shoulder muscle between her thumb and forefinger, she began to squeeze. She didn't have to squeeze very hard.

"Oww," he squealed, trying to bend away from her. The seatbelt didn't give him much room to move. "I'll talk, stop, owww…."

She let up a little. "Did you steal the paintings?"

"No, ya gotta believe me. I didn't."

"Where is the other painting?"

"My apartment."

"It had better be," Tig said. "If you lie to me, you aren't going to like what happens next."

The chipmunk nodded vigorously.

"Who gave you the paintings?"

"No one. I found them."

"Where?"

"In the trash bin in an alley. I don't steal nothin'. I find stuff, abandoned stuff. I sell it."

"Can you take us to the alley?"

"Ah, I think so."

Following the chipmunk's instructions, they drove to the alley behind Méi's art gallery, a narrow asphalt driveway with service entrances behind each building. The dumpster was half a block away, one of those big six-foot wide metal ones, green with two black rubber flaps to cover the trash.

Should she believe him, or was the chipmunk screwing with her? He could have stolen the paintings and claimed to find them, trying to avoid a burglary rap.

"They were in that there trash bin," he said, pointing with his head because his hands were still cuffed behind him. "I lifted the flap, and they were lying on top."

Tig opened the door. The alley smelled of urine and rotten food. The trash bin sat near a door with "Tony's Italian Ristorante" stenciled on it. Using a nitrile glove, she opened the trash bin's lid—the reek of garlic hit her. She held her breath, took a good look at the restaurant's trash, and saw nothing suspicious. She dropped the lid, got back into the back seat, and closed the door.

"When did you find the paintings?" she asked.

"Jeez, lady, I'm not so good with dates. Maybe a week ago? In the morning? Yeah, it was in the morning."

Tig signaled Liza, who radioed Jayden with the information, and turned back to the chipmunk. "Did you find anything else with the paintings? A photo of a Chinese woman and an African American man?"

"Huh?" he asked, looking surprised by the question.

Tig scowled at him. "What part of English don't you understand?"

"I understand it just fine," he said. "I didn't see no photo. Didn't take no photo. Why would I want someone else's photo, anyway?"

CHAPTER 30

HENRY'S HOUSE—SAME NIGHT

Henry finished his notes on Jupiter, closed his observation book's leather-tooled cover, and went inside to change into something more appropriate for the meeting. When the doorbell rang, he greeted Ari, studying him closely, and could detect no difference between Ari and any ordinary mortal. He even smelled mortal, like Cerissa did.

"You are her cousin?" Henry asked, guiding Ari into the drawing room. Cerissa had gone upstairs, leaving them alone.

"You've got that right. We share a grandmother on our Lux side. Her mother and my father are half-siblings—they each had a different human parent."

"I see."

"What has Cerissa told you about us?"

"Some." Henry offered Ari a chair by the fireplace and sat down across from him in his own leather armchair.

"Okay, it's like this," Ari said, taking the offered seat. "The Lux need humans to breed, and a few millennia ago, our leaders started the Great Experiment to see if our kind could live with a breeder."

"Breeder?"

"A fertile human."

"Before then?"

"You don't want to know. Anyway, in the past, the child of a Lux and human mating would be brought back to the Enclave soon after the child was born. So our leaders wanted to see what would happen if we were raised around humans instead."

"Cerissa told me she was kept in human form during her childhood and raised by her father's family."

"Precisely. But that's not what I'm here to chat about, old boy. Though there is a connection."

"And that is?"

Ari displayed a small black device. It reminded Henry of a stunted magician's wand. In his other hand, Ari held a small gold box. "We've developed technology to prevent our people from hurting a mortal bound to one of us. We couldn't let those we breed with become pawns between our political factions."

Breed with? But vampires were infertile. Henry stared at the wand, blinking rapidly. Should he say something? If Cerissa's wellbeing depended upon it, Ari needed to know.

He took a deep breath. "But I cannot give her children."

"Yeah, she told me. That's what makes this such a radical move. We don't know how the higher-ups will react, but we figure this is our best bet to protect her."

"What do you mean by that? What would your people do to her?"

Ari pursed his lips, looking at Henry long and hard. "Your guess is as good as mine. And with this, we think they won't be able to touch her even if they wanted to."

Ari flipped the lid on the gold box, and Henry looked at the crystals inside. They reminded him of tiny uncut diamonds.

"Virgin crystals," Ari said, and used the wand to capture a crystal.

"How does it work? I mean, how can a small crystal protect her?"

"She told me you were smart," Ari said with a nod. "Each Lux has a similar implant from birth. The crystal implanted in humans is different, but it's recognized by our implants. And it works both ways—it stops breeders from physically hurting any of us, or any of us from hurting them. It wouldn't be fair to leave us open to their violence with no way to defend ourselves."

"I see." If such a thing were available to protect mortals from vampires, Henry would have supported inoculating all of humanity. He didn't trust his own people—or himself. He had stared into the abyss of what he'd become too often to know willpower alone wasn't always enough.

"With this, I wouldn't be able to physically harm her?" Henry asked.

"You'd still be able to, ah"—Ari waved the wand—"you know...."

"Bite. I could still take her blood, but...."

Ari gave him a big, sloppy grin. "I'll adjust it to allow rough sex, including biting. And either of you can give permission to the other to up the ante—I mean, do you ever use a knife to draw blood?"

"There are some rituals...."

"Are they frequent or important? Never mind—I'll adjust for those too. But you couldn't cause any real physical harm—to her, or to any of us. And the same goes from us to you." Ari tossed the little wand in the air like a majorette twirling a baton.

Henry stayed silent, watching him.

"You don't have to decide now," Ari said, catching the falling wand. "Think about it—I can come back when you're ready."

"That isn't necessary," Henry replied. "I have already made up my mind."

Cerissa inched her way back downstairs when she heard Ari leave, using the bannister to steady her wobbly progress. She met Henry in the entryway.

He didn't have to tell her what he'd decided—she already knew.

The crystal would take time to sync to her. While it did, a shrill sound echoed in her head like static from an old-fashioned radio, and her vision blurred, the room reflecting like a fun-house mirror. The lights of the wrought iron chandelier seemed like blinding flares, the red-orange tiles beneath her feet shimmered, creating a hideous double image.

This was her first crystal. She hadn't anticipated how bad it would be.

He held out his forearm, showing her the small mark from the injector. "Ari said it would disappear within a day. For a vampire, it will be gone within the hour."

When she didn't say anything, he looked at her, like he was searching for something. "Are you all right?"

"No," she said, rubbing at her temples. "It's like having a wall thrust between us."

She pulled away and staggered into the drawing room. The noise in her head was deafening. She stopped by the river-stone fireplace with her back to him, resting her head against the rough-hewn mantel, gripping the wood to stay upright.

He followed her. "What do you mean, 'a wall'? The crystal is merely a protective measure—one that works both ways."

He rested a hand on her shoulder. His touch should have been comforting, but it wasn't. She lifted her head and squinted at him, trying to focus on his words. Her gaze wavered, and she gripped the mantel to steady herself.

"Both ways?" she repeated. "I don't understand."

"The crystal protects you from me as well. I still don't fully understand what you are. I've been concerned I might accidentally injure you by taking your blood. My instinctive knowledge of mortals—when to stop without hurting them—doesn't apply to you."

She put her hand to her head, trying to break through the fog surrounding her. Why did he think he might harm her? It didn't make sense. He was always so gentle with her, so careful not to hurt her when he bit.

He took her in his arms. "The crystal also allows me to find you wherever you are. If something happens to you, I could go to you."

"It has its limits. You can flash to where I am, but you're doing it blindly. What if I'm standing in sunlight?"

"Ari has adjusted the programming—I cannot come to you if you are in sunlight."

"Good."

He furrowed his brow. "Why are you not pleased?"

She pushed against his chest, stepping back. "I…I'm just in pain, Henry. I didn't expect it to be like this."

"If it's hurting you, I'll remove it." He drew his knife out of his pocket, flipped it open, and placed the blade point against the mark on his skin.

"Don't," she yelled. She lunged at him, wrapping her fingers around his wrist and knocking the knife away with her other hand. The white noise in her head increased. From the surprised look on his face, he was hearing it too. She released his wrist.

"The noise stopped," he said.

"The crystal takes a while to calibrate to me. While it does, it's not pleasant. That's how I knew…it started…the buzzing noise you heard… started in my head."

She leaned against the mantel again. Her stomach churned, the dizziness making her nauseated.

"The crystal allows me to hear what you are hearing?"

"Not exactly. It's tuning itself to me."

"But it stopped. I don't hear it now."

"We have to be in physical contact for you to hear it—skin on skin, near where the crystal is implanted. Once it's tuned to me, the noise will stop. For the most part, things will be as they were before," she said, rubbing her head futilely to stop the noise.

He stooped to retrieve the knife from the floor, folded the handle, and slid it into his pocket. "If the crystal is causing you pain, why don't you want me to remove it?"

"Ari's right—this is the best strategy we have right now. And the pain will go away with time; the noise will stop."

He took her into his arms again and stroked her back, the noise growing incrementally louder. She wanted it to stop, but she didn't want to let go of him.

"I am sorry it's causing you pain," he said. "What can I do for you?"

A good question. Why did everything have to be so difficult? She'd hope to enjoy a honeymoon period with him once they were past the hearing, but fate wasn't allowing them any time at all.

"I'm sorry," she said. "Maybe I should just return to Gaea's."

She stepped back, breaking from his arms, and the dizziness overtook her. He caught her before she fell, and eased her down onto the armchair.

"You're in no shape to drive. You're staying here," he said gently, kneeling in front of her, cupping her face in his hands. The love in his eyes was unmistakable.

She took a deep breath and nodded. Even with the pain, there was nowhere else she'd rather be.

CHAPTER 31

MORDIDA—SAME NIGHT

Jayden stood at the open door of the judge's private residence. The judge grumbled over having his dinner party interrupted and quickly scribbled his signature on the warrant. Jayden thanked him and folded the two-page document, slipping it into his jacket's inner pocket. The door closed in his face.

He returned to Liza's Roadster, climbed in, and told the navigation system to guide him to where the chipmunk—as Tig had dubbed him— lived. It turned out to be the rear unit in a duplex. Jayden drove down the long, narrow driveway and parked in front of the apartment's door, where the driveway curved to form a concrete pad. He suspected the back unit was originally a garage. Two hard patches of dirt, devoid of plant life, flanked the threadbare doormat.

His leather jacket had "POLICE" printed on the back, giving anyone seeing him fair notice he was on police business.

He knocked. From the sound, a cheap, hollow core door. No deadbolt. He turned the doorknob. Locked.

Well, you couldn't always get lucky. He didn't have a battering ram with him, and contrary to the movies, he wasn't going to bash it in—he had no desire to dislocate his shoulder.

A kick near the lock might do it, but why risk his knee?

He went back to the Mercedes and retrieved his crime scene kit. A wrench made short work of the knob, twisting it open with a snap.

He drew his gun and called out, "Police."

No sounds emanated from within, no scurrying, no toilet flushing, no window being opened. He cautiously entered and quickly searched the small studio apartment for occupants.

All clear.

The other stolen painting was propped against the wall, with junk nearby: a trash barrel of recyclables, a unicycle, and a pile of used sports equipment.

He shuffled through the junk and rummaged through drawers, looking for the other missing items: the photo of Méi and Razi, the framed art review, and the glass paperweight containing a peony petal. Razi had told him the peony petal symbolized good fortune. Perhaps it worked—the art gallery made good money.

Jayden opened the nightstand drawer and found a small plastic vial of pills by the bed. He bagged and tagged them, but nothing else of interest. Receipts from a recycling center were scatted on a makeshift desk. Those receipts seemed to confirm the chipmunk's story.

Jayden pulled his camera from the kit and snapped a few photos of the painting, the recycling receipts, and the room.

After carefully securing the painting in the passenger seat and ensuring he'd be able to shift gears without gouging it, he drove back to the Hill. There, he dusted the painting and frame for prints and lifted the few he found. The only good ones turned out to be the chipmunk's. The perp was in the system because of prior drug arrests. The other prints were too smeared to identify.

Jayden wasn't sure what to do with the painting when he finished, whether he should return it to Méi or take it to the mayor, and decided to lock it in the evidence room. They might need it for the trial, although he doubted there'd be one. The chipmunk had probably told Tig and Liza the truth—he was a trash digger, living off the discards of others.

Tig dropped the chipmunk off at the Mordida County Jail. The district attorney would handle the bail hearing. Back at the station, she carried in the painting the chipmunk had brought to the coffee shop. Jayden processed it for evidence and found nothing except the chipmunk's fingerprints, just like the one he'd recovered from the apartment.

Both paintings were unharmed, aside from some red sauce on the back of one frame, which looked and smelled like a three-day-old Italian dinner.

It made no sense. Why would someone steal the paintings and abandon them in the trash? What *was* the goal in that?

If Rolf had stolen the artwork, he would have shredded it to prevent the mayor from ever enjoying it, or squirreled it away somewhere private. Rolf had been Tig's only suspect in this case, and now that seemed unlikely.

After photographing the paintings and preparing a returned property receipt, she walked the short distance to the mayor's office carrying them, and knocked at his door. The mayor had avoided her since she demanded a vote of confidence. Tonight, he couldn't wiggle out of it.

"Come in," he said.

The look on his face was priceless. After a few stiff pleasantries, he held out his hands for the artwork, looking closely at each painting, running a fingernail over the dried marinara sauce on the frame, *harrumphing* twice, before setting them aside and taking his seat behind his desk. He signed the property receipt and returned it to her.

She eased onto the uncomfortable guest chair and asked, "Who knew you had outbid Rolf on the paintings?"

"The council did." The mayor kept his eyes directed at his desk blotter and shrugged. "I needled Rolf about it during one of our closed sessions."

Great. The whole council had just joined the suspect list. "Was the town attorney at the meeting?"

"Yeah, him, and whoever else Rolf told."

"Anyone angry enough with you to steal the paintings?"

The mayor looked at her, surprise apparent on his round face. "Besides Rolf? Marcus wasn't happy I didn't accept the original deal he negotiated with Henry, but I don't see Marcus doing something like this."

"Anyone else?"

"Not really, but you know how it is. In politics, someone is always mad at you."

Damn straight. She wasn't going to give his guilty conscience a free pass, and continued fixing him with a harsh stare.

His gaze drifted back to his desk. "But I can't think of anyone mad enough to steal," he added.

Good. He's feeling guilty. It serves him right. "How about Rolf? Is anyone pissed off at him, someone who stole the paintings to make Rolf look like a suspect?"

The mayor's face brightened. "Now that's an interesting idea. I'm not aware of anyone, but you might ask him."

She thanked the mayor for his time—a slight concession to his rank—
and returned to her office. She had considered asking him when he would
schedule the vote of confidence, but she wanted him to feel guilty a little
longer. If she confronted him too soon, his guilt might turn to anger.

Jayden had gone home for the night. She sat down at her desk and
phoned the district attorney. He agreed no charges would be filed against
the chipmunk, so the burglary was still an open case. She hated open cases.

If Rolf didn't steal the paintings, did someone else on the council want
to ramp up hostility between Rolf and Winston by framing Rolf? Liza was
perennially pissed at Rolf, but again, she didn't see Liza as a viable
suspect. Tig made a few notes in the case file about her conversation with
the mayor and considered phoning Rolf.

Her calendar popped open on the computer, interrupting her two-
fingered typing: an appointment to meet with Father Matt.

Damn, I almost forgot.

She would have to talk with Rolf another night; she had no time right
now.

Fifteen minutes later, she was at the Hill Chapel, sitting on the couch
in Matt's office. The room always seemed stuffy to her, with crowded
bookshelves lining two walls. A pretentious Englishman who used to pay
for her protection in the late 1800s had a study just like it.

Not that she thought Matt was pretentious. If anything, he was too
humble, too *peaceful*. Didn't he ever get mad at anyone?

He took the chair across from her.

"Thank you for meeting with me," she said. "Do you mind keeping
this conversation confidential?"

During the past four decades, she'd shared confidential information
with him on occasion, and had never regretted doing so.

He ran his hand over his closely trimmed beard. "I'm happy to."

"Good. Here's the confidential part: although the council announced
the resolution of Blanche's case, I still believe others were involved in the
attacks on Henry and Yacov. One lead involves a church called New Path.
We've already tried an internet search and found their website. Ever heard
of them?"

"Not off the top..." He went over to the bookshelf, pulled out a large
hardbound volume, and flipped through it. "They aren't listed in the
American directory of churches. Let me check an alternate spelling."

He flipped through a few more pages, his eyes taking on a glazed look.
"Wait a minute," he said, and abruptly snapped shut the book. At his desk,

he dropped the book and searched through a stack of files, picking out a blue-colored sheet of paper, which he read. "It doesn't mention a church…"

"May I see it?"

He handed it to her and sat back down across from her. She handled the one-page flyer by the edges to avoid leaving fingerprints, and read through its simple message.

A NEW PATH FOR YOU

Are you hiding who you are?

Pretending to be something you aren't?

Ashamed of what you've become?

We want to help.

Just like you, we were pushed into hiding. We were told our survival meant living in the shadows. We were told we must pretend to be like the sheep who walk the streets of every city. We were told to shut up, sit down, and sign a document none of us agreed with.

But we aren't sheep. We're wolves.

And wolves were meant to hunt.

You have no reason to be ashamed. You have no reason to pretend. You have no reason to hide.

A strong wind is blowing, and it will clear a new path for our kind. Be the wolf you were meant to be.

At the bottom of the page, the same post office box used by New Path Church. "Where did you get this?"

"A stack of these were left in our meeting room. Usually, people ask for permission to leave out announcements, and they include contact information for someone on the Hill. No one asked permission, so I took the stack off the table. I threw the others away and kept this one."

"What do you think it means?"

"Hmm." Matt took off his glasses and picked up a soft gray cloth from the table next to his chair. Cleaning them, he looked deep in thought. He wore glasses to hide a scar where windshield glass had sliced through his eyebrow when he was still mortal. He'd been in the car accident before safety glass and seat belts were in widespread use, and he'd told Tig the story one night over a game of chess.

He dropped the cloth back on the table. "Let's start with what I don't think it means. They aren't literally talking about changing in to a wolf. Yes, it's discouraged on the Hill, but changing into a wolf is not forbidden, so long as discretion is used." He returned the round glasses to his nose. "The key word is *hunt*. I think this is targeted at vampires who still like to hunt live victims. That's why I removed it. I didn't believe it compatible with the chapel's mission."

She glanced at the page again. "When did you find it?"

"About a week ago."

Damn. It was after Blanche was put down. Someone else on the Hill was hooked into New Path. The post office address on the flyer confirmed it came from the same New Path that picked up the parolees.

She laid the flyer on the couch and pulled an evidence bag from her pocket. "You're sure you don't know who left these out?"

"I'm sure. If it was something I learned in confession, I couldn't reveal the confidence, but I would tell you the confessional seal protected the information. I have no idea who left these."

"Thanks, father." She slipped the flyer inside the evidence bag. "If you think of anything later, or if you see these flyers left out again, please contact me. I need to talk to the person who is distributing them."

She took her time walking back to her office, lost in thought, considering the wording of the flyer. *Sign a document* could refer to the treaty. There were many who felt forced into agreeing to the ban on creating new vampires, but the flyer didn't mention expanding their numbers. Matt was right—the flyer seemed like slick ad copy targeted at those who were addicted to live feeding.

Or is the metaphor even deeper? Is New Path the group Petar heard about? A group to put the wolves in charge of the sheep.

She'd originally thought the "Jim Jones" reference meant New Path wanted to expand their numbers. In other words, kill mortals to create new vampires. Instead, could it be a group that wanted to decimate the mortal population and keep the rest for food?

Either way, finding out who was responsible for the flyer moved to the top of her to-do list. Then it dawned on her. Oscar's nest was one of the more recent signatories to the treaty. Had he felt "forced" into signing it?

Back at the station, she made a note in the investigation file—a question to ask Oscar if she ever got the opportunity—and then went into her small crime lab and treated the paper to raise any fingerprints. She used V-Trak to compare what she'd found to all vampires on record, but the only prints on the flyer were Father Matt's.

Fuck. Another dead end. At least the flyer provided two possible motives behind the attacks.

She sat down at the table in the squad room. But why use a church? And why attack Henry and Yacov? They weren't the only ones involved in negotiating the treaty.

No, something about the attacks felt personal, and attacking Henry three times made it very personal. But what? And how did it tie in to a church either pissed off over the treaty or seeking world domination?

She thought back to the email Blanche had planted on Henry. Did they want to start a war between communities that weren't involved in the church as a smokescreen? How would that help?

None of it made any sense.

Tig returned to the computer in her office and updated the case file.

A knock sounded at her office door and she glanced over to see who it was. Jayden stood in the doorway. He'd changed out of his uniform into jeans and a t-shirt.

"Hey, Tig," he said. "How did it go with Matt?"

She showed him the flyer and explained her thoughts. Talking about it didn't provide any greater insight this time.

"Why don't you call it quits for the night and come home?" He held out his hand to her. "You got the paintings back. That's something to celebrate. And besides, you can't work all the time. I've got a better way to spend the night."

She bet he did. Maybe giving her brain a rest would allow her to start fresh later. She took his hand and stood up. "What did you have in mind?"

"Why don't we take the police van and drive up to lookout point? I'll throw a sleeping bag in the back. We can watch the moon set and still be back before sunrise."

Yeah, it had been a while since they'd had a little outdoors fun. She grabbed her portable radio. With everything happening, she couldn't afford to be completely off the grid. But with any luck, they'd have a few undisturbed hours, too entranced with each other to watch the moon. She hooked her arm in Jayden's and they strolled out into the night.

CHAPTER 32

Henry knelt in front of Cerissa's chair and wrapped his arms around her. He felt bad for causing her discomfort, but he believed accepting the crystal was the right choice—for both of them. Stroking her hair, he held her close. She sighed against his shoulder and her body relaxed, softening into his embrace. Perhaps the adjustment wouldn't be a long one.

"I should go upstairs and get some sleep," she finally said.

"It's still early. May I make a suggestion? Lie here on the couch and use me as a pillow. I'll read while you sleep. Maybe if you take a catnap, you'll feel better."

The couch was covered in dark brown leather and had a mahogany frame. It faced the fireplace, with the two matching armchairs at an angle nearer the hearth. He pushed the heavy wooden coffee table away to make room and then retrieved a murder mystery from the library.

She grabbed one of the embroidered throw pillows and, turning on her side, put the pillow under her head on his lap. He stroked her hair with one hand and held the book with the other.

Her breathing soon became the soft, regular sound of someone asleep. He continued to stroke her hair absentmindedly, his focus on the mystery story he read, until his fingertips registered a sudden change, and he froze. Her hair had become short and coarse. He glanced down. She had transformed into a large *puma*, the species of cougar native to the Hill.

What brought on the sudden transformation? She'd never changed before while sleeping.

He fingered the fur around her neck. The cat yawned without opening her eyes, her sharp teeth inches from his belly. She settled and went back to sleep, occasionally moving a paw as if dreaming. Her clothes—a stretch

214

top and skirt—were undamaged from the transformation, but they looked strange on the cat, like a child had dressed a pet in doll's clothing.

She purred slightly when he stroked her thick blonde fur. Her appearance flawlessly mimicked the local *pumas*: the black outline of her ears, the white puff of her cheeks sprouting fine whiskers, even the lighter fur on her chest.

So beautiful.

He tickled a whisker, and she twitched her nose without waking.

Why did seeing her like this deepen his love for her? He wanted to know everything about her, and this was a part of who she was.

"*Mi amor*," he whispered.

The cat woke with a start. She scrambled to sit up, and he pulled back his hand. Cerissa shook herself; the clothing seemed to annoy her, and she struggled to remove it, using her paws to push the spandex t-shirt off over her head.

"Here, let me help." He freed her from the stretchy fabric and unhooked the bra. The cat took it the rest of the way off, using her teeth to fling it to the floor, and turned her attention to the skirt.

"Let me unzip it," he said, not sure whether she understood him. "You'll tear it."

He got the skirt off her, but she bit through the thong strap, pulling it off with her teeth. Now free, she stretched, bowing before him.

"Happy?" he asked. Her response was to head-butt his arm, the way a cat scent-marked its territory. He stroked her head and shoulders. She purred and rubbed against him again. She had a strong, musky odor, like a real cougar.

"Lie down," he said softly, and she did.

He kept petting her until she purred and dozed off again. While she slept, she changed back to her human form. As much as he enjoyed seeing her naked, he didn't want her to get cold, so he took the afghan off the back of the couch and covered her with it. When she woke, her head still lay on the pillow.

"Feeling better?" he asked.

"A little. The volume of the noise is lower."

"Is that a good sign?"

"Yes," she said, brushing the hair out of her face. "I dreamed I was running."

"Was something chasing you?"

"No, I was just running. In the woods, free, the noise was gone, and—"

He watched her eyes take in her naked state, and the fur on his sleeve, which she sniffed at. She sat up suddenly, pulling the afghan around herself.

"You are magnificent as a *puma*," he said.

She buried her face in the afghan. "How embarrassing."

"There is nothing to be embarrassed about, Cerissa. I accept what you are." He ran a hand over her hair, just as he'd petted the cat. "I loved seeing you as a *puma* tonight."

"You don't understand." She raised her face from the afghan. "Only young children morph in their sleep. It shows a lack of, ah, control. It must be the crystal."

"Perhaps it was the power of suggestion. I did refer to your resting as a 'catnap.'"

She leaned against him. He wrapped his arms tightly around her and kissed her. He was glad she hadn't followed her instinct to run away—this was something they needed to go through together. "Can you take the shape of other animals?" he asked.

Her grip tightened on him.

"Cerissa, what is wrong?"

"I don't know."

"You've never let me see your full Lux form. What do you look like?"

She didn't answer. In the time it took him to blink, she morphed back into a *puma*, jumped off the couch, and loped up the stairs to the bedroom. When he heard the door shut, he decided not to pursue the topic any further—for tonight, at least.

He had only seen her Lux six-fingered hand before. Was she a humanoid bipod—or something so strange he couldn't imagine it? Was that why she resisted revealing her true appearance?

Still, her lack of candor bothered him, like an itch he couldn't quite scratch. What else hadn't she told him? The trouble with her people over their relationship—it may only be the tip of a giant iceberg. And the Lux—could they be a threat, not just to him but to the community he built? He opened the book he'd been reading, but couldn't shake his conscience's whisper.

You can't protect both her and your town. At some point, you'll have to choose.

He closed the book. He had founded this town, building it from scratch, planting the first vineyard with his own hands. It was his life's work, a safe place for vampires to hide in the open. But he couldn't bear the thought of losing her. He didn't care what secrets she hid. He'd chosen her, and nothing would ever change his mind.

CHAPTER 33

At their weekly meeting, the council gave Tig the vote of confidence she'd demanded, but they refused to vote on her compensation package. Rolf's comments were just plain nasty—in spite of the vote, he made his opinion on her skills quite clear.

Afterward, she met with Winston in private.

"We want you to stay," the mayor told her, "but we can't vote on your proposal right now. Find out who Blanche was working with, and we might be able to do something."

"If you don't double my salary, I won't renew the contract. It's nonnegotiable."

"We understand. You have your options, and we have ours. Solve the shootings, and you'll get what you want."

No one on the council thanked her for the successful return of the stolen artwork. Yeah, she'd figure out who had sponsored Blanche's attacks, and right after, she and Jayden would move. *Screw 'em.* Other communities would appreciate what they had to offer.

After the vote, Rolf refused to discuss the art theft, refused to tell her who might have set him up, refused to cooperate in any way.

Late into the night, she and Jayden racked their brains trying to figure out how to investigate the vice mayor. If Rolf was behind the conspiracy, he was smart to take her on so openly. If she investigated him, and he learned about it, he'd scream it was payback.

Around one in the morning, Jayden started to drag. He looked drained. "You need rest," she told him. "Clock out and get some sleep. I'll see you before sunrise."

217

"I will, but I have a few things to do first." He gave her a quick kiss and then disappeared into his office.

So much for following her orders.

Two hours later, Ufa arrived. Now Tig had someone she trusted to follow the vice mayor when he left the Hill. She'd first fought beside Ufa during the Ottoman Wars, and they had remained loyal comrades.

His official status on the Hill was "visitor." The guards at the Hill's entrance sent her hourly reports—who left and who returned, along with the guest log. She put Ufa in the squad room, with a computer and a television to occupy his time. The hourly reports were forwarded to him, and she asked the guards at the gate to call her if Rolf left the Hill.

"You're not going to believe this," Jayden said, entering her office.

"You're still here?" Tig frowned at him. "I thought you were headed to bed."

He held up a file folder. "I hadn't cleared my email yet—and a good thing I looked."

"All right, quit grinning like a hyena. I'm not in the mood."

He still looked dog-tired, despite the smile on his face. She couldn't imagine what he had to be happy about. He spun the file in her direction, and she plucked it out of the air, not losing a single sheet of paper.

"We got the DNA report from the lab on the Cutter," he said. "The Ruthton case, the one where the woman was found dead in a hotel room."

She opened the file and scanned through the lab report. DNA was found on the plastic sheet under the dead woman's body. Male. "Is he in the state's DNA database?" she asked.

"You want everything, don't you? He's not been in prison—at least, not since they started DNA testing. The lab's expanding the search nationally."

"Good." She returned to her desk chair and put her feet up, reading through the report one more time. Jayden hadn't moved from where he stood in front of her desk. "There's more, isn't there? I can tell by your look."

"Yup. No corrupt DNA. I talked personally with the lab tech. All his tests were good—he didn't discard any sample as contaminated because of bizarre results."

She still couldn't shake her suspicions. "You think the Cutter is mortal, don't you?"

"The blood could be nothing more than a trophy. Maybe he pours it all into one big vat and bathes in it, like what's her name, the Countess of Blood."

"You're thinking of Elizabeth Báthory of Hungary. And as much as I'd like to believe your theory, it's unlikely to be a coincidence."

"Well, he's moved on. It's San Diego's problem now."

Tig shook her head. "If a vampire's involved, it's still our problem."

"But—"

"Just because they didn't find any corrupt DNA doesn't mean a vampire wasn't present at the kill. I hate thinking that way. I do." She closed the file on the DNA report. "He dodged all the security cameras when he left the hotel. How do you explain it?"

Jayden plopped onto her couch, stretching out his legs. "Maybe the security cameras were hacked."

Something worth considering. "I'll email the detective in charge and ask him."

There was an old American saying—when you heard hoof beats, think horses, not zebras. Here, it meant think mortals, not vampires. Being from Africa, zebras seemed more likely to her.

CHAPTER 34

HENRY'S HOUSE—THE NEXT NIGHT

Henry hung the towel over the shower's door and hurriedly zipped his black slacks, getting ready in his basement dressing room to save time. Cerissa would arrive any minute for their dinner date. He had suggested dinner out as an excuse to see her. Since the crystal had been implanted in his wrist four nights ago, she'd spent all but one night away from him.

Her thin excuse—getting investors—was like a pebble in his shoe. Now that she was his mate, the council couldn't kick her off the Hill. She shouldn't feel the pressure of time anymore. It had to be something else.

The one night he saw her, she had refused intimate relations, blaming the crystal, and continued to dodge his questions about her real appearance.

She seemed as uncomfortable showing him her Lux body as he was talking about his past.

Now, there's a thought.

If he demanded explanations, it would only push her away. She was still adjusting to the crystal and the bond created by his bite. He'd be patient, show her how much he loved her by waiting, by not pressuring her. Perhaps a romantic dinner out would put her in the mood to open up to him.

He buttoned his long-sleeve shirt and looked in the mirror.

Too uptight.

He unbuttoned the top two buttons, the stiff cotton fighting him, and opened the collar.

Still too uptight.

He unbuttoned the cuffs and pushed the sleeves back, rolling the cuffs.

Better.

Now he could blend in with any hipster.

He heard her car park in the driveway and hurried from the basement to greet her. She had suggested sushi when he mentioned it to her last night during their phone call. While he could cook anything—so long as it didn't require garlic—he had never learned the art of sushi.

He twitched his nose at the thought. He disliked the smell of raw fish. He had no problem cooking fish, as it stayed raw for only a short time in the hands of Chef Bautista. But preparing raw fish that stayed raw was another matter entirely.

Meeting her at the door, he said, "You look lovely, *cariña*."

She wore a sleeveless black dress, the short skirt slightly flaring from her waist, and carried a sweater draped over her arm.

"Thank you," she said, accepting a kiss from him.

"We're all set. Rolf and Karen will join us at the restaurant."

He'd been avoiding Rolf since the council hearing two and a half weeks ago. Even the night Anne-Louise arrived, he'd texted Rolf, asking him to leave a vial of blood in the mailbox so they wouldn't have to meet in person.

Henry had read through his lawyer's memo, coming to the conclusion that any dissolution of his partnership with Rolf would take years to complete. Even though he wanted to distance himself from his junior partner, it was either ask Rolf to join them or disappoint Cerissa, because no one else was available on short notice to satisfy the Rule of Two. He wouldn't risk violating any rule by going without an escort, and he refused to disappoint Cerissa. So he sucked it up and asked Rolf.

"I've been looking forward to seeing you all day," she said, sounding less than enthusiastic.

"Is there something wrong, *cariña*?"

He put his arms around her in a gentle hug. He could almost feel her sadness.

"I'm sorry, Henry. It's nothing."

"I am willing to listen, if something is bothering you," he said, escorting her to his car and opening the door for her.

She turned to face him. "I know it has been a few nights, since, well, since…"

More than a few, but he didn't correct her. "It's all right, Cerissa."

She smiled weakly. "I've been wanting to talk with you about something, but the crystal may be pushing it all out of proportion."

He kissed her cheek. "I'm happy to listen to whatever you want to say over dinner."

She gave him a one-armed hug before getting into the passenger seat. "Thanks, Henry."

He closed the car door. Was she finally ready to confide in him? He would listen and be supportive. Nothing she said could change his mind about her.

The lobby of Ichiban's Restaurant was elegantly decorated, a large tropical fish tank built into one wall. Cerissa should have known he'd pick a five-star restaurant. She stopped to watch the fish while he went over to check in with the hostess.

The aquatic creatures were so colorfully vivid—bright blues, shiny yellows, deep reds—and the shapes so fascinating. The smaller ones, like torpedoes, flitted around the outer edges of the tank, while the larger, spadelike fish swam with measured leisure.

If only she was as relaxed as the fish.

Courage. You can do this.

Henry had accepted everything she'd told him about the Lux. She had to have faith he'd accept her real appearance.

Then why did her doubts keep darting around like the tiny fish in the aquarium?

Yes, he was Catholic.

Yes, she looked like an angel.

Yes, that might shake his worldview.

But their love was strong, and they would get through this. If she laid the foundation over dinner, and it didn't go well, she could always step back and give him more time.

Chicken.

A large green moray eel poked its head out from under a rock, opening and closing its mouth as it breathed. It seemed to be watching her, as if it had read her mind and was demanding: *Will you or won't you?*

Henry returned from the hostess desk. "Do you plan on eating him for dinner?"

"Don't be silly. You know that's not the type of eel they make *anago* from."

Someone tapped her shoulder, and she abruptly turned around.

Karen gave her air kisses. "So what's the special occasion? Whatever it is, I'm just happy to eat out with Rolf along. He usually refuses to go."

Rolf scowled. "You have plenty of food at home. You don't need to eat at a restaurant."

Henry put his arm around Cerissa. "We are celebrating one month together."

"Really? It's only been one month?" Karen asked.

"If Henry says it, it must be true," Cerissa agreed.

The hostess interrupted the conversation by calling Mr. Bautista's name. "I'll see you after dinner," Karen said, giving Cerissa another hug.

She took a deep breath and shoved her fear aside.

I've got this under control. Nothing will go wrong.

At Henry's request, the hostess seated them at a booth rather than the sushi bar—less attention on what he wasn't eating. Rolf and Karen were at a table far enough away to give them privacy.

Cerissa ordered for her and Henry, and included both sushi and sashimi, but no rolls. She preferred her fish plain and neat, with cold saké to wash it down.

"You ordered enough to feed a small whale," Henry teased, after the waitress left.

"Enough for two—isn't that what I'm supposed to do?"

"True. But you don't have to overdo it."

"Pooh. I'll have no trouble eating it all. I love fish."

Henry smiled at her indulgently. "If I didn't know better, I would suspect you had dolphin in your ancestry."

She smiled back tentatively, but kept her mouth shut. They would talk about her ancestry soon enough.

The plate of sashimi and sushi arrived, and the waitress placed it between them. Cerissa welcomed the distraction. Small, empty plates sat in front of each of them. For a guy who didn't eat, he handled chopsticks like a master, placing two pieces of fish on his plate as cover, selecting the less smelly variety.

He could eat if he wanted to, but the food would remain undigested and rot in his stomach. Not a pleasant smell, Karen had told her. Some vampires had become masters at regurgitation in order to blend in with humans. Henry wasn't one of them.

She worked her way through the sashimi. Whenever she reached with her chopsticks, her bracelet rolled forward on her wrist, and she pushed it back until it was tight against her skin.

The moonstone reminded her of their bond and what she needed to explain to him. She had waited long enough. "Henry, I have something I need to tell you."

"What is that, *cariña?*"

Little pieces, like the fish. Little bites at a time.

She lowered her voice. "Remember I told you the Protectors were concerned about fang serum?"

"But they were wrong. You've had no problems from it. Aside from experiencing the sexual stimulant…"

Warmth flooded her cheeks. Why did she blush so easily around him? "Ah, there's more to it. I stole a sample of Blanche's fang serum and analyzed it. Fang serum contains a compound similar to the Lux morphing hormone."

"And you're just telling me this now?" He pressed his lips together, his irritation obvious.

She dipped a piece of salmon into a mix of soy sauce and wasabi, focusing her eyes on the fish, and not the angry look on his face. After she ate it, she said, "Ah, since I figured out a solution, I didn't think—"

He exhaled audibly. "You didn't think your wellbeing is important to me?"

"I do, but it turned out not to be a problem."

"And what was your solution?"

"Remember the hypo, the medication I take to stabilize my human form? It nullifies the effect."

"I see. What would happen if you didn't use it?"

"Nothing *bad*." She motioned with her chopsticks to emphasize her nonchalance. Having finished the sashimi, she moved on to the sushi. Using her chopsticks, she pinched a piece of *ami ebi*. She bit into the raw freshwater shrimp, which felt cool to her tongue, the texture like sinewy Jell-O.

She took a long time chewing it.

He crossed his arms. Once she swallowed the shrimp, he asked, "If it's nothing bad, why didn't you tell me sooner?"

"Well, fang serum forces me back to my native form. And you couldn't drink my Lux blood, so I didn't want it to interrupt our moment—"

He held up a hand. "All right. I understand, I think." He paused as if considering something. "Cerissa, what do you look like in your native form?"

She had thought about how to answer this question. Hell, she'd obsessed on it. "Ah, somewhat like a mortal."

"May I see?"

"Not here. Obviously." She took a quick breath. "What do you remember after you were shot?"

He furrowed his brow. "Waking and seeing you there. You were holding a knife and the silver bullets you removed from me. I remember the feel of your wrist against my lips—the warmth of your blood reviving me and something about the way you kissed me afterward." He closed his eyes, looking deep in concentration, and then he opened them. "That is all I recall until Yacov arrived."

"Do you remember seeing me when I left?"

"No—but later, when I slept, I had a strange dream. I saw an angel at my door. She told me to return—it wasn't my time to die yet."

He believed it was a dream!

"Why did you want to know what I remembered?" he asked.

"I'll explain when we're back at your house. Trust me, it'll make sense later." She picked up her saké cup and drained it. Right now, she had a bigger issue to deal with. "There's also something about the crystal I need to tell you."

He had raised the saké flask to refill her cup, and paused, lifting an eyebrow at her words.

Do it, Cerissa.

"Ari may have left something out when he explained the crystal to you."

On nervous impulse, she popped one of the deep-fried shrimp heads into her mouth. *Bad choice.* There was no way to daintily eat it. She used her hand to cover her mouth—the brittle antennae of the shrimp were sticking out. She did her best not to crunch too loudly.

Henry finished filling her cup. "What did Ari omit?"

"After the crystal finishes tuning to me," she said, talking behind her hand because her mouth was still full of crunchy shrimp head, "we'll be able to feel each other's strong emotions."

His eyes turned solid black with anger. Yeah, she felt that cold blast. *Not good.* It was starting already.

"You'll be able to read my mind?"

"No—" she began, and washed the shrimp head down with a cup of saké. Most people thought of anger as hot, but through the crystal, it was like being dunked in ice cold water. "Emotions only. Your thoughts will still remain private."

"But my emotions will not?"

"Neither will mine."

"And you didn't think this important enough to tell me before now?"

"Well, you can blame Ari for this one. He was supposed to tell you everything about the crystal. I only learned today that he hadn't and... Henry, I'm sorry. I thought you knew."

Henry closed his eyes and pinched the bridge of his nose. He took a controlled breath and opened his eyes.

"Cerissa," he began, his voice strained. "You will be in my head."

"Not exactly—"

"You will be in head. Just like my maker."

It took her a moment to register the real meaning of his words.

He thinks it will be like how Anne-Louise can call to him, can get in his head and have a hold over him.

It wasn't. It wouldn't give Cerissa any power over him. In fact, she would be stripped just as bare to him.

"Henry, no. No, it's not like—"

Before she could finish, Rolf walked up to their table. "There's been another shooting," he said, his voice low.

"Who?" Henry asked.

"Méi," Rolf replied.

"Is she all right?"

"Henry, she's—"

"Dead," Henry finished.

Rolf set his phone on the table in front of Henry. "At the art gallery. The shooter escaped. I received a text from Tig."

Henry looked stricken. He must have been close friends with Méi. A flash of his grief invaded Cerissa's mind, a gray fog descending over her consciousness, leaving a bitter taste, like turmeric in her mouth, that made her want to cry.

She read the text message upside down: *homicide mei gallery bring dogs*

Rolf returned the phone to his pocket. "Tig needs help with the search. I have to leave to get the dogs and take them to the gallery."

Henry's face suddenly lost all expression and his grief withdrew from her mind like an offshore wind had blown the gray fog away. Vampires could cut off from their feelings when they needed to—how else could they do some of the things their nature required?—but until that moment, she hadn't guessed how completely he could disassociate from what he felt.

Henry got the waiter's attention and hastily paid the bill. As they rushed out, she took his hand and squeezed it. She wanted to flood him with her aura to take his pain away, but she knew that wouldn't help—not in the long run. He had to feel his own feelings. For the millionth time since she met him, she felt out of her element, unsure how to help him in the face of such heartbreaking news.

CHAPTER 35

MORDIDA—FIVE MINUTES LATER

Henry put the Viper in gear and sped toward the gallery. A dark grief threatened to engulf him. To fight it, he had to stay focused. He had to stay calm. He had to stay clearheaded. Tig would need his help to find Méi's killer, and then the killer would pay the ultimate price.

Cerissa touched his sleeve. "Henry, what can I do?"

"Nothing," he said. "Méi is—was—created by Anne-Louise."

"She was your sister?"

He didn't want to focus on what he'd lost, but Cerissa deserved an answer.

"*Sister* is not an accurate description." A cold chill wrapped around his heart, forming an icy wall between him and his grief. "Méi was turned in 1864, many years after I was. She was from China. She came to San Francisco to work in a laundry—instead, she was sold into prostitution. Syphilis was rampant at the time and working as a prostitute was a death sentence. Anne-Louise rescued her from that."

"Were you still living with Anne-Louise then?"

"No." He pulled into the left-hand turn lane, driving on autopilot. "I had been on my own for many years. I first met Méi when Anne-Louise and I reunited for a short time, after I sold my New York restaurant. Méi and I got along well, which struck Anne-Louise as funny. You see, the sense of family mortals share is rare among vampire siblings."

He paused as he made the turn, the memory of him and Méi laughing together rising in his mind's eye—a happy moment they'd shared. He fought to stay focused on the road before he did something reckless. "When I started buying land on the Hill, Méi did as well. She was my friend."

"Henry, I'm so sorry. I wish I had met her."

"She was an extraordinary artist. There will never be another one like her."

He drove the Viper into the parking lot, grabbing the space reserved for the "owner" of the Bautista Art Gallery. "I am half owner of the gallery. She owned the other half," he said, anticipating Cerissa's question. "Méi and her mate, Razi, manage it."

Méi *used* to manage it. He couldn't bring himself to say the words or leave the car; he couldn't bring himself to do anything that would make her death real.

Cerissa felt Henry's grief invade her mind again, his control fraying as he spoke. He must have cared deeply for Méi. When he stayed frozen behind the steering wheel, she laid a hand over his and said, "Maybe we should return to the Hill. Let Tig and Rolf handle this. There's no reason for you to go in there."

"This is something I must do."

"Henry, the killer could still be nearby."

"I'm not afraid of him."

Those words seemed to spring him into action. He got out of the car, and she had to run to keep up with him, her high heels tapping on the pavement.

As they entered the gallery, Zeke walked briskly past her, tipping his black cowboy hat in greeting, with council member Frédéric following him in the direction of the parking lot. Both were armed, and Tig shouted after them to establish a perimeter guard. A mortal wearing a police uniform stood at the front door, already on guard duty.

On the marble tile floor lay a mummified body. Nearby, Tig swiped a cotton swab at a spot of blood, collecting a sample. She dropped the swab into a bag and labeled it, while Jayden took photos of the crime scene.

If Cerissa hadn't been told Méi had been killed, she wouldn't have known who it was. The jewelry lying in the debris provided the only clue. Jade earrings hung from her ears, and a jade necklace wrapped around the dry, shriveled neck. She assumed they belonged to Méi. The Chinese associated the gem with beauty and virtue.

Tears rolled down Henry's cheeks. Cerissa gripped his hand and held it. She wanted so desperately to comfort him, but how? Perhaps her aura would help, just a little bit for now, until they got home and he could grieve in private.

A female voice she didn't recognize broke the silence. "Henry, I had no idea you had such feelings for Kim Han."

Henry spun around. "Méi!"

Cerissa turned too, and saw a tiny woman standing behind them.

"You are unharmed," he roared. He grabbed Méi in a hug, lifting her off her feet, burying his face in her straight black hair as he spun her around, her small feet dangling. She wasn't even five feet tall.

Henry's joy washed through Cerissa's mind like the woodsy scent of a dense forest, the taste of ripe berries on her tongue.

"Put me down," Méi demanded, in a voice belonging to a drill sergeant. "Now."

"Of course." He slowed his spin and set her on her feet, returning his arms to his sides, regaining his normal dignity. "We had been told you were dead."

"I am dead, fool, but the silver bullet didn't hit me, so I'm still a vampire." Méi smirked at Henry, a sparkle in her eyes allaying her harsh words. Her English was tinged with the song of her native language. Then her smile faded, and she motioned toward the corpse. "Not true for Kim Han."

"What happened?" he asked.

"Stupid assassin," Méi said. "Couldn't tell one Asian from another. Kim was Korean, not Chinese."

Cerissa shook her head. Tig had meant "homicide *at* Méi's gallery." Why hadn't the chief used a complete sentence? A few more key taps would have avoided Henry's heartache.

Henry brushed back a few stray hairs that had come loose from his ponytail during his spin. "What happened?" he asked.

"Kim wanted to see a painting, to buy it," Méi said, gesturing toward a vivid oil painting of two large calla lilies, one painted in a deep red-purple, and the other an intense cerulean, each with a lemon-yellow stamen. The striking work of art had a bullet hole in it.

"My new exhibit," Méi continued. "I emailed Kim to meet tonight. She liked it and bought it. I left the room to run her credit card, heard a loud bang, and ran back here."

"Why do you think he meant to kill you, and not Kim?" Henry asked.

"When he saw me, he wasn't happy."

"He swore at her," Tig said, joining the conversation, the small evidence bag in her hand. "And he tried to shoot her."

Méi nodded. "I dodged the bullet, drew my dagger, and threw it at him. Hit his arm. Clumsy of me. I meant it to go through his heart. He dropped this." Méi showed Henry a photo; Cerissa could see it too. In the photo, Méi stood next to an African American man, his hair in long, thin braids, each tied off with colorful beads. He was twice as wide as Méi and half again as tall.

Henry handed the photo back. "But otherwise you are fine?"

"I would be better if the imbecile hadn't ruined my painting, not to mention killing a paying customer."

"I am sorry about Kim," Henry said, "but I am glad you are unharmed."

"There was no doubt he would fail. I saw him a split second before he fired. Plenty of time to avoid the bullet. Whoever is doing this has hired dimwitted mortals."

"You're sure the shooter was mortal?" Tig asked.

"Absolutely. A vampire would not have been so stupid, mistaking Kim for me."

Tig took the photo back from Méi. "And this is the one that was stolen?"

"*Shi*," Méi said with a sharp nod.

The man in the photo appeared from the gallery's back hallway. "Yes, that's the one," he agreed.

Tig turned to Henry. "Thanks to Méi's dagger, we have the killer's blood. Rolf is bringing the dogs. We may be able to track him. It's a long shot, but if the killer is stupid, he may be hanging around, hoping for a second chance. That, or we trace him back to where he parked his car. If security cameras are nearby they may have caught his license plate number." Tig turned back to Méi. "You're sure it was a man?"

"I could smell him. A mortal male. Wore a mask. Six feet tall." She pivoted her flattened hand, indicating "more or less."

"Weight?" Tig asked.

Méi paused for a moment. Her lips moved silently, like she was doing the math, converting numbers. "One-eighty? Not sure."

"That's okay. It's more than we had before." Tig rushed off to join Jayden, who had dug the bullet out of the injured painting.

"I am glad you didn't chase him," Henry said.

"*Cào*. I would have, except for Razi." Méi gestured toward the tall man standing behind her. "The shooter fired again before running off. I dodged the second bullet by ducking into my office. Razi insisted I stay there until Tig arrived. He was right. Better position to defend." Cerissa suddenly felt Méi's gaze land on her. "Who is this?"

Henry gave a little nod in Cerissa's direction. "Dr. Cerissa Patel. Cerissa, this is Chen Méi and her husband, Razi."

"Ms. Chen," Cerissa said, inclining her head and giving a slight curtsy. Even if Henry hadn't already told her that Méi was his sister's name, she knew the Chinese tradition placed the surname first. "I'm glad to see you both are unhurt."

Cerissa raised her gaze and offered her hand to Razi to shake. He gripped her hand lightly in greeting. Almost seven feet tall, he was a large, muscular man, with a gentle bearing. The braids he wore softened the effect of his size.

"So this is the new one you are sleeping with?" Méi asked.

"Cerissa is my mate, yes," Henry said. "I hope you will welcome her to the family."

"I would love to. Are you offering a taste?" She clicked her fangs and smiled a toothy grin at Cerissa.

"No," Henry said, hastily wrapping an arm around Cerissa and pulling her tightly to him, almost taking her off her feet.

Was this why Henry hadn't introduced them before? He was glaring at Méi disapprovingly.

Méi gave a little bow. "Ignore me. I'm just annoyed. We were supposed to open the new exhibit tomorrow night."

That may be, but the circumstances didn't excuse Méi's lapse of etiquette.

The artist's gaze locked on Cerissa again. "I've heard you stole Henry's heart. Quite a feat. He hasn't had one for two hundred years," she added with a laugh.

"Méi." Henry made her name sound like a warning.

Rolf's arrival stopped any further discussion. "Henry, I need your help with the search."

Two excited dogs whined and Cerissa glanced in the sound's direction. Mort and Sang stood at the entryway, straining at leashes Karen held.

"If you'll excuse me," Henry said to Méi.

Cerissa went with Henry to the front of the gallery, kneeling down to pet each German shepherd. They greeted her with doggie kisses.

Rolf scowled, his eyes taking on a mean, pinched look. "They aren't pets. Leave them alone."

Cerissa ignored him, running her hands over each dog's back. Her aura attracted them—she could be a real Dr. Doolittle, and with these two, she wanted to be.

Tig joined the group, carrying three bulletproof vests, and distributed one each to Rolf and Henry, before putting on her own. Karen handed Rolf the leashes and kissed him.

Cerissa didn't want Henry going with them. What if the shooter was out there, waiting to strike again? Henry must have sensed her fear, because he whispered to her, "I'll be fine. The shooter is long gone by now. Stay here."

"But Henry—" she began.

"Please. Do not argue. Stay here," he whispered.

She started to object, but he held up one finger. The determination on his face was too clear. He wore a heart shield anytime he left the Hill, and with the extra protection of a bulletproof vest, the only vital organ unprotected was his head. She didn't like it, but she had no choice. She accepted a kiss from him and stayed in the gallery with Karen. Jayden joined the group, strapping on the vest he carried, and the search party left.

"Henry's been one of the targets," Cerissa told Karen. "He shouldn't be out there."

"Yeah," Karen said. "But there's nothing you can do about it. He would have dug in his heels even more if you'd argued with him in front of Rolf and Tig." Karen paused, shrugging. "Come on, I'll show you around the gallery."

"Frédéric, return," Tig said into her portable radio, and glanced around while she waited. Lined with upscale businesses, the street stood quiet. In this section of Mordida, most shops closed by nine on weeknights. Henry and Rolf whispered among themselves. The dogs obediently sat next to their master.

She looked up the street one more time. The Mordida police hadn't arrived yet, the only good thing to happen tonight. Zeke and Frédéric had searched the area when they first arrived—no sign of the perp.

Frédéric sauntered back from his post by the parking lot. Why couldn't he hustle? He stopped in front of her and leaned in close.

"Yes, chief?" he whispered.

"Stay here and guard the door."

"My pleasure, chief," he said, a hint of sarcasm in his tone, before taking his post in front of the door.

Was he being nasty because of the vote of confidence she'd asked for? Council members could be a pain in the ass, but they all served as reserve officers when she was short-staffed—it came with the gig. At least Liza was worth her salt, even if she wasn't available tonight.

Tig turned away and caught Rolf's eye, motioning toward the cloth she held. She had no choice; she had to work with the vice mayor despite his attitude toward her—the only tracking dogs on the Hill belonged to him. The vampire sense of smell might be superior to mortals, but she couldn't run along with her nose to the sidewalk, sniffing at the trail. Rolf insisted Henry help because he didn't trust anyone else with his dogs.

She allowed each dog to sniff the blood sample. Mort ran a circle, nose down, around the sidewalk before he let out a yelp, tugging at the leash Rolf held. Sang moved as fast, and with her nose to the ground, pulled Henry in the same direction.

"Let the dogs lead," Tig said quietly.

With their guns drawn, she and Jayden ran along flanking them. The dogs kept moving forward when the blood trail ended a few feet outside Méi's gallery. Tig didn't like it. They were out in the open, nowhere to hide. She kept watching for any sign of movement and sniffed the air as they ran. No scent of mortals nearby, but the smell of frying garlic was strong.

Must be that Italian restaurant down the block.

She consciously stopped breathing. Now was not the time to succumb to the foul fumes of that mutant rose.

As they approached the corner of Fifth and Grand—a blind intersection—she took a quick breath and whispered, "Slow the dogs."

The dogs veered right. She ran ahead, holding up her hand to tell Rolf and Henry to stop, and hugged the stucco wall, peering around the corner—an empty street, except for a parked car. Further down the block was a city parking lot. Had he parked there? Maybe they'd get lucky and there'd be video cameras. She took a breath.

Damn that garlic.

She couldn't smell any mortals, but she couldn't tell for sure.

She motioned for Rolf to move forward slowly. Mort turned the corner and strained at the leash. Henry and Sang followed behind. They traveled fifty more feet along the side street before the dogs came to a dead stop outside a closed bakery.

Sang jumped up on the building's wall, scratching at the stucco between two plate glass windows advertising fresh breads and pastries. Mort joined her, the two dogs whining excitedly, creating too much noise. Tig motioned to Rolf to pull them back as she looked toward the roof.

How could a mortal go straight up a building?

Garlic. Dead end. A glint of light reflected off metal above her head.

"It's a trap!" she yelled. "Over here."

She jumped through the bakery window, shattering the glass. Rolf and Henry each scooped up a dog and leapt inside after her. But where was Jayden?

Gunshots sounded. She smelled his blood in the night air and leaned out the window, firing up at the shooter. Jayden was on the ground.

"Cover me," she shouted at Rolf.

She swung outside onto the wall and scaled the one-story building. Rolf's bullets whizzed past her. The rooftop shooter ducked back behind the parapet of the building.

You're mine, asshole.

Crab-walking the stucco wall, her fingernails extended like claws, Tig climbed toward the roof at an angle, moving away from where she'd last seen him. He wouldn't expect her there, not with Rolf's barrage of bullets keeping the shooter back. In a flash, she vaulted over the parapet and landed on the flat roof, drawing her gun, looking for the perp.

Where was he?

The rooftop was vacant. She spotted a service ladder on the other side and ran to it, looking over the edge where the building backed onto an alley.

A mortal disappeared into a Toyota beater, and the driver smoked the tires. She aimed and fired—the bullet shattered the car's rear window. She couldn't leap a hundred feet onto a moving vehicle. The car continued to roar down the alley. She fired again, aiming for the tires, got the rim instead, the metal-on-metal sound echoing through the alley. Duct tape covered the license plate.

Holding on to the ladder, she vaulted onto the parapet, ready to jump—if she ran fast enough, she might catch the car.

Henry's voice stopped her. "Jayden needs you."

She clenched the rails of the ladder, suppressing the desire to scream her rage, torn between two duties: capture whoever was behind these attacks, or save Jayden.

Jayden took priority. She loved him too much to sacrifice him on the Hill's altar.

She sprinted across the roof and glimpsed Henry cautiously reaching for the burner knob on a camp stove, turning it off. A frying pan, sizzling with cooking garlic, had created the smell and masked the shooter's scent.

Jayden lay on the sidewalk, a pool of blood beneath his leg. Fear twined around Tig's spine, the chill grabbing her gut. She leapt from the wall to Jayden's side.

Rolf was on his knees with his palm over Jayden's wound, his fangs out. The vice mayor panted like he was about to lose control.

"We're sitting ducks here," Tig said. "Let's move him into the bakery."

When Rolf didn't release Jayden's leg, Tig grabbed Rolf's shoulder and pulled him back, knocking him onto his ass. She carefully lifted Jayden into her arms, and he said, "Fuck, fuck, fuck," as she stepped across the window frame and laid him on the floor inside, away from the broken glass.

Why hadn't Rolf offered Jayden his blood? Sure, under ordinary circumstances, the Covenant forbade it, since she and Jayden were blood mates. But these weren't ordinary circumstances. She could have caught the killer if Rolf didn't have a stick up his ass.

She bit her wrist to feed Jayden. He sucked weakly, his breathing labored.

Not good.

Her blood wouldn't repair this kind of damage. With her other hand, she ripped the radio off her belt. "This is Chief Anderson. Officer down. Bakery store. Fifth and Grand. I need a bus and backup."

"Roger that, chief," came the voice over the handheld.

"And put out an APB for an older-model Toyota with a shot-out rear window."

"Roger."

Jayden looked so pale. Then it dawned on her. Had Rolf held off giving Jayden his blood to prevent her from pursuing the killer?

She eyed Rolf, who stayed on guard, straddling the window's opening. Mort and Sang lay inside the bakery near their master. The two dogs suddenly stood up, whining. She heard it seconds after they did: the sound of running. Rolf raised his gun, and, with her free hand, Tig reached for her own.

Cerissa appeared at the broken window. "Rolf, put that down before you hurt someone."

The envoy pushed Rolf's gun aside and stepped past him, with Razi right behind her.

"What are you two doing here?" Rolf demanded.

"When the search party didn't come back, I knew there was trouble," Cerissa said, a look of grim resolve on her face when her gaze reached Jayden on the floor.

Henry landed on the sidewalk behind Cerissa. The smell of garlic lingered faintly in the air, but not much of it. Tig squatted next to Jayden. Cerissa dropped her medical kit on the tile floor across from Tig and, kneeling, wrapped her hands over his leg, applying pressure. Jayden moaned.

"Why didn't you stop her?" Rolf growled, following Razi into the bakery.

"Hey, man, I tried, but she was determined," Razi replied. "She snuck out the back door to Henry's car to get her bag and did an end run through the parking lot. Frédéric saw her and yelled for me to follow her. He stayed at the gallery, guarding the door."

"That's no excuse," Rolf snarled, clenching his fists, his knuckles white.

Why was Rolf so angry? Tig looked over at him. "Rolf, guard the window."

The vice mayor didn't move.

"Now," Tig ordered him.

"Fine," he said, returning to the sidewalk.

Perhaps this was the excuse she needed to put him on inactive duty. She would consider it later, once Jayden was okay. For now, she had to manage the situation.

The pool of blood beneath Jayden grew larger.

"Will he live?" Tig asked Cerissa. "His sucking is weak—he may not be taking in enough blood to keep him alive."

"Get this off him," Cerissa said, indicating the bulletproof vest with the motion of her chin. "I need to see where he was shot."

Tig pulled back one of the straps, while Henry helped with the other one. Henry lifted Jayden slightly to move the vest back. Jayden grimaced with pain and released Tig's wrist.

"It's okay, baby," she said, putting her wrist back to his mouth. She caressed his head, and her heart constricted. "Everything's going to be okay. You're going to be okay. You have to be okay."

"Henry, I need your help. Press here," Cerissa said, releasing Jayden's leg so Henry could replace her.

The doctor used scissors from her medical kit to cut through Jayden's pant leg. The fabric was drenched in a deep scarlet, the oval stain growing faster than it should.

Tig looked up when Rolf inched back into the room, his gaze fixed on Jayden's blood. The room smelled strongly of it. "Rolf, go stand on the sidewalk and watch for the ambulance," Tig said.

Henry pulled the pant leg off. Cerissa applied a large gauze pad to the wound and put pressure on it again.

"The first bullet hit the vest, knocking him backward," Cerissa said. "The next bullet went straight through his thigh, where the vest didn't cover. Downward trajectory; it may have shattered the bone. We won't know until they get him into surgery."

Jayden moaned again.

"See—she is of no use here," Rolf said from the window. "Probably not even a real doctor."

"Shut up, Rolf," Tig said, staring at him to make sure he got the message. "Let Cerissa work without distractions."

He scowled again, but closed his mouth.

"The ambulance will be here soon," Tig reminded the group. "I don't want to explain why civilians are involved. Henry—you and Razi return to the gallery with the dogs. Rolf is officially a reserve officer, so his presence can be explained."

"And I happened to be in the area," Cerissa offered, continuing to press on Jayden's leg. "No one will question a doctor providing help."

"Cerissa will ride in the ambulance," Tig added. "Henry, you can meet her at the hospital."

When the sound of sirens grew nearer, Tig broke Jayden's hold on her wrist. "That's enough for now," she told him.

She stroked his forehead, wishing she could do more. It had been a trap all along, and she had walked right into it. How had she been so stupid to let this happen? The council was right. She wasn't cut out for real police work.

Maybe I should pack up Jayden and take an easy security job with another community.

He looked so pale, and spasms of pain shook his body. She pressed the back of her hand to his cheek—his skin was cold and moist. Fear shot through her again. Would he survive the night? She didn't know what she'd do if she lost him because of her mistake.

CHAPTER 36

MORDIDA GENERAL HOSPITAL—SAME NIGHT

Jayden slowly opened his eyelids, pulling against the sleep gluing them together until they snapped open. Now he was awake, in a hospital bed, and that was when the pain hit with full force.

Fuck. Had a train hit him, followed by a sixteen-wheel semi and a herd of cattle?

Cerissa stepped within view and placed a small box with a red push button onto his palm. "The morphine pump remote is right here," she said. "If you're in pain, press this. It's time released, so you can't overdose."

"Thanks," he croaked. "Where's Tig?"

"Hunting whoever did this to you." Cerissa patted his shoulder. "Tig stayed until you came out of surgery, to make sure you were all right. She was worried."

"Water?" he asked. His mouth was dry, the back of his throat sore, and his jaw joint tender. What had they stuck down his throat during surgery?

She lifted a pink plastic cup, putting the straw into his mouth. He took a couple of long pulls. The suction made his teeth ache. "Thanks."

"You're going to be fine. I spoke with the surgeon—the bullet missed the bone, but it shredded your leg muscle and tendon. The surgeon was surprised the damage wasn't worse—Tig's blood must have repaired the severed veins."

"Yeah, I'm lucky," he said, letting the sarcasm show. He took another pull on the straw she offered. "If I was one of them, I wouldn't be here."

Cerissa looked surprised and returned the cup to his hospital tray. "You want Tig to turn you?"

Did he? If the treaty was changed, would he take the plunge? He scrubbed at his eyes, wiping away the sleep matted in his eyelashes. The IV line, which was stuck in the back of his hand, bent with the motion. Now his hand hurt too.

"I don't know what I want," he said. "But sometimes I think Tig would respect me more if I was one of them."

Cerissa shook her head. "I can tell you this: she told us that you're better than she is at police work."

"Nice lie, but I'm a cop, remember? Even stoned on morphine, I can spot a lie."

Henry walked into the room. "No, she's not lying." He handed Cerissa a paper coffee cup. "Tig thinks very highly of you, as do we all."

Pain cramped Jayden's leg. He hit the pump remote again. His head swam as the pain receded, and he closed his eyes.

"Henry, why don't you wait for me outside?" Cerissa said. "I won't be long. Jayden needs to rest." After Henry's footsteps receded, Jayden felt her hand on his shoulder again. "It's kind of hard living with them, isn't it?"

Yeah, she had that right. Stronger, faster, superior in about every physical way he could imagine. "They're sure better than us mere mortals."

"They aren't better, just different," she said. "They have their limitations, too. And they need us."

"Then why does it feel like…" Like what? "Like I can serve and protect, but not sit at the table with them?"

"You're not alone. Others feel the same way." She took a drink of her coffee. "Change is coming, but it may be slow."

Jayden coughed to clear his throat, and she offered him more water. After the sip, he said, "When you live forever, you can take your time."

She looked sympathetic. "Maybe the council needs to hear how you feel."

Yeah, like he could go before his bosses and tell them how fucked up their system was. The council would never listen to him. "Thanks, but I'll suffer in anonymity."

She patted his arm. "We can talk about this when you're better. Get some rest. I'll come back during the day."

"Thanks—I'll hold you to that."

He closed his eyes and drifted off.

Tig had refused to leave the hospital until she saw Jayden in the recovery room. Once she did, and after the surgeon assured her he'd be fine, she couldn't wait any longer—she had a job to do. Returning to the art gallery, she finished collecting the evidence, including the camp stove on the roof. Jayden's blood still covered the sidewalk below.

I should have done more to protect him.

It was four in the morning before she reached the Mordida crime lab. After greeting the DNA lab tech on duty, she handed him the small bag containing the swab. "Got a blood sample for you to run."

"What happened?" He signed the evidence list, documenting his role in the chain of custody.

"One of our residents was attacked. She stabbed the assailant before he escaped." If she told him about Kim Han's murder, he'd ask about the body. Better to keep it vague. "The perp circled back and shot one of my officers. I'd like to get the results quickly."

"You want to know if he's in the DNA database?"

"Precisely."

"For a boy in blue, I'll jump this to the front of the line. I may have results by tomorrow, thanks to our new SNiP machine."

At her insistence, Sierra Escondida had donated money so Mordida's lab could buy the fastest DNA analyzer available. Their investment just might pay off.

"Thanks," she said. "Call me, day or night."

She glanced at her phone. Four fifteen. She couldn't put it off any longer. After a quick call to Father Matt, she drove back to the Hill, parking in front of the modest ranch-style home Kim Han had leased on a quarter acre of land where the valley flattened out.

Tig waited in her police van, staring at the well-manicured rose trellis, which framed the house in white blooms.

Too cheery a house for the news she was about to deliver.

Kim had joined their community about forty years ago, having barely scraped together the buy-in fee, and took the smallest house available. Tig had run the background check at the time—all clean, or Kim wouldn't have been allowed in.

Her death was likely wrong place, wrong time.

Still, Kim had done well for herself since joining the Hill. No family to notify—her maker was dead—but she had a relatively new mate, Jessica, the relationship only five years old.

Tig glanced in the rearview mirror when the lights from Father Matt's car flashed behind her.

No more putting this off.

She marched up the stone path to the front door and pressed the doorbell. Father Matt and Yacov's wife, Shayna, wordlessly joined her on the porch. Father Matt was there in his professional capacity, while Shayna would offer Jessica a shoulder to cry on during the day, after Tig and Matt left.

When the door opened, Kim's mate took one look at the three of them. "No," Jessica said, her hand shooting to her mouth, a look of disbelief on her face, her head shaking. "No, no, no…" She started to crumble.

Father Matt moved fast to catch Jessica before she hit the floor and helped her to the living room couch. Pale with shock, Jessica kept repeating "no" over and over again. Shayna went to the kitchen and returned with a glass of water for the widow.

Tig took a seat opposite them. She hated this part of the job most.

"I'm sorry to inform you that Kim was killed tonight. You have our deepest condolences."

Unshed tears finally flowed from Jessica's eyes, and Shayna was quick with a tissue. "How?" Jessica asked, her voice cracking on the one word. "I—I went to bed when she left to see Méi…"

"The man who killed her broke into the art gallery while Kim was there with Méi. Kim was alone when it happened. Méi wounded him, but he escaped." Tig looked over at Father Matt, and he nodded, encouraging her to continue and get this over with. Neither of them had much time—dawn would arrive shortly. "Right now, we suspect the killer was targeting Méi. But to help our investigation, I have a few questions for you. Are you willing to answer them right now?"

Jessica straightened her slumping shoulders and cinched her bathrobe. "If it'll help, I'll do what I can."

"Did Kim have any enemies?"

"No one I'd call an enemy," Jessica said, then paused to blow her nose. "We had problems with one of our neighbors. They kept putting their trash cans in front of our home. But we worked it out."

Not something worth killing over. "As the day goes by," Tig said, "if you think of any reason someone would do this to Kim, please email me. I'll see it when I wake tonight." Jessica nodded. "Do you have any family you want us to call? Someone you can stay with when you leave the Hill?"

Jessica's face grew red, her eyes narrowing, her tears flowing again. "You arrogant bitch. Kim isn't dead, what, six hours? And you want me off your precious Hill already."

"I'm sorry, I didn't mean it that way—"

"I don't want to be made to forget her. I loved her. This is my home, our home. She's still here—I can still smell the fragrance of her perfume." Jessica stood and bolted over to a table filled with knickknacks. She picked up a clay pot. "Kim made this when we took a pottery class together. And this," she said, holding a small brass replica of the Golden Gate Bridge, "we bought this on our trip to San Francisco. And this"—she gently cradled a pair of glazed swans—"she gave me this when we got married. And you want me to leave my home behind like it never happened?"

Tig had heard it all before. Some mates wanted their memories wiped right away, to forget, to take away the pain. Others resisted—not this vehemently—but this was the first death since mortals began clamoring for equal rights. She opened her mouth to apologize again, but Father Matt held up his hand.

"That's not what the chief meant," he said. "No one is rushing you. You'll have time to grieve, to figure out what you want to do next."

"Next," Jessica spat out. "Next means losing her forever. I want to remember, I want to know how much I loved her, I want...I want her back," she said, collapsing into a chair and sobbing into her tissue.

Father Matt cleared his throat, getting Tig's attention. "Chief, I know you have to leave, to keep your investigation moving forward. Shayna and I will stay with Jessica."

Tig stood. *Is this how Jayden would feel if something happened to me?*

"I'm very sorry for your loss," Tig said, and left.

Climbing into the police van, she ticked through her mental to-do list, stuff she needed from the council. She had warned them—the attacks weren't over. Now they couldn't deny it.

She didn't want to lose anyone on her watch, not an innocent bystander, not a founder, and certainly not Jayden. The council had better start listening to her, or she would pack up Jayden and leave. She wasn't going to lose him because of the council's foolishness.

She took a deep breath. The pain of leaving the hospital, of not being there when Jayden woke, dug at her heart. There wasn't enough time to go back and then return to the Hill by dawn. *Damn it.* She hated the powerlessness of daytime sleep, the sun's ever-present threat to her life. What she wouldn't give to be mortal again and have a normal life with Jayden.

But that wasn't going to happen.

She looked out at the early morning sky, the first orange glow of sunrise peeking over the distant hills beyond eastern Mordida. She was done wishing for things she couldn't have, but she would demand the things she could, starting with an end to the council's fiction that the Henry/Yacov case had closed with Blanche's death.

By tomorrow night, she'd put her strategy in front of the council. And if they didn't do what she asked, they could find someone else to be their police chief.

CHAPTER 37

MORDIDA GENERAL HOSPITAL—AFTER SUNSET

"Twelve hours lost to day sleep," Tig grumbled to herself as she strode down the sterile white hospital hall. The smells of death and dying and chemical sanitizers invaded her nose. The soft quiet was broken by the tinny public-address system, the dinging monitors, the hushed voices.

She hated hospitals.

With help from the front desk, she found Jayden's room—his *private* room. That was one thing she had accomplished before leaving last night. The Hill could afford to give Jayden some privacy while he recovered.

Cerissa sat by his bed and raised a finger to her lips when Tig walked in. The envoy stood, gesturing toward the hallway. "He's doing better than can be expected," she said, keeping her voice low as they left the room. "His vascular system is healing rapidly. The doctors don't know what to make of it."

Tig nodded. Her blood was responsible. She would give him another cautious dose tonight. He needed just enough to speed along his healing. Without fang serum, too much might kill him—permanently.

"Is he in pain?" Tig asked.

"No, the doctors have him on a morphine pump. But he's feeling a little, well…"

"A little what?"

"Sad?" Cerissa cocked her head, as if considering something. "No, he's feeling ashamed—ashamed he got hurt, ashamed for being mortal."

"He has no reason to be ashamed."

"Tell him that. It would help if he heard it from you."

Good advice. Tig glanced back into the room. Jayden still slept. "Thank you for staying with him. You can leave now if you want."

"He just dozed off. Henry is driving over with Father Matt, but I need dinner…"

"Under these circumstances, Henry can return to the Hill without a vampire escort. He can go back in your car." Then it occurred to her— Cerissa might not want to go straight home. "And if you want to stop somewhere for dinner, I'll cover for you and Henry with the town council. Thank you again for looking out for Jayden."

"You're sure? I can grab dinner here at the hospital. I'm happy to stay."

"Matt and I will be here. Go home and rest." Tig walked toward the elevator alcove, the envoy following her. "You've given enough of your time. I appreciate it, and I suspect Jayden does too."

With the threat of a whipping still hanging over his head, Henry knew he couldn't afford to violate the Rule of Two by going into Mordida alone. He slid into the passenger seat of Father Matt's metallic blue Prius. The car's nickname made popular by *South Park* seemed appropriate: Pious. Matt was a religious man, but in a good way, and he was the only priest Henry trusted.

Henry's knees bumped against the dashboard as Matt drove the car around the large fountain in Henry's driveway and back to Robles Road.

"Thank you for driving, father."

"No problem." Matt turned right, toward the Hill's gate. "How are you and Cerissa doing? You were there last night when Jayden was shot."

"I—" Henry began, and stopped. Since rising, he'd obsessed on what Cerissa had disclosed at the sushi restaurant. The emotional connection—that was bad enough, but what else hadn't she told him? He needed to talk about it, but how could he say what troubled him without spilling Cerissa's secrets?

"What is it?" Matt asked. "You know you can talk with me."

"It's just… I don't want to violate Cerissa's privacy."

"Then talk about you. What's troubling you?"

"Cerissa has been keeping secrets from me." There. That was general enough—nothing too damning about it.

"How long have you two been dating?"

To Henry's mind, she'd become his girlfriend the night they first made love, but they had started dating a few weeks before that. "Almost seven weeks, if you include the time I was under house arrest."

"You've seen her a few times each week for about four weeks?"

"More in the last two weeks, but yes, you're correct."

"Henry, relationships take time. You're not going to learn everything about her overnight. She'll open up to you when she's ready. At this stage in your relationship, it's normal to have secrets. Discovering more about the other person you fell in love with is half the fun."

"I know, but…"

"But what?"

"She hasn't told me the full truth about her family."

"And are you keeping secrets from her?"

A shiver ran through Henry, the kind mortals described as someone walking over your grave. He looked at his hands. "I have not told her everything about my past."

"You've lived over two hundred years, counting the time you were mortal. It takes a while to unpack all that history. If you told her all the bad things you've ever done, it wouldn't be good for either of you."

Henry remained quiet. Could Matt be right? There were moments Henry wanted to bare his soul to Cerissa, to confess every sin, to beg her to stay with him despite his past transgressions.

"And she is, what, twenty-nine?" Matt asked.

"More or less," Henry said, skating around the truth.

"As you come to trust each other, you'll naturally reveal more of your past. If you jumped right in and unburdened your soul, well, I've had clients who did, and it's not healthy." Matt ran a hand over his beard. "They think, 'confess everything—if my mate is going to reject me, let them do it now before I'm in too deep.' Any of that strike a chord?"

"I guess."

"And then they bare all and it's overwhelming to the other person."

Was Matt correct? Had Cerissa been right to hold off telling him? Maybe she needed time to feel comfortable enough to trust him with all her secrets.

Matt paused as he changed lanes. "Not to mention after the way Anne-Louise turned you, you've always had a bit of a trust issue with women."

"Father, that isn't fair. Anne-Louise has nothing to do with my concerns about Cerissa."

Matt stopped at a red light and glanced over at Henry, raising an eyebrow. "Give yourself time. And give Cerissa time. If there is anything you needed to know right now, she would have told you."

Jayden drifted for a while on a morphine cloud. He woke when the sound of someone talking in the hallway invaded his drug-induced dreams. Was Tig here? He had no idea what time it was. He pressed the control, raising his hospital bed so he could sit up.

"Anyone out there?" he called out, his voice thin and raspy.

Tig strode into the room. "I'm right here, baby. How you doing?"

She leaned over and kissed him. His lips were dry and cracked, but she didn't seem to care. He could only imagine how he looked. Fuck, he hated having her see him weak and helpless.

Sliding her arms around him, she hugged him and asked, "Are you feeling better?"

"I'm getting by." The morphine was keeping the pain at about a five on the doctor's damn one-to-ten scale. "Cerissa was here."

"She just left to meet Henry. Father Matt should be here soon, and he'll stay with you when I have to leave. I wish I could stay all night, but I have to swing by the forensics lab, make sure they don't kick us to the back of the line. And after that, I'm meeting with the council."

Yeah, the job came first. He was a cop; he understood that was the deal. There were plenty of occasions he'd had to sacrifice time with her to get the job done.

"It's okay," he said. "Don't worry about me."

"I do worry about you because I love you, Jayden." She squeezed his hand. "I don't say it often enough, but I do. And I need you. I value you— for exactly who you are. But I don't know how to tell you what you need to hear for you to understand that."

"Cerissa told you," he croaked. If he could have scrubbed his hand over his face, he would have. But after the first time, he'd learned not to move the IV lines stuck into the back of his hand, and Tig was holding the other one.

"Cerissa said you were feeling down about getting hurt. There's no reason for you to feel bad. It could have happened to anyone."

"Yeah, but if it had been one of you, you'd be healed by now."

"Not from silver. Those bullets were silver. If one of us had gotten hit, we might be in worse shape than you." She ran her hand down his arm. "But Jayden, you aren't any less for being mortal. I see you no differently, and I'm getting pissed off that this town is making you feel bad about who you are."

He took a deep breath. Yeah, hearing that did help. Then his leg cramped, the pain shooting up to an eight. He scrunched his eyes and fumbled for the morphine pump's remote on the hospital tray.

"What can I do?" she asked.

He dropped the device back on the tray and opened his eyes. "Give it a moment. I'll feel better."

She gifted him one of her rare smiles. "I got a better idea—how about some more elixir of Tig?"

She bit her wrist and offered him the pooling blood.

"Almost as good as morphine," he said with a harsh laugh, before latching on to her wrist.

The taste of her blood always surprised him: a sharp metallic bite with a sweet edge. More satisfying than the richest dark beer, it gave the same exhilaration as a double espresso followed by a mellowing hit of pot.

He sighed around her wrist and relaxed into the pillow. The pain in his leg faded and the skin around the stitches tightened as the blood worked to heal the area.

Her phone buzzed and she yanked it out of its holder, glancing down at the caller ID. "It's the lab," she told him, and swiped the screen.

"You have a hit on the blood results?" Tig asked the caller. She held the phone out, like she'd put it on speaker.

"You're going to be surprised," the caller said. "I know *our* chief will be interested."

"Who is it?"

"I've emailed you the report. Read it and call me back."

Tig took her wrist back then tapped the phone a couple of times, and her eyes grew wider as she read the lab results.

"What is it?" Jayden asked.

"The man who killed Kim Han—we have a match for his DNA," she told him.

Finally, a break. It was about time. When she didn't say anything more, he asked, "So who is it?"

She slowly shook her head. "You'll never guess. Not in a thousand years."

CHAPTER 38

HENRY'S HOUSE—SAME NIGHT

Henry transferred from Father Matt's very small car to Cerissa's somewhat small car. The plan was to spend the evening with her at the hospital, but it turned out Tig didn't need them, so they returned to his house. He heated the frozen *arroz con pollo*, which was left over from the dinner he made her earlier in the week.

His phone rang as Cerissa finished her meal. He glanced at the caller

ID and the corners of his lips dropped. Why her—why now?

"Good evening, Anne-Louise," he said with a frustrated exhale.

"That's it. I want you and Méi on a plane tonight."

He jerked the phone away at the sound of her shrill voice, tapped the speaker icon, and placed the phone on the kitchen table. "I've put you on speaker. I'm here with Cerissa."

"I don't care if you're there with the Queen of England. You and Méi are to return to New York tonight."

"Méi is no longer under your control. I doubt she'll agree."

Anne-Louise huffed. "I'll deal with her. My children will obey me, do you hear me?"

Oh, he heard her. Red clouded his vision. This was just too much. Cerissa motioned for him to bring the phone closer.

"Anne-Louise?" Cerissa said.

"No. I'll not listen to you this time. He'll come to me. It's the only way I can protect him. There is someone trying to kill my children, and I won't allow it. Do you understand?"

"What I understand is you signed an agreement with Leopold. You can't demand Henry's presence in New York."

"I don't care. Leopold can sue me. By the time it's worked out, Henry will be in New York, and the threat will have passed."

"Yes, but then you'll have to relinquish all claim on Henry's blood."

"My dear girl, what are you prattling on about?"

"The penalty clause in your agreement with Leopold. Did you read it?"

"That's what I have lawyers for."

"If you insist *we* go to New York tonight, you'll lose all claim on Henry. Your lawyer should have told you."

"Why you little—"

"It's not my fault if you didn't read it."

"Wait. I will find it and read it now."

A *thunk* followed—Anne-Louise had dropped the phone. Henry hit mute. "Have I told you lately how much I love you?"

"Not enough." Cerissa smiled weakly. "The last few nights have been stressful."

"I'm back," Anne-Louise announced. Paper rustled, like she was flipping through the pages, and Henry unmuted the phone.

"Section 10," Cerissa said.

"I found it," Anne-Louise snarled.

"You're worried about Henry," Cerissa said. "And he appreciates your concern. You're trying to look out for his best interests, but this isn't the way to do it. Tig has a sample of the killer's blood. We hope it leads her to whoever is behind this."

Henry didn't give Anne-Louise a chance to argue it. "Cerissa is correct. Thank you for your interest in my welfare." He swallowed, the words clotting in his mouth. "I will take precautions. You have no need to worry."

"I—" Anne-Louise began.

"And if the threat is from someone in New York," Cerissa said, "you could be placing him in danger. You wouldn't want to bring him harm, would you?"

"Of course not."

"How does this sound?" Cerissa asked. "He'll send you a text each night before he goes to sleep, letting you know he's fine. Would that help?"

"I don't seem to have any choice in the matter."

"I promise," Henry said. "I'll text you. Goodnight."

He hit the disconnect button and left the phone on the table.

Cerissa dropped her face into her hands. "Good grief, that was close."

"You did wonderfully." His phone buzzed and she raised her head. An email from Frédéric. He started to dismiss it, but Cerissa stopped him.

"Rein in your mortal?" she repeated, reading the subject line. "May I see that?"

Why not? He handed the phone to her. She punched the preview to open it and he read it over her shoulder.

The subcommittee has gotten out of hand. Mortals on the council? Never! Mortals have already screwed up this world. We can't let them screw up our domain. Put your mate back in their place.

"Well, isn't he a piece of work," she said. "Do you mind forwarding it to me?"

"You don't think—"

"I'm just being cautious."

He did as she asked and then stuffed the phone into its case on his belt.

She laid her head back on her arms, and he stroked his hand over her hair. "Would you like a back rub?"

"Yes, please," she mumbled against her arm.

He stepped behind her chair to rub her shoulders, using his thumbs to relax the muscles around her neck, while she cradled her head in her arms. He kept massaging her. Ten minutes later, he wondered if she'd fallen asleep.

"Cerissa?"

She abruptly straightened up. "Oh."

"Are you all right?"

She rubbed her eyes. "I was dreaming about something I forgot to tell you. I was going to tell you over dinner last night."

"Yes?"

"Ah, Anne-Louise is investing in the lab. Leopold let her. She kind of twisted his arm when they negotiated the agreement, to sweeten the deal."

He pursed his lips. If the deal were any sweeter, Anne-Louise could open a candy store. "She always finds another way to screw me."

"I asked Leopold to reconsider, to let you invest too, but he wouldn't hear of it. Especially now, since we're mates."

He sighed and knelt next to her. "I have the better part of the deal."

"I think so too." She hugged him tightly. "Do you mind if I sleep here? I need some rest. In the morning, I'll go back and see how Jayden is doing."

"Of course you may sleep here. I will join you until sunrise."

She put her hands flat on his chest. "Sleep. I need sleep. Once the noise from the crystal stops...."

He wrapped his arms around her again. "We do not have to make love. I would be content to hold you as you fall asleep."

"Okay, then," she said with a tired smile.

"I'll join you in but a moment. I just want to clean up down here."

He watched Cerissa climb the stairs to the bedroom.

Their bedroom.

At first, he had been in a hurry to have her move in. But her delayed disclosures made their relationship taste like a wine that wasn't ripe for bottling.

Do we need more time before I ask her?

She was so brave going up against Anne-Louise. She had saved his life—three times—at risk to her own wellbeing. She was smart, beautiful, and self-sacrificing. The more he learned about her, the more he loved her. Maybe Father Matt was right.

Maybe I know everything about her I need to know.

His phone buzzed. Tig had sent out a reverse-911 text, announcing a series of community meetings. Something important must have happened. He scrolled through the long text, which listed the meeting places, including Rolf's house. Tomorrow, Henry would take Cerissa to that one.

And very soon, he'd ask her about the next step.

CHAPTER 39

After spending another day at Jayden's hospital bedside, Cerissa met Henry at Rolf and Karen's place. The ten o'clock meeting hadn't begun yet, but Rolf's living room was already filled to capacity with community members milling about. Cerissa accepted a kiss on the cheek from Henry.

"Do you mind if I speak with them alone?" he asked, pointing to where Rolf, Frédéric, and Yacov stood.

"Go ahead. I'll grab us seats at the front."

Folding chairs in orderly rows occupied half the room. Cerissa eased onto one in the front row. Her eyes went wide when she saw who rested in the chair next to her, his leg stretched out and wrapped in a rigid removable brace.

"Jayden, what are you doing out of the hospital?"

"An amazing recovery," he said, laughing. "That's what the doctors called it. Two nights of blood from Tig sped up the healing process. She checked me out tonight against doctor's orders—they wouldn't sign the papers. They couldn't believe what their own eyes told them."

"You should be resting, not here."

"Don't worry—my leg's much better, but it still hurts. I'm taking the next week off. What's the use of having sick leave if you can't use it?" He adjusted the position of the brace he was wearing. "You know, sometimes I aspire to be a slacker."

Cerissa laughed. From what she'd learned about Jayden, it was anything but the truth. "So what's this meeting about?"

"A lot." He leaned in close, bracing himself against one crutch. "I don't want to steal Tig's thunder, but I can tell you this," he said, his voice lowered. "We suspect San Diego is the focal point for whoever is behind this."

"San Diego?" Cerissa repeated, recalling what Ari had told her a while back—Rolf frequently went to San Diego.

From behind her, someone cleared their throat. Cerissa jerked her head around to find Gaea standing there. "Well, my dear, I wondered when I might see you again, but I didn't guess it would be here," Gaea said primly, her hands on her full hips. "You've been away from the house a lot."

Cerissa stood and gave Gaea a hug. She ignored the looks she got from some of the other vampires. As Henry's mate, close contact with another vampire was discouraged, but there had to be an exception for one as old and trusted as Gaea.

"It's good to see you," Cerissa said.

"You look fit. Is Henry treating you well?"

"Yes, of course."

"I expect you to spend a little time at home soon and catch me up on what's been happening. I heard you and Henry were there when Jayden was shot."

"Henry was. I arrived afterward."

"You can't fault me for being worried. Leopold would never forgive me if I let something happen to you."

"Nothing's going to happen to me."

"And you, young man," Gaea said, glaring at Jayden. "You should be more careful."

Jayden didn't get a chance to reply. Tig took her place in front of the group and announced, "If everyone would take a seat, we can begin."

Cerissa gave Gaea a hug goodbye.

"Hey, girlfriend," Karen said, grabbing the chair on the other side. She leaned in and whispered, "I've got some real juicy gossip. The mayor really blew it."

"How?"

"Lying to the community—boy, they won't forget that come next election. Rolf told me it was the mayor's idea to tell everyone the investigation was over."

Cerissa shrugged. Finding out who was behind this and ensuring Henry's safety were more important than local politics.

Tig watched the mortals scurry to find chairs. Her fellow vampires, in their typical manner, were slow to take orders. The two founders continued an intense conversation with Rolf and Frédéric—the power core in the room. She stood in front of Rolf's granite fireplace, looking out over the room. Why did Rolf need all this space? His living room was large enough to serve as a formal ballroom, with its marble tile floor, two crystal chandeliers, and four French doors overlooking the pool.

If the vice mayor could afford to live in a palace like this, why did he begrudge her the raise she requested? Her home was a shack in comparison.

She glanced at her phone. Time to get this meeting going, or she'd be late for the second one. Well, there was one way to get their attention.

"We know who killed Kim Han," she announced. The vampires stopped talking and turned in unison to look at her. "Now if you'll take your seats...." Good. The power core grabbed the chairs nearest to them, and the fifteen others followed suit. "I'm holding small meetings like this tonight and tomorrow night so everyone can attend at least one meeting."

She waited a beat, focusing intensely on Rolf.

"The Carlyle Cutter killed Kim."

A buzz of expletives shot through the room, the mortals expressing their astonishment. The vampires sat there immobile.

"As you'll recall, the first Cutter killing occurred two months ago. A week after Blanche was apprehended, the third victim was discovered in Ruthton.

"I suspected there might be a link between the Carlyle Cutter and our community, so I spoke with the detectives in charge of the Ruthton case. The public doesn't know the Cutter is draining his victims after torturing them." She paused, letting the information sink in. "He's creating adrenaline-spiked blood."

"What does that mean?" Karen asked hesitantly.

Hmm. Rolf had been at the council meeting where it was discussed. He must have used better lip glue around Karen than Tig had given him credit for in the past.

"Good question," Tig said. "Fear and pain cause a chemical change in blood. It tastes like blood from a victim who was chased and trapped. Adrenaline-spiked blood is sometimes sold on the black market, mostly to older vampires who developed a taste for it before we became more civilized. It's unlawful for a community member to buy it because of the inhumane way in which it's obtained. The normal penalty is a large fine."

Tig scanned the room again—no one reacted, so she continued. "The council passed an emergency ordinance last night increasing the penalty. Because of the particular viciousness involved, if anyone is caught buying

Cutter blood, they'll be banned from the community. And if anyone is found to be directly involved in the Carlyle Cutter killings, he or she will be staked."

The humans let out a collective gasp, and Rolf asked, "Do you know the identity of the Carlyle Cutter?"

"Not yet," Tig said.

Gaea waved her hand in the air, like she was signaling a waiter. "My dear, are you saying the Cutter is a vampire?"

"No," Tig said, shaking her head. "His blood is definitely mortal. What I'm saying is a vampire may be behind the Cutter's actions—pulling the strings. We have good reason to believe Chen Méi was the real target. Now that another founder has been targeted, we suspect Blanche was not working alone."

"What's your game plan?" Frédéric asked.

Tig nodded to him, acknowledging the prompt. He already knew the answer—he had been present during the closed session last night when she revealed her next steps to the council.

"We're intensifying our attempt to rule out suspects," she said. "For that reason, each of you may be interviewed. The council expects your full cooperation."

"Chief Anderson," Yacov said, rising to his feet. "I appreciate your efforts, my friend, to find the person or persons who are behind these crimes. But in establishing this community, we didn't create a police state."

"Of course, Founder. No one will be compelled to talk with us, but we'll have to intensely investigate those who do not cooperate. It's in each person's best interest to talk openly with us so we may rule them out and move on."

She waited to see if there were any more questions. When no one spoke, she said, "At the next council meeting, I'm asking the council to install a perimeter-monitoring system along the wall, including motion detectors and surveillance cameras. The man who shot Dr. Patel came in by foot. We found the shooters' ladders against the wall—on both sides. And we still don't know how Blanche got back in—she didn't come through the guard gate—so we're considering trip cameras along the mountain ridge."

Henry stood, his hands folded in front of him. "Chief Anderson, we all appreciate your hard work, your efforts to keep our community safe, but we should embark on this course with caution and much reflection. In our zeal for safety, we can become prisoners of our own means."

His concern was a familiar one; she'd heard it all before. Most vampires avoided having their picture taken. A visual record made it harder to assume a new identity when the current one became too old to maintain. She had come up with a compromise that should pass muster with the community.

"The mayor is sensitive to your concerns, Founder. There will be no cameras at the entrance to the community, but anyone scaling the wall is entering illegally. So that's where I'm proposing we place security cameras—along the wall. If you have a better idea on how to keep the intruders out without sacrificing privacy, we're interested in hearing it."

"I recognize the dangers we face," Henry said. "I'm only saying we should proceed with caution."

Tig bit back her reply. There'd been too much caution already, and now a member of their community was dead.

"Are there any further questions?" she asked. Hearing none, she added, "Thank you for your attention. Captain Johnson or I will be in touch to schedule an interview."

CHAPTER 40

TIG AND JAYDEN'S HOME—LATER THAT NIGHT

Jayden snagged an ice pack from his home freezer and wrapped it around his leg. He hobbled into the family room, which formed one big room with the kitchen, and made his way to the computer in the corner. Ignoring the pain, he eased himself into the chair to check his email. A few clicks later and he had the printout in hand.

He pushed away from the table and awkwardly plopped onto the slightly worn couch. Covered in a woven pale green fabric—a color he liked and Tig hated—the couch was the first piece of furniture they bought together.

Before he moved to the Hill, Tig had lived in a small two-bedroom house. When he moved here three years ago, she'd rented this larger house for them both, and they bought all new furniture, except for the bedroom. The Danish modern set from his apartment was new enough that they decided to keep it.

Tig even tolerated his love of old comic books. He'd framed and hung his favorites on the family room's walls, including his 1937 *Detective Comics* issue featuring Batman.

Sometimes he felt like Robin to Tig's Batman. Tonight, he felt more like Sherlock Holmes. He proudly laid the printout on the coffee table and shoved a pillow under his leg to raise it—the damn thing was throbbing again.

He'd overdone it, going to the meeting at Rolf's. Tig had dropped him off at home before she headed to the second meeting so he could rest, but he was determined not to fall asleep. Everything was happening too quickly. He wanted to talk with Tig when she returned, so he turned on the television, increasing the volume to keep himself awake.

His eyelids started to droop, but opened fast when he heard the clunking sound of the automatic garage door.

"In here," he called out, when Tig came through the kitchen door that connected to the garage.

"You should be in bed," she said.

Picking up the remote, he clicked off the television. "I'm fine here. How'd it go?"

"About as well as the first."

He rearranged the pillow under his leg, trying to stop the pain. Nerve damage *did* take longer to heal, even with vampire blood to boost it. She brought him another ice pack and adjusted the pillow for him.

"Better?" she asked.

"Yeah, thanks." He relaxed back onto the couch again.

"Mind if we talk business?"

"Why do you think I waited up? I'm in no shape for sex," he said with a laugh.

She smiled at that and lowered herself onto the edge of the coffee table. He liked making her smile.

"Have you received any response from your email to New Path?" she asked.

"The church appears to be on hiatus. Autoreply message said they were doing 'missionary work' and unable to reply right away."

"That makes no sense."

He shrugged. "It is what it is. But I did finish looking into Henry and Yacov's histories, to see if Yacov had any blood relationship to Henry's grandsire. I went back as far as the records we have and found zilch. I think they come from different lines entirely."

"Okay, we can tick that box."

He tapped the stack of printouts next to her on the coffee table. "And I pulled the airport records while you were at your meeting."

"You're supposed to be resting."

"Marcus emailed me a signed warrant. With Kim's death, everyone's become much more cooperative. I sent it to the tower, and the night controller emailed me the flight logs for both Rolf and Frédéric."

She quickly flipped through them. "From his travel permits, we already knew Rolf was in San Diego a lot," she said, topping it with a whistle.

"Yeah, just because he pulled a travel permit didn't mean he actually traveled on that date. The flight logs confirm it."

"But there's more. One flight matches with the first prisoner release date confirming he was there at the time. Did Maggie finish the chart I requested?"

He pointed to the computer—he'd left it open on the screen. "She matched the gate logs to Rolf's request for travel permits."

Tig moved to the desk chair. She *tsked* as she scrolled through the spreadsheet, glancing back and forth between it and the airport logs.

"Just what I suspected," she said. "He didn't get travel permits for every trip. He flew to San Diego on all the prisoner release dates and the date the guard was killed—he hid a lot of his travel."

"From what I can tell, Frédéric wasn't near San Diego on the key dates. He was only there twice in the last year. Not much."

Tig swiveled the desk chair to face him. "So we keep our focus on Rolf for now."

"Has Ufa discovered anything about Rolf?" Jayden asked.

"Not yet. Aside from his dinner out with Henry the night Kim Han was shot, he's been a real homebody lately."

"Did you see Maggie's note? Liza's been off the Hill a lot, and some of it in San Diego. Do you want Maggie to track her travel dates?"

"Shit. Maybe I should check the rest of the council, just to appear balanced—and the town attorney, too." She turned to the computer and tapped at the keyboard. "I'll ask Maggie to do it."

"One more thing," he said, holding his phone. "A text message came in while I was in the hospital. I didn't see it until tonight. The knife used to kill Norman, the prison guard, had dried blood under the handle."

"So what? His throat was sliced. Not surprising his blood flowed under the handle."

"It wasn't *his* blood."

Tig's eyes grew wide. "Whose blood was it?"

"Remember the Cutter's first victim, the one from Carlyle, the one he got his name from?"

"Yes...."

"They matched the blood under the knife handle to the Cutter's first victim. The Cutter killed the guard."

"Fuck." Tig threw down the airport logs she still held. "This nails it. The Cutter *is* linked to the attacks on Henry and Yacov too, and not just Méi."

"Yeah, but I have one question."

"What?"

"With Blanche dead, who's pulling the strings now?"

After the meeting at Rolf's house, Cerissa said goodnight to Henry and drove back to Gaea's. Glancing at her watch, she decided there was time. She wanted to talk with Ari—she had recorded Tig's report, but couldn't wait for him to view the video. He needed to hear the latest now.

She left her car parked along Robles Road and hiked to the mountain trail behind Gaea's house. Flashing back to the Enclave—the pivot point for all their instantaneous transport—she set the device in her watch for Florida and flashed directly inside Ari's house. He'd left his protection screen turned off again.

Sloppy.

The house was dark, the computer room empty. Where was he? Ari was one of those programmers who usually worked into the wee hours of the morning. She prowled down the hall, looking through each open door, until she reached the master bedroom.

She peered in. It was dark, but she could see the outlines of two people in bed, a woman asleep next to Ari.

Oops.

Cerissa scrambled back quickly, but he threw off the sheet and bolted from the room, grabbing a pair of boxers before closing the door silently.

"What are you doing here?" he asked in an angry whisper. He stepped into the boxers, covering his nakedness in lime-green martini glasses.

She propped her hands on her hips, just like Gaea did when annoyed. "If you can drop in on me unannounced, I can do the same."

"Come in here." He ushered her into the living room of the house he rented. She looked around—she hadn't been in this room before. Chrome and white leather furniture dominated, with a television on one wall.

Jeez, was he a walking caricature of a playboy? A little dated, though…or was 1960s Hugh Hefner back in style?

He went over to a glass-top sideboard and mixed a drink for himself. "Help yourself."

She examined the bottle of Macallan—aged fifteen years. Young for a scotch, but she needed a drink. Badly. "A lot has happened in the past week," she told him.

"I saw the vids." He settled back onto a leather lounger, stretching out his long legs. "Nice job on Jayden's first aid, by the way."

Pacing back and forth, she swirled her drink and looked into her scotch glass. Nothing there was going to help, but she took a sip anyway.

"Look, kid, sit down and tell me what's got you so worked up."

She parked herself on the white leather couch and explained to Ari what she'd recently learned. "If a vampire is using the Cutter, we have to stop him. Can you imagine what will happen if humans trace the Cutter back to someone on the Hill? It will destroy my community."

He scratched his belly and belched, then got up to raid the bar fridge, setting out sliced salami, cheese, and crackers. He made himself a plate, motioning for her to serve herself. She wasn't interested in food.

"Just what do you think you can do about it?" he asked, and chomped down on a cracker and cheese sandwich.

"We could use some of our, ah, resources—to help."

"Ciss, are you out of your silly little mind?" He waved a slice of salami at her before popping it into his mouth. "Notwithstanding our little ploy with the crystal, you're still in deep shit if the Protectors find out you're keeping house with Henry—"

"I'm not living with him."

"You're just making booty calls, I know, but you didn't let me finish. The Protectors can detect when our technology is used—you'll just double the trouble you're in."

She took a sip of the golden-brown liquid in her glass. "There must be some way we can help."

"I know you mean well, but you can't meddle," Ari said. "You're a Watcher. Observe only—not that you've been doing much observing."

"I can't sit back and let something bad happen to Henry—"

"I know, kid, but you can't use our technology to interfere." He made a stack of cheese and salami wedged between two crackers and shoved the whole thing in his mouth. He managed to add, "Them's the rules," without spraying crumbs.

She started pacing again. "But we're interfering already—we're supposed to figure out who's behind the VDM, so the Protectors can stop them."

"Yeah, that's a sanctioned op. But without the Protectors' blessing—"

"Well, Tig thinks whoever is behind the assassination attempts is controlling the Cutter. What if the Carlyle Cutter is working for the VDM and the VDM is trying to assassinate the founders of Sierra Escondida?"

"Got any proof?"

"I don't need proof." Her glass was now empty. She poured another drink and shot it down. "Just tell the Protectors the Cutter might be involved with the VDM, and you can use our technology. That should get them off your back."

"Okay, kid, I'll consider it."

"And you can always use human tech."

"What good would that do?"

"For one, have you continued to track Rolf's flights?"

"Rolf? You think he's involved with the Cutter?"

She slammed the scotch bottle down on the counter. "I don't know— that's why I'm asking."

"Okay, okay, calm down. Don't break the bottle; that stuff ain't cheap. I set up a search-and-retrieve program on Rolf's flights. I haven't looked lately."

"Can you run a report?"

"Not today. I'm booked solid."

"I saw."

He gave her a sour look. "I should be able to get it to you in a day or so."

"What about Frédéric?"

"I've been tracking him, but I haven't seen anything that points to him."

"How about this?" She took out her phone and showed him Frédéric's email.

"Oooh, I like the part about putting their mates in their place. Is Henry going to put you in your place?"

"Ari, I told you—"

"Just cool it, kid." He stared at the email again. "Well, his attitude toward mortals kind of fits with the VDM. You got anything else on him?"

"Not anything I haven't already given you. What about Blanche?"

"What about her?" Ari asked, stifling a yawn.

"We need to find out who she was working with."

"Already tried. I didn't buy the council's announcement, especially after you told me about the email she left in Henry's pocket."

"Huh? And you didn't tell me?"

"While you've been mattress-dancing with Henry, I've been working. I ran a check on all of Blanche's bank accounts, any phones she had under her name, and a few aliases I discovered, as well as her past four apartments. Bottom line—she traveled a lot. No pattern, though she did spend time in San Diego. The most interesting part was a transfer of half a million dollars into her bank account after she shot Henry and took a photo of him lying on the ground."

"So who paid her?"

Ari popped another cracker sandwich into his mouth and shrugged like he wasn't impressed. "A religious group called New Path."

"We need to tell Tig about New Path."

"She already knows."

"You're tapping Tig's phone?"

"Phone, email, the works—I even have a keystroke logger on her office computer. Someone has to watch out for your butt."

"So who's behind New Path?"

"I'm still working on that. Whoever opened the bank account was crafty. I haven't traced it to any live human beings—or dead ones. It stops with a numbered account in a little country known for its privacy laws."

"Which shouldn't be a problem for a computer whiz like you."

"It is if they keep their records on paper instead of in a computer."

"What about Blanche's phone?"

"Burner phone—paid for with a no-name credit card, one you can buy through any grocery store."

"What about Barney Morrison and the other names I gave you, the ones from the investor presentation?"

"Nothing so far. But the VDM has been cagey. I don't expect—"

Footsteps in the hall stopped the conversation. "Who's that?" came a sleepy-sounding voice. The woman pointed at Cerissa.

"Why, Reeta, my little angel," Ari said, rising and quickly joining the woman at the archway. She had a robe wrapped around her. "This is my cousin, Cerissa. She's having a little domestic problem and stopped by to get my advice."

"At four in the morning?"

"That is when domestic problems often arise, my sweet."

Cerissa stood. "I'm sorry to disturb your sleep. I didn't realize Ari had company. I'll leave and talk with him tomorrow."

Ari waved a finger at her. "Just remember what I said, Ciss. Your job is to watch, not investigate. You can't use our tech—" he began, and then glanced over at Rita. "You can't put your nose into things that aren't any of your business. You'll get it cut off each time. And noses are hard to grow back."

CHAPTER 41

SIERRA ESCONDIDA POLICE DEPARTMENT—TWO NIGHTS LATER

It took Tig two nights to interview twenty Hill residents, resulting in a lot of legwork with few results. Jayden was still recovering, and she refused to let him accompany her—he needed to heal.

The council members were last on her interview list in case something new popped. She'd only get one chance at each of them, and tonight was her shot at Rolf.

He had disappeared from the Hill last night. Ufa tailed him to the airport, booked a private charter, and followed him to San Diego. Ufa had yet to report in. She tapped her fingers, anxious to hear from him.

At her request, Jayden had called Karen during the day and found out Rolf was in San Diego on business, visiting with distributors.

Yeah, right. Like she believed that explanation.

Rolf was due back tonight. Based on the airport logs, Tig now had a good reason to talk with him. She sent an email asking him to meet her at the police station when he returned.

Rolf's reply insisted they meet a few hours before dawn at his winery office. She preferred talking to him on her own turf, but since she didn't have enough evidence to arrest him, she agreed to his terms. At the appointed time, she trod through the winery corridor alone.

But she wasn't stupid. She had backup nearby. Just in case he went entirely rogue.

She had tried phoning Ufa so she could talk with him first. But he wasn't responding to her calls. Had something happened?

Maybe I should delay the meeting.

Rolf's office door was open, and inside it sat two elegant wooden desks, one empty, one with Rolf behind it. The richly appointed room seemed a bit jarring, a bad combination of old world and modern. Rolf motioned to a chair in front of his desk and then brought his fingers together in a steeple, reminiscent of the same pose the mayor frequently adopted.

Too late to cancel now.

She remained standing, took out her phone, and hit record. He didn't question it—as a reserve officer, he knew the protocol.

"What did you want to discuss?" he asked.

"Your flights to San Diego. Why are you going there so frequently?"

"Business. I meet with our wine distributors."

She dropped the chart Maggie prepared on Rolf's desk. "That's a lot of distributor meetings. I've spoken with a few other winery owners. When I told them how often you go to San Diego to entertain distributors, they laughed."

"They would," he scoffed, handing the chart back to her after barely glancing at it. "They're amateurs."

She leaned on his desk, shortening the distance between them. She had to flush out her quarry before someone else was killed. "Come on, Rolf. You were in San Diego the nights the shooters were released from prison. You didn't pull travel permits. Why?"

He scowled. "Just a coincidence."

"And you were in San Diego when the prison guard was killed."

"What prison guard?"

Did he sleep through all her reports to the council? Or was he being intentionally obtuse? "Blanche's boyfriend, the guard who knew all three parolees involved in the attacks. You flew to San Diego right after the dance ended, you were there in the early morning hours when the guard was killed, and then you flew right back, in time to set up Henry at the baseball game."

"Again, just a coincidence." He fluttered his fingers like he was brushing lint off his shirt. "I flew to San Diego to bring some of our clients back for the baseball game."

"Then why didn't you pull permits for your travel?"

"Too much *verdammt* paperwork."

"Seriously, Rolf. You voted to have Henry whipped for breaking the rules. What makes you think you're exempt?"

"I'm on the council, that's what."

She stared at him, looking for any tell behind his arrogance. Nervousness sat in the lines around his eyes. "The guard was killed by the Carlyle Cutter."

His eyes widened. "What the fuck are you talking about?"

"You heard me. The Carlyle Cutter killed the prison guard. Tell me, Rolf, were you there? Did you drink the adrenaline-spiked blood from the kill?"

Rolf shot to his feet, leaning his fists on the desk, his angry face inches from hers. "Enough. I want you to leave."

She must have hit a nerve. "Rolf, talk to me. If you're innocent, tell me the truth about San Diego."

"Go to hell. If you know what's good for you, you won't repeat this nonsense to anyone."

"If you were there on business, why are you so angry?"

He slapped a hand on the desk. "What I do in San Diego is none of your business!" he shouted.

"It is when you don't pull travel permits."

He pointed at the door. "Enough. Leave."

"The evidence points at you, Rolf. This is your chance to explain yourself."

"There's nothing to explain."

She straightened up and crossed her arms. "So which will it be? Burned alive or a quick stake through the heart? Confess now and the council might be lenient, spare you the painful death you deserve."

"This conversation is over." He grabbed a briefcase and strode out. "Lock the door when you leave," he called out behind him.

She stood there stunned. He hadn't reacted until she asked about adrenaline-spiked blood. He'd been nervous, acting all cocky to cover it up, until she spoke those words. Then the rage came out.

Her question must have really rattled him, if it made him stupid enough to leave her alone in his office. There was nothing to stop her from searching his desk and computer. She phoned Zeke and told him to join her. If Rolf came back, she wanted someone on guard at the door.

She pulled her keys out of her pocket and moved to Rolf's side of the desk. The flash drive on her keychain—she had wondered when it would come in handy. She flipped it open and plugged it into a USB slot on Rolf's computer. He'd left without locking the screen. When she tapped the space bar, the screen saver disappeared, replaced by the desktop.

"Where's Rolf?" Zeke asked, when he arrived at the door.

"He left. Keep an eye on the hall and yell if he comes back."

"What're you doin'? We don't got no warrant."

"Don't need one. He invited me here and left." She opened the hard drive browser and found what she wanted—all Rolf's email and his work calendar, in one file.

Zeke scratched his head. "But you don't got a warrant. We can only grab stuff in plain sight."

"A mere technicality, one the council isn't going to care about." She surfed through the other folders, but didn't find anything else of interest. She copied his correspondence files, just in case, then closed the browser and ejected the flash drive. Rolf underestimated her.

"There," she said, holding up the thumb drive. "The answers to our questions may be right here."

It was after four in the morning when Henry switched on the console in his game room and logged in to *Zombies from Hell*. After all the stress he'd been through, killing zombies seemed like good, clean, relaxing fun.

Cerissa had just left for Gaea's to meet a small group of potential investors who were on the Hill and had questions about her project. His phone rang. Did she miss him so much she couldn't wait and called while she drove? He paused his on-screen character; he didn't want the rat-a-tat sounds of gunfire from the multi-player video game interrupting the call.

He glanced down at the caller ID and, seeing Rolf's name, decided he should program a special ringtone for Cerissa.

Did he really want to talk to Rolf? He and Rolf hadn't settled things between them. Then again, if it had something to do with the winery, it would be irresponsible to ignore the call.

He punched the connect button. He'd fake the cordiality he didn't feel until he found out what Rolf wanted.

"Rolf, where are you? We have a good zombie battle going. I think the other team is from another community; they are excellent players."

"Tig was just at the winery."

"So?"

"The stupid bitch wants to know why I've been in San Diego so frequently."

Henry took a deep breath. "What did you tell her?"

"What we agreed. I was there to meet with distributors."

"Did she believe you?"

"No. I think we have a problem."

"What do you mean *we* have a problem? There is no *we* here—you made that clear from the council dais."

"I did what I thought was best for you. But that doesn't matter now. You have as much to lose in this as I do."

"Now that's where you're wrong."

If anything, all Henry had to lose was the community's respect, and with the way his reputation had been tarnished in front of the council, it might be better for him to have the whole thing come out now. Rolf, on the other hand, had a lot more to lose.

"Henry, you have to help me," Rolf begged. "If they find out, they'll think you were in on it."

"They will only think that if you stab me in the back again."

"I won't. But I need your help or Tig will dig deeper, and neither of us wants that."

Tig heard the outer door of the police station buzz. She looked up from the computer screen in her office. Rolf's calendar was open on her desktop computer, and Henry stood in her doorway.

She quickly hit the shortcut, switching the screen to her desktop view, and stood up. "Founder, I wasn't expecting you."

Henry settled into the guest chair. "I'll answer your questions about Rolf, but you must tell no one."

"I can't promise confidentiality." She picked up her phone and started recording their conversation, tipping it to show Henry.

He reached over and punched pause. "If you want to talk off the record, I'm happy to do so. It has nothing to do with the crimes you are investigating. But it would ruin Rolf politically if others learned the truth."

"You think I care about Rolf's political career?" She laid the phone on her desk, still paused. She didn't have much choice if she wanted to hear what Henry had to say.

"I know Rolf hasn't been diplomatic in his criticism of your investigation."

"This isn't payback." Tig resumed her seat and tapped the paperwork on her desk. "These dates—his trips to San Diego are just too damning. The shooters all came from the San Diego prison, and a prison guard connected to those shooters was murdered. Rolf was there on four key dates."

"Circumstantial evidence." Henry unclipped his phone from his belt. "Tell me the dates you are concerned about."

She handed him the list with dates. He displayed something on his phone and offered it to her.

An appointment on his calendar read: *San Diego - Rolf / Wine Connoisseurs LLC.*

She selected the second date—another wine distributor appointment.

"I was with Rolf on those occasions," Henry said, holding himself with an air of authority. "He met with no one connected to the murders."

Tig shook her head and handed the phone back to him. "He's your friend. It's normal for you to cover for him. But Henry," she said, exasperated, "he tried to kill you."

"I will tell you the truth, and you will keep it confidential."

"I can't make that promise, but I will do this: if no other evidence leads to Rolf, I won't have any reason to tell anyone else."

"Just remember, it would be unfair for you to use this information politically."

Yeah, right. Rolf hadn't been fair with her, but Henry expected her to take the high road. Still, she couldn't burn a source, especially a founder.

"I understand," she finally said. "Go ahead."

"It is like this: banked blood doesn't satisfy him. He still needs blood from the vein."

"Henry, really—" she began, and then pursed her lips, recalling something from Rolf's jacket—the special file she had on each member of her community. Before Rolf moved to the Hill in the 1950s, he'd been tied to a vicious attack on a mortal in South America. The mortal had survived. When Rolf was vetted for membership sixty-five years ago, Henry had given his personal pledge that nothing like it would happen again if Rolf joined the Sierra Escondida community.

She would review the file to confirm her memory after Henry left. Perhaps he'd built his story on Rolf's history to give it credibility. She wasn't sure whom to believe. Everything he said could still be a lie.

"Tig, you must understand. He only goes to areas outside the treaty, which is why he's chosen San Diego."

"So he can combine business with his habit?"

"I'm not lying." Henry paused, averting his gaze to the side, like he was considering something. When he returned his focus to her, he added, "After the council's vote, I looked into dissolving our partnership. Rolf doesn't know yet. I only tell you this so you'll understand. I'm not lying for a friend. Whatever friendship he and I used to have, well, it's been strained to the point of breaking."

She took in a deep breath and forced it back out loudly. "I'll take your word for now. But if any new evidence arises…"

"I understand. You'll do your job. But I'm convinced nothing connects Rolf to the attacks." Henry stood up. "Thank you for your time."

As soon as Henry was gone, Ufa appeared at her office door. Why hadn't he reported in before this?

"I have the answer you seek," Ufa said. "I was waiting in the other room and heard what Henry told you."

"Was he telling the truth?"

"I have no way to know whether Henry lied—he may believe what he told you—but his story is not the complete picture. Your vice mayor has a big problem. A very big problem indeed."

"And that is?"

"He's addicted to adrenaline-spiked blood."

CHAPTER 42

Henry stacked wood in the drawing room's fireplace over a mix of smaller sticks and newspaper. After another day's sleep, the evening had turned unseasonably cold for late May.

He was ready for a relaxing evening at home with Cerissa. She'd come over as soon as the sun set. She had no meetings tonight, no investors to woo.

Father Matt's suggestion echoed in his mind. *Take your time, get to know her, don't demand all her secrets right now.*

What about his secrets? He certainly had enough of them, including the one Tig now knew. Would Cerissa forgive him his past transgressions when she found out? Forgiveness didn't come naturally to him. He had to work at it.

But what about her? She'd forgiven him for the whole Anne-Louise blunder. Perhaps the Lux were the forgiving type. After all, Cerissa knew he had a long past, but never seemed bent on digging it up.

Maybe she did accept him for what he was.

Tig posed a different problem—her job was to question everything, forgive nothing. Even if Tig hadn't believed what he told her last night, he was certain Rolf had nothing to do with Kim Han's death or the Cutter—which meant the real culprit was still out there.

That alone was a good reason to stay here tonight. He didn't like the idea of becoming a prisoner in his own home, but for the moment, why go into town and invite trouble?

At least the crystal had stopped tuning to Cerissa. When she arrived at his doorstep, she'd eagerly greeted him, wrapping her arms around him and kissing him deeply.

So far, the whole emotion thing hadn't been as intrusive as he'd feared. Only her extreme emotions drilled through his mind in a way he couldn't ignore. The rest of the time, it wasn't much different from reading Cerissa's feelings from her face, voice, and scent—except now, he experienced phantom sensations of temperature, smell, and color to go with the emotion. Her eagerness as they kissed had the scent of evergreen, with a shot of sizzling heat.

He didn't want to carry her off to the bedroom right then—well, he did, he desired her very much, but he didn't want to be *that* kind of man, who thought only of sex—so he cooked dinner for her and suggested they spend some time relaxing by the fireplace.

He lit the match under the kindling and remained kneeling in front of the hearth, to make sure it didn't sputter out.

The fire grew, the flames licking around the logs. In short order, he felt warmed to his core, comfortable and cozy. The crackle of the dry logs, the smell of the fire, reminded him of happier times in his childhood. The stack of unread newspapers next to his chair beckoned to him. He left the fireplace and eased back into his cushy leather armchair, snapping open a newspaper. He glanced at Cerissa over the top of it.

She was reading a novel, oblivious to his gaze. She looked tasty, sitting in the chair opposite his, sipping tea and reading. She had gone by the public library and checked out a book he considered to be one of the most inaccurate pieces of trash ever written, but he kept his opinion about Bram Stoker's *Dracula* to himself. Giving a mental shrug, he settled deeper into his chair, and returned his attention to the *Wall Street Journal*.

He was on page ten when she interrupted his reading. "Henry, may I ask you a question about vampires?"

Had she not been so adorable, he might have been annoyed. "Does that count as a question?"

"Very funny. I was just wondering about something," she said. "Some of the stories are myths, right? I've seen you wear a crucifix. And Father Matt handles the host with no ill effect."

"Father Matt has a collection of holy objects, from a variety of religions. He serves communion and handles holy water. None of those myths are true."

"Except silver *is* deadly."

"Yes. Which is where the misconception about crosses came from."

"I don't understand."

"Crosses and other religious symbols were frequently made of silver.

Hold up a silver cross and a vampire will back off. Hold up a wooden cross and the person doing so will not live to tell the tale. Thus, mortals assumed it was the cross, when it was the silver."

"But how do you explain using the host to keep a vampire at bay?"

"You are reading fiction. Do not expect it to be accurate. But perhaps there is even an explanation for that. The chalice holding the host was often made of silver. Place a silver chalice filled with the host near a vampire, and once again, the silver threatens harm. Father Matt uses a gold chalice. You'll notice we have spared no expense in using gold where silver would normally be the metal of choice."

She crossed her arms. "What about turning into a bat?"

"Am I to have no secrets from you?" he asked brusquely.

"I thought you were in favor of full disclosure."

He glowered. She was right, but he didn't want to talk about it. A particularly loud crackle of the fire punctuated the silence.

"Is it true?" she asked.

He exhaled sharply, refolded the newspaper, and laid it aside. "You should be aware such things are not openly discussed in the community. Transforming into a bat or a wolf was a way to escape danger. We no longer hunt humans, so we no longer need to transform to flee when the hunt goes bad. Transforming is associated with those times and not spoken of. Some of the younger vampires have never tried to change; perhaps they cannot. Transforming within the boundaries of the Hill is discouraged."

"I'm sorry if I hit a nerve. I didn't expect it to be a touchy subject, considering you chose *Rancho del Murciélago* for the name of your home."

"I named it 'Ranch of the Bat' a long time ago. With the cave of bats on the ridge, it seemed funny at the time, but attitudes have changed in the past hundred years."

"Interesting," she said, looking thoughtful. "So you don't have to worry about conservation of mass like I do."

"No."

"I wonder why."

"One could speculate we supernatural creatures are immune to the laws of physics."

"You've seen me morph," she said, her deep green eyes twinkling in the firelight. "I would love to see you change."

He frowned. What she asked was distasteful to him, and it hardly seemed fair—he had yet to see her Lux appearance. With everything that had happened, he hadn't pressured her to show him, and after the hiatus caused by the crystal, he wasn't about to sabotage his chance at making love to her tonight by raising it.

She leaned toward him and laid a hand on his knee. "Please?"

"If I show you, you must promise not to tell anyone, not even Karen."

She held up her hand like she was swearing an oath. "I promise."

For her, he'd do it. And maybe after seeing him change, she'd feel more comfortable revealing her true appearance.

Cerissa waited while he strode to the center of the room. Without preamble, he vanished, his clothing dropping to the floor.

A small bat wiggled out from underneath his shirt. He stretched his wings as if yawning and took flight. He circled the room a few times. The light from the fireplace threw flickering shadows on the ceiling when he flitted by her. He bounced around as he flapped—his flying seemed erratic. Maybe he was rusty at it.

Or was that how bats flew? She'd never seen one up close.

She stretched out her arm, making her hand into a flat landing pad, but splaying her fingers. She wasn't sure if he could land on a flat surface or would need a perch.

On his next swoop, he made an awkward landing, jumping from one finger to the next until he had a firm grasp on her index finger. He swung forward, hanging upside down, rapidly flapping a bit until he firmly gripped her finger. Once secure, he folded in his wings.

She slowly raised him so they were at eye level and gently touched his wing, sweeping her fingers across the thin, leathery surface. It was softer than she expected, and she ran the back of one finger over the fur on his chest.

His male member woke up—prominently in view.

"Aren't you the cutest little thing?" she said, cooing at him and eyeing his bat penis, which was bigger than she'd expected for such a small mammal.

He hissed and took flight again. Okay, maybe she shouldn't have called him "cute." He'd told her he didn't like it. How was she to know he'd be able to understand her and take offense?

She smiled to herself.

He is darling as a bat.

He circled again and landed on her shoulder. He had a slightly musky scent, a pleasant aroma. The way he crawled along her shoulder tickled. She quivered as he edged further underneath her hair.

"Oww," she yelled when he bit her neck. She pushed him off, forcing him to take flight. "You didn't ask permission to bite."

Annoyed, she held her hand over the wound to keep the blood from running onto her clothes.

He circled a few more times before landing and transforming back. He stood there before her naked, the glow of the fireplace dancing on his copper-brown skin.

"Do not call me cute," he said.

"I'm sorry if I insulted your manhood, but you should ask before you bite."

"You're right. I apologize. But as long as..." he said, gesturing toward her neck.

"Fine," she replied with a sigh, rolling her eyes.

He removed her hand from the wound, licked the blood from her fingers, and then kissed the wound itself. The small bat bite didn't provide a large enough opening to allow him to truly feed, but it sent shivers along her spine as he gently sucked. And from the way his erection brushed against her, it was arousing him, too.

The doorbell rang. "Damn," she said. "Double damn."

"Are you expecting company?" he asked, gathering his clothes and shielding his thick length from view.

"No. I take it you aren't either. I'll go see who it is."

She waited a moment while he ducked into the library with his clothes in hand and then went to the front door to see who'd interrupted a promising moment. She ran her fingers through her hair, moving a long lock to cover the small holes left by the bat bite. If the interruption wasn't long, they could pick up where they left off.

She turned on the monitor connected to the security camera. The video display revealed Gaea standing on the porch, clutching a small package to her chest.

Why would Gaea stop by without calling first?

"Good evening," Cerissa said, opening the door and giving Gaea a hug. "Won't you come in?"

"Of course, dear, but I can't stay long. Dylan is in the car." Gaea paused and sniffed the air. "I hope I'm not interrupting something."

"Ah, nothing," Cerissa said, smoothing out her hair, making sure a lock still covered the bite. "No, nothing at all. We were just reading by the fireplace."

"Good evening, Gaea," Henry said as he entered the foyer. His clothes were not as neat as he normally wore them, but he looked passable.

"Good evening, Henry. I was telling Cerissa I hoped I wasn't interrupting anything."

"Not at all. Would you like to come into the drawing room and tell us why you are here?"

"Actually, I only stopped by to give Cerissa this." Gaea held up a small package. "It arrived during the day. I tried calling, dear, but your cell phone went to voicemail."

"I'm sorry I didn't hear the call." Cerissa accepted the package Gaea offered her. "But you didn't need to deliver this."

"Dylan thought it looked important. I'm taking him into town to celebrate the end of the semester for him. He has only one more year of community college left. Winston is joining us there."

"Please congratulate Dylan for us. And thank you for bringing the package."

"It was no bother to stop by."

After Gaea left, Cerissa examined the package. The return address was from the manufacturer of her car. She set the box on the entryway cabinet, opened it using the pocket knife Henry offered her, and took out a letter.

"What is it?" Henry asked.

She skimmed the letter. "Looks like my car has been 'recalled.'"

She handed him the letter. "The fuel injection system on your car has a problem," he said. "They will repair it free of charge and replace it with this part." He pulled back the box's flaps to reveal a cylinder sealed in shrink-wrapped plastic. "Call the number in the letter, and they'll tell you which mechanic to take it to."

She took back the letter and placed it in the box. "I guess I'll have to go into Mordida soon to get it fixed. But not right now," she added, wrapping her arms around Henry's waist.

"Indeed. Right now, I need to feed."

He pulled free of her grasp, and she followed him into the kitchen, puzzled. He had already fed for the evening. Why again?

He took one of her silvery blue bags out of the cupboard and heated a pot of water. "Just like you burn calories when you change into a *puma*, I need more blood when I become a bat or wolf."

"What happens if you don't get it?"

"It weakens me." He shrugged. "It's another reason I don't do it too often—the cost isn't worth it. And as I said before, it's embarrassing—"

She raised her hands. "Don't worry. I won't tell anyone."

After downing the warmed blood, he rinsed his mouth and took her in his arms, his lips softly touching hers, excitement growing inside her as he deepened the kiss.

"Where did we leave off?" he murmured, nuzzling her neck and licking the bat bite again, his nose buried in her hair.

About forty satisfying minutes later, they were curled around each other in bed, enjoying the afterglow. She lay on her back, staring at the ceiling. Henry's head rested on her shoulder. His hair, unbound and silky, flowed over her skin.

"The look on Gaea's face when she caught the scent of blood was priceless," she said.

"There should not have been much. The bite was so tiny." He propped himself up on his elbow, raising a finger to touch the small bite.

"True, but she caught the scent anyway."

"A good thing she didn't come by a few minutes earlier while I was still circling the room."

"Or a few minutes later." She ran her fingers through his long hair. "Of course, we could have ignored the doorbell."

"So are you satisfied now you've seen me as a bat?"

"Oh yes. You are so darling like that."

"Cerissa," he said, his voice carrying a warning not to continue.

"But you were so cute, with your itty-bitty—"

"Cerissa, don't say it."

"—little bat—"

"Cerissa," he said sternly, grabbing and tickling her.

"…fangs."

She changed what she was going to say at the last second. She rolled over to escape, and he pinned her on her stomach, straddling her legs, and tickled her.

"Henry," she said between muffled laughs, "all right, I give up. I won't call you cute."

"Promise?" he asked, pausing, his fingers barely touching her skin.

"Absolutely," she replied, still giggling.

"Very good." He stopped tickling and released her.

"I won't call you cute," she said, sliding off the bed, "until I'm at least ten feet away from you." She ran to the door of the bedroom. "And you were sooo cute." Turning, she ran out of the room.

Henry didn't wait. Lightning fast, he chased after her, and from the stairway balcony, he could see her duck into the drawing room. He slid down the bannister, leaping to stick a perfect landing by the open drawing room door. He peered around the doorframe. The fire was now embers.

His nipples tightened from the chill in the air. That wasn't all that had shrunk. Perhaps he should have grabbed a robe first.

He stepped into the room. No sign of her. He sniffed the air and detected the fresh scent of her blood. She hadn't gone far. He took another step into the room. Where might she be hiding? *Hmm.* The library or the music room were likely possibilities. Or should he go through the kitchen, taking the back hallway? She was less likely to expect his approach from there.

The sharp pinch to his butt took him by surprise. He jumped and turned toward her. With a giggle, she was off at a run. How had she masked her scent enough to carry out a sneak attack?

"You do live dangerously," he called after her as he pursued her upstairs. She'd almost made it into the bedroom when he caught her around the waist and plopped her down at the foot of the bed, laying her back.

He bent over her and pinned her arms. He tried to look menacing as he asked, "Whatever shall I do with you?"

She panted, out of breath, and couldn't stop laughing. "I don't know," she said. "But I'm sure you'll think of something."

He couldn't resist a challenge like that. He released her arms and pulled her to the edge of the bed, her knees bent, her legs dangling. He had purposely bought a bed with a low footboard and placed a blanket chest in front of it. Kneeling on the cushioned chest, he spread her legs and kissed her inner thigh.

"Henry?" Cerissa lifted her head in time to see him caress her thigh with his lips.

His eyes locked on hers. "I want to taste you, *carina*. May I?"

Why not? He'd already had a sip of her blood earlier, but a second one wouldn't hurt anything. After all, he deserved his prize for catching her.

"Taste away," she said, lying back and looking at the ceiling. What would a thigh bite feel like? Being so close, would the heat flow faster to her core?

He slowly placed long, lingering kisses along her inner leg, building the anticipation, flooding her with wet warmth, except he didn't bite. He kept going, until he reached the apex of her legs. Spreading them further apart, he wrapped his hands around her thighs and slid her closer to his mouth.

"Henry, what are you doing?" She raised her head to look at him again.

"Relax, *cariña*. Relax and enjoy."

His long, firm tongue knew just where to go. When he licked her, she arched her back, inhaling deeply, sensations of pleasure shooting through her.

Oh my. This is the type of taste he meant.

He licked again, flicking his tongue through her folds, sucking her nerve bundle, raking it with his teeth, somehow keeping his fangs sheathed. She laid her head back and closed her eyes. It was exquisite, to lie there and do nothing as he began to draw moans of pleasure from her.

But was this only a warmup? She'd experimented some with other men, but none with his skill, and none who brought her to climax this way. "Henry—"

"It is all right, Cerissa," he said between licks. "Let it happen."

She closed her eyes and surrendered to him. Her breathing became more labored until the feel of his tongue was her entire focus, the sensation building, wobbling on the razor's edge of coming.

He captured her once again between his lips, sucking gently and tonguing her until the feelings exploded and she bucked her hips, almost dislodging him as she came.

He held on and used his tongue to chase every last spasm of pleasure from her, then slowed down, giving her one more lick before kissing her inner thigh—but even then, he didn't bite.

He used the sheet to wipe off his face, and crawled beside her, taking her into his arms, kissing her forehead.

She felt like warm honey, melting into his arms. "You were wonderful," she said against his chest.

"I am glad you enjoyed it."

She hesitated for a moment. "Could I do something similar for you?"

"When you're ready. There is no rush," he said, still holding her.

He'd been so good to her. How could she tell him she'd never kissed a man there before? She knew the basics, but what if she couldn't make the magic happen for him the way he did for her?

She could almost hear Ari's voice in her head: *Courage, kid. You got this.*

She inhaled deeply and kissed Henry's chest, taking a quick nip at each of his nipples. Slowly, she alternated between planting small kisses along the way and biting at his tight abs. She followed the trail of black hair pointing like an arrow to below his waist. She wasn't sure what to do next. She timidly licked his erection like one would lick an ice cream cone.

Henry put his hands behind his head so he could watch her without interfering. After a few licks, she sucked on him, running her tongue around the tip, and looked up at him for reassurance. He smiled back at her and nodded.

"Ah, I've never done this before," she said, and gave his erection another lick.

Never before? He liked being her first, sharing something new with her, and her eagerness to please sent a thrill buzzing through him.

He let her explore on her own. Lick after lick, the pleasure built, but her tentativeness became too much for him. She teased without giving full pleasure.

When he could take no more, he pushed back against the headboard so he could sit up. Guiding her to take him fully in her mouth, he gently showed her how to slide up and down on him.

He didn't think he could get any harder, but watching her full breasts move as she kneeled over him sent a rush of blood to his already engorged *pené*.

With his guidance, she grew more adventurous, working her warm, wet mouth back and forth on the full length of him.

Her hair fell forward, covering her face, and he parted the strands to see her lips wrapped around him.

She found her rhythm, pressing her tongue's tip along his length as she moved, until he teetered on the edge of orgasm. Should he pull out and plunge between her legs to finish? He didn't know how she would react if he came with her lips around him. But when he started to pull away, she wrapped her arms around him and held on tight as she continued to suck.

That was the signal he needed. He could take no more—he threw back his head and let the air rush out of his lungs as he cried out, pulsing inside her tight mouth as she sucked him dry.

She continued licking and sucking until he touched her hair and said, "That was excellent, *cariña*."

"Really?" she asked, looking up at him shyly.

"*Si*, yes, *ja*," he said, grabbing her and pulling her into his arms. "Absolutely wonderful."

She snuggled in close to him. He stroked her hair, her naked breasts pressed against his side, her cheek on his chest.

She raised her head and looked at him. "But you didn't get to bite," she said. She sounded concerned, as if somehow she'd failed.

"*Mi amor*, believe me when I tell you this—you were perfect. I didn't need anything more than what you did."

She seemed reassured, and snuggled back against him, running her fingers across his pecs. He kissed the top of her head and closed his eyes, allowing himself to drift off.

He was so lucky to have her. Her real appearance didn't matter—who she was inside did. She'd revealed her true self in so many small ways— from her acceptance of him, to the way she handled Anne-Louise, to her compassion for Jayden when he was wounded.

Father Matt was right. His curiosity could wait. When she was ready, she'd show him her Lux appearance. And he had faith it would be very soon.

CHAPTER 43

THE ENCLAVE LAB—THE NEXT DAY

Cerissa worked in the cramped lab at the Enclave, performing the delicate task of genetic surgery. If she had another batch of genetically modified eggs incubating soon, it would double the number of clones producing blood by next year.

A few hours later she wrapped up surgery, returned the embryos to their liquid nitrogen tank, and then harvested and packaged blood from the existing clones into shiny blue bags.

Finished with her work, she flashed to Henry's home and left the bags on his kitchen counter. Since her car was in the shop, Henry had promised to give her a ride to Gaea's tonight. She had a midnight appointment to meet a new group of potential investors. They were visiting from Rancho Valley, a winemaking area east of San Diego County.

By the meeting's end, would she have enough money to build the lab? She hoped so. It would keep the Protectors happy if she did.

She climbed the stairs to the master bedroom and checked her email—still nothing from Ari. He had promised her a report on Rolf's activities, but so far, nothing. Probably still in bed with Reeta.

Henry had offered to make chicken mole tonight. All day, her mouth craved the rich sauce. She checked the time—seven forty. The lengthier spring days meant he stayed underground longer. With half an hour before sunset, she had enough time for a hot shower.

Tonight she'd tell Henry everything she'd been holding back. He hadn't raised it again, surprising her with his patience, but he deserved to know, to see her Lux body. If she took her time and told him her theory behind the Lux's origins before showing him her wings, he'd understand.

He had to.

But what if he rejects me?

Her gut churned. It took real courage to let someone see who she was—and her *amma* hadn't made it any easier for her. But no, she wouldn't let that fear stop her.

I have to show him who I am.

She loved him too much to hide the truth from him any longer. And if he reacted badly—if he rejected her—she would just have to find someway to deal with it, no matter how painful.

Thirty minutes later, finished with her shower, she opened the closet door. She had started keeping clothes at Henry's. It gave her options in case their plans changed.

Is this how couples start living together? One garment at a time?

She selected a casual shirt and capris, and placed her phone in her pants pocket. Later she would change into business clothes for the investors meeting.

Looking at herself in the mirror, she considered removing her contact lenses. She was about to bare her soul to him. She could blink to turn them off, but an inadvertent blink could turn them on. She couldn't risk recording this discussion.

"Cerissa!" Henry yelled, followed by the distant sound of his feet slapping the basement staircase from the crypts below. The kitchen door slammed against the wall, the *bang* echoing to where she was upstairs.

"Cerissa!" he yelled again.

She hurried to the stairway balcony, buttoning her shirt along the way. She could remove her contact lenses later.

"Cerissa!"

She glanced at her watch. Eight ten—the sun had set less than twenty minutes ago. It usually took him longer to get ready for the evening. From the balcony, she watched him run through the foyer. Only half-dressed, he held his cell phone in one hand and a shirt in the other. Panic filled his eyes, his frantic emotions surging through her.

"I'm up here, Henry. What's wrong?"

"Oh-thank-God-you're-all-right." He raced upstairs, grabbing her in a bear hug, and spun her around the same way he had Méi.

"Hey, take it easy," she said, trying to regain her footing. "What's going on?"

He set her down and brushed the hair from her face. "I received an email saying you'd been kidnapped and demanding a ransom." He let go of her and looked at his phone. "They said they had my mate."

"What?"

He showed her the email. After reading partway through it, she said, "One of your friends has a pretty warped sense of humor to send this."

But as she got further into the email, the room started to spin. She leaned against the hallway wall and slowly sank to her knees.

No. It can't be true.

Henry knelt next to her on the floor and took her hand. "Cerissa, what is wrong?"

"They have Karen. They think they have me, but they have Karen."

"I don't understand."

"I loaned her my car today." Her heart beat wildly, thumping against her ribcage, as her mind pieced together the facts. "Karen's car was in the shop. She needed to go into Mordida today to get it from the dealership, and you told Rolf I would drive her. But since mine needed recall work, I called her and she offered to drop off mine when she picked up hers.

Dylan promised to give me a ride in the morning to get my car."

"You didn't go with her?"

She shook her head, not believing her own words. "Karen said she'd get a ride to her dealer from the recall mechanic. I left my car parked at her house before she woke this morning, and I transported back to the Enclave."

"You haven't spoken to her all day?"

"I've been in my lab. I didn't think to call her."

"Is it possible they don't have Karen?"

"The kidnappers gave you the location where you'll find my car," she said, showing him that part of the email. "If they have my car, they must have Karen."

Cerissa buried her face in her hands, tears flooding her eyes.

Henry phoned Rolf. Cerissa sat on the rug, huddled in on herself, and he squeezed her shoulder before going to his office. She shouldn't have to listen to this call.

"Rolf, have you heard from Karen?" Henry asked, collapsing onto the chair at his desk.

"Not yet. Is she with Cerissa?"

"No." There was no easy way to say it. "From what we can tell, she may have been kidnapped."

"What are you talking about?"

"I received an email demanding a ransom."

"Why would they send it to you? That makes no sense."

"They think they have my mate." He propped his elbows on his desk, holding his forehead in his hand, his shirt slung over his shoulder, unwilling to believe what was happening. "I'll forward the email to you. We need to call Tig."

"How could they mistake Karen for Cerissa?"

"She was driving Cerissa's car."

"But Karen doesn't look anything like her. Skin color alone—"

Henry rubbed his forehead. "I don't know how to explain it."

"What do the kidnappers want?"

"The precise amount in my Swiss bank account—they are sending a clear message. They have information about me they should not."

"Send me the email."

Henry disconnected the call and forwarded the email to Rolf. The Swiss bank account only held the amount Leopold had refunded. Henry rarely left any money in the account for long because he used it as a temporary parking place to transfer funds in and out of his brokerage accounts. But since he was waiting for the market to dip again, he had held off rebalancing his portfolio. The full sum was still in his account.

He didn't want to believe Leopold was behind the kidnapping, but he was the only one who knew the exact amount.

Henry's phone dinged again—another email from the kidnappers. This one had a video file attached. Henry opened it and watched a short, silent video of Karen. She appeared scared but unharmed. It looked like she was in a windowless room. The text message was more ominous and threatened to kill her, slicing off one body part at a time, if he didn't follow the instructions precisely. He hit forward and sent it to Rolf.

"I'll see you in a moment," Cerissa said over the phone. "Use the front door. Knock." She clicked off the call and, taking a deep breath, stood on trembling legs. She leaned against the wall. Her hands shaking, her mind not willing to accept the truth, she took a step forward and then another, walking her hand along the wall for support, headed for Henry's office.

Everything will be all right. We'll find her. She'll be okay. She has to be okay.

Henry sat at his office desk, looking at his phone. "Another email from the kidnappers," he told her.

She grabbed his phone and read it. Watching the video of Karen broke her heart. It should have been her. Tears threatened to explode from her eyes, and she blinked rapidly to keep them from falling.

"Ari is on his way," Cerissa said. "He's an expert in computers and should be able to trace the emails."

Henry slipped on his shirt, buttoned it, and then looked at her strangely, furrowing his brow. "Can you find Karen?"

"God, I wish I could, but she hasn't been tagged." Cerissa glanced at the phone, the freeze frame of Karen's scared face staring back at her. "I didn't think, it didn't occur to me to have her tagged."

"Tagged?"

"It's a more advanced form of GPS, smaller than the crystal in your arm. I could find her and transport her to the Enclave if she'd been tagged."

The doorbell rang. She ran downstairs. Henry followed her, and she opened the door. Ari stood there, dressed for clubbing in an expensive blue sports coat, the sleeves rolled, a Rolex prominent on his wrist.

"Hey, Ciss."

"I'm so glad you're here."

He gave her a quick hug. The smell of cologne and cigarette smoke clung to him. "You look terrible, kid." Ari slipped his arm over her shoulder. "Hi, old man," he said in Henry's direction. "Where's your computer?"

"My office," Henry replied.

Cerissa rushed upstairs. Ari followed at her back, keeping pace with her. "Look, Ciss, don't worry. We'll get your friend back. There's not a computer on this planet that can hide from me."

She rounded the corner into Henry's office. "Can you do it without getting into trouble with the Protectors?"

"No worries, sweet cheeks." Ari plopped into the chair behind Henry's desk and turned on the computer. "I've been fooling them for so long that they'll never see my fingerprints on this one. Most of what I need to do can be done without resorting to things that break their silly little rules. The Protectors can't stop me from using the best brain nature ever gave a Lux."

She stood next to Henry, chewing on her lower lip, waiting for the computer to finish booting. Ari placed a briefcase on Henry's desk and took out a laptop and a selection of devices. Underneath Ari's laptop was a thin binder. He handed it to her. "Here's the report you wanted."

She quickly flipped through it but couldn't focus on the words. All she could see was Karen in the hands of the kidnappers. Anxiety crawled along her arms like ants marching toward food. She brushed at them with the edge of the report; it didn't stop the feeling. She closed the report and looked at Ari. He'd already connected his laptop to Henry's computer.

"It'll save time if you give me your passwords," Ari said, handing Henry a pad of paper. "I'll need both your firewall password and the password for your email account."

She watched over Henry's shoulder. He wrote it out: "Computer = Cerissa" and "Email = miamor."

"You two got it bad, don't ya?" Ari said. "But you couldn't have made it easier for a hacker. When this is all over, I'll give you Ari's primer on passwords and computer security." He turned back to the screen, which was working its way through the opening protocol. "Eeks," he said, when the microprocessor data rolled past. "We need to get you on a faster operating system. This thing is five generations old. Okay, which emails have you received from the bad guys?"

She reached across Ari and opened Henry's email program, showing him the two emails they'd received so far. The second one included the video file. She picked a flash drive out of a collection Henry kept on his desk and plugged it into the computer to download the video. "We might be able to use the video to identify where they're keeping her."

"Good idea, Ciss. Guess I'm not the only one who got some brains in this family." He clicked the touchpad on his laptop, launching a diagnostic program. "Okay, gang, leave me alone. I assume you want a brick and mortar address where the email originated?"

"And the device, whether it is wireless or fixed, and any identifying signatures, and," she said, glancing over at Henry, "there's probably a keystroke trap or some other back door on Henry's computer. They have his Swiss bank account number, they know the amount, but haven't transferred any money out, so they're missing some codes."

"Cerissa," Henry began, and then stopped, uncertainty on his face. "Leopold knew the account number from the wire transfer."

"How?"

"The money in that account—it's the amount I paid Leopold. He returned it, but I haven't reinvested it yet."

Her knees buckled out from under her.

"Whoa, girl," Ari said as Henry caught her and helped her over to the couch under the window.

"It can't be Leopold. It can't be." She shook her head, the dizziness threatening to overcome her mind. "He'd never try to hurt me."

Henry stroked her back. "I understand, *cariña*, but Leopold is the only one besides me who knows the amount."

"Wait. It can't be him. If it was Leopold, the kidnappers would know they don't have me."

"You could be right." Henry sounded hesitant. Then he seemed to pull himself together. He stood and offered her his hand.

"I have this," Ari said, his eyes still focused on the laptop's screen. "I'll call when I get something."

"Thanks, Ari," she said. Once she and Henry were in the hallway, she asked, "What now?"

His phone rang before he could answer her. He took the call and pressed speaker. "Henry," Tig said without preamble, "does Cerissa have a second set of keys for the car?"

Cerissa nodded.

"She does," he said.

"Bring them to Rolf's. We're establishing the command center at his house."

"We will be there in five minutes."

Henry went outside to get the Viper out of the garage, and Cerissa grabbed her medical kit along with the second set of keys, still clutching Ari's report under her arm. She ran into the kitchen, scooped up a few blue bags, and threw them into the black leather bag containing her medical supplies. Henry hadn't fed yet.

The recall letter lay on the table in the foyer, next to the brass bowl Henry kept his keys in. She slipped the letter into her purse. Maybe, just maybe, Tig could use the letter to track the kidnappers. It had to be a setup, to get her off the Hill and vulnerable.

Why, oh why, did I let Karen go alone?

No, blaming herself wouldn't help anyone. Rescuing Karen was the priority. Cerissa ran out into the night and jumped into Henry's car. With Tig in command, they were a team. And somehow, they'd get Karen back.

CHAPTER 44

ROLF'S HOUSE—FIVE MINUTES LATER

"How can I help?" Cerissa asked Jayden.

When they arrived at Rolf's house, Henry left her standing at the edge of the cavernous living room while he grabbed one end of a long table the mayor was dragging.

"Give me a sec," Jayden said, stepping back as Henry and the mayor dropped the table where Tig pointed.

Jayden placed his laptop on it and added a radio base station. Tig resumed shoving furniture out of the way haphazardly. Liza and Zeke carried a large whiteboard into the living room, propped it on two chairs, and, at Tig's direction, went back for a television.

"Here," Jayden said, handing Cerissa a computer cable. His leg was no longer in a brace, but he would rub it occasionally. "Do you mind plugging this into the whiteboard?"

"Glad to."

The cable connected the board to Jayden's laptop. She grabbed an extension cord from his kit and powered up the board. Other reserve officers—some of them members of the town council—began trickling in. Even the town attorney was there.

Once the TV was propped up on a couch, Cerissa shoved the flash drive into the TV's USB port and loaded the video of Karen, using a remote control to play it.

The image of Karen filled the screen.

"Pause it," Tig said.

Cerissa stopped the video and Tig moved closer to the TV. The high-resolution screen displayed fine details, including the fear lines on Karen's face.

"Behind her is a concrete block wall," Tig said. "She's in a commercial building or a basement. If she's in Mordida, it's more likely to be a building. There are no basements in the lowlands; the water table is too high."

"It looks like the paint job is old," Liza added.

"See that chip in the paint?" Tig pointed to an area on the wall. "At least seven colors. It's probably over fifty years old."

"So we're looking for an older building," Liza said.

Tig nodded. "Play it."

Cerissa started the video again, watching from beside Henry, taking his hand. Seeing Karen so scared left a big, gaping hole in the middle of her chest, and Henry's distress invaded her mind as a bitter taste, like acid at the back of her throat.

When Tig finished viewing the video, Cerissa took the recall letter out of her purse and offered it to Tig. "Karen was taking my car to this mechanic, Harry & Roy's Service." Cerissa pointed to a sticky note attached to the letter, where she'd written the mechanic's address after phoning for an appointment. "This is the recall notice."

Tig grabbed gloves from the crime scene kit sitting at Jayden's feet and handled the letter by the edges. "How was it delivered?"

"In a box, with a car part. I used Gaea's address to register the car; the box was delivered there. Karen took both the box and the car part with her this morning."

Henry pointed to the address in the letter. "The return address on the box was the same."

Tig looked back at the letter. "Who has touched this?"

"Only Henry and me."

Tig took the letter over to where Jayden sat at the worktable, his laptop open and working. Cerissa followed her.

"Dust this," Tig said. "Run any fingerprints you get."

Jayden slipped on gloves before accepting the letter from Tig. "The address of the mechanic," Jayden said. "It's close to the location given in the kidnapper's message."

"Check it out," Tig said. "Cerissa, is there anything else out of the ordinary that's happened recently?"

Cerissa had already asked herself the same question a hundred times since the first email came through. "No, nothing."

"No one has tried to follow you? No stranger approached you in town?"

"I haven't been off the Hill much. A meeting with my architect, lunch with Karen, dinner with Henry—no one approached me, no one I didn't already know."

"If you remember anything, anything at all, speak up. It could save Karen's life."

Tig took the remote control from her and walked away, joining Liza and Zeke to watch the video one more time. Cerissa turned to Henry. She felt so helpless.

"We'll get her back," he said, squeezing her hand. "Are you all right here? I want to speak with Rolf."

Rolf was standing toward the back of the living room talking with the mayor and Frédéric. Her throat was so dry and tight that she could only nod her agreement.

Henry gave her hand one more squeeze and then strode off. She grabbed a chair and pulled it up next to Jayden. He dusted the letter with black powder and pressed a sheet of plastic over the raised fingerprints.

Cerissa hugged her purse tightly to her chest. It felt wrong to sit here and do nothing. "Tell me if I can do anything to help."

"Will do," Jayden replied, never taking his gaze off his work. He plugged a hand scanner into the laptop and scanned the prints. A program opened on the computer's screen. He clicked the mouse and started a search.

"No luck," he said a few moments later, inclining his head toward the computer screen. "The only fingerprints are yours and Henry's."

Cerissa hugged her arms tighter around herself. Why couldn't they have gotten a break? Her head felt like a monsoon wind was blowing through it; her thoughts buffeted about, the voices of those around her muffled, and she jumped at the *thump* made when Liza and Zeke dropped an ice cooler on the floor next to the worktable. A strip of masking tape affixed to the cooler had been labeled "banked blood."

Rolf and Henry stood to the back of the room, Rolf motioning frantically, both of them speaking in hushed tones. The mayor and Frédéric had left them and joined the group huddled around Tig. The others in the room seemed to be avoiding Rolf.

Jayden posted information to the whiteboard. He copied the address from the kidnapper's second message and added a map of the location where the next instructions would be found.

Tig stood at the whiteboard, her back to Cerissa. "This is where Karen was supposed to drop off Cerissa's car," Tig said, using her finger to draw a circle on the map. "The mechanic's address in the recall letter—the car's in a parking lot next to it."

"What do you have in mind?" Liza asked.

"We have less than fifty minutes before Henry has to be at the car by eleven. Zeke—I want you to leave now. Get over to the mechanic's shop and reconnoiter." She turned toward the mayor. "You go with him. I want to know if there are any mortals in the building. Use stealth—don't let anyone suspect you're nearby."

Zeke tipped his cowboy hat before putting it on. "Right, chief. Winston and me, we'll be careful—they'll never know we came and went."

"Good. Call me when you're finished. Then circle back to here." Tig pointed at a location near Cerissa's car. It was on a side street—they wouldn't be visible from the parking lot. "We'll meet you there."

While Tig gave directions, Jayden added a flow chart of the prior assassination attempts to the whiteboard's display.

Cerissa recognized most of the key events, but four were new to her. "What are those dates?" Cerissa asked Jayden.

"The first three shooters were ex-cons. Those were the dates they were released from San Diego's prison."

"And the fourth date?"

"The prison guard who knew all three prisoners—it's the date he was killed."

289

Jayden added visual representations of the people involved and their connections, including a silhouette representing the kidnappers. When Karen's picture appeared, Cerissa's throat tightened again.

She took Ari's report out of her purse and stared at it, trying to keep the tears from spilling down her face. At first, the words were a blur. Then she started reading it in earnest. She looked up at the four dates. Her mind spun.

It couldn't be. No. Impossible.

She needed to talk to Henry, but he was trying to comfort Rolf. As if Rolf needed any comfort.

Cerissa looked over to Tig, who was speaking into her cell phone. Should she tell Jayden? She needed to talk to someone. She couldn't sit on this information.

"Rolf," Tig called out, "what's Karen's cell number? Mordida PD will try to track it for us." Tig repeated the number Rolf gave her and hung up. "He'll call back."

Jayden added a new projection to the whiteboard. "This is a satellite map of the area where Cerissa's car is parked. Keep in mind it isn't a live feed; it could be a few weeks old."

Rolf and Henry stepped closer to the whiteboard, joining Tig and the others.

Tig touched the whiteboard and expanded the map to cover most of the board. "I want snipers here," she said, pointing to a building near the parking lot. "And here. Another team will be on the ground. If Zeke and the mayor find nothing, we might be able to glean something from the car to tell us where they have Karen."

"We can't go in there as a group," Rolf said. "The instructions were clear—Henry must go in alone."

"That's what you want, isn't it?" Cerissa stood, the legs of her chair scraping the marble floor. They all turned to look at her.

Rolf pointed at her. "This is your fault. The kidnappers wanted you, not Karen. If you had never come here, Karen would be safe."

She ignored him and pushed her way through the group to look at the whiteboard. She touched the flow chart, the board cold and smooth as her fingertips enlarged the page and pushed the map aside. "You were in San Diego on all these dates, Rolf."

Rolf turned red with anger. "Henry, if you don't make her shut up, I will."

Henry lightly gripped her shoulders. "Come with me," he said.

"Henry—"

"I trust you," he whispered near her ear. "Now trust me."

She narrowed her eyes at Rolf, but went with Henry.

"Fucking bitch!" Rolf yelled. "She's wasting our time. It's her fault if Karen is killed."

"Cerissa," Henry said, when they were out of earshot of the others. She kept glancing over her shoulder at Rolf.

He gently cupped her chin and turned her to look at him. He could feel her anger and anxiety through the crystal, but she had it all wrong. "Listen to me."

She thumped the report against his chest. "Jayden told me their investigation was focusing on San Diego, and then I read this."

He opened the report and skimmed through it. All the dates Rolf had gone to San Diego, including the two dates Henry had accompanied him, although his own name wasn't in the report. Ari had been thorough, but not perfect. The map showed cell tower pings tracking Rolf to a neighborhood not too far from the prison for each date he was there.

She pointed at the map and said, "Rolf was in San Diego when the shooters were released from prison. He was there when the guard was killed, too. On each date—he was near the prison, near where the guard was killed. Why?"

Henry tucked the report under his arm and looked directly into her eyes. He had to convince her she was wrong. "Cerissa, Rolf is not behind this."

She shook her head. "He set up everything. Tig was right—he wants you dead. That's why he invited you on the horseback ride; it's why he suggested you go with him to track Kim Han's killer. He's the one who hired the shooters—that's why he was in San Diego."

"Cerissa, enough. I'm going to tell you the same thing I told Tig, but you must tell no one, not even Karen."

"Tig's discussed this with you? Why didn't you—"

"He was live feeding."

"Live feeding?"

"This can go nowhere. It would destroy his run for mayor. He must still feed from a live mortal. Banked blood doesn't fully satisfy him. He needs to supplement it with blood direct from the vein."

He had downplayed it to Tig, too, holding back information about Rolf's real problem. He couldn't tell Cerissa everything.

But I promised her I would hide nothing from her if she asked.

He had to reconcile his duty of loyalty to his friend—his former friend—with his promise to Cerissa. But in light of what had happened at the council hearing, did he really owe Rolf anything?

Yes. I'm an honorable man, even if Rolf is not.

Cerissa scrunched her eyebrows together. "What do you mean it doesn't fully satisfy him?"

"He can get some nutrition from banked blood, but he needs—"

"Adrenaline." Comprehension filled Cerissa's eyes. He should have known she'd figure it out. "Rolf's addicted?"

"I guess you could call it an addiction," Henry replied. "It's why he's so rigid in his views—every human is a temptation for him."

"But why San Diego? You can't tell me it's a coincidence."

"San Diego has areas outside the treaty, and many of our distributors are located there. He makes up an excuse for Karen about seeing distributors and flies the winery's plane there when he cannot hold out any longer."

"But it's against the Covenant."

"Not if he's outside our jurisdiction. But it *is* socially frowned upon—especially his inability to control it. It would sabotage his political career in the same way a drug addiction takes down mortal politicians. Other council members may do it on occasion—take a vacation, do a little live feeding. But Rolf's hooked, and his lack of control—"

"He cheats on Karen?"

"He says he does not have sex with them. He does not kill them. And he tips them well."

"He tips them? As if that makes it all right?"

"When you eat salmon, who gets paid—the fisherman or the fish?"

She glared at him. "If he's hooked on live feeding, he could be part of the group who wants to turn this country into one big cattle ranch to serve his needs."

Henry rolled his eyes. "Rolf would never be part of such an abomination."

"How do you know he isn't lying? That's one of the trickiest ways to lie—admit to a different peccadillo."

Why did she keep pressing this? He didn't want to say it out loud. He wasn't hooked like Rolf, but he did enjoy an occasional free-range feed.

I owe her the truth, at least—the truth about me.

He rubbed his eyes. "I know, because I have on occasion gone with him."

"You what?"

"I have joined him on occasion. He feeds and returns to the Hill. He never met with any other vampires."

"Why didn't you say something before this?"

"Everyone has their secrets, as you well know. It was not for me to reveal Rolf's secret."

"You said every human is a temptation for him—even me?"

"Especially you." He gently stroked her jaw. "He feels an overwhelming desire for your blood, and it makes him angry."

"My aura—he is affected by it. That's why he wanted me off the Hill."

Henry brushed his fingers along her arms. How to explain it quickly? They really needed to return their attention to Karen's rescue. "After the dance, after being near you all evening, it's why he had to fly to San Diego right away, why he was there when the guard was killed. The desire to feed was driving him crazy."

"I had no idea I was affecting him that way."

"Henry," Tig called out. "I need to go over the plan with you."

"I'll be right there." Lowering his voice, he said to Cerissa, "I know Rolf. I know him so well I can say my next words without doubt: he is not the one behind this."

"But what about Ari's report? Tig should have it. Ari didn't use our technology—there's nothing in it she can't see."

Henry took the report and returned to where the others were gathered, Cerissa following at a distance.

Rolf scowled at her. "What is she still doing here?"

Tig stepped between them. "Since this involves your mate, you should sit this one out. We'll take it from here."

"Tig's right," Liza said. "You're too close to this. Let us do our job." She grasped Rolf's shoulder. "We'll get Karen back, I promise."

Rolf clenched and unclenched his fists, but he stepped back, turning away from them. "We're wasting time."

Tig put her hand in the small of Rolf's back and pushed him a few paces toward the kitchen. "Rolf, go feed. Fill the tank—that goes for everyone." She gestured toward the ice chest. "Full rations. We'll need to be in top shape tonight."

Rolf growled and stalked off.

Henry glanced at the ice chest. He needed to feed, too, but he had no appetite. Not with Karen missing and his friend in agony.

Tig returned to the whiteboard. "All right, here's the plan," she said, and mapped out her strategy.

Henry forced himself to quit thinking about Rolf. Karen was the important person now. They had to save her. But something kept bothering him as he listened to Tig.

So far, the kidnappers had communicated by email. Why not send the ransom instructions electronically? It didn't make sense to meet in person. Unless the kidnappers wanted him away from somewhere, or near somewhere, or wanted them chasing their tails so they would miss something important.

"It's a trap," Henry finally said.

"The car?" Tig asked.

"Yes. They didn't want Cerissa and they don't want the money. If they wanted money, they would have stayed with email; it's faster. They want me, isolated, away from the Hill. They already tried three attempts to kill me, which Cerissa thwarted."

"Three?" Tig asked, her eyebrows almost to her hairline.

"Two. I mean two," he said. "Yacov thwarted the third. It doesn't matter." He swept his hand out, as if pushing aside his mistake. "The kidnappers are using her as bait to lure me to the car. My guess is they want me dead. The car is either rigged to explode, or there will be an ambush there. It's why they've set the rendezvous for eleven—so most mortals will be home in their beds when they attack."

Tig seemed to consider his words. "Henry, may I speak to you privately?"

"Of course."

She strode across the room away from the others. He followed.

"You should have this," he said, giving her the report when she stopped. "Cerissa's cousin prepared it—he's the expert who is working on my computer right now, trying to track the kidnapper's emails. The report covers everything we already discussed."

Tig thumbed through it. "I found initials in Rolf's calendar for those dates. And cross streets. They aren't the shooters' initials. What are they?"

"I suspect they are the initials of his victims and where he found them. If he finds one he likes, he may go back again, calling the person to him." Tig didn't look convinced. "What is it you wanted to discuss with me?" he asked, anxious to change the topic.

Tig explained her plan to him. Henry pursed his lips and agreed. He didn't like it—too much could go wrong—but he couldn't think of a better plan. And he was willing to do anything to get Karen back. No matter the risks.

CHAPTER 45

ROLF'S HOUSE—MOMENTS LATER

Tig used the whiteboard to diagram her plan. Henry would be the bait. "He'll arrive by motorcycle," she told the others. "Better maneuverability, less chance of being trapped."

Her phone rang. "Yes?" she said into it. The Mordida police tech gave her a quick report. The last signal from Karen's cell phone was over eight hours old, coming from a tower near the location of the car. She thanked him and disconnected the call.

"The kidnappers must have destroyed the phone or the battery's dead," she told her team. "I want the rest of you to leave now and get to the rendezvous spot. Cerissa, would you please go with Jayden in his car in case we need a doctor?"

"Of course."

She turned to the town attorney. "Marcus, normally you aren't part of our field team, but I want you with us in case we need a warrant written up. You can go with Jayden and Cerissa."

"No problem, Tig, whatever you need. I have my iPad with me and a judge on speed dial."

She wished Ufa was still on the Hill to help, but she'd paid him and he left the night she learned Rolf's secret. As the others headed for the door, Tig strode into the kitchen to tell Rolf they were leaving. Henry followed her.

"You'll stay here," she told Rolf.

He downed the last of his drink and threw his mug into the sink. "The only way you'll keep me here is in silver chain. So either arrest me now, or I'm going with you."

Henry put his hand on Rolf's shoulder. "We trust you. You'll drive me to the house to get my motorcycle."

"Are you sure, Henry?" she asked.

"I'm sure. I want Rolf to drive me."

Tig narrowed her eyes. She wanted Rolf sidelined until Karen was rescued. She still didn't trust him.

"I know what I'm doing," Henry added, letting go of Rolf.

She eyed Rolf coldly. "Just remember. I'm in charge of this operation. You're an observer. I expect you to follow my orders to the letter."

Rolf screwed his face into a sneer. "Get Karen back. If you fail to do that, you'll never give another order, because I'll kill your career."

She lunged at Rolf, twisting his arm and pinning him face-first against the wall, her other arm wrapped around his throat in a chokehold. "I've had enough of you and your threats. Now here's one for you. I know Henry whitewashed what you do in San Diego."

She eased off his throat so he could speak, but kept him pinned to the wall.

"You…you," Rolf sputtered.

"You're not flying there to do some innocent live feeding. You're going there to hunt." She spat the words out with all the disgust she felt. Videos Ufa took had shown Rolf chasing a man until the poor mortal collapsed from terror and exhaustion. The images were burned into her mind's eye.

"How dare you—" Rolf started.

She tightened her arm around his throat again. "You're addicted to adrenaline-spiked blood. If I find out you're involved with the Carlyle Cutter, I'll stake you myself."

With a shove, she released him, banging his head against the wall. When he turned to look at her, his cold blue eyes radiated his hate. She stared at him as she backed out of the kitchen, leaving Henry to deal with Rolf. She couldn't protect people from their own stupidity. If Henry still trusted Rolf, well, that was his problem, not hers.

Henry jumped onto his motorcycle and sped toward Mordida, barely keeping his speed legal. Fifteen minutes until the kidnapper's deadline—

not much time to rendezvous with Tig and still make it to Cerissa's car by eleven o'clock.

Fear knotted in his stomach—fear that any mistake would cost Karen her life. He wanted to push the bike faster but couldn't, not without attracting the attention of the Mordida police, a delay he couldn't risk. He glanced at the bike's side mirror. Rolf followed in a white Escalade—Rolf and Karen each owned the same model SUV, but in different colors.

Henry skidded to a stop at the rendezvous point. Tig stood by Jayden's police car, an iPad in her hand. Cerissa remained huddled inside the car. Jayden handed Henry a bulletproof vest. He put it on under his leather jacket, so the kidnappers wouldn't see it. The area around them was deserted, the businesses closed, the streets empty.

"No one was at the mechanic's shop," Tig told him.

"It's the God's honest truth," Zeke added. "We got in through an open window. Shop's been in business for over twenty years from the looks of it—must be named after the owners. Roy's dead; we found an old funeral program tacked to the wall. Looks like Harry's been running it."

Tig held up a business card from Harry & Roy's Service. "It's not the number in the recall notice."

Henry took the card from her. "So the shop owner was not involved."

"We found Harry's home address," the mayor added. "A team should check him out."

Henry glanced at his watch. In four minutes, he had to leave. "We don't have time."

Tig pointed at the satellite map on her iPad. "Henry's right. I'm going to need everyone here and in position. Red team—Liza and Frédéric—will be in Jayden's car and parked here, about seventy yards from Cerissa's car." She moved her finger, sliding the map and pointing to another building. "Blue team—Zeke and Winston—will be positioned nearby. I'll be on that roof." She indicated the building closer to them. "This way, we'll have a clear shot at anyone who approaches the car. Henry, keep in mind where we're positioned. Try to stay out of the line of fire."

"I understand," Henry said, the knot in his stomach cinching tighter.

The car with Zeke and Winston took off. Liza and Frédéric, with Rolf under strict orders to stay out of it, drove to a street on the far side of the parking lot in Rolf's Escalade. Cerissa and Marcus stayed behind with Jayden. Tig scaled the wall of a nearby building, a rifle strapped to her shoulder.

Two minutes remained before the time set by the kidnappers. Henry started the bike's engine and took a deep breath, gripping the handles tightly, determination coursing through his veins.

This has to work.

Wearing a Bluetooth earpiece under his helmet, he phoned Tig. "Can you hear me?" he asked.

"Roger," she said.

With his helmet's visor up, he revved the engine and took off.

Cerissa's car was easy to spot, the sole car in a deserted parking lot. He sped toward it—five yards away, he caught the scent of explosives.

He veered from the car and gunned the bike's engine, the blast's heat wave at his back. The concussion wave came next, sending him off balance. He laid the bike down sideways, skidding across the parking lot, the bike rotating a half-circle.

When he stopped moving, his injuries were minor, but the position left him exposed. He scrambled out from under the bike and looked around.

"Hold it right there," a man called out.

Henry stood and raised his arms. "I'm unarmed. Where is my mate?"

Tig's advice had been to go along with the fiction they had his girlfriend. When the kidnappers realized they had the wrong person, they might kill Karen.

"We're going to take you to her. Keep your hands in the air."

Two men—both armed—left the shelter of a large van parked by the curb. Henry could see a third peering around the side.

"Is she all right?" he asked.

The men stepped across the sidewalk to the black asphalt of the parking lot, both guns pointed at him. "So far," the taller one said. "If you cooperate, she'll live."

"What do you mortals want? I'll pay any price to get her back. I just need time."

"We'll tell you when we get where we're going. Now turn around." The two gunmen continued to approach.

Henry didn't turn around. "I'll go with you, but I need to know where we are going."

"I said turn around."

When Henry didn't, they both raised their guns and fired.

❋

Before the gunshot sounded, Henry vanished—the signal Tig was waiting for.

"Mortal," she said into her headset, then waited a beat for the others to prepare. "Blue team, left target. Red team, right."

From the flat rooftop, she watched the gunmen in the parking lot look around frantically. With Henry out of the line of fire, she and the other shooters had clear shots. She put her target in the cross hairs, her fingernail pointing perpendicular to the direction she aimed.

"Now," she said, and squeezed the trigger.

The sound of five volleys filled the silent night air, and pepper balls hammered each of the gunmen. Henry's one-word message told her which ammunition to use—garlic concentrate or capsaicin pepper.

The impact of the balls sent the gunmen to their knees. A red cloud of the potent pepper powder, released on impact, surrounded them. They grabbed for their eyes, rubbing them, and retched.

"Go," Tig said.

Winston and Zeke vaulted into the parking lot, knocked the two men onto their stomachs, and handcuffed them. The men continued to roll on the ground, gasping for air. Liza ran from her position by Rolf's Escalade to collect the perps' guns and shoved the weapons into her waistband.

Tig jumped from the rooftop she was on, landing close to the parking lot.

The third man, hiding behind the perps' van, edged open the driver's door, got behind the steering wheel, and shut the door. The length of a football field separated Tig from him. Rolf and Frédéric, who were stationed closest to the van, reached the driver in seconds.

"Wait," Tig called out, breaking into a run.

Rolf punched straight through the side window and peeled back the glass. The van's engine started, the driver's terrified face visible through the windshield. Frédéric gripped Rolf's shoulder, like he was trying to restrain the vice mayor, but Rolf was too quick. Whipping his silver knife off his belt, Rolf held the driver's hair with one hand, and then used the knife to slit the driver's throat.

Tig arrived a moment too late. "Rolf!" she yelled. "I told you to stay back."

Rolf didn't respond.

Both carotid arteries had been severed, the throat cut all the way to the spine. Vampire blood wouldn't save the driver. Now Tig had only two perps to question.

Fuck it. She looked away in disgust, mad at herself. Rolf had no business being here—she should have stood her ground. And Frédéric—why hadn't he tried harder to stop Rolf?

Turning to the mayor, she barked, "Go get Rolf's Escalade. We'll need it to transport the bike. Liza—get those two in Jayden's back seat." Jayden had driven up in his police car, along with Cerissa and Marcus. "Zeke—search the suspect's van and see if it has GPS navigation. The navigation system will tell us where it's been." She looked back to Rolf, pointing a finger at him. "Get away from the van. Now. And you," she said, tossing her keys to Frédéric. "Bring the police van."

Rolf stomped off. He stopped at where Henry had vanished, gathered Henry's clothes, and lifted the helmet.

Henry looked up at Rolf and took flight. He circled a few times. When the mayor arrived with the Escalade, Rolf put Henry's clothes on the front seat. Henry flew in, transformed back, and got dressed.

No one said a thing about his ability to become a bat. A few even looked impressed.

At least Tig's plan had worked so far.

He could feel Cerissa's sense of relief. Buckling his belt, he got out of the Escalade to help Rolf load the motorcycle into the back. Zeke and Liza passed by, carrying the handcuffed prisoners, and dumped them into the back seat of Jayden's police car. Rolf stared at the two men, anger frozen on his face.

Satisfied the bike was secured, Henry hastened over to look at the prisoners. Cerissa joined him, slipping her hand into his and squeezing it. He squeezed back.

Liza removed the clip from one of the confiscated guns. "Silver," she said. "Those two were sent to kill."

She slammed the clip back in and handed it over to Tig.

Tig put the guns in the car's trunk and joined Henry. "Are you okay?"

"I'm fine." Henry stared at the two men. He didn't recognize them. "But those two—will they be in shape to be questioned?"

Jayden limped over, carrying a small packet. "This will help," he said, holding two towelettes. "Antidote wipes."

"Let them suffer," Rolf snapped.

Tig stepped between Rolf and Jayden. "Much as we'd like to do that, we need them to answer questions before their accomplices guess what happened. They didn't act alone."

Jayden wiped the pepper powder from their faces. "The effects will wear off shortly." He closed the car door. "We can leave now."

"Liza—you drive the perp's van back to the Hill," Tig barked as she opened the Escalade's door. "Frédéric—you drive mine and take Marcus with you. I'll drive Rolf's."

Henry pulled Cerissa away and asked quietly, "Your aura—can you compel them to tell the truth?"

"Not my aura, but there is a way using Lux technology. I could read their minds with it, but they have to be willing participants. The touchstone won't work if they aren't willing, even if I could use it, and I can't. It would reveal too much to Tig and the others."

"What if I convinced Tig to let you talk with the men alone?"

She shook her head. "The Protectors can detect our technology when it's used outside the Enclave. They could whisk me away before I got the answers we need."

"What if you took the men to the Enclave?"

"Henry, I wish I could do something, you don't know how badly I do. But the Protectors would know I brought in unauthorized subjects. And that assumes I can get them away from Tig in the first place."

He pondered the alternatives. "Rolf will want to employ old-fashioned means. I have never been convinced torture works or produces reliable results, but Rolf will be willing to do anything to get Karen back. We don't have time to let the men wait and contemplate the possibilities of impending torture, to see if that breaks them."

Tig pointed to the south. "Henry, do you hear those sirens? Someone must have heard the explosion and called the Mordida police. We need to leave. Now."

He nodded and escorted Cerissa to the police van, the car Frédéric would drive. He refused to put her in Jayden's police car with the kidnappers. "Have you heard from Ari?"

"He hasn't found anything yet. The kidnappers pinged those emails through so many sites that it's taking him longer than he expected it to, but Ari will find them soon."

He opened the passenger door for her. "Do you mind riding back with Frédéric and Marcus? Rolf shouldn't be in the same car with a mortal right now."

"Whatever you need me to do, I'll do," she said, then got in and closed the door.

Zeke jogged up. Tig rolled down the Escalade's window and accepted the wallet Zeke handed her. "No navigation system," he said. "Nothing in the van, but I went through his wallet. Just his driver's license, a few credit cards, and cash."

"Okay—you and the mayor go question the shop owner," Tig said. "See if he knew anything about the plan or where they have Karen. We'll take the perps back to Rolf's. Call me when you get an answer."

Henry climbed into the back seat of Rolf's Escalade. From the snippets he caught while talking with Cerissa, Tig and Rolf had argued over who would drive. Tig must have won, since Rolf was riding shotgun.

Tig reached through the open window and stuck a portable police light on the roof, then plugged it into the power socket. After triggering the siren, she led the caravan at full speed back to the Hill.

Henry held on in the back seat, the front wheel of his motorcycle lying across the folded half-seat next to him. The smell of burned rubber permeated everything.

When his phone dinged, they were almost at the gated entrance to the Hill. Another email from the kidnappers had come through. No message this time—instead, it contained a new video. As he watched it, his hand shook with anger. In the video, a masked man was doing unspeakable things to Karen with a knife. Henry passed the phone to Rolf, who played back the video.

"No!" Rolf roared, the sound of his fury filling the Escalade. He banged his fist on the dashboard, his jaw muscle bulging. "*Miene liebling*, no!"

Henry silently balled his fists, clenching his jaw hard enough to crack teeth, anger welling as every muscle in his body rigidly held back his own explosion.

Karen was being tortured because those men wanted him dead. If it wasn't for him, Karen would be safe.

Those men would pay. Every single one of them would suffer. He'd personally see to it—no matter the cost.

CHAPTER 46

Tig sped past the Hill's wall, leading the way to Rolf's house, leaving the guards at the gatehouse gaping bewilderedly as the convoy charged up Robles Road.

How could I let things spin so out of control?

She was torn between two bad choices: capture the men, or let Henry go with them.

She couldn't sanction the latter. Those men were there to kill Henry, either in the parking lot, or soon after if he'd gone with them, and Karen would still be captive.

There had been no other way to play this, and blaming herself was a distraction she couldn't afford.

Focus.

From Rolf's description, Karen was in the hands of the Carlyle Cutter. The Cutter had just started his first cut above her breast. If he followed his standard MO, Karen had a terrible few hours left to live.

Rolf posed a different problem. He kept repeating over and over, like a mantra, "They will die."

She slid her hand to the back of her belt and flipped off the safety switch on her stun gun. If needed, she would put him out of commission until she was done grilling the kidnappers.

She didn't have time to take the prisoners to the police station. Not only was Rolf's house closer, but the command center equipment sat in his living room. She drove the Escalade onto Rolf's circular driveway and slammed on the brakes, stopping near the front door.

"What room can we use to interrogate them?" she asked him, opening the driver's side door and jumping out.

303

"The basement. They will be closer to their graves there."

She pulled the stun gun off her belt, not quite pointing it in his direction. "Stay here."

"I'm going with you," Rolf said, his voice a cold growl.

"No you're not. You're not thinking clearly. Stay here or I'll tell Jayden to drive the prisoners to the jail."

He pounded his fist on the dashboard, cracking it.

She slammed closed the Escalade's door. Crossing in front of it, she kept her vision locked on Rolf. Henry put both hands on Rolf's shoulders, leaning forward to say something to him.

Good. Henry should be able to keep Rolf seated for the moment.

Jayden's car screeched to a stop behind the Escalade. The assailants' van with the dead kidnapper, driven by Liza, parked behind Jayden. Frédéric, Marcus, and Cerissa in Tig's van arrived last.

"Where do you want them?" Jayden yelled, pulling one of the handcuffed men out of the police car. Liza had already jumped out of the van and placed the other perp in an arm lock.

"The basement."

Tig followed them, with Frédéric on her heels. She grabbed a couple of straight-back chairs from the dining room and carried them downstairs.

She stopped Marcus in the foyer. "Wait up here. It's better you don't know what I have planned for those two. And keep Cerissa with you. I don't need an audience."

"Understood," Marcus said.

Jayden and Liza herded the captives downstairs and into two separate windowless rooms. The basement walls were lined in unfinished brick, signs of green algae creeping along the brick from water intrusion. She placed a chair in each room. Her plan was to divide and conquer.

"Strap them tight."

Liza came out first. "Here's his wallet."

Tig looked through it, Frédéric breathing over her shoulder, watching. No ID, but two thousand in cash. Was that his price for being a kidnapper?

Cheap bastard.

She strode into the room with the first prisoner. Liza had done a good job using zip ties to strap him to the chair. Tig got within inches of his face and said, "You will tell me what I want to know."

The guy looked like he was about to piss himself. "Ah, ah, I don't gotta tell you nothing without a deal."

"A deal? This is a competition, not a deal. And let me tell you what you're competing for. We have your friend in the other room. The first one to talk dies the least painful death. If I weren't so short on time, I'd take you to heights of pain you never believed possible. But I need this information now. So you have an opportunity to be spared what you rightfully deserve."

"You won't hurt us. You're police. I'll sue if you do."

She hit him in the stomach. He tried to double over, his face purple in agony, but the zip ties were unforgiving. Tears streamed from his eyes, and he gasped for breath.

She leaned in again. "Don't let the uniform fool you. You won't live to sue, and no one here will help you. This is why."

She held up her phone and played the video of Karen.

The man blanched. Still struggling to breathe, he said, "The director said he wouldn't kill her."

"The director?"

"The guy said to call him that." He struggled to suck in another breath. "Never gave his name."

Shit. "Where is the woman being held?"

"Don't know. The driver had the address."

"The one who was killed?"

"Yeah. Frank and I was just hired guns."

Wait. Rolf had killed the only one who could lead them to Karen? Had he done it on purpose? That didn't add up. His rage at seeing the video had been genuine. Rolf wasn't that good of an actor.

"How many other men are working with you?"

"Ah, the director and two other guys. The three of 'em were there when we left. Really, that's all I know."

She straightened up, towering over the man. "I'm going to talk to Frank now. If you change your mind, tell Captain Johnson to come get me. Perhaps your friend will want to be spared what I have in mind for the loser."

She gave Frank the same treatment. He started babbling right away. "I don't know how to get there," he whined, panting hard and gulping air. "They blindfolded us until we was inside."

"What did the building look like?"

"I told you, we was blindfolded. I didn't see it from the outside."

Inches from his face, her fangs bared, her lips pulled back, she shouted at him, "What did it look like from the inside? How many stories? How old was it? What was it made of? You know more than you think you do."

305

"Ah, concrete bl-blocks," he stuttered, his scent souring. "One story, ah, like those old shops from the 1950s."

"Go on."

"Windows at the top of the concrete blocks, high up. No windows on the building's sides. Only front and back."

"So it's not at the end of the block. Keep going. How many rooms inside?"

"Two. It's like a machine shop. Where they make stuff."

"Describe the layout."

"In the large room, the front room, there's old equipment, a drill press, scrap metal, ah, junk like that. The other room in back is an office. They have her in the office."

"Were there other buildings across from this one?" Tig asked.

"In front. Tall buildings across the street. Newer buildings."

"I thought you couldn't see out."

"The building she's in—the windows have been painted over, but some of the paint is thin. They kind of stood out over us."

"What else did you see?"

"Don't kill me and I'll tell you."

She grabbed his shoulder and squeezed the joint until he screamed. When she relaxed the pressure, he gasped for air, his eyes squished shut against the pain. She kept her hand there in case more persuasion was necessary.

"What did you see through the window?"

"The building, the building," he said, "behind the building was an alley. We drove down it to get to the parking lot. I could tell when we'd turned off the paved street onto the alley—the road is bumpy there, like potholes. But—but I didn't see a street sign and I ain't been there before. That's all I know, I swear. Really. Don't hurt me again. I've told you everything."

Tig let go of him and left. She briefed the others and then went back in, certain there was more she could get from this one.

Cerissa paced in front of the command station in Rolf's living room. Why was she banned from the basement? On one level it made sense—she wasn't a police officer—but how could she help if she didn't hear what the kidnappers confessed?

The town attorney, whom she hadn't been introduced to yet, grabbed a bag of blood from the ice chest. "I'll be in the kitchen if anyone needs me," he told her.

After he left, she continued to pace, not knowing what else to do.

When Henry entered the room, his anguish cut through her bones, flooding her heart with pain. "What happened?" she asked.

He strode past her and stood in front of a large picture window, his back to her.

"Henry, what did they tell you? Is Karen all right?"

She laid her hands on his back, fighting the overwhelming waves of distress rolling off him. Had something horrible happened?

"Henry, please, what is it?"

His anguish suddenly vanished, like a scalpel had severed their link.

She stepped back, her hand rising to her mouth. Had they killed Karen?

Oh God, let it not be true.

"H-henry?"

"Another video arrived." He turned to her, his face a blank. "Why did you let her go alone?"

She recoiled at his words. "I, I was going to meet her there, but she offered... I didn't think there would be any trouble."

The cords in his neck knotted tight enough to snap. "What you are—you could have stopped the men the same way you stopped Blanche."

Her throat constricted.

He's right. This is all my fault. How can I fix this? I have to fix this...

She turned away and collided with Rolf, who shouldered her aside. In rapid fire, Rolf told Henry what Tig had learned from the gunmen about Karen's location.

Cerissa rushed over to Jayden's computer and began searching for land use maps on the internet. The maps would show Mordida's commercial and manufacturing areas, maybe give them a clue of where to look.

Nothing.

The maps weren't available online—only in person. At this hour, how would they find someone who worked for Mordida's planning department? They didn't have time. They needed the maps now.

Wait.

Cerissa took a shaky breath.

The lab.

She had purchased copies of Mordida land use maps when she first started hunting for a location for the lab. Where were they? She ran a shaky finger across her phone, looking for the stored documents she'd scanned.

There.

She shoved a cable into her phone and began transferring the first map to Jayden's computer. When she finished, she projected it on the whiteboard.

"Henry, we need Tig."

He stopped talking with Rolf and looked at her. "Why?"

"I think I have a way to find where they're holding Karen."

Tig ran her hand over the large map projected on the whiteboard. While Cerissa worked loading the other maps, Tig had sent Liza to the basement with strict instructions—let Rolf ask his questions, but don't let him kill them. She'd even confiscated his silver knife and handgun. He'd get both back later if he behaved himself.

She glanced over at the sound of footsteps—Rolf, Henry, Liza, and Frédéric returning from the basement. Marcus followed them into the room.

"Anything new?" Tig asked.

Rolf shook his head, a grim look on his face. "Nothing. They are either liars or worthless. We have all we're going to get from them."

"Jayden is watching them?"

"Yes," Liza replied.

Tig gestured toward the whiteboard. The map showed streets with blocks color-coded based on zoning districts. No street addresses were shown. "We're looking for an area where office buildings abut older manufacturing—"

"Check for industrial zones," Cerissa interrupted.

Tig looked over at her. "Explain."

"Manufacturing is only permitted in industrial zones. The high-rise buildings would likely be zoned commercial. Look for a large lot zoned commercial, across from an area zoned industrial."

Tig quickly located three possible sites on the map and then looked over her shoulder at Cerissa. "Can you pull up satellite pictures for these locations?"

A satellite map for one of the areas soon appeared on the whiteboard. It didn't have all the requisite features. "Next," Tig said.

The keys clicked as Cerissa typed and the next map appeared.

Tig shook her head. "No, this isn't it. The buildings aren't right."

More typing. Tig held her breath. If this wasn't it, they were back at square one. The wait cursor quit spinning and the satellite map materialized on the board. She looked at the two buildings. A city street divided them.

"Zoom in," Tig said, containing her excitement. The satellite photograph showed a tall office building across the street from a row of one-story manufacturing buildings with flat roofs. "There. There is the alley," Tig said, pointing to where it ran behind the one-story building. "What's the address?"

"Three-fifty block of Grand Avenue," Cerissa said.

Rolf stopped his pacing. "It's three hours to dawn. We must move now." He turned toward the door.

"Stop. We will plan this carefully." Tig laid Rolf's knife and gun on the command station table. "You get those back when we leave." She turned to the whiteboard. "The kidnappers may have booby-trapped the building to kill Karen or us as soon as we charge in. We need someone to reconnoiter. Rolf, you'll go in first and identify which building she's in by the scent…"

Tig stopped before saying "of her blood." A mortal police officer who worked for the Hill had entered the living room.

"Ah, chief, you called for assistance?" the officer asked.

"Can you transport the prisoners to the town jail? I need Jayden with us. Liza will take you to where they are."

"Sure, chief," he said, and left with Liza.

The rest of her team began throwing out ideas on how to get Karen out alive if she wasn't already dead. The room was filled with the din of their voices. As they argued, Tig's phone rang. "Yes?"

"Nothin'," Zeke said. "Owner didn't know nothin' about it. He said some guy was sniffin' around, wantin' to know if he had any empty garages for rent. Owner told 'em no."

"Did he remember the guy's name?"

"Chuck," Zeke replied. "No last name, no paperwork, neither. We asked."

"All right. Meet us at First and Hope. We're leaving here shortly," she said, then hung up.

Marcus tapped her arm, and she turned to him. "As soon as you have a confirmed address, I can get a judge to sign the warrant."

She looked at him like he was crazy. "I'm not waiting for a warrant. We've got exigent circumstances to go in without one."

"Well, Tig," Marcus said, sounding uncertain, "I should still file it with a judge to make the courts happy."

The courts were the last thing on her mind. "Just stay here and listen to the radios. You'll know the address when we do. But I'm not waiting for a warrant. When we find Karen, we're going in."

Cerissa went over to Henry and whispered, "I'm going with you. If Karen's hurt, you're going to need a good doctor at the scene, and not that quack Dr. Clarke."

He clenched his jaw and nodded.

She turned away so he wouldn't see the tears in her eyes. She couldn't blame him for how he felt—it was all her fault—but she couldn't believe Karen was dead. Tig had told them the Cutter worked slowly, methodically carving his victims—so there was a chance Karen was still alive.

Cerissa rushed outside to make sure her medical kit was in Jayden's police car. Finding it, she grabbed the injector, dialed for the stabilizer, and jammed it against her throat. The stress was screwing with her control.

Her phone rang. She almost dropped the injector trying to answer it.

"Kid, listen carefully," Ari said. "You have to tell them to quit using email. Now. Whoever is behind this has hijacked all email sent or received by Henry. They get a copy of everything."

"That's how they knew the amount Leopold paid back."

"And when to strike. They have access to Henry's calendar. They've taken the long view. The dates on these back doors are more than nine years old. They're on the wineries' main server, not Henry's computer—that's why it's taken me so long to find them. I'm betting someone who used to do IT for the winery sold them out."

"Got it. What about phones?"

"Stop using them—they may be tapped as well."

"I'm changing my cell phone to the Enclave's frequency. Call me on it if you learn something."

She ran back to the command center. Everyone was gathered around Tig at the whiteboard. Cerissa charged past the open doors of Rolf's living room and blurted out, "Henry's emails have been tapped, maybe our phones."

Tig whipped around. "How do you know that?"

"I spoke to Ari, our computer tech. The kidnappers have read every email Henry sent or received during the past nine years. Your own email may be compromised as well."

Jayden walked into the room. "The prison's records were hacked too," he said.

Tig's face lit up, a cross between anger and comprehension. "The Cutter's Ruthton crime, the security video, the morning he left the hotel, the video was erased and looped." She turned to Jayden. "I received confirmation earlier today. A hacker with sophisticated skills must be involved."

"Shit," Jayden said.

Tig took out her phone and shut it off. Everyone else followed her example. Cerissa pretended to—she couldn't risk missing a call from Ari.

Tig clipped her phone back on her belt. "That's why we never received any of the emails Yacov tried to send us, his emails listing the suspects. They scrubbed them. Someone on that list must be involved."

Rolf looked like he was ready to implode. "The plan calls for us to communicate by phone."

"We can deal with that," Tig replied. "I upgraded our radio system—we have enough encrypted radios in the police car. Even if the kidnappers have a scanner tuned to police frequencies, they won't be able to decode the signals. Let's get moving."

CHAPTER 47

Henry stared past Tig, looking out the driver's-side window of the Escalade. They turned into the alley driveway behind a row of aging manufacturing buildings painted an indeterminate brown. Some buildings were connected by common walls; others had small walkways separating them. A shared rutted parking lot about fifty yards deep flowed between the alley and the buildings.

He should never have lashed out at Cerissa. She wasn't to blame at all. The kidnappers wanted him, and everyone else was collateral damage. But in his mind's eye, he couldn't quit seeing Karen as the man sliced into her. Awake in the video, Karen screamed against the duct tape over her mouth.

He tried to vanquish the image from his mind.

The lit-up high-rises on Grand Avenue loomed over the row of one-story buildings. On his side of the alley, a similar group of one-story buildings mirrored the ones on Grand, but faced Hope Street with a parking lot behind them.

Tig braked, and Rolf opened the back door and slid out. He skulked behind the row of buildings where Tig suspected Karen was being held, sniffing at the air like a scent hound. Rolf slipped past four buildings before freezing when he came to the fifth.

Two short bursts of static emanated from the radio—the signal Rolf had found Karen. Rolf huddled under one blacked-out window facing the alleyway. If the prisoners' stories could be trusted, the room behind it held Karen. Tig drove along the alleyway and parked deep into the parking lot behind the opposite buildings, using a large trash enclosure to partially shield the Escalade from view.

Henry watched Rolf through the driver's-side windows. Security

312

cameras protruded from the building and pointed at the closest parking lot and the back door.

Henry ran his hands through his hair, dislodging the leather string holding his ponytail in place. He began winding and unwinding the string around his finger. The leather bit into his skin, but the pain didn't alleviate the powerlessness he felt.

Rolf sprinted to the next building, cutting a wide arc to avoid the security cameras' field of view, and circled back to where Tig had parked, stopping at Henry's open window.

"She's in there," Rolf said tensely. "The smell of her blood is strong."

The unspoken words hung between them—*Rolf doesn't know whether she's alive.*

Henry transformed into a bat. Dizzy from the change, he blinked at the blackness enshrouding him. Hunger stabbed at his stomach. He should have fed at Rolf's house, but he couldn't think of his own needs then—not while he knew what Karen was going through.

Crawling out from under his clothes, he took flight and squeaked, using the sound's echo to locate the building. He landed on the light fixture above the back door, gripping the rod jutting out from the concrete wall. He flapped his wings to maintain his balance as he settled in to hang there.

Once he had his wings folded in, a rock smashed against the door. Tig had pitched it with exquisite precision.

He waited for the door to open. Nothing. A few moments later, another rock banged against the door. This time, the door opened. The muzzle of a gun poked out first. Then a man's head appeared. The man looked around. Above his head, Henry quickly crawled across the doorframe to cling to the inside ledge.

The man pulled his head in and closed the door. He hitched his pants and sauntered down the hall, disappearing into the front room.

Henry took flight and bobbed through the dark hallway, past the door of the back room, which was open. He looked in and saw no one besides Karen, so he circled around and went in.

Karen was strapped to a desktop, either passed out or recently dead—he couldn't be sure. The bastard had carved the word "NEVEr" and a diamond shape on her stomach. Fingers were missing.

What kind of a sick asshole did such a thing to a woman? He circled one more time and flew less than a foot above her—his radar detected signs of warmth in her veins, and his ears caught a weak heartbeat.

Alive.

No smell of explosives, no trip wires—probably no booby trap. He swooped into the hallway, flittered past the second door, and landed on the ground next to the open doorway, peering in. Two men played cards while Karen lay dying.

His rage flared. Should he kill them now? They deserved a painful death for what they'd done to Karen. But his conscience wrestled with his anger and slammed it to the mat. Karen needed help—now. And Tig needed the men alive to find out who was behind this.

He sucked it up and flew back to the exit door, which was now locked and alarmed. He transformed back into a man and studied the keypad's swipe pattern. The four most frequently touched keys were covered in dark smudges, easily discerned by his enhanced vision, and he guessed at the code's order. On his third attempt, he deactivated the alarm.

He propped the door open with an abandoned crate. Transforming back to a bat, he crawled onto the crate and spread his wings, taking flight through the two-foot opening. He wobbled weakly as he flew—he needed blood, and soon.

At the Escalade, he had trouble transforming back. He pushed at his skin, willing it to change, demanding that it change. His bones elongated, a momentary expansion, and then he collapsed back like someone had released their finger from the spout of a half-filled balloon.

I have to do this for Karen.

He pushed again, forcing the change through, until he stood on two human feet. His dry skin crackled, his hunger clawing at him. He ignored it all and briefed Tig while he dressed.

Tig radioed the others and explained the layout and the plan. "Henry and Rolf will enter through the back and protect Karen. Jayden, pick me up on Hope Street, where the sidewalk cuts through. I'll lead the team through the front door on Grand Avenue. We'll need the battering ram."

Henry read between the lines. Rolf wouldn't be with the team at the front door. Tig didn't trust him to leave any kidnapper alive, and she shouldn't trust Henry either. Given the chance, he'd kill each of them after seeing what they'd done to Karen.

Cerissa clutched the shoulder strap of the seatbelt tightly, every muscle in her body tightly wound. From the passenger seat, she watched Jayden slowly drive his police car along Hope Street, paralleling Tig's progress in the alley. Streetlights cast long shadows on the asphalt. The old concrete-brick buildings were dark, not a single light on inside.

Her heart constricted as Tig described Karen's condition over the radio. "She's alive, but we don't know the extent of the injuries yet. Henry and Rolf will take the back door and protect her."

I have to fix this, I have to fix this, I have to...

When Jayden braked, Cerissa grabbed her med kit and bolted from the car.

"Wait," Jayden called. "Take the EMT kit too."

The car's trunk popped open. She ran to the back and grabbed the soft-sided zippered case marked with a red cross and slid it over her shoulder. Next to it was a green oxygen bag. She snagged it too and took off down a walkway between the buildings. Tig dashed past her, running in the opposite direction.

At the edge of the building, Cerissa stopped and whistled, getting Henry's attention. He motioned for her to go back. She ignored him and ran from the building to the Escalade, huddling behind it with him and Rolf.

"Stay here until the men inside are secured," Henry whispered angrily.

"No way," she whispered. "Don't even think of reverting to your old-fashioned ways. I'm going in with you."

"Very well, but let us lead." He reached for two of her bags to carry. "I know where they have Karen."

Tig's signal came over a portable police radio—the team at the front door was in position. Henry and Rolf sprinted to the building, slipping through the open back door. Cerissa ran close on their heels and slid to a stop when she entered the dingy office.

Hopelessness and grief swirled in her—and those were just Henry's emotions. Her own dark guilt threatened to engulf her as her vision narrowed.

Karen lay naked, eyes closed, strapped to an old metal desk. Her skin matched the desk's gray color. Blood dripped from her hands, forming two pools on the floor.

Henry signaled Tig over the radio. A loud crash filled the air—the front door hitting the ground, the footsteps of Tig's team running into the other room. Shouts of "freeze" and "on the ground" were followed by a short scuffle.

The noise shook Cerissa out of her shock. She ran to Karen's side and placed two fingers on her neck.

A pulse—she has a pulse.

Carefully, she peeled back the duct tape gagging Karen. Henry stood guard at the door. Rolf had stopped halfway into the room, his gaze fixed on Karen's mutilated body.

"They will all die for this," he said icily. He bolted from the room, shoving past Henry.

"She's still alive," Cerissa told Henry. She frantically flipped the latches on her med kit and grabbed her hypo. "She needs your blood, and she needs it fast. I'm going to give her a stimulant to wake her."

"I'll get Rolf." Henry moved toward the door. "I can't feed her. She isn't my mate."

"We don't have time." She dialed in the combination for epinephrine, which would treat Karen's shock and hopefully wake her. She looked up at Henry. "Without your blood, Karen will die."

Cerissa pressed the hypo against Karen's neck, injecting the stimulant. Karen roused, a desperate moan passing between her barely parted lips.

Henry glanced toward the door. Angry voices sounded from the other room, followed by the crash of furniture. Was Rolf fighting with Tig?

"Now," Cerissa demanded.

Resigned, he used his pocket knife to cut his wrist and placed the wound against Karen's lips. It wasn't the first time Karen's lips had touched his skin. At the end of their one and only date, Henry had shared a brief kiss with Karen, and at the time, he'd felt nothing. Now, the cold touch of her lips caused a deep sorrow to well in his chest.

At first she fed weakly, moaning against his skin, but as his blood worked to heal her, she sucked more vigorously. He looked at what the Cutter had done to her and didn't have the heart to tell Cerissa. Vampire blood wouldn't fix the damage he saw.

Cerissa ignored the look on Henry's face. She had to stay focused to save Karen's life.

Five fingers were missing—two on one hand, three on the other. She tied a light tourniquet at the wrist of each hand to stop the bleeding and wrapped gauze around the raw stumps. Then she grabbed Henry's free hand and pressed it over Karen's wounded fingers nearest him. "Apply pressure," she said. "We need to stop the blood loss."

Karen moaned louder and tried to move away, but the straps stopped her.

Cerissa wrapped a blood pressure cuff around Karen's arm, and the reading confirmed what she already knew—the loss of blood was straining Karen's heart, close to killing her.

Cerissa had two bags of clone blood with her. But where to place the transfusion needle? She couldn't use an arm; she didn't want to increase the blood volume there and have it bleed out through Karen's missing fingers. She palpated for the subclavian vein by Karen's breastbone, found it, and slid in the intravenous needle.

To start the flow of blood, Cerissa clamped the bag with the other end of the tube, puncturing it. She hung the bag on a nail protruding from the nearby wall. The blood slowly moved through the tube. The gravity feed wasn't fast enough to do any good. Cerissa took the blood pressure cuff off Karen, wrapped it around the blood bag, and pumped it up, putting it under pressure to force the blood to flow faster.

She crossed her mental fingers. Clone blood hadn't been tested on humans yet. To survive, Karen needed human blood as much as she needed Henry's blood. Without it, Henry could accidentally kill her.

While Cerissa was undergoing envoy training, Leopold had warned her: never flood a mortal with vampire blood without either human blood to dilute it or the bite. Undiluted vampire blood would run out of injuries to heal and attack healthy organs, feeding on them, trying to turn the person without the catalyst.

She slapped gauze pads on the worst stomach cuts. Some of the shallower ones had healed already, thanks to Henry's blood, leaving behind a scar that would forever scream the Cutter's message. She lifted the gauze from around one finger—the wound was clotting.

Something must have interrupted the Cutter. He had been methodologically removing each finger, alternating between hands. The fingers were lined up on the table next to her. Cerissa swept them into a sterile bag and placed the bag in her med kit.

Karen began to shake violently—signs of shock, despite the stimulant. Cerissa reached for the hypo and stopped. It contained other medicines, but she wasn't sure how they'd affect a real human.

Instead, she unzipped the green bag and removed the small oxygen canister. A tube-style mask allowed Karen to keep feeding from Henry. Cerissa connected the mask and opened the flow of oxygen.

A sleeping bag lay in one corner. She wrapped Karen in it, trying to warm her, and used an old phone book to elevate Karen's feet.

Cerissa gritted her teeth as white-hot anger flooded through her.

I have real medical equipment at the Enclave instead of this primitive shit. Why can't I use it? Because of some stupid non-interference rule?

She looked up at the sound of Henry collapsing to the floor and dashed around the desk, kneeling by his side. He was so pale—he needed to feed.

Her last bag of clone blood: save it for Karen, or give it to Henry?

"I'm okay," he mumbled. "Help Karen."

His words decided it. Cerissa ran to the next room and stopped at the doorway. Rolf and Tig were circling opposite each other. The rest of the crew stood between Rolf and the tied-up prisoners.

"They deserve to die," Rolf said icily. "I have a right to kill them."

Tig's hands were raised in front of her. "Stand down, Rolf. Now."

Rolf lunged at the chief and Tig landed a roundhouse kick, sending Rolf flying.

"Rolf!" Cerissa yelled. "Karen is alive and needs you!"

He ignored her. He jumped to his feet and charged at Tig.

How can I stop this?

Cerissa desperately looked around. A long metal pole lay by the door. She grabbed it and ran up behind Rolf, whacking him on the back with all her strength.

He staggered and dropped to his knees. Tig backed off, and Cerissa grabbed his collar from behind. The other vampires mumbled their opinions on her sanity, the collective sentiment being that she must be crazy.

"Rolf!" she yelled into his ear. "Karen needs your blood!"

He swung on her, but she sidestepped quickly.

"Rolf, stop. Karen needs you."

He bared his fangs at her and lunged.

"Karen's alive," she yelled, but he kept coming like an angry bear in attack mode.

She backed up, looking around for a way to defend herself without morphing. "Karen—" she started to scream at him.

He grabbed her, his fangs heading for her neck. She wrapped her hands around his throat, holding him back. This wasn't going to end well.

A flash of motion and a *thunk* vibrated through her. Rolf's chest mashed her against the wall and he dropped to his knees, taking her with him, her hands still wrapped around his throat.

Tig raised the chair she'd swung, poised to whack him again if he got up.

Cerissa pushed and rolled away from him, getting unsteadily to her feet. "Drag him in to where Karen is," she said.

The others pounced as a group to restrain him. They followed her to Karen, pulling a struggling Rolf with them.

Henry was back on his feet. He'd reopened the wound in his wrist and was trying to feed Karen again. When Rolf saw that, his eyes widened and the message got through.

"Let me go!" Rolf yelled.

They did. He ran to Karen's side, sliced his wrist open with the silver knife from his belt, and shoved Henry out of the way.

"Zeke, Liza," Tig barked. "Take the captives to the police car. Cerissa—should I call an ambulance for Karen?"

"No. I can take care of her wounds."

Tig nodded and left the room. Tig hadn't seen the extent of the trauma—the sleeping bag covered Karen's hands and stomach, masking the worst of it.

Cerissa took Karen's vital signs. "She's as stable as she's going to get here. You can move her."

Rolf cut the straps and carried Karen to the Escalade. Cerissa followed closely behind with the oxygen bottle and blood bag. Henry gathered the emergency bags, and then dashed ahead to open the rear doors, the space empty. The damaged motorcycle had been left at Rolf's.

Rolf lovingly laid Karen in the back cargo space, tucking the sleeping bag around her. Cerissa climbed in. "That's enough of your blood for now," she told Rolf. "I'll ride with her."

Rolf clenched his jaws. His determination to stay at Karen's side was written on his face.

"Rolf, get in the back seat," Tig ordered him, then grabbed Rolf's arm, pulled him to the passenger door, and shoved him in. "Sunrise in sixty minutes. We don't have much time. Jayden will return during the day to collect what evidence he can."

Henry loaded the emergency bags in next to Cerissa and stood at the open hatch door. "Cerissa, I'm—"

She shook her head. "Not now."

He grabbed her wrist. "Cerissa, this was not your fault."

Through the crystal, she felt his remorse. He let go and closed the back hatch.

It didn't matter if he no longer blamed her; she still blamed herself.

Rolf leaned over the seat and stroked Karen's auburn hair, brushing it away from where it was matted on her face, stuck to dried tears.

The desperate tenderness with which he touched Karen sent a tidal wave of sadness through Cerissa. She struggled to ignore it by concentrating on Karen, taking her pulse, listening to her heart, checking her bleeding stumps, doing what she could as Henry drove them back to the Hill.

I have to fix this.

But how? If she used Lux technology, the Protectors would find out. They would confine her to the Enclave, even take her wings. She'd never see Henry again.

Why did her choices always come down to duty or love? If she followed orders, Karen would suffer. If she listened to her heart, Karen would be fine, but she'd lose Henry. She didn't know how to mend this without sacrificing either her friend or her mate.

How do I choose between them?

Karen roused, moaning, and began thrashing her head from side to side. Cerissa snugged the sleeping bag around her tighter.

"No more," Karen begged. "I'll do whatever you want."

"You're okay. The man is gone. You're safe."

"Stop, please, stop. No, not again…" Karen let out a wail, a wail of deep pain and despair.

Cerissa blinked back tears and her heart fractured, shattering like glass into red fragments so small that no Lux technology could fix it.

CHAPTER 48

ROLF'S HOUSE—TWENTY MINUTES LATER

"Take her to her room," Cerissa directed, following Rolf as he carried Karen through the foyer. The four were alone in Rolf's house—Tig and her team had continued on to the Hill's jail with the prisoners.

Karen had passed out during the drive. Rolf climbed the stairs, careful not to jostle her, the oxygen bottle tucked under his arm, the empty transfusion bag resting on Karen's stomach.

Hurrying past Rolf's living room, Cerissa saw the ice chest, and rushed in to snag a packet of donor blood. She tossed it to Henry. "You need to feed."

He didn't bother taking time to heat it or pour it into a mug. He ripped off one corner with a fang and drank it down cold, squeezing the bag so it squirted into his mouth. She grabbed another one and took it upstairs to Rolf, who accepted it without comment. Henry followed her shortly, another bag of blood in his hand, the color returning to his face.

Rolf sat on the bed next to Karen, gently stroking her leg.

Cerissa opened her med kit and took out surgical tools. She stopped when she got to one she was forbidden from using on a human.

I'm supposed to protect mortals from harm.

A duty drummed into her head since she was a child. But what was her duty *after* they were harmed? What then?

Am I just supposed to stand by and watch Karen suffer because she's human?

According to the Protectors, that was the rule. Interference was forbidden unless it served the greater good.

Screw that. Who are the Protectors to decide who will suffer and who will not?

She wasn't going to let Karen experience a lifetime of pain because of her. Not if she could do something about it.

Being raised by her father's family had indeed changed her—for the better. Humans mattered, and not just the survival of the race. Each one mattered. She could no longer be the objective observer, the watcher standing apart. When she got her medical license, she'd taken an oath to save life and minster to the ill and injured. That oath trumped her duty to the Lux.

She shook her head. How could she ever have considered doing nothing as an option?

The image of Henry's crucifix filled her mind's eye. Now she understood his view on sacrifice. To be worthy, the sacrifice must be her choice, not something demanded of her. But would he understand why she chose to save Karen, even if it cost her everything they had together?

Knowing Henry, he would.

She motioned for Rolf to move aside. "You need to feed before you give her more blood. Go outside while I treat her wounds. I need to focus on my work and not worry how what I do affects you."

"I'm not some fainting mortal. Do what you must."

She stared back at him. She wasn't going to use a forbidden regenerator in front of him. It was one thing to save Karen; it was another to let Rolf see things he shouldn't. "Please. Go feed and let me work."

Rolf gave her a stony glare, but left the room.

Cerissa looked over at Henry. "Both of you stay out. I'm going to use some advanced techniques, and he can't see what I'm doing. So keep him out."

"I'll do my best," Henry replied. "Will she be all right?"

"I can heal her body," Cerissa said, grasping the regenerator tool. "Can you or Rolf make her forget what happened to her?"

"Not without removing her memory of Rolf." Henry took another swig from the bag of blood he carried. "To wipe her memory of the torture, we would have to remove all memory of her life here."

Cerissa walked him to the bedroom door. "Okay. I know what I have to do."

There was so much more she wanted to say to him—so much to explain. But there was no time. Karen needed her.

She closed the bedroom door and returned to Karen, peeling back the sleeping bag, which stuck in places where some of the deeper wounds had continued to bleed and clot, holding the fabric like sticky glue. Thanks to Henry and Rolf's blood, some of the shallower cuts had already healed.

The word "NEVEr" was now written in a combination of bright pink scars and dark red, crusty lines.

But vampire blood wouldn't regenerate severed fingers or heal Karen's mind, and neither would the forbidden tools in Cerissa's medical kit. She needed the surgical suite at the Enclave to repair everything.

Karen stirred, her face contorted in pain.

Time to go.

Cerissa ejected her contact lenses. She dropped them into a tray in her medical kit that would upload the videos of Karen's rescue to Ari. She wanted him to know what happened. Normally she'd use a compartment in her phone to upload the videos, but she'd left the phone downstairs in her purse.

She grabbed the oxygen bottle, laid it on Karen's stomach, and flashed them to her lab at the Enclave.

Karen roused and asked, "Where am I?"

It was more of a moan than a clear question. From the sound of it, she was having trouble breathing.

"You're in a surgical center," Cerissa told her. She laid Karen on the exam table. It wasn't a match to Karen's body shape—it was designed for the Lux—but it would have to do. "Relax and try not to breathe too deeply for the moment. I need to change the oxygen bottle."

The atmosphere in the Enclave was thinner than Karen was used to. Cerissa replaced the tube mask with a sealing one, covering Karen's nose and mouth, and turned on the oxygen.

She attached a monitor to Karen's chest, tracking her heartbeat and blood pressure, and connected the IV line in Karen's subclavian vein to a nozzle protruding from the infirmary wall. She introduced both a paralytic and an anesthetizing agent into the IV line. Karen's blood pressure was still adequate. There was no need for another transfusion just yet.

Once Karen was sedated, Cerissa got undressed and morphed to her Lux form. The backless surgical scrubs she threw on accommodated her wings. With the flip of a switch, a sterile field surrounded the treatment table where Karen lay.

Using a regenerator tool, Cerissa began the tedious process to regrow bone and tissue the Cutter had hacked away. All cells carried complete genetic memory. The trick was to convince them to multiply and transform into the cells needed for regrowth. The first part was easy; the second part was more difficult, and took an accomplished surgeon. She was good, but out of practice. It would take her longer than she liked, but that was the price of excellence.

Henry watched Rolf pace back and forth in front of Karen's bedroom door. How much longer could he keep Rolf from disturbing Cerissa? Rolf had drunk two bags of blood, was working on his third, and kept running one hand through his hair, his forehead wrinkled, his eyes filled with grief.

"Give her time," Henry said. "She's a skilled doctor. She—"

The ringtone stopped him. He took his phone off his belt and punched the side button to see who was calling. The startup screen began to cycle, turning it on. It was then he realized it wasn't his phone ringing. He'd shut his off earlier.

"That must be Cerissa's phone." He put his ear to the door. It wasn't coming from Karen's room—it seemed to be coming from below them. "Wait here," he said, and then hurried downstairs to search for the sound.

"You can't answer Cerissa's phone," Rolf called after him. "It might be bugged."

"Her phone has an extra layer of security—I'll explain later."

But how would he explain it? They were all keeping too many secrets.

He tracked the sound—the ringing seemed to come from the foyer. Cerissa had gotten into the habit of leaving her purse on his foyer table and, in the chaos of the evening, had set her purse on a similar table near Rolf's front door.

"Where's Cerissa?" Ari demanded when Henry answered her phone.

"We have Karen back. Cerissa is upstairs with her."

"Then write down this address. I located the computer the kidnappers used to send their emails."

Henry found a pen and pad in Cerissa's purse and wrote as Ari dictated. Then he stared at it. "That's where we found Karen."

"I'm not surprised—the videos had to be uploaded on-site or near there. I'm going to keep working to see what else I can discover. Did you find a computer there?"

"We didn't have time to look. We had to get Karen back here quickly. Sunrise is less than fifteen minutes away."

"Is Karen okay?"

"She was badly injured—mutilated by those bastards. Cerissa will tell you about it later."

Henry dropped the phone into her purse and took the stairs three at a time, racing back to the hallway outside Karen's room. Rolf stood there, his ear pressed against the door, the palms of his hands splayed against the white painted surface.

"This isn't right," Rolf said. "I should be in there with her. She needs me. I can feel it." He reached for the doorknob.

Henry grabbed Rolf's arm. "Think. She's had enough blood. Much more, and you risk killing her."

Rolf shook off Henry's hand. "And without my blood, she may die. I have to know she's all right."

Rolf grabbed the doorknob again. Henry wrapped his arms around Rolf's waist and pulled him back, trying to restrain him without hurting him. Rolf threw himself at the door, ramming his shoulder into it and breaking the frame. His momentum dragged them both into the room before they lost balance. Henry landed on top of him and rolled off. Rolf sprang to his feet, stopping at the foot of the empty bed.

"Where is she?" he screamed.

Henry took a guess: "Cerissa has taken her to where she can perform surgery."

"Where? How?"

"Rolf, calm down. Karen is in good hands."

Rolf growled and swung at Henry. He missed. "Where is she?" Rolf screamed, and lunged again. "Tell me where she is!"

Henry sidestepped. He grabbed Rolf's shirt, plowing him into the wall. The dry wall dented and cracked from the impact.

Rolf crumpled onto the floor into a ball, white dust raining on him. Henry stepped back, scrubbing his hand over his face.

I can't let him find out about Cerissa.

Rolf sprang to his feet, swinging his fists, the silver knife at his belt still sheathed.

Henry ducked. Why hadn't Rolf gone for the knife? Had rage so clouded his mind he'd forgotten it? Or did Rolf still value their friendship in spite of everything?

I know I do. Even after everything with the council, I shouldn't. But Rolf is still my friend. I can't draw a weapon on him either.

He raised his arms to deflect Rolf's fist, but moved too late. The blow split his lip open. He ignored the pain radiating through his face and landed a solid punch to Rolf's stomach, putting all the force he could behind it. Rolf doubled over and fell to his knees.

The sound of bones cracking had accompanied the blow—except it wasn't Rolf's bones.

Henry's right hand dropped limply to his side when he pulled away. *Madre de Dios.* A sharp pain radiated up his arm, agony avalanching through his mind. He dropped to his knees and grabbed Rolf left-handed. Struggling to his feet, he dragged Rolf to the hallway balcony.

I don't have the strength for this fight, my friend.

Giving blood to Karen and transforming into a bat had drained him—it would be a while before the human blood he drank restored him to full strength.

Getting a firm one-handed grip on Rolf, he propelled his friend over the hallway balcony to the floor below. Rolf landed on his back with a crunch on the white marble. He lay there spread-eagle, one leg bent back, not moving for at least a minute.

Please forgive me.

Henry wiped a trickle of blood from his lip and licked it off the back of his hand. Rolf slowly, painfully, rolled over. It was only a matter of time before Rolf healed enough to re-engage the battle.

Henry slid his left wrist under his immobile right hand, centering his hand over the crystal. Painful shocks radiated out as he worked his fingers open.

He had never tried this before. Cerissa had warned him she didn't know what would happen to him, being a vampire. It was a risk he had to take.

"Take me to Cerissa," he said.

A moment in nothingness, like dreaming while wide awake, and then he stood in an operating room. Small and enclosed, windowless, it looked like a cave carved out of rock. He took a breath—the air was cold and thin. Were they at high altitude?

He focused on the people in the room. Karen was naked on the surgical table, some of her missing fingers already restored.

Then he focused on the surgeon. Her back was to him.

Long white wings grew from her shoulders and trailed to points just above the floor—like angel wings painted by the old Renaissance masters.

Wait—

Angel wings?

Cerissa sensed his presence before she saw him. She raised the top of her wings and fluffed them with annoyance.

Damn. Double damn.

She didn't need this right now. She set down the regenerating tool and touched a panel on the computer next to the table, turning on a translation program. She spoke in her language as the computer translated. Her Lux mouth was unable to form the sounds humans made.

"You didn't have to take this risk. Go back," she sang, turning to face him.

"*Madre de Dios,*" Henry whispered.

He stood there, transfixed. *So beautiful.* Not human, but elegant and exotic, with iridescent blue skin, the way some Caucasians were faintly pink. Straight white hair hung down her back to her waist, held back in a series of clips. It flowed to the side when she turned to look at him. Her eyes, large and round, like waif eyes in a Keane painting, were the color of molten silver.

She seemed to shine. On her forehead, a multifaceted eye, like a

DARK WINE AT SUNRISE

round-cut diamond, radiated three shades of brilliant blue. Light from her third eye created a halo effect. She quickly raised her hand to cover it.

Why cover such beauty? He took a step closer. The urge to stroke her soft-looking feathers overwhelmed him.

He took another step and stopped. He'd seen those wings before. It hadn't been a dream. The angel at his door, the angel who told him it wasn't his time to die after Blanche shot him…

That angel had been Cerissa.

My angel.

A ripple of fear shot through him, a ripple of fear she'd feel through the crystal. He dropped to one knee and bowed his head.

Jesucristo. He crossed himself. *No, it can't be true. There must be some other explanation—*

"Why are you here?" she asked. He looked up at her. Her big eyes blinked once, the tips of her wings ruffling.

He struggled to find the words. "Rolf is—uncontrollable—he needs reassurance Karen will live."

"He knows we're gone?"

"I couldn't stop him. He broke down the bedroom door."

Cerissa opened a nearby drawer and tossed him a black onyx bracelet. She said something, her language sung rather than spoken.

"There's no way to explain our disappearance," the computer translated. "He might as well see for himself. Tell him to put on this bracelet."

Henry nodded, but he couldn't contain his fear. He had to ask.

"Are you an angel?"

She cut him off with the trill of a musical note, which the computer translated. "I don't have time for this."

He reached out to her, but before he could rise, she punched a series of buttons on a panel. The transport device whisked him back to Karen's room.

CHAPTER 49

Still kneeling, Henry pressed his eyes closed. There had to be another explanation. Cerissa couldn't be a real angel. She would have told him if she was a heavenly being.

At the sound of a grunt from the doorway, he opened his eyes. Rolf clutched his chest with one arm as he crawled into the bedroom. Henry slid an arm around Rolf and lifted him, walking him to the bed.

"Where the fuck did you come from?" Rolf demanded, gingerly sitting on the edge of Karen's bed. "No vampire power transports clothing."

Henry slapped the bracelet onto Rolf's wrist. "Put this on."

Rolf suddenly bolted to his feet, flailing with one arm at the empty air. "Get away from her!" he yelled.

"Rolf, what's wrong?" Henry asked, gripping Rolf's shoulder and pulling him back to the bed.

"Karen's on a table and some strange thing is hovering over her." Rolf tried lunging again, but he doubled over in pain before he got farther.

Henry grabbed Rolf's wrist, his unbroken hand covering the bracelet. Henry stood still when he heard Cerissa's voice.

"You're not here," Cerissa was saying. "You're wearing a communication device. It allows you to see the surgical center in my lab. Now shut up and let me work. You may watch, but you can't interfere. I'm regenerating the skin, muscle, and bone that were cut away. This will take time. You'll have to be patient."

Rolf eased onto the bed again, holding his ribcage. Henry kept contact with the bracelet so he could hear too.

"Will she be okay?" Rolf asked.

"Yes. Now shut up."

328

"Cerissa, can you hear me?" Henry asked.

"Yes, Henry."

"It is almost dawn."

"Then take Rolf below ground and go to sleep. I'm busy."

"Will it break the link if we leave Karen's room?"

"He can walk around with the communicator and still see me—he can watch until he goes to sleep. Now I must insist you two stop talking to me so I may concentrate. This isn't easy work. I'll bring her back when I'm done. She'll be at Rolf's when he wakes."

The surgery took a couple of hours. Finished, Cerissa returned the regenerator to its stainless steel tray and checked Karen's vitals. The numbers looked stable—no sign of any reaction to the transfused clone blood.

Exhausted, she collapsed onto a backless chair, hungry enough to eat anything—even the vegetarian cuisine her people dined on. She reached into a nearby refrigerator and took out a bottle. Not her favorite—she had lived too long in human form—but she sucked down the green liquid, ignoring the bitter taste.

The tough part came next: healing Karen's emotional trauma. The Carlyle Cutter was a sociopath, a true sadist—he knew too much about what he was doing and how to inflict pain while keeping the victim alive. The odds of Karen's psychological survival weren't good, not with those emotions lurking in her brain.

After resting, Cerissa adjusted the environmental controls, changing the atmosphere in the room to one suitable for humans, and morphed back to her human form. The scrubs she wore hung too loosely. She cinched the tie around her neck so the top wouldn't expose her breasts and then touched the computer panel, triggering the antidote to bring Karen back to consciousness.

She eased the oxygen mask off Karen's face. Soon, Karen's eyelids fluttered.

"How are you feeling?" Cerissa asked.

"I'm...." Karen's face transformed from peaceful to puzzled to fearful, until she shut her eyes tight, grabbing Cerissa's hand, squeezing it painfully.

"No..." Karen said, the high-pitched word trailing off.

Cerissa rapidly tapped on Karen's forearm, trying to ground her in the present. She couldn't let Karen focus on the torture just yet. Not until she was connected to the touchstone.

"You were injured," Cerissa said quickly. "Rolf and Henry gave you blood. Their blood helped a lot, but not enough. You've been through surgery. You're fine, physically."

"No…" Karen repeated, tears welling. Then she shook her head, a quick twitch, like she was trying to suppress the memory.

"Listen to me; listen to my voice. There's one additional injury I want to heal, if you agree. Your memories of what happened to you—"

Karen twitched again but remained silent.

"I can desensitize those memories and help you process the emotional trauma. The kind of trauma you've suffered—unless we do something about it, the memories will keep coming back, crashing into your awareness and forcing you to relive the emotions in the present."

"I—I don't understand."

"I know it sounds far-fetched, and I'll explain more later, but for now, the choice you have is whether you want me to stop the memories from flooding you with painful emotions."

Karen continued clutching Cerissa's hand. A single tear formed and slowly descended down Karen's face. "Help me," she pleaded, scrunching her eyes shut again, taking in air in short, gasping bursts.

"Do you want me to make the emotions stop? It may not seem like a fair question, but the sooner I do this, the less difficult it will be. Each time you think of what happened, it duplicates the emotional memory. If I did this a week from now I would have to chase all the duplicates."

"You can really do this? I'm not dreaming it? I'm not going to wake up—"

"You're awake now. You're healed physically. I want to give you a shot at healing emotionally. Do you want it?"

"I want to see Rolf."

A good sign—Karen still felt connected to Rolf. "It's after dawn. You won't be able to speak with him for another eight hours, and if you agree, we'll be done with this process long before he wakes."

"You really can stop these memories from coming back?" Karen's voice trembled, and she gulped another short breath.

The device had never been used on a human before. The Lux had invented it to heal the emotional trauma they sometimes suffered at the hands of humans. But it was the only way Cerissa could help Karen—it had to work.

"You'd still have the memories," Cerissa said, "but they'd be integrated and stored properly in your brain. It would feel like they were someone else's memories, like you had watched a movie and it hadn't happened to you."

"Then do it. Please, do it."

"I'm going to need your help. First, you hold this," Cerissa said, handing Karen a black jasper stone. "The brain stores memories chemically. This touchstone reads those chemical changes."

She attached a lead from the touchstone to the computer. "It's connected to this device. I take your hand in mine. Simple."

She wrapped her hand around Karen's—she needed to be in contact with the touchstone for it to work—and used her other hand to trigger the computer program. "With computer assistance, I'll locate the memory, test it to find its limits, and reprogram the emotion associated with it. I have to take my time with this so I don't reprogram more than I should. Picture each memory as residing on the surface of a soap bubble. There are millions of these bubbles, and they carry fragments of different emotional memories. We're looking for the fragments from the last eight hours or so."

She pressed another button on the computer console. A drug designed to keep Karen calm and relaxed during the process flowed into her veins through the IV.

"I'm giving you some medicine to make it easier for you," Cerissa said. "I need you to concentrate on each memory. The good news is you only have to do this once. After we're done, the traumatic emotions will be gone."

Once Karen's eyes were closed, Cerissa morphed to her native form, and placed the oxygen mask back on Karen's face.

Opening her mind, Cerissa connected neurally to the touchstone. Her viewpoint spun as she suddenly saw herself through Karen's eyes. A sharp pain pulsed through her brain, a side effect of using the device. Cerissa took a deep breath to control it and steeled herself for what came next.

With the computer translating, she prompted Karen to remember what she could of the kidnapping. In order to erase the memories, Cerissa had to see, hear, and feel the memory, from Karen's vantage point. And not only the visual and auditory memories, but the sensory memories encoded in the limbic part of the brain, the ones Karen's body remembered even if her mind had blotted them out. It wasn't easy to relive what Karen went through, but it was worth it to spare Karen the emotional hell of reliving the torture for the rest of her life.

As the memories unfolded, Cerissa fluttered her wings. The Cutter was nothing if not methodical. When Karen first passed out from pain, he'd used a "popper"—amyl nitrite—to wake her before resuming the torture. He took his time making the cuts, which prolonged the torture but probably saved Karen's life.

How could one human being do this to another? Had he no empathy at all?

Apparently not. Halfway through, the Cutter removed his mask, letting Karen see his face. The way he revealed himself was sadistic, as if to say, *I can show you who I am because you're going to die anyway.*

Fear rippled through Cerissa and her feathers rose—the Cutter wasn't among the men Tig had captured. He was still on the loose.

In Karen's memory, the Cutter brought his face inches from Karen's, and spoke for the first time. "My name is Chuck. And it's my privilege to deliver you unto death."

Cerissa pressed a button, using the computer to take a freeze-frame image of him. Even without the photo, she would never forget his face.

As the memory continued, a *ding* sounded. Chuck picked up a phone, his thumbs flying. A text message? Who was he talking with? Had someone warned him of Tig's progress?

Somehow Cerissa had to get this information to Tig. But how?

An hour later, Cerissa finished the procedure and removed the touchstone from Karen's hand.

Karen appeared to be resting comfortably, eyes still closed, face relaxed. Cerissa morphed back to human form and transitioned what she had experienced into a compartment of her mind far from her waking consciousness.

She checked the time. Six hours had passed. Why hadn't she been interrupted by one of her colleagues? Or had the Protectors already found out, and decided to leave her undisturbed?

It didn't matter. It was done. Karen would be all right.

Cerissa changed clothes, removed Karen's IV line and oxygen mask, and prepared a large envelope containing photos of the Cutter she'd taken from Karen's memory. After scooping Karen into her arms, Cerissa pressed a button on the control panel and transported them back to Karen's bedroom.

CHAPTER 50

Cerissa gently laid her friend on the bed and went looking through the closet for something to dress her in. She didn't want Karen waking disoriented and naked. Cerissa found a soft cotton nightshirt, dressed Karen in it, and slid her under the bed covers.

It wasn't long before Karen asked, "Where am I?"

"Your bedroom. You're safe. You're well. Everything is all right."

"Where's Rolf? He was here, giving me blood..." Karen squinted. She seemed puzzled, like she was trying to make sense of the sequence of events.

"It's daytime," Cerissa told her. "Rolf will wake in about seven hours. You'll be able to see him then." She took Karen's hand. "You were badly injured during the kidnapping. Both Henry and Rolf fed you when you were rescued. They fed you all the blood they could without hurting you, but it wasn't enough to heal your injuries."

Karen splayed her fingers, her gaze fixed on them. "I don't understand—I don't feel hurt."

"I—I repaired your fingers. Remember, I'm a doctor as well as a research scientist?"

Karen flexed her hand. "Shouldn't I be in a hospital?"

"I'm going to explain everything to you. In the meantime, are you hungry or thirsty? You should try to eat something if you can."

"I'm hungry, I guess."

"Wait here. I'll go downstairs and get you something to eat."

"Sure," Karen said, closing her eyes and yawning.

Cerissa went downstairs to make lunch. Through the kitchen wall, she heard the sounds of Sang and Mort whining. She found the dog chow in the pantry and went outside. An automatic water bowl had kept them watered, but their food dishes were empty and had been tossed around the outdoor dog run. She slipped open the latch and kneed her way past the anxious dogs to fill their bowls.

When she returned to the kitchen, she washed her hands and made Karen's lunch. She then retrieved the dogs, bringing them upstairs, and carried a turkey sandwich, apple slices, and ice tea on a tray. The dogs eagerly ran ahead, jumping on the bed, and nosed Karen awake.

"Stop that. Get down," Cerissa said. The dogs jumped off the bed. "Sit."

They sat, their plaintive brown eyes looking for reassurance.

"It's okay," Karen said. "They're just glad to see me."

The dogs watched as Cerissa placed the tray table across Karen's lap. She slipped an arm around Karen, helping her to sit upright. Karen ate slowly, still groggy from the anesthetic. When she finished, Cerissa lifted the tray away. The dogs had lain down on the rug, and with Cerissa's movement, they stood up, on guard.

"What do you remember?" Cerissa asked, sitting on the bed next to her.

"It's all kind of jumbled. I remember the kidnapping and being knocked out. I don't know with what. They grabbed me before I could get to my gun and threw me into the back of a van. One of them held me while the other injected something into a vein in my hand. Ten seconds later, I was out." She stopped to take a sip of her tea. "I woke in a room with everyone in masks. One of them took videos with his phone. They had me look into the camera, and they called me Henry's mate. Since I was driving your car, they thought I was you."

Cerissa nodded. "The ransom demand was emailed to Henry. What else do you recall?"

"I—I," Karen stuttered, looking puzzled. "He cut me, he cut my fingers. Why don't…"

"I desensitized and reprocessed your emotional response to the memory."

"Seriously? You can do that?"

"What else do you remember?"

"I only remember pieces of the rescue. I remember feeding off Henry, and then Rolf, and being in horrible pain. I remember thinking I was going to die, and then wishing I would die."

Cerissa squeezed Karen's hand. "But you didn't."

"Then I had this strange dream. Maybe it was from the anesthetic. You and I were in this strange place, with strange instruments. Except it wasn't you, it was this...well, an angel, and she had your features but not quite, and she was blue. Not solid blue, but kind of translucent. She had wings and this brilliant blue mound on her forehead—it had facets, like a sapphire, and it glowed."

Karen took another sip of tea. "I watched the pretty halo it created. She asked me a lot of questions, and then I woke up here. Strange dream, huh?"

Oh damn. Karen had fixated on Cerissa's third eye—it wasn't an eye used for seeing the real world; it was a sensory organ through which the Lux connected. How would Cerissa explain it? Karen's eyes had been closed whenever Cerissa looked at her, but perhaps Karen had gone in and out of consciousness while Cerissa reprogrammed her emotional memories. It could happen.

What to do now? She'd risked everything to save Karen's life. But this...telling a human about the Lux was forbidden. Her people had lived on this planet for over four thousand years by keeping themselves secret, by protecting the truth of their existence.

She'd violated that law when she told Henry. At the time, she had no choice. She was now bonded to him, and with the crystal tying them together, the Protectors couldn't touch him.

And then there was Rolf. All Rolf had was a glimpse of her back and a glimpse of her lab—he knew nothing of the Lux beyond that.

But what should she do about Karen? Tell her friend and disobey one of the highest commandments? This time, she wasn't trapped, and this wasn't just a little glimpse. If she told Karen the truth, it would be a willful decision to go against the Lux.

Should I lie to her? Tell her it was a hallucination induced by anesthesia?

That would be the easiest fix. She was already in deep enough trouble with the Protectors. Telling Karen would only make it worse.

But if she lied to Karen, how could she call Karen her friend? Her whole life she'd done her duty, obeying the Lux orders mindlessly, living the lie. As a small child, she'd been taught to hide what she was, first from her father's family and then from the other humans she'd fostered with and grown close to over the course of her life.

The big lie was always a barrier between her and any mortal friends. Just as it had become a barrier between her and Henry. She couldn't hide who she was anymore from those she loved.

And then it dawned on her.

The difference between mindless duty and free will: free will is all about making hard choices.

She'd made a hard choice when she took Karen to the Enclave to heal her, and now she faced another one. But what if she told Karen the truth and Karen pulled back in horror? Cerissa wasn't sure she could survive the pain of one more rejection. The way Henry had bowed to her in fear—she cringed at the memory.

No, I can't think of that right now.

She looked at her friend. She trusted Karen. She cared about her. She had to take the risk, no matter the outcome, and as much as she cared for Karen, the risk of rejection didn't feel quite as terrifying as it had with Henry.

Cerissa took a deep breath and let it out. "It wasn't a dream. It's time I told you the truth."

"Truth?"

"Henry has known since I was shot—there was no way to keep it from him once I was injured. Rolf knows now. He learned last night. What I am."

Karen laughed. The sound was magical. "Right," Karen said, shaking her head. "You're some sort of supernatural being who can perform medical miracles?"

"No, that's not quite right." Cerissa looked at her human hands, the missing sixth fingers making her feel incomplete. "I'm natural, for what I am, but I'm not from this planet. I can change my appearance and hold mortal form. The bluish creature you saw is my true form."

Karen wrinkled her brow. "You're serious."

"I am."

"Where were we?"

"You were in the infirmary in my lab at the Enclave—it's a secret place where my people live. I had to change to my native form to use the medical instruments. They aren't designed for human hands."

Cerissa spread the fingers of one hand and let them morph. She gingerly touched Karen. Her two blue thumbs wrapped around Karen's hand, her four blue fingers resting on Karen's palm.

Karen's eyes widened and she lifted Cerissa's hand, bringing it closer to her face, examining it, carefully bending each finger, tracing the delicate underside of the finger with her own, until she reached the fourth joint. Then Karen's face took on a serious look Cerissa had never seen before.

"Oh my God," she said in a reverent whisper. "It was you."

Karen stared at the blue six-fingered hand. Cerissa impulsively caressed her friend's face, human skin feeling like sandpaper.

"You're an alien?" Karen asked.

"Well, ah... My people aren't from this world. That's all I really know."

"You're not here to hurt us? You see all those movies about aliens enslaving us—I mean, you're nothing like that, you're...you're my friend."

Cerissa chuckled. "I'm not here to hurt anyone. Think of us as castaways, stranded on this planet. We've been here a long time. If anything, we're committed to ensuring humans don't destroy this world." Cerissa reluctantly removed her hand from Karen's face and morphed it back to human. "I can't hold it partway for long."

Karen lifted her ice tea glass, her hand shaking slightly. "This is real?"

"Very real. We have tissue regenerators to regrow damaged tissue from adjoining cells. Like a lizard can regrow its tail, we can convince your genetic material to replicate the missing tissue."

"I see. And you did this using...ah—"

"Medical technology."

"Technology your people invented?"

"Yes."

"And only Henry, Rolf, and I now know about you?"

"Yes," Cerissa said, then hesitated. "I hope you'll keep my secret."

"After all you've done for me, you bet I'll keep your secret. Even if we weren't friends, I would."

"So we're still friends?"

"Of course we are. Don't be silly." Karen smiled, her intensely serious look evaporating. She looked like the old Karen. Stretching out both arms, she focused on her hands again. "But my fingers don't have an even color."

"The new skin has never been exposed to the sun. As you tan, it'll match better."

"That's a relief. I don't want to be blotchy for the rest of my life."

Cerissa smiled, suppressing a laugh. "Then you're all right with this?"

"Cerissa, you saved my life. Of course I'm okay with this."

Tears filled Cerissa's eyes. Karen hugged her. "Don't cry," Karen said. "We'll keep your secret. Don't worry."

"I'm not worried, just relieved. I was so afraid you might reject me. Rolf was ready to kill me last night. He is so xenophobic."

"That's just Rolf. I'll take care of him. We'll protect you and keep you safe here."

Those were the strangest words Cerissa had ever heard. Did she need a human to keep her safe? Until she thought she might lose her friend, she didn't realize how much Karen meant to her. With her mind more at rest, the full weight of her fatigue hit her.

"Would you mind if I lay on the bed next to you? I'm about to drop on my feet. I haven't slept in thirty hours."

Karen patted the comforter. Cerissa went over to the other side of the bed and collapsed onto it. It felt so good to lie down. "Will you be all right?"

Karen kissed Cerissa on the cheek. "You get some rest. I'll be fine. Mort and Sang will protect me."

"Thank you," Cerissa said, and then drifted off.

She woke to the sound of Ari's ringtone. She'd left her purse downstairs. The dogs started to follow her, but she told them to stay—Karen was still napping.

"Ciss, you silly-headed cow," Ari began as soon as she said hello, "how could you even think of doing what you did without getting my help? I'm beginning to think you're a fucking moron. How many times have I told you to remember the eleventh commandment? Namely: don't get caught."

"How do you know what I did?"

"I've got a tap on the reports going to the Protectors, and your name figures prominently. Why didn't you call me first? I could have hidden what you did ten dozen ways. Now there'll be hell to pay."

"Then so be it." She'd known the risks when she did it. "I'm done hiding."

"Kid, have you lost your mind? I've seen Watchers confined to the Enclave for *years* for smaller offenses. Not to mention the emotion-wiping thing you did—it's not approved for humans. What you did is so over the top; they're going to be pissed. You can't play god. They don't like anything that smacks of playing god."

"How do you know?"

"I've been in hot water with them before. I know how they think. You, on the other hand, have never so much as bent the rules before. This will work in your favor, but it leaves you with no idea how to play the game. You're going to need me. And here is my first piece of advice: get your ass back to the Enclave. Report to your Guardian and explain to her what happened. Get her on your side, and do it before they come looking for you."

"But I need to talk with Henry first." She glanced at her watch—sunset was still two hours away. "He's not up yet."

"I'll deal with Henry. Leave your phone there, and I'll call him before I turn myself in.

"I don't know. I should be the one to tell him."

"You don't have any time to spare. You need to go *now*, not ten minutes from now!" Ari yelled in her ear. "I can delay the report a few hours at most. Time enough to allow you to get to your Guardian first, if you leave now."

The line went dead. Years of confinement? After the way Henry reacted when he saw her wings, maybe it was for the best—he'd never be able to accept her.

After writing out a note to Henry, a big emptiness settled in her chest. It was her own fault anyway. She should have shown him her Lux appearance sooner, then they might have had a chance—she would have been able to explain it her way. Now, that chance had sailed away like a feather in the breeze. She squared her shoulders and flashed back to the Enclave, ready to face the Protectors, come what may.

CHAPTER 51

ROLF'S HOUSE—THAT NIGHT

Upon waking, Henry flexed his hand. The fractured bones had mended while he slept. In a night or two, his hand would be fully healed—but what about Karen?

He waited for Rolf to rise. Rolf should be there when they learned whether the surgery had been successful. A short while later, Henry heard the younger vampire open the door to the adjacent basement room. He followed Rolf upstairs toward the sound of barking dogs.

Rolf took the stairs two at a time and ran straight to Karen's bedside, scooping his mate into a gentle hug. "*Liebling*, are you okay?"

Henry stopped at the bedroom's doorway. His gaze swept the room.

No sign of Cerissa. He didn't want to intrude, but he had to know what happened while he slept.

"How are you feeling, Karen?" Henry asked.

"I'm okay. Cerissa did a great job." She held up her hands, showing him. "Rolf," she said, "you're going to have to accept what she is. She's my bestie."

"Yes, *libeling*," Rolf replied, and continued to tenderly touch Karen's face, like he needed to reassure himself she was real.

Karen looked over at Henry. "Please give us some time alone, okay?"

"Of course," he replied, "but can you tell me where Cerissa is? I need to talk with her."

"Oh," Karen said, rubbing her eyes. "She got a phone call and hightailed it out of here. But she left this for you."

Karen held up a large manila envelope and Cerissa's phone. He thanked her and went downstairs to open it alone.

He sat on the living room sofa and read the note:

Dear Henry,

The man who tortured Karen is still alive. He wasn't among the captured. Enclosed is his photo. I extracted it from Karen's memories when I reprocessed her emotions. She won't be haunted by what the Cutter did to her.

You need to know the Cutter was in communication with someone while he had her—I saw him sending text messages, but I couldn't read them.

What I did for Karen, taking her to my lab and restoring her body, it violated the rules I live under. I've returned to the Enclave to try to work it out. Use my phone to call Ari as soon as you receive this. He'll explain.

I'm truly sorry. Even if we never see each other again, know that I love you with all my heart.

Cerissa

Fear shot across his skin, the hair rising on the back of his neck. He phoned Ari and arranged for them to meet at his house. The Viper was still parked in Rolf's driveway. He got in and sped home.

Ari was waiting in the drawing room when Henry arrived, sitting in Cerissa's armchair.

He strode into the room and brushed his sore hand over the crystal in his wrist, ready to transport to her. "Get up. We have to go after her."

"Hold on there, old man." Ari raised his hand. "You're not going anywhere."

"What do you mean? She's in trouble because of me. I have to do something."

"You need to put on the brakes and stay calm. I'll go to the Enclave to see what I can do for her. But this isn't going to be easy."

"Why? What will your people do?"

"It depends. She's never done anything like this before, so they may be lenient." Ari shrugged, sending a lock of wavy hair onto his forehead, and he brushed it back. "Then again, they may be pretty pissed. But the last thing you should do is go charging in there after her. You don't know the politics."

"Politics," Henry said. "You expect me to stay here and do nothing?"

"If you want to help her, that's precisely what you'll do. The only reason I came here is so you wouldn't go off half-cocked."

"There must be something—"

"Not right now. And don't use your email or computer until I can replace them with secure technology. I'll take care of it after I get Cerissa straightened out."

"If I can't help right now, when?"

"You'll know when the moment is right."

"And just how will I know that?"

"Trust me," Ari said, pointing at his own wrist. "You'll know."

The crystal. Henry took a deep breath and sat down across from Ari. "Then you're going to tell me the truth."

"The truth about what?"

"Why does Cerissa look like an angel?"

Ari rolled his eyes. "You really want to do this now?"

"I need to know."

"Okay, old man. I'll tell you if you promise not to tell Cerissa."

More secrets? No, if Henry and Cerissa had any chance, there could be no secrets between them. "I cannot make such a promise."

Ari pursed his lips, appearing to consider it. "It's your head. She's not going to be happy."

"Tell me anyway."

Ari grabbed his phone from his belt, pulled off the t-shirt he wore, and seamlessly morphed into his Lux form, fanning out his white wings and singing a short phrase.

"We *are* angels, Henry," the phone translated.

341

Henry froze. Seconds ticked by. He didn't blink, didn't breathe, didn't think. After seeing Cerissa's Lux form, he had told himself there had to be another explanation.

"You okay?" Ari asked, raising his pale brows over his oversized molten eyes. "Henry?"

An angel. She told me there was nothing else I needed to know. I believed her. I trusted her. I—

Henry buried his face in his hands, and the words came pouring out. "*Madre de Dios.* I made love to an angel. If not for my prior sins, then for this I will surely burn."

"Hold on there," Ari said, rustling his wings. "We're not that kind of angel."

Henry reached for his crucifix where it lay underneath his shirt, ripping a button off in his haste to grasp it.

Ari waved one hand. "Don't worry. It's not a sin to make love to our kind of angel."

How could it not be a sin?

And then the answer crashed through Henry's mind like a freight train, taking out everything in its path.

No, she cannot be.

He gripped the crucifix so tight that it sliced his skin. He opened his hand and looked down at his bloody palm. "What kind of angel are you?"

"The fallen kind."

Did he really black out? One moment, the angel Ari was across from him. The next, Henry was lying on the couch, the human Ari peering into his face, offering him a glass of blood.

He slid away from Ari, but accepted the glass, taking a deep draw on the room-temperature liquid. Ari must have gone into the kitchen and retrieved one of the blue pouches.

"Feeling better?" the shirtless Ari asked.

Henry edged further away. "She lied to me."

"No, she didn't."

Henry set the half-empty glass on the coffee table and slouched back on the couch, his head braced in his hands.

"She told you the truth," Ari continued. "That first night, she told you two hundred of us fell from the sky, and we had to mate with mortals to have children. If you'd been to Sunday school a little more often, you would have recognized the story of the Bene Elohim."

Henry rubbed his temples. "But she said her people didn't know what they were."

"During the past few millennia, it's become popular to imagine we're stranded astronauts—aliens from another world. That's Cerissa's view. But I've read the ancient texts, and I'll tell you this—I believe we're fallen angels."

"You were cast out of heaven?"

"Four thousand years is a long time. Given the stories from the fall, we can't be one hundred percent sure whether we were cast out for wrongdoing, or put here intentionally to help mortals. Our ancestors are dead now; we can't ask them."

"Angels cannot die."

"Think again, Henry. If what the old ones said was true, we lost immortality when we landed in this godforsaken place and mated with mortals. Personally, I believe we're the descendants of those who got the boot for being prideful."

Henry ran his hands through his hair, stripping the rawhide string from his ponytail. He began winding and unwinding it around his finger, the implications sinking in. Haltingly, he said, "If Cerissa is an angel, I cannot lie with her again."

"A fallen angel, Henry. There is no sin in 'lying' with her, as you so quaintly put it. Trust me on this one: there is no inherent sin in sex. Sex can be used to sin, but it isn't inherently wrong to lie with Cerissa, or any other person."

"I cannot. Never. Again." He stared at the glass of blood where he'd placed it on the coffee table. "I have drunk angel blood," he said, burying his face in his hands again. "I will burn forever."

"Take a chill pill, man. You drank *human* blood. Not angel. Trust me on this one. You couldn't drink her real blood."

"I do not know—"

"That's right. You don't know." Ari shook his head. "I shouldn't do this, but sometimes I can't help myself."

Henry watched as Ari transformed back into an angel. The angel spread its wings and stepped toward him. Frozen in place, Henry waited for whatever was to come—he deserved to die for making love to an angel.

Ari's hands gently touched both sides of his head, the tips of his wings wrapping around Henry.

"Bless you, Henry," Ari said softly, then brought his lips to Henry's forehead in benediction, a kiss of peace.

A feeling of wellbeing flooded through Henry, like a cleansing waterfall. It washed away his fear and shame and left only his love for Cerissa.

"Now you see," Ari said. "You can still have a relationship with Cerissa if you want it. Nothing I've told you changes that. You just have to release all those fears you cling to, and never let them return."

CHAPTER 52

SIERRA ESCONDIDA POLICE STATION—LATER THAT NIGHT

Tig sat across the conference room table from the threesome. Karen was between Rolf and Henry. At one end of the long table, Méi sketched, filling in color detail, the paper clipped to an easel, the artist's pastels in a long box next to her. Karen had finished describing the Cutter, and Méi was putting the last touches on her drawing.

Karen waited, looking peaceful, holding Rolf's hand. After what Karen had been through, how could she be so calm? Rolf looked more stressed than Karen did, the small lines around his eyes deeper than they should be.

Tig had shown Karen photos of the kidnappers who had been captured or killed. The man who had taken a knife to Karen was not among them, which confirmed the prisoners' stories, and was why Méi's services were needed.

"Before we show you the drawing," Tig said to Karen, "is there any detail you want to add? It may help to close your eyes. Do you see any moles? Scars? Anything?"

Karen closed her eyes. "No blemishes. He was a good-looking guy, considering."

"Okay, you can open your eyes and look at the sketch. If necessary, we can adjust it after you see it."

Méi screwed up her face in anger and pointed at Karen. "My work is perfect, if *she* described him well."

Temperamental artist. Tig couldn't use a sketch artist from Mordida's police department without explaining too much. "I'm sure your drawing is perfect, Méi. But sometimes seeing the sketch can trigger memories in the witness, and we adjust it accordingly."

"Humph," Méi replied. "Bad art, to do it that way."

"Show the picture to Karen, okay?"

Méi laid the drawing on the table in front of Karen. The level of detail Karen had remembered was mindboggling.

The sketch depicted a man with neatly trimmed short brown hair, parted on the side, a small mustache, light brown eyes bordering on hazel, fair skin with a pinkish undertone, a straight nose, square jaw, and high cheekbones. There were wrinkles around the eyes, but not many. Karen had guessed he was in his thirties.

And the face looked like no one Tig had met before.

Karen glanced at her lap and then looked at the sketch on the table again. "That's him."

"You're sure? You don't want to change anything?"

"No, that's him. That's the Cutter." Karen slewed her eyes toward Rolf. "I—There's something else I forgot to tell you."

"Give me a moment to turn on the recorder."

Karen had already told the story of the kidnapping and confirmed the same height and weight descriptions Méi had given from the attack at the gallery. Tig had recorded the interview but paused it when Karen finished, while Méi sketched. Tig turned the recorder on again. She signaled Karen to start.

"His name is Chuck. I mean, that's what he said his name was. He introduced himself before he started cutting me."

The same name he'd given to the mechanic. "Did he say anything else?" Tig asked.

"Ah, he said something like: *This is what you get for living with a bunch of mortal-loving vampires.*"

"Those were his exact words? 'Mortal-loving vampires'?"

"Yeah, I'm sure."

Something about the phrase sounded familiar, not the exact words, but the sentiment. Tig couldn't put her finger on it. "I have one more thing I want to show you."

She swiped at her iPad, waking it up, and tapped the photo, then turned it so Karen could view it. "We found this on the kidnapper's computer. This may be why they thought you were Henry's mate."

The image showed a newspaper report from the society section, a picture of Henry and Karen together at a Vasquez Müller Winery party. The headline read: "Is the Hill's Most Eligible Bachelor Taken?" The caption identified Henry by name, but not Karen.

"Oh, that," Karen said. "Rolf couldn't go. He had a prior commitment out of town."

Yeah, right. Tig knew what kind of commitment he had. "So you went with Henry?"

"We didn't *go* together," Karen said, glancing over at Henry.

Henry picked up the iPad and skimmed the article. "The winery sponsors an exclusive winetasting event for local restauranteurs, and the press is invited. We couldn't cancel when Rolf became unavailable, so Karen and I hosted it. We told them no cameras, but the *Mordida News* reporter used his phone's camera when we weren't looking."

"Yeah," Karen said. "I called the paper the next day and demanded a retraction, but they refused. I told them I wasn't Henry's girlfriend, that I was the PR director for the winery, but they didn't care."

"It wasn't worth bringing legal action," Henry added. "It would only stir it up more."

"Thank you, that helps." Tig took the iPad back and focused on Karen. "Now, is there anything else you remember?"

"I told you about the Cutter texting during it?"

"You did."

Karen shrugged nonchalantly. "Well, that's all I can recall."

"Don't apologize. Your memory is better than most under the circumstances. And it's possible you may remember more about the kidnapping as time passes. Please write down everything you remember, and send it to me."

"Sure, but I doubt it." Karen pushed her chair back.

Something seemed terribly wrong with Karen. She was acting too blasé, too disconnected from what had happened.

"Karen, do you mind if I speak with Rolf alone for a moment?" Tig asked.

"Ah, sure, whatever."

Méi gathered her art supplies. "If you don't need me, I'll leave too."

"Thank you for your service," Tig said.

Henry remained seated. "I'd like to stay, if you don't mind."

Why was Henry glued to Rolf? Tig waited for Karen and Méi to leave before saying anything. Once alone with the guys, she got right to the point. "I think Karen's in shock. She is much too calm. You should take her to see Father Matt."

"Before Cerissa left, she prescribed some medication for Karen," Henry said. "You're probably seeing the effects of the medication. If Karen needs help, we'll take care of it."

"And where is Cerissa? I wanted to interview her too."

"She had a family emergency and had to leave town once Karen was found. I don't know when she'll be back."

"That sounds serious."

"It is. Do you need anything else from us?"

"No. I'll get the sketch distributed to all the treaty communities."

Henry raised an eyebrow. "Won't doing so tip your hand?"

"I'd rather the Cutter know we're after him than have him attack another community. Everyone needs to be on the alert for him."

"What about mortal authorities?"

"I'm going to tell them he's a person of interest in an attempted homicide and kidnapping. That's the best I can do. I can't say it's related to the Cutter. How would we explain vampire blood healed Karen's cuts? And I can't involve them in Kim Han's death, either."

Henry paused, looking thoughtful. "What happened with Kim's mate?"

"Father Matt handled it. Jessica left the Hill last night. Her trust fund wasn't very large yet, but Kim left everything to her, so she'll be provided for. She's relocated to San Francisco."

A mortal mate from the San Francisco community would keep an eye on Jessica and make sure she had a smooth transition from her so-called "accident" that had resulted in her "amnesia."

Henry rubbed his chin. "Of course, the homeowners association will pay her the value of the remaining lease on Kim's house once the board finds a new tenant." He pursed his lips. "I know some of the mortals thought she should be allowed stay."

Tig stood. "That's Yacov's problem, not mine. If there's nothing else, I need to get this sketch sent out. Thank you for coming in with Karen."

"One more thing," Henry said, motioning for her to sit again. "The ransom amount the kidnappers demanded was the exact amount Leopold paid me to settle a dispute between us."

Anger sizzled through her like a cold fish on a hot rock. "You're just telling me this now?"

"Cerissa seemed certain Leopold wasn't involved, and the computer expert found a Trojan on my computer. As you know, a virus has been collecting data from my email and forwarding it to a hacker. So the kidnappers may have learned the amount through emails Leopold and I exchanged."

"Anything else?" she asked, trying to keep her anger from leaking out.

"What do you plan to do with the kidnappers who are in custody?" Henry asked.

"I have to turn them over to mortal authorities. Karen may have to testify at trial. Jayden can cover our involvement."

Rolf scowled at her. "They are guilty. We should kill them."

Tig thrummed her fingers on the table. As much as she'd like the solution to be that easy, it wasn't. "Putting them in a mortal prison is the best option. If mortal authorities apprehend the Cutter, his cohorts can testify in court. I suspect they'll fall all over themselves to cut a deal." She thrummed the table again. "Now, is there anything else you need to tell me?"

Henry glanced at Rolf, who shook his head.

"And neither of you know who this man is?" Tig pointed at the sketch of the Cutter.

"I understand why you're asking," Henry replied. "But no. We don't know him."

She narrowed her eyes. They better not lie to her. "Just remember, the whipping post is still on the table. If either you or Rolf go after the Cutter on your own, the council will not be pleased."

She saw them out and then returned to her office. After running the sketch through her scanner, she initiated a program to compare the image to all California mug shots. Nothing.

She didn't like what Henry had told her about Leopold and the money. Had the Cutter been seen around Leopold? Worth checking out—she emailed the sketch to Rick in New York.

Afterward, she drafted a message to the other communities. This required just the right spin—enough to get a response, but not enough to spook whoever was behind the Cutter.

Henry waited by Rolf's Escalade. Rolf had encased Karen in a bear hug the minute they were outside, and seemed unwilling to let her go.

Karen pushed back at his chest. "Rolf, release me. I'm fine."

"You did an excellent job," Henry told her.

"Piece of cake, with the Cutter's photo you guys put on my phone. The only time I was nervous was when I glanced at it." She tried to wiggle out of Rolf's arms, and when that didn't work, she pinched him. "Let me go."

Rolf released his grip on Karen. "Do you think Tig believed her?"

"I watched Tig the entire time," Henry said, opening the door to the Escalade for Karen. "She showed no sign of doubt. And why would she? We've done everything we can to help her solve this."

Karen stepped up into the passenger seat. "Any word on when Cerissa will be back?"

"None. Her cousin told me I must wait. I'm going to give her a few days to get this straightened out, and then I'm going after her."

Rolf climbed into the driver's seat. "What can you do? With the technology the Lux have, you're no better than a caveman."

Henry's throat tightened. He loved Cerissa in spite of what she might be. And he would never abandon anyone he loved.

"I don't know. But I'm going to figure it out."

CHAPTER 53

THE LUX ENCLAVE—THREE DAYS LATER

Cerissa woke in the eight-by-eight-foot cell—barely enough room to stretch her wings out. It was carved from rock on three sides, and the fourth wall consisted of a clear material, like acrylic but a hundred times stronger. The barrier provided no privacy. Not that the Lux prized privacy. Still, the idea lingered the way colored dots did after a flash of bright light.

Ari paced in the cell next to hers. The rock between them kept her from seeing him, but she could tell he paced from the sound of his feet slapping rock. She rolled off her small cot, and her stomach growled.

The Protectors had ordered no food for the prisoners. They weren't being cruel; they were ensuring the two were too weak to morph and escape. It made no difference that she and Ari had turned themselves in voluntarily three days ago. When it came to the Protectors, rules were rules.

But understanding their logic didn't stop her stomach from protesting.

At least the Protectors hadn't ordered them banded. The small gold-colored wristband, embedded with crystals, inhibited the ability to morph. The band was used to keep children locked in one form. It was tuned so the band could only be removed by the person who fastened it on, usually their Lux parent. She would rather go without food than be humiliated that way.

She raised both hands to her head, massaging her temples with twelve fingers, feeling light-headed from the lack of food. At some point they would question her. What could she do to convince them the path she'd chosen was the right one?

She wanted her freedom, to choose her own destiny. But leading a revolt wasn't her style. She was a scientist, not a revolutionary. Besides, the price of revolution was death—death for those who rebelled, and death for those who defended a way of life that was no longer defensible.

I don't want my freedom at a cost to others.

Wasn't there another way? What about telling the truth?

My truth. Do I have the courage to tell them my truth?

Not until she faced the fact she wanted a life in Sierra Escondida separate from her duty to the Lux did she begin to see her truth. And despite her fear, her fear of rejection and punishment, she had to accept the truth about herself—she wanted her own life, one that included love and friendship with people who knew what she was.

The look in Karen's eyes, the look of acceptance when Cerissa revealed her true self, that look had soothed a place deep within her that still felt tender from *amma*'s rejection so many years ago.

Cerissa settled onto the cot again. Was she being naïve? Wouldn't the Protectors dismiss her truth, belittle her for not sacrificing everything to the Lux? They'd never accept her the way she was. They'd only accept her blind obedience.

She shook her head. It didn't matter. Telling the truth was the first step in her journey to freedom—whether the Protectors believed her or not, whether the Protectors accepted her or not, whether it meant the loss of everything dear to her…

If only I had told Henry the truth, shown him my Lux body before he fell in love with me.

She ruffled her wings.

Should have, would have, could have.

Wishing wouldn't change the past. She wanted to believe he still loved her, but then she pictured the look of fear in Henry's eyes when he dropped to his knees, and a sliver of despair crawled up from her belly, wrapping itself around her heart.

Would she ever see the look of love in his eyes again?

And did it matter? The Protectors weren't likely to let her return to him.

The sound of movement in the corridor stopped her internal debate. A gaggle of Guardians approached. That could mean only one thing.

The Assembly of Protectors gathered in the largest room in the Enclave, located right below the mountain peak, a room big enough to host the entire Assembly. The Assembly's seats were elevated on a curving stair-stepped platform, much like a college lecture hall. The first row was reserved for the highest-ranking Protectors.

Cerissa flittered the tips of her wings, waiting for the inquisition to start. It reminded her of Henry's hearing before the town council. His penalties had—mostly—been negotiated in advance.

Not here. The Scythe of Justice, a long bronze pole topped with a curving, sharp blade, stood mounted in stone. It was only displayed when it might be used.

Would they really take her wings? Surely they wouldn't do anything so drastic. If they took her wings, she'd lose the ability to morph into human form. She'd have to stay confined to the Enclave for the rest of her life, unable to go out among humans, unable to bear children, unable to have the life she wanted.

And worst of all—she'd never be able to make love to Henry again.

The Guardians parked Ari next to her. He hadn't spoken one word to her during their confinement. Now he ignored her.

They stood in the center of the large cave. The late afternoon sun, shining through a skylight in the top of the cavern, lit her like a spotlight. She looked up at the sunlight. Would it be the last time she saw it?

The moonstone and amethyst bracelet still encircled her thin wrist, her six fingers the only thing stopping it from sliding off. With her other hand,

351

she fingered the stones moving from one to the other like beads in a rosary. The Guardians had tried to take the bracelet from her. It was the only time she fought back, and they let her keep it.

Cerissa glanced over at Ari, but he refused to look over at her. He stared straight ahead as if he could see the Protectors who sat in the shadows around them. The sunlight's glare made it impossible to see the Protectors— there was no way to read their wings, to know what they thought or felt, while Cerissa's every reaction would be laid out for all to see.

"Why did you do it?" The first question shot out from the Assembly, sung in the Lux's language.

"I love her." The ambiguity in their question allowed her the choice, and she chose first to defend healing Karen's wounds. "Friends help friends—it's through relationships that humans grow as individuals. By relating to humans, I become more in tune with their thoughts and feelings, more empathetic to them. Isn't that our goal?"

"Your assignment was to learn about the vampire communities, to uncover their threat, without violating your orders."

The speaker was one of the Protectors Cerissa didn't know well. What would persuade her?

"That's not our only goal," Cerissa replied. "You wanted my generation raised among humans, to help us better relate to them. Well, my human father taught me this: a real friend assists in the time of danger."

An old Hindu proverb, one of the hundreds she had heard as a child.

"What about what we taught you?"

"But this is what you taught me," she said, the backs of her wings rising, signaling her disagreement. "If I'm to learn what it means to be human, then I must be true to those relationships—I can't sacrifice them on the altar of objectivity."

"Instead you would sacrifice your duty to us."

"Karen was *tortured* because I was fulfilling my duty. The kidnappers meant to take me. She was an innocent bystander. My very presence on the Hill interfered with Karen's life."

Cerissa stepped forward. The Guardians moved to stop her.

Time to roll the dice and let them see the first truth for themselves.

"I demand the right of touchstone," she said, and looked toward the black polished stone displayed on a raised pillar a few feet from her.

A gamble. Letting them see the truth could backfire—they might conclude the Cutter's cruelty didn't justify violating the rules. She stepped forward and grasped the stone, the Guardians flanking her.

Each of the Protectors had a similar stone in front of them; each would slip her hand over it to see what would be revealed.

The shock of using the touchstone could be disorienting—if having an icepick shoved through your forehead could be described as disorienting. Cerissa eased into it, letting the pain wash through her until the memories opened up like paintings hanging on a long black wall, each painting a shining image illuminating the darkness as she whipped past it in her mind.

When she found the one she wanted, she let it bloom forth, thrusting it into the Protectors' minds: Karen's memories of what the Cutter did to her.

Cerissa spared them no sensory detail. The Protectors experienced everything, from the first knife cut above Karen's breast, to her terror, her helplessness, the pain in her wrists as she tried to break free of the plastic ties holding her to the table, her screams muted by duct tape.

They smelled the bitterness of the amyl nitrite reviving her and watched the knife rise and come back down, the intense pain as her flesh became a living message board.

During the worst parts, when the Cutter started hacking off fingers, the shuffling and fluttering of wings filled the cavern with noise.

When it ended, one of the Protectors stood and began ranting. "This proves it. What I've said all along. Humans are evil. They are demons who shouldn't be suffered to live. We should take control of them and put a stop to this once and for all."

A chaos of voices broke out.

Agathe, the head of the Assembly, trilled loudly. The chaos stopped, and she said, "Then we'd be no better than the vampires we're trying to stop."

Another voice from the Assembly disagreed. "The vampires want to subjugate mortals. We only want to protect them from the evil within themselves—use the touchstone to reveal those who are truly evil, and then we destroy them to protect the others."

A small chorus of voices seemed to concur.

Cerissa trilled right back at them. "It won't work. Humans would resist captivity. They would fight back, and you would end up destroying all of them."

Agathe raised her hand again, stopping the debate. "Cerissa is right. If we take away their free will, their ability to do evil, there is no opportunity for them to redeem themselves. Do not forget why we are here—to earn our own redemption, not to subjugate an entire race of beings."

The Assembly once again filled with the sound of competing songs. The schism within Cerissa's family was an uneasy one—some believed if the Lux proved themselves worthy, they'd be released from this godforsaken planet. Others believed rescue would never come—whoever abandoned them here had long forgotten them.

"The woman you healed—she isn't your only transgression," said Sevin, the Protector who was responsible for Cerissa's assignment. "You violated orders and revealed to a vampire what we are."

Cerissa froze. Did they have the original videos of her confessing to Henry, the ones Ari had edited? Or was it a trap—were they merely making an educated guess?

Doesn't matter—I need to get it all out in the open.

Cerissa threw her shoulders back, spreading her wings. "I was trapped and had to make a quick decision in the field."

"You should have returned to us for approval," Sevin said sternly.

Cerissa turned in the direction of Sevin's voice, still unable to see her. "There was no time to consult the Assembly. I was injured and couldn't leave."

She reached for the touchstone again, letting it show the Assembly how she'd saved Henry's life, her mistake in revealing what she was to him, and his promise not to tell anyone.

When the memory finished playing out, Sevin stepped forward into the light, her wings showing no mercy—only stern determination. "Your field decision doesn't justify hiding the revelation from us."

Cerissa flittered the tips of her wings again. "It was done. There was nothing you could do."

"The Assembly could have ordered his death—put an end to the threat."

"And how is that fair or just? My mistake shouldn't condemn him."

"And then you compounded your transgression by bonding with him."

"You don't understand the vampire communities," she said. "They don't trust mortals who aren't in a relationship with a vampire—the loyalty bond is how they maintain control of their secret society. They would never have accepted me in the long term unless I mated with one of them."

She didn't try arguing for true love between her and Henry. So many of the Protectors had been born in an era where romantic love didn't exist—or was a rarity. They wouldn't appreciate what she felt for Henry.

And after seeing her real appearance, she couldn't swear Henry still loved her.

"But it didn't end there, did it?" Sevin asked. "You let Rolf see you as Lux, and you told Karen what we are."

"Why can't you get it?" Cerissa asked. "Your generation was raised apart from humans. You've made mistakes because you didn't understand them. It's why you wanted my generation raised by them."

Cerissa took a deep breath, trying to quiet the fear lurking in her lungs. "You don't know what it's like, being raised with them, living with them, but always hiding from them. I want a life where I don't have to hide. I want a life of my own choosing. Your experiment—you've made my generation more humanlike than any before us, and I claim the human right of free will, the right to disclose who I am to those I care about."

A shocked silence fell over the Assembly. It was soon broken by the sound of movement on the stairs, and someone stepped into the light.

Cerissa flared her wings in shock when she saw who it was.

Amma?

Cerissa's mother strode up to Agathe, pointing a finger at her chest. "I told you this would happen. The more our children are around humans, the more they identify with them. This is your fault."

"Deveshi, leave the room. Cerissa is your daughter. You cannot be part of this decision."

"I can't?" she snapped. "You made me an unwilling participant in your horrible experiment. How dare you say I can't be part of the decision to deal with its aftermath?"

Agathe pointed toward the door. "Leave. Now."

"Not before I have my say. You reap what you sow. You wanted more humanlike, more relatable, Lux children. Well, then, you must let them embrace that side of their lineage." *Amma* looked in Cerissa's direction. "I'm proud of you, daughter. You had the strength to do something I could not."

Amma turned her back on Agathe and strode back into the darkness, her wings fanned out, signaling her pride and determination. The shock Cerissa felt turned into a warm glow.

Amma cares? She really cares about me?

"We have heard your words," Agathe said to Cerissa, "and the words of your mother." Agathe then turned to look at Ari. "What about your supervisor? Ari, why didn't you report to us? It was your duty to inform the Assembly when Cerissa violated her orders."

Before Ari could speak, Cerissa cut in. "He didn't know. I hid it from him. He didn't know I planned on bringing Karen here, he didn't know I planned on mating with Henry—he knew none of it."

The first half-truth she'd told the Assembly—she felt almost ill from it, but couldn't let her mistake condemn Ari. Sometimes compassion had to override absolute honesty.

Ari fanned his wings out full, the one on her side stretching protectively across her shoulders. "I'm her supervisor, and I take full responsibility."

"Then you shall share in her fate," Sevin replied. She stepped forward out of the shadows, striding past Agathe, and lifted the Scythe of Justice. Guardians grabbed Cerissa by the arms. "Spread your wings," Sevin said, circling around behind her.

Cerissa struggled, trying to turn to face Agathe. "You can't do this. You don't understand—if I can't morph, if I don't return, Henry will tell them the truth. You'll never be able to get another one of our kind past their gates."

Sevin sang a single note—in a human, it would be a laugh. "Then we will have to kill Henry."

"You can't do that," Cerissa screamed, twisting against the hands holding her.

"We can and we will."

Ari cleared his throat. "Henry's under her protection. He has a crystal, tuned to her."

A murmur shot through the Assembly.

"You can't kill him without first killing her, and you can't kill her," Ari said calmly, his usual flippancy gone. "You'd lose control of all Watchers if you did. The death penalty is only meted out to those who kill another Lux."

Sevin lifted the scythe and pounded its blunt end loudly on the cavern floor. "Silence. You think you have made fools of us. Well, Cerissa, we may not be able to take your wings if you are to complete your assignment, but nothing stops us from taking Ari's." The Guardians pushed Ari to the rock floor, his wings held out, the scythe rising over him.

Cerissa shot out her wings, extending one far enough to cover Ari's back. "Have you become so like humans that your first answer is to kill and maim?" She tried to break free of the Guardians who held her. "You're no better than the Cutter. If you take Ari's wings, I won't help you!"

Another wave of discordant songs echoed through the chamber, the Assembly arguing among themselves. Agathe stepped forward, spreading her wings, and caught the scythe with both hands before it could fall on

Ari, raising her voice above the din. "Sevin, it is not for you to decide. It's a decision for the entire Assembly."

Agathe wrestled the pole from Sevin's grasp and pounded the scythe's blunt end into the rock floor's cylindrical indentation, leaving it standing there. To the Guardians, she said, "Keep them here."

Agathe led the Protectors out of the cavern. Cerissa had no strength left, and swayed, letting the Guardians who gripped her keep her upright as she listened to the soft shuffling of wings and feet.

They were gone for hours. The skylight at the top of the cavern had grown dark, and lights embedded in the rock wall glowed. After the Assembly paraded back in and resumed their seats, Agathe stepped forward, Sevin slightly behind her. Sevin raised her wings at the shoulders, signaling her disagreement with what Agathe was about to say.

"The Assembly is not without mercy," Agathe said softly. "You were inexperienced and made mistakes because of it. For this, you will be spared, as will your supervisor. Our leniency is dependent upon full disclosure. You will tell us everything, including how you did it. The Assembly will not be deceived again."

"Understood," Cerissa agreed. When Ari said nothing, she nudged him with her foot. "Ari, you agree too."

"Fine," Ari said, speaking toward the rock floor. "I agree."

Agathe inclined her head at Cerissa. "Your acts cannot go unpunished. We will not take your wings—however, punishment will be meted out. Your friend Karen—you reprocessed her emotions and now hold her memories within your mind. You also saved her from her scars, so you will now bear the scythe's scars. Take her to the ground and spread her wings."

The Guardians forced Cerissa down and held her wings out to the side. The scythe sliced through Cerissa's back, the soft area at the base of her wings, and the burning pain radiated with such intensity that it took all her willpower not to scream out.

When the scythe was lifted, she was unprepared for the pain's return, sobbing wordlessly when the blade sliced through the base of her other wing. After it was lifted for the second time, Agathe carried the scythe to where Ari lay, and through her own sobs, Cerissa heard Ari's sharp intake of breath. His splayed wings overlapped hers, and by the way they shook, she knew the same thing was happening to him.

It was like having it happen to her all over again, to hear Ari struggle against the pain, until he too lost the battle and sobbed.

At the edges of her pain, her mind recognized the soft rustle of a vampire moving swiftly. "Keep your hands up and apart," Henry demanded. "Move them one inch and I'll cut off your head."

Through her tears, Cerissa glanced around to see Henry gripping Agathe, holding the scythe's blade against her throat.

"Child of Lucifer," one of the Assembly called out.

The Spanish translation was momentarily delayed. Someone had turned on the translator for him.

Damn. Cerissa would have to deal with that later. In spite of the burning pain in her back, she rose on her elbows and twisted to see him.

"Henry," she said. His name was repeated over the loudspeakers, delayed by the computer's translation. "Henry, it's all right."

Agathe wrapped her hand around Henry's. "Violence is not necessary."

"I told you to stand still," Henry said, his voice a low growl, and the scythe's blade dug into Agathe's neck, a rim of dark blue blood appearing above it.

"Henry, don't."

Hurting Agathe would only make things worse. Cerissa sat up, turning to face him so he wouldn't see her bleeding cuts any longer. Her limp wings dragged on the ground, sending pain shooting through her.

"How is he able to draw my blood if he's under her wings?" Agathe demanded.

Ari rose on his elbows. "I set the crystal to let him—he's a vampire, for heaven's sake."

But why hadn't Agathe morphed into another creature to slip from his grasp? Henry shouldn't be able to hold her if Agathe wanted to escape.

Then Cerissa saw the glint of gold on Agathe's wrist. She turned her head to glare at Ari. "You gave Henry a crystal band?"

"Hey, with you, I figured he needed all the help he could get."

"Cerissa, can you walk?" Henry asked her, the scythe still pressed against Agathe's neck. "I'll take you from here if I have to kill this one to do it."

"Violence will not help your case." Agathe stood calmly in Henry's grasp, her voice stern.

"See what they are?" Sevin said angrily. "How they solve their problems?"

Henry brought the blade closer to Agathe's throat again. "Your hypocrisy is appalling. The evidence of your violence is on Cerissa's back."

Sevin took a step toward Henry. "Cerissa's punishment is not your concern."

"Henry, please don't…" Cerissa said.

Ari struggled to sit, dark blue blood running down his back. "Feed her. He won't back off until he knows she's okay."

Agathe gestured with her eyes, and a Guardian swept in carrying a jug of bright green liquid, poured a glass, and handed it to Cerissa. She greedily guzzled it. Relief flooded through her as she reknitted the muscle and grew the sliced skin together.

"Feed Ari," she insisted, raising the glass to the Guardian. While Ari drank, she folded her legs and leaned forward so Henry could see her back was healed, except for two long, thin scars. The scars would forever mark her transgressions.

"Agathe," Cerissa said, "please offer Henry sanctuary."

"Sanctuary?" Sevin yelled. "He brought his violence to the Assembly. There will be no sanctuary."

Agathe cut off Sevin's rant. "Mr. Bautista, you are bound by the crystal to Cerissa, yes? That is how you transported here."

"Yes," Henry replied.

"Then you have sanctuary here. We will not harm you while you are here, and you may leave when you are ready. I give you the word of the Assembly."

"You can't hurt him—the crystal won't let you," Cerissa said for Henry's benefit. She took the empty glass from Ari and held it out for a second serving.

Henry still firmly gripped Agathe, and he directed his gaze at Cerissa. "I won't let them hurt you again."

"They aren't going to do anything more to me. Please release Agathe."

"Cerissa speaks the truth," Agathe said. "Nothing more will happen to either of you."

Cerissa rose to meet his gaze. "Please, Henry."

His solid black eyes still showed his fury, but he gave a brief nod. "Then give Cerissa sanctuary, too."

Sevin sputtered, a sound like hitting an off-tune note. "It's unheard of."

Agathe held up her hand. "Cerissa has sanctuary here until she leaves again."

Henry pressed his thumb against the crystal of the band on Agathe's arm, and when it opened, he snatched it off and pocketed it. Lowering the scythe, he pushed Agathe away. He looked so strong, so beautiful, standing there holding the scythe like some ancient warrior, his hair tied back, his eyes shining with power.

"Take her back to her chamber," Agathe said, motioning toward Cerissa. "Ari will join me while I talk with Mr. Bautista in private. The Assembly is dismissed."

Agathe began to leave the chamber.

Henry stepped closer. "Cerissa goes nowhere without me."

"It's all right, Henry," Cerissa said. "Please. Let me go."

"Cerissa, I will never let you go. I love you."

"After seeing—me…you still love me?" she asked, her pulse pounding.

He raised an eyebrow. "I'm here to rescue you, am I not? Of course I still love you. I never stopped loving you."

Her heart lightened.

Ari made a sound like a whistle, and the computer translated. "As cute as you two are, you need to follow Agathe's orders if we have any chance of resolving this. Henry, come with me."

CHAPTER 54

THE LUX ENCLAVE—MOMENTS LATER

Henry eased onto the couch in the rock-walled room they led him to—a small room compared to the cavern they'd been in. The tapestry-covered couch circled the room, and its back rose to the bottom of his ribcage. He glanced behind the couch—no one hiding there.

The scythe they'd used to slice into Cerissa's back rested against the cushion next to him. He kept it as a symbolic gesture—he wasn't going to let them use it on Cerissa again.

Ari morphed to his human form, still wearing a sarong-type garment, the transition quick. If Henry had blinked, he would have missed it. Ari reclined on the couch opposite him, and Agathe positioned herself next to Ari, her wings draped over the couch's back. Agathe still looked like a blue angel.

If he had to, Henry would use the crystal embedded in his wrist to find Cerissa. For now, he would listen to what Agathe had to say. If a long life had taught him anything, it was this: never forgo a chance to listen to your enemy.

Another angel-like creature entered carrying a tray, and offered him a choice of three glasses—two containing the green liquid Cerissa had drunk, the other one a glass of blood.

"Thank you." He accepted the glass intended for him and sniffed it. It smelled like blood from Cerissa's clones. He touched the bland liquid to his lips—a small courtesy sip—and placed the glass on the nearest table, which folded out from the couch.

Ari downed his drink in two long gulps. Setting his glass aside, he said, "We have a bit of a problem."

"Why did Agathe slash Cerissa's back?" Henry asked, angrily gesturing at the scythe.

"She...er... I mean, we..." Ari said, glancing over at Agathe. "Cerissa told you what we are. We didn't tell the Protectors, and we kept a few other secrets from them, such as your bond with her, that she let you take her blood."

None of it justified what they did to her. Henry scowled at Agathe. "Barbaric, for a so-called advanced race."

Agathe held out a pink crystal on the flat of her hand. When she sang, it translated her words. "You wouldn't have liked the alternatives any better."

"I won't leave without Cerissa."

Ari raised his hands, urging caution. "Don't push the Protectors. They're going to let her return to Sierra Escondida in a few days."

"If they don't—"

"They understand. But you need to understand this: because you and Cerissa are bound by the crystal, they can't hurt you."

"I heard Cerissa when she said it the first time."

"You didn't let me finish. They can't hurt you without killing her first."

Agathe shook her wings. "If you betray us, I will not be able to hold back the Assembly. They will demand her death."

Henry slowly nodded. He wasn't stupid; he understood the politics.

Ari turned toward Agathe, looking skeptical. "Oh, come on. What does it matter if humans find out now or twenty years from now? We can't keep our existence secret much longer. Mortals are making rapid technological progress—they're bound to detect us soon. If it gets out early, the Assembly won't kill her."

"Silence." Agathe cut the air with her hand. "They were very close today to executing both of you."

Henry scowled again. "You would kill her for revealing herself to me? She always spoke of her people as being moral. You leave me with grave doubts about that—and whether I can trust your form of morality."

Agathe stood and flapped her wings.

Trying to intimidate him? Try again. He could always cut the crystal from his wrist. Then he'd have a fighting chance. After seeing what they did to Cerissa, they were lucky he didn't slaughter them all.

"You are in no position to judge." Agathe did a funny gesture with her wings, wiggling the arched tops. "Keep your silence, and she'll be fine."

He crossed his arms. "What are your intentions toward Sierra Escondida?"

"Your treaty communities won't be touched so long as they aren't a threat to humanity."

"Cerissa told me about the VDM rumors."

"When Cerissa returns to you, will you help her ferret out the source of the rumor?"

"If such exists, I want the movement destroyed."

"Then we are finished here," Agathe said, turning to leave.

"Not quite." Henry took his phone off his belt. "You make threats, but want me to trust you. Trust must be a two-way street. This is what will happen if you betray my trust and do anything to harm Cerissa or my people."

Henry hit play on his phone. In the video, Cerissa confessed to the Lux's existence, and morphed her human hand into the Lux six-fingered hand. He had recorded the entire conversation.

"Meaningless," Agathe said impatiently, the movement of her wings emphasizing her attitude. "Humans will believe they are seeing a special effect, like in their movies. We have discounted such before."

Henry paused the video. "But my people will believe the founder of Sierra Escondida," he said, inclining his head. "And there is more you need to see."

He resumed playing it. In the video, the image cut to him speaking toward a camera. He gave the GPS coordinates of the Enclave and urged his communities to attack the Lux, before the Lux destroyed them.

Agathe spread out her wings, a look like rage on her face. "How did you get our location?"

"Mortal technology can be very useful," Henry said, clipping the phone to his belt again.

Comprehension spread across Ari's face. "This isn't the first time you've been here. You used the crystal to find Cerissa when she was operating on Karen."

"Precisely. I had my phone with me—"

"And it automatically connected to our Wi-Fi system," Ari said, looking up at Agathe. "I told you we needed better computer security, even out here."

"When Cerissa didn't return two nights ago, I checked the GPS coordinates on my phone. Since your base is located inside a tall mountain in the Andes, my guess is you can't move it easily."

"We will destroy the video before you can show it," Agathe said.

Henry made eye contact with Ari. "What do you think? Will you truly be able to destroy all copies?"

"If they're on the dark net, maybe," Ari said. "If you've copied them to flash drives…"

"Precisely. Hard media cannot be reached, not without finding each copy. If I'm killed or simply disappear, the copies will be released to every vampire community, worldwide. You could torture me, but even if I gave you the current locations, you couldn't get to all of them in time."

"We don't torture people," Agathe said loftily.

Henry narrowed his eyes. "What do you call what you did to Cerissa?"

"That was punishment, not torture."

"Call it what you like. If you threaten us, my people will believe me, and you'll find yourself at war with all vampires. You know where our communities are located, and now we know where to find you. This puts us on equal footing."

"Well done, old man." Ari chuckled. "Couldn't have done better myself." He looked at Agathe. "The Assembly doesn't have a choice. You have to send him back now. If you don't, it's an act of war."

"Silence. That is not for you to decide." Agathe looked toward Henry. "If we allow you and Cerissa to find the vampires who are plotting against humanity, you will not release the video?"

"You have my word—you do nothing to harm my people or Cerissa, and your secret is safe."

"Not just your word, Mr. Bautista. You release your video, and Cerissa's life will be forfeit."

Placing a hand over his heart, he gave a little bow to Agathe. "Détente through mutually assured destruction. Just remember—you can't fight a battle on two fronts. If you want to defeat the VDM, you can't engage in a war with all vampires."

Agathe fluffed up the top of her wings. "Even accidental release will be punished." She strode to the door. "I will return."

Henry sank back against the couch, a fraction of the tension in his shoulders easing. Maybe it would work out after all.

Ari laughed. "Well played."

"Perhaps." Henry rubbed his forehead—too much to process. He thought he'd come to terms with learning the Lux were fallen angels, but seeing a room full of Lux... "She once told me you live a millennium. When you die—do you return to heaven, or go to hell?"

"Ah, Henry, I have bad news for you."

"You mean the fact Cerissa is a descendant of fallen angels is good news? I am still growing accustomed to your *good news*."

"It's like this, old man. We can't go to hell because we're already there."

Henry grabbed the glass of blood and drank the remainder.

"Take it easy," Ari said. "Nothing has changed."

Henry set the empty glass on the table, and it immediately refilled itself with blood. Ari must have caught the look on his face, because he quickly added, "A hospitality glass. Don't worry, Henry, it's technology, not magic."

Why was it easier for Henry to believe in science than magic? Because he desperately wanted to believe in a rational world, despite what he was?

"You tell me I'm in hell," Henry said, shaking his head, "and you expect nothing to change?"

"Not to get theological on you, but haven't you detected the absence of *that which is*?"

Henry closed his eyes. He'd tried—really, he'd tried—to sense the presence of God. He'd always failed. The problem had to lie with him. "It's because I am evil."

"Vampires aren't evil. This world—this place—what you call *God* is powerless here. By your theology's definition, that makes this hell."

Ari's argument ran against everything Henry believed in. "This can't be hell," Henry said. "It can't be."

"Take a breath, dude. That's as deep as we're going to get right now, or we'll run around in circles."

Henry looked at the empty glass he held, streaked with rivulets of blood. "Is my existence the proof this is hell?"

Ari laughed. "Pride, Henry, arrogance, to think you're the proof. We don't know why this place exists; we don't know why we're here. We do our best with the tools we have to keep real evil from winning."

"You fight Satan?"

"Satan, Lucifer—both of them died many millennia ago. Two different angels. Straw men—they weren't what your churches made them out to be."

Henry started to object, but Ari cut him off.

"Revisionist history is popular in hell. Whoever wins for the moment rewrites the history. Religionists are known for recreating myths in their own image, and for promising things they can't deliver. It's happened over and over again. You can't think clearly if you believe their myths—you lose your ability to question their illogical reasoning. But just hear me on this: all religions are wrong; all faiths are right."

"Did you just attack my religion?"

"No, Henry, I didn't. You'll see."

"A demon like me? A child of Lucifer, as your people called me. What will I ever see of God?"

"You aren't a demon, old man. I've told you already. The real demons are those that lurk in the heart of all people, the potential for it. We've made it our business to fan the flames of love and compassion instead, to do those little things we can to make this a better place. It's part of our mission."

Henry raised the glass to take a deep draw on it again. "Love and compassion? I'm not impressed by the love and compassion of your people."

"Yeah, don't forget I was on the receiving end, too. Alatus Lux may translate into 'winged enlightenment,' but we don't always live up to our name."

"Indeed," Henry said, pinching the bridge of his nose against the tension roosting between his eyes. "If it hadn't been for the crystal, I cannot imagine what they might have done to Cerissa. When her pain came ripping through my mind…"

"She told me you were having trouble adjusting to the crystal." Ari stood and went over to what looked like a computer terminal. He typed something in. A panel slid back, and he removed a box and handed it to Henry. "Whether you believe we're in hell or not, believe this: you're better off with Cerissa in your life. So what will it be, old man? You say you love her. But can you truly make peace with what she is? Because if you can, I have a present for you that will help."

CHAPTER 55

SIERRA ESCONDIDA POLICE STATION—TWO NIGHTS LATER

Tig stared at the whiteboard in the squad room. Listed underneath the Carlyle Cutter's name was the information she gleaned from the kidnappers. Their stories were close enough—she had no doubt the man who tortured Karen was still on the loose, and DNA tests confirmed it.

When she interrogated the kidnappers, they had revealed their deep fear of the man who was in charge. None of them knew his name, although he had referred to himself as "the director." The kidnappers called him psycho—he enjoyed too much what he did to the woman they had captured.

In accordance with modern police practices, she'd shown them a six-pack: five sketches of men from Méi's portfolio, plus the sketch of the Cutter, all laid out on the table. Each kidnapper picked out the Cutter and had nothing to add to Karen's description.

A possible first name—"Chuck"—was listed on the whiteboard as well.

Jayden had yet to hear from the prison. They had no clue who tampered with the inmates' files. The trace on Henry's emails, the sabotage of the prison's records, and the alteration of the hotel security video all pointed to someone with a great deal of sophistication in computer hacking.

Leopold was looking less like a suspect. Rick had confirmed no one matching the Cutter's description had been seen at the Collective. And no other community or local police agency had responded to her "person of interest" bulletin.

The puzzle pieces seemed too disconnected: a religious group called

New Path, a serial killer who was mortal, a hacker, the dead Blanche, and rumors of war.

Jayden had searched the laptop they recovered from the scene of the kidnapping and found only the news report about Henry and Karen at the winery event. Tig couldn't use Mordida's police lab. She didn't know what they might find on the computer about vampires.

The computer expert who had helped Henry, the one who tracked the Cutter's location, had been unavailable due to a so-called family emergency. So had Cerissa.

Tonight, Ari had appeared at the door of the police station, offering to help. Henry swore Ari could be trusted. Henry's judge of character was usually spot on—except when it came to Rolf.

She put Ari at a desk in the squad room so he could examine the laptop the kidnappers had used. Technically, she needed to have Ari vetted before using him, and have Matt loyalty-bond him—since Ari was mortal and not an envoy—but she needed answers more than she needed approval from the town council. She would talk with the town attorney later to get it done. Everyone was so cooperative now. Even Rolf.

Thanks to Ufa, Tig knew Rolf's secret—and that was worth ten times what she'd paid for Ufa's assistance. Last night the council had unanimously passed a proclamation praising her for Karen's rescue. They then voted to approve the security cameras she wanted. Rolf made the motion. He even withdrew his motion to bring in someone to "help" her and publicly apologized.

Whatever doubts she had about Rolf... Well, if he had been part of the plot, he would have known they had the wrong woman, and his relief at getting Karen back hadn't been faked.

Last night's council meeting had been an emergency session called to deal with the aftermath of the kidnapping. Tonight, more mundane matters were on their agenda. Tig had asked Jayden to cover the meeting for her, grateful she could count on him. His leg still bothered him; sitting through a meeting would be light duty. One of them had to be there or the council might do something stupid.

From what the kidnappers told her, the Cutter had left shortly before the rescue, which meant someone had warned him. Her crew hadn't communicated anything about Karen's rescue by phone or email, so the hacker didn't get it that way. If there was a rat, it was likely internal, someone who was at Rolf's house that night, which meant her longer list of suspects, including Oscar Nolan, was off the table for now.

Shit.

She rubbed her forehead. She didn't like the idea that one of her crew had sent the warning message, but added a note to the whiteboard, with a list of those present at Rolf's house during the investigation—a short list including Liza, Zeke, Frédéric, Marcus, Winston, Jayden, Rolf, Henry, and Cerissa. All the council members were on the list except for Carolyn, who had been out of town and missed the whole thing.

"Got it," Ari called out.

She walked around the work table to where Ari worked at the kidnapper's laptop, and looked over his shoulder. "Got what?"

"They were using an app linked to a web-based program to monitor texts."

"They weren't receiving them on their phones?"

"Using the web-based program meant they didn't have to rely on one phone—anyone monitoring the computer would see it."

She read the first in a series of messages:

> 9981 2:30 p.m.: The bird is in the coop. Video made. Will send it later.

"What's that number?" Tig asked, pointing at 9981.

"The web program abbreviates the phone number, using its last four digits: 9981 is the number at the location where you found Karen, the number the Cutter used to send the videos; 2242 is off-site—the conspirator asshat who monitored your activities."

Tig continued reading the messages.

> 9981 (Cutter) 8:20 p.m.: Video sent.
> 2242 (Conspirator) 8:21 p.m.: OK.
> 2242 (Conspirator) 10:36 p.m.: You have wrong bird.
> 9981 (Cutter) 10:38 p.m.: ???
> 2242 (Conspirator) 10:40 p.m.: Hold for now. Do nothing.
> 9981 (Cutter) 10:43 p.m.: Can't. Crew is on way to mechanics.
> 2242 (Conspirator) 10:46 p.m.: Warn crew. Setup. Dragon bringing snipers.
> 9981 (Cutter) 10:48 p.m.: No phone. If caught, eliminate driver.
> 2242 (Conspirator) 10:49 p.m.: Ok.

Rolf had killed the driver. Was he back on the list again?

2242 (Conspirator) 11:53 a.m.: Plan B.
9981 (Cutter) 11:54 a.m.: Got it.

She glanced up at her timeline on the whiteboard. Henry received the video of the Cutter carving-up Karen at 12:01 a.m. Plan B must have turned the Cutter loose on Karen.

2242 (Conspirator) 1:15 a.m.: Two captured, driver dead.
2242 (Conspirator) 1:16 a.m.: Where are you? Sterilize coop.
2242 (Conspirator) 1:17 a.m.: You fail, you don't get turned.
You want to be a god, you better fix this.

She stopped at the phrase "be a god." Only one person on her list would talk like that.

9981 (Cutter) 1:26 a.m.: I won't fail. Text me if they leave.
2242 (Conspirator) 2:46 a.m.: The dragon has left the tower.
Kill the bird. Sterilize and abandon coop.

Tig read the last entry. "That's when we left Rolf's house. The conspirator ordered the Cutter to kill Karen."

But why hadn't he? Had he received the message too late and scrambled out of there minutes before the rescue?

"Want to know who sent it?" Ari asked.

"You can tell?"

"But of course—genius always wins out in the end. I have the full phone number, I can get the owner's name if it's registered. I just have to hack into the phone company's records."

Usually she would look the other way. But a federal crime? Not good if they tracked the hack back to the Hill.

"Will the feds find out?"

"Now I'm hurt."

Okay, so Ari was conceited. Most experts were. She didn't have time to assuage his feelings; this was the best break so far. In her gut, she already knew who the conspirator was, but the council would need hard proof.

"Give me the number. I may have a faster legal way."

He pointed at the screen and read it out to her.

"You're sure about the number?" she asked.

"You betcha—proof enough for a courtroom."

She used her phone to do a reverse search in the community directory. Nothing.

"Let me check V-Trak," she said, grabbing her iPad.

"And I'll hack the phone company," Ari said. He had continued to type while she tried her phone directory. "Let's see who finishes first. Loser buys dinner," he said with a wink.

Yeah, and you're buying.

She logged onto V-Trak on her iPad and typed in the phone number. A name popped up, an alternate phone number for one of the Hill's residents.

She'd guessed right.

"Got it," she said. "Councilman Frédéric."

Amazing what she could get done with the right team. When you hunted the lion, you didn't do it alone. It took many spears to bring down a savage enemy.

Now the pieces, how they connected, rapidly fell into place. Frédéric knew Rolf had bid on the paintings the mayor purchased. He'd been in the closed session where Winston had bragged about winning the bid, and knew stealing those paintings would push Tig in the wrong direction, focusing her investigation on Rolf.

Frédéric also knew Rolf hated Cerissa and opposed her presence on the Hill, making Rolf a likely suspect for the kidnapping—*if* the Cutter had successfully kidnapped Cerissa. Frédéric might even have known of Rolf's feeding problem.

But why did he do it? She'd worked with Frédéric for fifty years. He'd been on the council since Henry and the other founders resigned to let a new generation manage the community. Sure, Frédéric occasionally had some strange ideas: aggrandized Zeus, didn't like mortals being free. But no indication he was a traitor to the Hill.

The flyer—*be the wolf you were meant to be.* What did it mean to him to be a wolf? She thought about Petar's rumor and the fake email Henry found, the one Blanche left behind—war was coming. Were the vampires who wanted to dominate and control mortals the wolves who would take over the sheep?

She shook her head. Yes, the pieces fit. But why had Frédéric been so stupid as to use a phone registered with her? Or had someone set him up? Only one way to answer that—she'd take him into custody and question him.

She glanced at the time on her iPad—the town council meeting had been in session for about twenty minutes. "Copy the string of messages and email it to Liza and the mayor with an explanation. I'll need their approval to hold Frédéric, since he's on the council."

"Consider it done, chief."

"And you owe me dinner," she replied.

She wouldn't say no to a little fresh donor blood—the doctor could siphon off a pint easy enough. She charged for the door, grabbing her two-way radio along the way.

"I need immediate back up," she told the dispatcher. "Call Zeke and Jayden. Have them meet me in the hall outside the council chambers. Text Liza and warn her we're coming in to arrest Frédéric. Do not contact Rolf. I repeat, do not contact Rolf."

She found Zeke waiting for her at the council doors. He must have been attending the meeting. Jayden came out seconds later.

"Frédéric is behind the kidnapping," she told them. "Zeke, I need you to go in the back way and block the rear exit from the council chambers. Jayden—you're with me. We want him alive to answer questions. Go for lower body shots if you have to."

"No garlic capsules?" Zeke asked.

"Last thing I want is overspray hitting the other council members—we can't afford collateral damage." Not if she wanted to keep her job. "Zeke, radio me as soon as you're in position."

Less than thirty seconds later, Zeke's voice cut through the radio static. "I'm ready."

"Let's go," Tig said to Jayden.

She was barely past the council doors when a loud crash echoed through the room. Frédéric had been thrown off the dais by Rolf, who was using the desk to launch himself into the air.

She sprinted to where Frédéric lay on the floor, arriving moments after Rolf landed on the traitor, straddling him. Rolf wrapped his hands around Frédéric's throat, trying to take his head off the hard way.

Liza stood and shouted, "Rolf saw the message on my phone."

If someone had done to Jayden what the Cutter did to Karen, she'd react the same way, but Tig needed Frédéric alive. She aimed her gun at Rolf's bulging neck muscles—if she fired, the silver bullet would exit on the other side away from where Frédéric lay.

"Release him," she ordered Rolf. "Now, or you'll be paralyzed for weeks."

Rolf kept his eyes directed at Frédéric's face. "It's his fault we didn't get to Karen sooner." Rolf lifted Frédéric and slammed his head against the tile floor. "'Can't you smell Karen's scent on the driver?' he asked me." Another lift, another head pound. "'Smells like he fucked her,' he said."

So that was what drove Rolf to kill the man in the van. Frédéric had been at Rolf's elbow and must have whispered his poison to Rolf before Tig was in hearing distance.

Pounding Frédéric into the floor once again, Rolf said, "I have the right to kill him."

"If the council agrees, you can deliver Frédéric's death blow," Tig said. "After I question him. We need to find out whether anyone else is involved."

"You think this asshole has friends?" Rolf growled, twisting Frédéric's neck.

"That's what I need to find out. Easy there." She cocked the Beretta, the barrel still pointed at Rolf's neck. A vampire would hear the sound. She used her free hand to grip Rolf's arm, yanking on it. "We need Frédéric to talk. Don't crush his throat."

Rolf gave a snort and abruptly released Frédéric, still straddling him.

"Okay, now stand up slowly," Tig ordered him, lowering her gun so it now pointed at Frédéric.

Before Rolf could move, Frédéric spat at him. "Mortal lover," Frédéric snarled. "Bunch of fucking mortal lovers."

Rolf's fist struck, breaking Frédéric's nose. Tig raised the gun, pointing it back at Rolf's neck. "Okay, Rolf, you've made your point. Ease off him now."

Rolf used the back of his hand to wipe away Frédéric's spit, cleaning his hand on Frédéric's shirt. Afterward, he slowly bent forward to stand, his eyes solid black.

Frédéric raised his hand, but instead of striking Rolf, he grabbed Rolf's silver knife from his belt. Tig pivoted and shot a bullet through Frédéric's ankle. He howled.

"You're not going anywhere," she told him. "Move again and I'll shoot the other leg." She said to Rolf, "Get off him—you're in my line of fire."

Rolf dismounted. Frédéric rolled onto his stomach, facing her and pushing up to his knees, the knife still in his hands. He panted, his face contorted with pain. "You want information?"

"Who are you working with?"

DARK WINE AT SUNRISE

"Let me go, and I'll tell you."

"Not likely," Tig said, as Liza circled behind Rolf, her own gun at the ready. "You can't fight your way out of here. But there may be a way to avoid the death penalty." Tig glanced toward the mayor, who nodded. "We can do a deal if you talk. Tell us who the Cutter is, where to find him."

"You got lucky with Blanche. How did you get me?"

"Your text message to the Cutter."

"Damn mortal technology," Frédéric grumbled.

"We know a lot," she said. "We know about Jim Jones."

His eyes widened ever so slightly.

"Yes, we know all about him, but I want you to confirm his identity," she said, bluffing. She wanted to keep him talking until she could disarm him. "Jim Jones is an alias, after all."

"If you knew his real name, you wouldn't need me to confirm it. By the time you find out, it'll be too late," he said, twirling the knife. "He has plans for you, he does indeed. He has plans for all of you."

At least she now knew the ringleader was male. She aimed the gun at Frédéric's other leg. "Put down the knife," she demanded.

"You mean this?" he asked. He continued rising on his good knee. She shot that leg, stopping him from attacking anyone with the knife, but before the bullet connected, he twisted the knife, the point facing his own heart. With a flick of his wrist, the silver knife plowed into his own chest, and with a bullet hole through both legs, he lost balance and fell forward, driving the knife through his heart, the blood burbling out underneath him, his body convulsing. He turned his face slightly.

"I'm just one god among many," he mumbled. "We will prevail."

And the light faded from his eyes.

Tig holstered the Beretta and signaled to Liza and Zeke to remove the body. She didn't like Frédéric's message, but at least the council's leak was now plugged.

Or was it?

She looked at the remaining council members. None of them were on her original suspect list. She had no reason to suspect them now that Frédéric had been exposed. Plus, she had their backing. She had no intention of leaving now. Not with a conspiracy to stop—a conspiracy that seemed to threaten the peace among all the treaty communities.

But how many other Hill residents were now part of it? Frédéric had been working in her backyard all this time, sowing his poisonous seeds among the Hill's vineyards.

It didn't matter. She planned on plucking every last weed he'd planted until she finally staked Jim Jones and ended this madness once and for all.

CHAPTER 56

THE ENCLAVE—MIDNIGHT, SAME NIGHT

Cerissa looked in the mirror again to make sure she hadn't forgotten any detail of her human appearance. Hair, eyes, nose, skin tone—all as they should be.

She looked at her hands. She'd forgotten to get rid of her sixth finger when she morphed. A week at the Enclave shouldn't have affected her memory; she'd been morphing into human form on and off for over two hundred years. Besides, her human appearance was set by her father's genes. It should have been automatic.

A stressful week was no excuse for failing to completely transform her hands. She morphed each hand again so only five fingers remained.

She missed having her sixth fingers—she always did in human form. In her mind, the extra fingers were still there, much like an amputee's phantom limb, but it was a small sacrifice for following her own path, for making her own home among the vampires.

She shrugged on her jacket. Her back still twinged with pain whenever she twisted the wrong way. Maybe the feeling would fade with time, even though the two curving scars would be there forever.

Even on her human body.

By order of the Protectors, she had to recreate the scars and carry them on her human form, a reminder of her transgressions.

One more glance in the mirror—everything looked fine on the outside, even if her insides were a churning mess.

During her last two days of captivity, she'd pitched her argument for free will among the Lux. No one yelled, "Off with her head"—still, it was a little like *Alice in Wonderland*. Her nest mates looked at her as if she was crazy, giving her a wide berth, while the Protectors grilled her with questions, some sheer nonsense, like whether Henry *really was* a good cook.

At least they seemed willing to listen to her.

Amma hadn't returned to visit her. Somehow, Cerissa understood— *amma* bore her own pain from Cerissa's childhood, and didn't feel connected to Cerissa the way a human mother might, she didn't feel the same human need for connection, for emotional closeness, that Cerissa did.

But *amma* would be there when Cerissa really needed her.

The Protectors hadn't allowed her to speak to Henry before whisking him back to Sierra Escondida. But he hadn't returned to her of his own accord, either. Not that it would have been a good idea to return, still, the thought lingered.

She knew the crystal was still in his wrist. The vibe from the crystal disappeared when he slept, and popped back on when he woke, though something about it felt more distant, like something was dampening the crystal's clarity.

And no one at the Enclave would tell her what happened after she left the Assembly cavern. Ari assured her Henry was okay, but nothing else. The Protectors fluffed their wings whenever she asked, irritated by her repeated question, so she stopped asking.

Knowing Henry, a deal had been struck. But what did he have to negotiate with?

The question gnawed at her.

The only logical thing she could think of was his relationship with her. Had he traded their bond for his freedom? But then why keep the crystal? Just to protect himself?

No, I can't believe that.

He'd never trade her for his freedom.

In front of the whole Assembly, he had declared his love for her. She had hung on to those words, clinging to them for the remainder of her captivity.

For all her life, she'd believed that people only loved her when she did what they wanted her to do, when she was who they wanted her to be. It was a constant battle to fight against that insecurity, to fight against her fear of rejection, to fight against what she'd always known. But Henry and Karen—and even *amma*—had now given her a reason to believe otherwise. She had to put that old hurt, that false belief, to rest.

And it began with believing Henry did love her, despite whatever reservations he felt after seeing her wings.

Ari had replaced Henry's computer yesterday and moved his email to a secure server. An hour ago, she had sat at the desk in her room at the Enclave and wrote an email to Henry, telling him she would return tonight after midnight.

She took a deep breath and glanced at her watch. The digital readout clicked over one more minute: 12:01 A.M.

Her punishment had officially ended, her freedom restored.

Touching the watch's face, she flashed to Henry's driveway. The white plaster fountain, a woman holding an urn, burbled merrily in the center of his cobblestone driveway. Wild sage perfumed the dry night air—she would always associate the scent with the first time she met him.

Then she glanced at the porch and her breath caught in her throat.

Candles in small paper bags lit the way to his dark oak doors, welcoming her once again.

But this time, the door flew open and he rushed down the steps to meet her, grabbing her and lifting her off her feet in a whirlwind spin. His lips crushed against hers, his tongue claiming her mouth while his pulse raced against hers.

She clung tightly to him. When she came up for air, she whispered against his neck, "I'm so sorry."

"It's all right. I understand now why it was so hard for you to show me. Ari told me what you are."

"Damn it," she said, taking a step back to look up at him. "Tell me he didn't."

"He said you're a fallen angel."

"I swear, that cretin, I'm going to kill him. He had no right to tell you—" She stopped herself, taking a deep breath. "Henry, please, don't listen to him. He told you one explanation. Some of my people believe the story he told you."

"You don't?"

"You might say Ari and I go to a different church."

"But your own words—the night I took your blood, you told me your people do what God does not. I should have listened then."

"I was speaking metaphorically." She bit her lip. The time for withholding was over. "You guessed we were ancient astronauts, stranded here without a way to get home. That's what I believe. It explains a lot. One biological sex—possibly our ancestors only sent one sex to explore outer space. And the technology we have—ancient technology, still more advanced than what you have today. Given how we look, we might have started the rumors about angels."

"But if you are an angel...."

"*Fallen* angel—don't forget that first word. And after breeding with humans for four thousand years, we have a lot of human DNA. It's overpowered by our Lux DNA. I mean, we can morph into other life forms, but with each new generation, we have to perform more genetic surgery to keep our native DNA dominant."

He looked so somber. Weren't her words getting through to him?

"So we're Lux," she added. "But we're also part human, too."

He tilted his head toward the stars and his eyes glazed over for a moment. "Ari said this world is hell."

"I told you not to listen to Ari."

He paused for a moment, the same way he had a hundred times since she first met him, and he reached for his crucifix, rubbing the small symbol. What could she do to convince him?

"I have made my decision," he said, returning his gaze to her, his eyes intensely serious. "Fallen angel or lost astronaut, hell or not hell, sin or no sin, none of it matters. I love you and I won't let any of it stop me from being with you."

He accepts me? He really accepts me unconditionally?

A shot of joy buzzed through her, but before she could respond, he dropped his crucifix and reached for her hands.

"And I think you should move in with me."

"Move in?" she repeated, her mind spinning.

Now that the Protectors knew about their bond, she had no reason to say no. She loved him. But move in with him? Was she ready for this next step so soon?

She looked into his dark brown eyes, the pupils growing larger the longer she waited. The image of him holding the scythe flashed through her mind. She sucked in a deep breath.

My predator. My hero.

She wrapped her arms around his neck.

"Yes, Henry, yes," she said, leaking tears and pressing her lips to his again.

When the kiss ended, he brushed his thumb over her lips and said, "I have a few conditions."

Conditions. She let out a breath, her shoulders dropping, her gaze casting downward.

How could I forget? All love is conditional.

"What is wrong?" he asked.

"I—I—" she began, focusing on a crack in one cobblestone, a crack mirroring the one forming in her heart. "I thought you accepted me for who I am."

"*Cariña*, I do. Please forgive my bad choice of words. That is not what I meant, truly." He stroked her cheek with the backs of his fingers. "My love for you is not conditioned on anything. But if we are to live together, share space, shouldn't we agree—in advance—to what our expectations are? That is all I meant to say. I suspect you have expectations, too."

She heaved a deep sigh of relief, the crack mending, his touch comforting. Would the wound her mother left her with always be so sensitive? Maybe it wasn't Henry's unconditional acceptance she needed; maybe it was her own acceptance, her own belief that she was loveable just the way she was.

Besides, he was right. She did have a few expectations herself, and smiled a little at the realization. "Okay, you go first. What are yours?"

"I have learned there are rules your people are supposed to abide by. I expect you to comply with them. And I want your promise—before you break one of those rules—that you will consult with me before you do."

"Henry, I can't promise that. If I had to break one of the Lux rules to save Karen's life again, I would in an instant. There may not be time to consult."

He looked thoughtful. "Then I want your promise to consult with me if there is time."

She nodded. "I understand, but I won't promise I'll do what you tell me to do."

"Knowing you as I do now, I would not expect it any other way. And there is one other thing. I value order in the house."

She raised an eyebrow. "Yes, I know, you're a neat freak. I get it."

"You can agree to live that way?"

"Yes, but on one condition." She smiled and looked away, realizing she'd just used the dreaded word. "I'll need a room of my own, somewhere I can be messy and not worry about what you'll think. What I really need is a lab, so I don't have to go to the Enclave every day. The lab there is so small, and it would help—"

He held up his hand. "The basement has some unfinished rooms. One could be converted to a lab easily enough. They already have plumbing and electricity, but are windowless. Would that be a problem?"

"That would be perfect. I prefer a lab without windows, and being in the basement, I would be nearer to you during the day, wouldn't I?"

"There are times when you are overly sentimental."

She looked into his eyes. "I like the idea of being near you."

"Oh, you're going to be near me."

He wrapped his arms around her and kissed her deeply.

"As far as the lab," he added, "keep the door shut and I won't see how messy you have it."

"Beast," she replied, smiling.

"Then we have a deal?"

"Yes, we have a deal."

She snuggled against him, her head resting on his shoulders, her fingers slipping under his shirt to trace the outline of his firm pecs, and she looked out at night sky, finding the North Star. She had her compass again.

Warmth filled her heart, and she took a deep breath, inhaling the spicy cologne he wore, the scent awakening her longing for him. God, how she'd missed the touch of his lips, the taste of his mouth, the feel of him inside her, the brush of his emotions against hers through the crystal—

Wait.

It hit her then—the crystal had gone silent.

Her mind had experienced his feelings as a combination of sensations. His happiness had been like the green of a brightly lit forest, the earthy smell, the taste of ripe summer berries, the breeze light and pleasant. His love had wrapped her in warm red blankets, the taste of cloves and cinnamon on her tongue. And his anger had been like being dropped into dark, ice-cold water, a freezing blast through her mind, a bitter taste in her mouth.

Now that she was in his presence, she should have been experiencing his strong emotions. But it was like being locked in an isolation tank, completely cut off from him. He looked happy, his kiss wasn't faked, but if he was happy, why didn't she feel it?

She stepped back and looked at him. Something horrible must have happened. Why else would his emotions be shut down?

"Is Karen all right?" she asked.

"She's fine. But this evening, Tig identified Frédéric as the traitor."

Cerissa's eyes widened. "Frédéric?"

"Yes, and he committed suicide before Tig could interrogate him. But from what he said before he died, he wasn't the mastermind behind this. Part of the deal I struck with Agathe is that I will work with you to find the VDM—which may be who Frédéric was working with. I wish I had better news."

"Is that why I can't sense your emotions? Or did you remove the chip from your wrist?"

He pushed up his sleeve and showed her a polished tungsten bracelet wrapped around his wrist, over the embedded crystal. The bracelet was different from the communicator or the crystal band. This slate-gray one was designed to dampen the crystal.

"Ari gave it to me," Henry explained. "'You're too young a couple to be connected at the emotional hip'—his words, not mine. I had grown accustomed to the crystal. There was something about feeling your emotions, too, that was…good. But Ari thought we should have some, how did he put it: 'head space.'"

She smiled. She couldn't help it. At times Ari could be so irritating that she wanted to slap him upside his pointed little head, but deep down, he cared about her wellbeing.

"And, in the end, I agreed," Henry continued. "This will let us learn each other, *cariña*, the old-fashioned way."

"And we all know you're an old-fashioned kind of guy," she said with a slight smirk. She would miss feeling Henry's emotions, but this was the much healthier route. It would give them time to be normal and to grow together until they were ready to be more closely connected.

But instead of responding to her teasing, Henry grew suddenly serious. He took both her hands and raised them to his lips. "I said some harsh words to you during Karen's rescue. I was upset after seeing what the Cutter did to Karen." He kissed her hands again. "It was unfair and unfounded of me. Please, *cariña*, accept my apology."

"I forgive you," she said, hugging him tightly to her.

"You have no idea what the past week has been like for me." His arms wrapped firmly around her. "I've missed you so much. I lost all interest in the things that usually bring me joy." He pulled back and looked directly into her eyes. "Cerissa, I love you with all my heart."

"I love you too," she said. She touched his face, the smooth skin a joy to feel with her fingertips. "Each day I was gone, as nightfall came, I felt sad I wouldn't see you, or make love to you, or hold you, or talk with you, or play with you." She looked down at the driveway's rust-colored cobblestones. "And I was so afraid that, after seeing me in my Lux form, you wouldn't want me anymore. I'm sorry I kept my appearance secret for so long."

"Cerissa, look at me." With one finger under her chin, he tilted her head so their eyes met again. "When I was at the Enclave the first time, while you were performing surgery, had you not cut me off and sent me back here, you would have heard me tell you how beautiful you looked."

"Really?"

"Really." He held her face between his hands. "*Cara de ángel, mi ángel.*"

"You don't mean that. I don't have the face of an angel—the wings, maybe, but—"

He kissed her passionately, hungrily, feasting on her mouth, and it sent a welcome shiver through her, one she felt deep in her soul.

"*Mi amor*, I want to make love to you and make you mine again."

She pressed her cheek against his shoulder and looked out at the North Star. "Well, what's stopping you?"

He bent to her, his soft lips caressing her neck. "Nothing."

A Note from Jenna

Thank you for reading *Dark Wine at Sunrise*. I hope you enjoyed it.

The adventures of Cerissa, Henry, Tig and Jayden continue in Book 3 of the Hill Vampire series, *Dark Wine at Dusk*.

When the VDM attacks again, Cerissa's happily ever after with the man of her dreams must take a back seat to her mission.

Henry is quick to pick up the gauntlet. He'll do anything to help his beautiful spy capture the conspirators who are determined to enslave mortals.

But as Henry's secret past rears its ugly head, it not only threatens their mission, but risks their love—and their very lives.

With Tig and Jayden working hard to discover who is behind the attacks, there will be plenty of action and excitement as they work together to solve the mystery of the VDM…

And, of course, Cerissa and Henry's sexy-times will continue to heat-up the page. Get ready for (as one reviewer put it) "one of the most inventive love romps I've ever read."

Happy reading!
Jenna Barwin
https://jennabarwin.com

P.S. Reviews are always welcome, and not as fattening as donuts. Please consider telling your friends or posting a short review on your favorite review site.

Acknowledgements and Dedications

To my husband Eric—thank you for all you do to make my life as a writer easier, including all those marvelous dinners you cooked while I stayed glued to the computer, pounding away at the keyboard.

To two wonderful author colleagues—Caitlyn O'Leary and Ophelia Bell—thank you! You both have been extremely generous with your time and knowledge about the indie publishing world.

To Tari Lynn Jewett and our #CharmedWriters group—your support and companionship during writing sprints make the frustrations melt away.

To my early beta readers—Kay H. and Pat H.—thank you for putting up with my learning curve, and for your gentle suggestions. And especially to Pat for your help with some of the medical stuff. Any errors in medical treatment are mine, not hers.

To my editing team—it takes a team to polish a story and ready it for readers. Katrina, Trenda, and Arran—you are all fantastic! Any errors in grammar, clarity, or plot are mine, not theirs. Their full names are:

• Katrina Diaz-Arnold, Refine Editing, LLC
• Trenda K. Lundin, It's Your Story Content Editing
• Arran McNicol

And thank you to my book cover designer, Momir Borocki, who did an outstanding job on the cover design.

There are many other wonderful people who have helped me improve my writing, and also helped me tackle the business of being a writer. The generosity of other writers, who have freely shared their expertise, is greatly appreciated. Thank you everyone, for your support and help!